A KIND OF DYING

'Meldrum is a superbly plausible creation. Riddled with contradictions and uncertainties, he is shrewd but obstinate, cynical yet humane, full on the one hand of his own self-worth, prey on the other to that peculiarly Scottish sense of inferiority that makes him at once such engaging and exasperating company . . .

'Anchored by its powerful central character, *A Kind of Dying* functions on one level as a highly accomplished crime novel, well written, well paced and well plotted. But at another level altogether it also serves as the vehicle for penetrating observations about the state of millennial flux in which our oddly class-ridden yet egalitarian Scottish society finds itself . . .

'In *A Kind of Dying*, Jim Meldrum's company has again proved to be as thought-provoking as it is entertaining. This must surely consolidate Frederic Lindsay's claim to be one of the most interesting thriller writers around.'

James Jauncey, *The Scotsman*

'Lindsay is a master at catching the small detail and giving it a shining lustre that may or may not turn out to be fool's gold. He tantalises with the nuts and bolts, while building the real creation behind the reader's back. I'm off now in search of the other Jim Meldrum novel, *Kissing Judas'*.

Vincent Banville, *Irish Times*

About the author

Born in Glasgow, Frederic Lindsay now lives in Edinburgh. He has served on the Literature Committee of the Scottish Arts Council, and is actively involved with PEN and the Society of Authors. He has written for the theatre, radio, tv and film, and is the author of five previous highly-acclaimed novels. His most recent novel, *Kissing Judas*, the first to feature Detective Inspector Jim Meldrum, was published by Hodder & Stoughton in 1997.

A Kind of Dying

Frederic Lindsay

CORONET BOOKS
Hodder and Stoughton

First published in Great Britain in 1998
by Hodder and Stoughton
A division of Hodder Headline PLC
First published in paperback in 1999
by Hodder and Stoughton

A Coronet Paperback

10 9 8 7 6 5 4 3 2 1

ISBN 0 340 69536 6

Typeset by Hewer Text Limited, Edinburgh
Printed and bound in Great Britain by
Mackays of Chatham PLC, Chatham, Kent

Hodder and Stoughton
A division of Hodder Headline PLC
338 Euston Road
London NW1 3BH

For Elspeth

An evil life is a kind of death.

> Ovid: *Letters from the Black Sea*, III, c. 5

Life's a comedy, just enjoy the joke.

> Ray Finewater

WITNESS

We were all drunk, if that's an excuse. I expect it has to be, don't you? Not in a court of law, but it won't come to that, will it? Not when— What you're after is more important than anything that happened that night, isn't that right? I mean, I know what this is about. I read the papers. It wouldn't make any kind of sense for you to get sidetracked. Different if – if the worst had happened that night. Christ, of course I don't know! I've never wanted to know. But it didn't, did it?

. . . Not for a judge, but in a church, in front of a priest, eh? Then being drunk might count for something. In your favour, I mean.

Trey must have been as drunk as the rest of us – four, I said, didn't I say? there were four of us coming back from the exercise. You know that's what we called him? Trey – his father had called him that and it had stuck from when he was a kid. Must have been, drunk, I mean. He'd put away as much as the rest of us. More, probably. Trey always had to be the best. Didn't matter what it was. Pistol, rifle, automatic weapons, cross-country, tactics, map reading. Drinking. Didn't matter. There should have been a war for Trey. A real one, I mean. Not the bog-trotters. In Europe or the desert, out East maybe. He'd have been brilliant – started another SAS, been a David Stirling, finished up a general, I shouldn't wonder. One of the good ones, like his grandfather. That would have suited him down to the ground.

He worshipped his grandfather. Hated his father. But I expect
you know that.

We'd made one stop after we left. Stopped to piss against
a wall. Then Trey jumped up on it. The other two didn't
hesitate, got up there after him and the three of them ran
along the top howling like loons. A dry-stone wall, snow
between the stones. We were on top of a bloody mountain,
for God's sake. There wasn't a moon and there wasn't any
way to make out what the drop was on the other side. Kill
yourself any way you want, I told them. But they went on
about me not joining in. You know how it is, any chance to
have a go at you, doesn't pay to show weakness. Not that it
was, weakness, I mean. Bloody stupid isn't brave. Not the way
I'd choose to go, I told them. Count me out, if you want to kill
yourselves. Didn't stop them. All the way down they gave me
stick. The road coming at me in big loops out of the dark. I'm
trying to drive, you stupid bastards, I told them. Got on my
nerves, tell you the truth.

We passed the hotel on the corner at the bottom and I turned
right on to the main road. Going south, Glasgow direction, into
the village, boarding-houses, cafés, gift shops. In the summer,
full of berks getting off buses. Quiet in the winter. Even quieter
at night. One street, blink and you'd miss it. We were almost
out the other end of the place when I spotted them, first sign
of human life, four of them, waving their arms about, maybe
they were singing, the one on the outside carrying a plastic
bag, carry-out from the hotel bar, I imagine. Four of them, four
of us. That's fair, isn't it? Four on four.

I turned the wheel and pulled the car across on to the
pavement in front of them. Didn't need to explain what I
had in mind. We'd done something like it – not exactly,
but something like, before. A yob hunt. I switched off and
stamped on the brake, jumped out before the car stopped. All
the crap I'd taken, I was in a tearing rage. I ran round the car
to get stuck in – and as I came round I had this glimpse of one
of them – his face, you know, in the light like a photograph,
that's not right, like a . . . something. Very clear, I mean. On
its own, that's the way I saw it. On its own. I was aware of
the other three. All in shock – what's going on? Help! They

knew we weren't stopping to say hello girls. About nineteen?
Twenty? The age we were. But it was this one guy I saw first
– fair hair, a ski kind of hat pulled down over his forehead, it
was cold that night. Clear in the light and then Trey hit him
and his mouth . . . exploded. Blood shot out – and I saw a
hole where his teeth had been. A black hole in the middle of
his face. With a bat, a baseball bat. I don't know – no, I hadn't
seen it before. I didn't need a weapon. Not for yobs. Christ, we
were trained. I mean we could have taken any four civilians
apart with our bare hands.

What do you mean? Had I a stick? It's a long time ago, five
years. I don't remember. Maybe I picked up a stick in the
woods. That must have been it. What I'm saying is, I didn't
get out of the car with any weapon. Didn't need one. I don't
know why Trey—

Everything froze when Trey hit him. One of them was
saying, 'What the hell are you playing at?' And somewhere
in the middle of it, wham! And the words went on to the end
of the sentence – *playing at.* Only there wasn't any point in
them – not from the moment the hit went in. Next thing the
four of them turned and ran like rabbits into the woods. Did
I say? That bit of the road ran by woodland. And that was it
as far as I was concerned. Bloody funny. Scared the shit out
of them. I threw back my head and laughed.

It was Trey who got the torches out of the car. 'Come on!' and
he was off with us following him. Torches? We'd used torches
on the exercise. That's why they were in the car. Baseball bats?
No, of course we didn't. I don't know why Trey had it in the car.
All I can tell you about is me, I didn't have a weapon, like I told
you, I picked up a stick. Not very brave? Suppose they'd had
knives? You have any idea how many of these bastards carry
knives? I suppose you do . . . Fire power, eh? Rule of war –
have more fire power than the enemy.

It was what we call tight terrain. Trees close together and
then a bit where they'd been felling so that you were scrambling
across broken branches. And there were soggy bits, the ground
split with streams and soft going. You'd have thought it would
have turned us back. And it was cold – I had just a jacket on.
Didn't matter. Didn't feel the cold. The old adrenalin had started

pumping. Hunting instinct, natural to us humans. After a bit, I
realised we'd got split up. When I stopped and looked round,
I could see the torches of the others shining among the trees.
I was breathing hard – I could see the white of my breath in
the torchlight. Funny thing is, that's all it took to bring me
to my senses. Out in the middle of sodding woods in the
winter. It was silly. I wanted back into the warm and get
on our way. Anyway, I remember thinking, running around
in the dark we'd no chance of catching them. No chance.

I was on the bank of a stream and I turned the wrong way.
Easy to do. I thought I was heading back to the car and instead
I went further. About ten yards and the stream widened out
into a stretch of water . . . There wasn't a moon so it was hard
to tell, I was on the edge of a dark space, maybe an actual
loch. I shone the torch on it to see and there he was – up
to his shoulders in the water staring at me. His mouth was
open and I could see the stumps where his teeth had been
knocked out. I thought, poor bastard, he'll freeze to death,
there was ice at the edge of the water, I don't know how
long he'd been in there, he must have walked into it in the
dark and stayed, bloody stupid place to hide, but you don't
think straight, not if you're frightened enough. You ever been
frightened that way? Blind panic, not a bad way of describing
it. I put out my hand – that's right, I did have a stick, come
to think of it, must have had because the idea was if he got a
grip on the end of it I could pull him out.

I didn't hear Trey coming. It was the man in the water who
gave the sign. His eyes moved. All the time he'd been staring
up towards me, but now he looked to the side. Not his head,
just his eyes, so that they showed white in the torchlight. And
that was the thing, you see, even when I turned my head and
listened and heard the noise of someone coming I kept shining
the torch full on his face. It was only when I heard Trey's voice,
I jerked my hand up. I thought he must have seen, but 'Get that
bloody light out of my eyes!' he said. 'Any luck?' I asked him,
then I realised he was shining his light in *my* face and that
meant the guy in the water could see me. I turned my back
on the water. 'One of them was moving fast,' he said, 'must
have been local, he knew his way.' He was up close to me

by this time. I kept my light off his face. 'Let's get back to the car,' I said. He didn't pay any attention, might as well not have spoken. I told him, 'It's bloody freezing.' 'Fuck!' he shouted. And he swung the bat at a branch about head height, and it flew apart, rotten with being near the water, I suppose. It made a noise too, like hitting a melon – or someone in the head. Almost the same moment, I heard the man in the water whimper. 'Others were blundering around – if Roddie hadn't been making such a racket himself I'd have got one of them.' And Trey clubbed the branch backhanded again with all his strength. 'At least one of them.' As he turned the torch beam turned with him – out to the loch. I saw the man in the water, the shape of his head, the white glimmer of his face. But, of course, I knew he was there. Trey missed him. The torch beam went on, over little waves like folds in silk, and I stared down the path it made for what seemed an hour until I just turned and walked away. It was the only thing I could think of to do – and, thank Christ, Trey came after me. When we got back to the car, the others were inside drinking out of the flask, wondering what had kept us.

Tell you a funny thing. That wall at the top of the mountain they jumped up and ran along? One time, year or more afterwards, I was coming back from a trip north and I recognised it. I mean, coming round a bend, the way the road turned, I just knew. I was on my own so I stopped the car and got out. When I looked over the wall, I felt sick. That night there hadn't been a moon, remember, so you couldn't really see what was below, but you'd had a kind of sense of the ground not too far underneath – it had been the snow on the wall I thought made it a stupid risk. But it was treetops underneath – and the ground a long way below. A long way. I remembered Trey running along the wall laughing, and thought it was a toss-up that night whether he killed or got himself killed.

Sorry. That doesn't have anything to do with what you want.

It just came into my head.

BOOK ONE

The Comedy Begins

CHAPTER ONE

Maybe Meldrum hadn't opened enough bottles of wine in his life, that was possible; but it was out of his experience for the corkscrew to hit something like a knot in a plank. It spun round but wouldn't go in any further. He pressed it in hard, then realised he might push the cork down into the wine. He swapped handles and wound up the counterscrew. Half the cork came out neatly. He dropped it in the pedal-bin. The half still in the bottle was brown with a dark centre, not crumbling at all though scarred a little in the middle.

'What are you doing?' Harriet asked. 'What's taking so long? You've been in here for ages.'

'Something wrong with this cork.'

She came in from the door and stood beside him. 'You should have opened it before.'

'I opened three.'

'There are four of us.'

'I thought that would have been enough. But then I'm only a policeman. I hadn't calculated on how much lawyers drink.'

'I'm a lawyer,' she said. And before he could answer, went on quickly, 'Try it at a different angle.'

'What?'

She took the corkscrew from him and set it into the left side of the cork. 'I can't turn it,' she said after a moment. She gave it to him, holding the corkscrew on at an angle. 'Or, of course, you could try another bottle.'

When he arrived back with the opened bottle, there was a little cheer from the guests, husband and wife, Harriet's friends. She'd known the wife since they'd been students together at Edinburgh University. In the way of these things, she wasn't so keen on the husband. Meldrum didn't much like either of them.

He couldn't believe how quickly they went through the fourth bottle. He nursed his glass, defying them to ask for more. At the critical moment, just as Harriet scowled at him and opened her mouth, he said, 'I'll make coffee.' He moved fast, but her voice caught him on the way to the kitchen.

'And a brandy,' she said. 'A brandy would be nice? Or we have—'

But he lost the rest of it as the kitchen door shut behind him.

At least there wasn't any trouble with the cork. He poured three glasses while he made the coffee. Thought, Fuck it, and poured one for himself. Drank it, and carried out the tray with the cafetière and three glasses of brandy.

When they were leaving, the husband, who at fifty was about twice as old as his wife, stumbled on a step as they went down the stairs. Looking back at Meldrum watching from the landing, he held up his car keys and said, 'Good job you're off duty. Or it would be, *Right, my son, you're nicked.*'

For the impersonation, he exchanged his Edinburgh middle-class accent for some Southern English village's PC Plod. His reason for this could be known only to himself, but Meldrum took it as intended to be some kind of insult. 'A policeman's never off duty,' he said.

'Eh?'

'I'll phone and shop you. Soon as you've gone.'

Fat Man swayed and thought about that until his wife reached out and took the keys from him.

Waving them off, Harriet said through a clenched smile, 'That was bloody rude.'

He grunted agreement. 'He's a clown.'

'Not him. You.'

'Silly bastard was drunk.'

'But not stupid. He knew perfectly well you were insult-
ing him.'

Meldrum closed the door, wondered about going back into
the living-room and finally followed her into the bedroom.
She was sitting at the dressing-table, brushing her hair.

'Not *perfectly*,' he said. 'Might work it out in the morning.
If he remembers anything when he wakes up.'

He was quite pleased with that, until in the mirror he saw
the expression on her face.

Later, though, they made love, which was nice. Never let
the sun go down on your anger, as his mother used to say.

Afterwards, she murmured something which he didn't
quite catch.

'Love you too,' he said, being ready to go to sleep.

'I asked, Did you have a brandy? . . . Thought so,' she said.
He felt her arm come round him and the heat of her body
as she cuddled up against his back. 'You should have more
sense at your age.'

Which was sufficiently older than her, though not twice
– so there was one difference between her friend's husband
and him.

The other being, of course, that he wasn't Harriet's husband;
or anyone's, come to that. Not any more.

CHAPTER TWO

Meldrum went to the house by right, as to so many before it. He, and those who went with him, held an invitation issued by bad luck or passion or simple evil. There wasn't any way of knowing which it would be, not when you went there first.

The sun had been shining all the way down the coast, but when they came in sight of the little town there was a cap of grey cloud pulled down over its grey stone houses.

'I've never been in this bloody place it wasn't raining,' Henderson said, and scrubbed the side of his head with the palm of his hand. He was about thirty with red hair cropped close at the sides, and a nose that looked as if it had been broken once and badly set.

It was the first time he'd spoken since they left Edinburgh. Meldrum hadn't broken the silence, interested to see how long it would last. He wasn't a man who liked flattery or even a lot of conversation; but he was accustomed, without thinking about it, to the usual mode of subordinates trying to impress, what you might call a kind of determined pleasantness. To the lucky, it came naturally. He hadn't ever found it easy himself; but at Henderson's stage, an ambitious detective sergeant impatient for the next step, he'd done his best. That kind of game went with any hierarchical organisation the way a smell of shit went with keeping pigs. Except that, it seemed, Henderson didn't feel any need to try. He wondered why.

The house was big with a wing on either side; very solid,

prosperous, made of stone with bay windows and crow-step gables. The kind of house built for merchants before the First World War to show the world how well things were going with the buying and selling. Fresh from the farm, Meldrum's grandmother as a girl had been, as they said then, in service; in a house he imagined as something like this. One of the first tasks the housekeeper gave her had been to crawl round the carpet in the drawing-room and comb out the tassels. No vacuum cleaners or dishwashers then; fortunately, in compensation people came cheaply. The house as a community; pantry boys and tweenie maids and large families; stirring with footsteps and voices.

Standing with Henderson in the hall, Meldrum was struck by the silence. All the doors off the hall were closed. Looking up the wide staircase, banisters on either side oiled to a sheen by hands' grip, he could see as far as a landing. There was a big painting on the wall up there, hills and sky varnished to a uniform dullness, and a table with a tall vase that as far as he could tell from below seemed empty of flowers. The sour-faced woman who'd let them in had gone up to fetch her mistress. Maybe instead she'd lowered herself out of a window and run off. He listened but couldn't hear a ticking from the grandfather clock by the front door. Perhaps it had run down. Beside him Henderson cracked his knuckles, left hand, then right. The sound made Meldrum glance aside in irritation, and when he looked back she was there. Mrs Bellman, the missing man's wife. First name, Willa.

Unusual name. While he was thinking that, she had left the landing and was moving down towards them. When she stood in front of him, he looked down at her, which was what he would have expected. It was what he was used to, being over six feet in height. All the same, his first impression stayed with him, which was of her as very tall and commanding. She was slim with dark hair and a strong face. Her eyes were blue-grey, very light and clear. It was a colour he associated with men's faces, the colour he'd seen in an uncle's eye when he was a child. The 'marksman's eye', an officer had told his uncle, who, on the strength of that as much as any talent, had become a sniper and killed men from ambush.

'Hilda said policemen. But you're not the ones who were here before.'

'Detective Inspector Meldrum. This is Detective Sergeant Henderson. The local people have asked for help.'

'Not before time,' she said. 'My husband has been missing for four days.'

As they followed her across the hall, Meldrum thought that for any ordinary family four days wasn't long to call in the cavalry; weeks for some; for most never – unless, of course, a body turned up. Other things being equal, bodies were guaranteed attention.

The room she led them into was small, just about large enough to take a couch and two chairs, with patio doors, at a guess replacing French windows, that showed a view of lawns and a glimpse of the sea. At the back of the house, it was a morning-room; facing the sun, which, for the moment, wasn't shining.

She waved them to seats on the couch. Big men, Henderson sweating and bulky, himself lean but tall, it made Meldrum uncomfortable, like one of two puppets set down side by side. Perhaps by accident, she'd taken a chair by the glass doors so that he had to squint against the light.

'Didn't the other one – Jackson, was that his name? – didn't he tell you all about it?' she asked.

Her name was Willa Bellman. According to the local police, she was fifty-one years old. Like newspaper reporters, they'd put an age to everyone. He wondered if they'd had the nerve to ask her, or if they'd got it somewhere else. On the Saturday, four days earlier, she and her husband John, older than his wife by ten years, had played host to a family party. Their younger son, twenty-three-year-old Alistair, known to the family as 'Trey', had arrived just before lunch with his sister whom he'd gone to pick up at the airport. Ruth had turned twenty-one that day, which was the reason for the party. The four of them had eaten outdoors, the weather being fine and warmer than was usual here in early summer.

'No,' she said. 'Nothing unusual. We stayed out on the terrace, just talking, catching up with what the two of them had been doing. We had some drinks. I suppose I should tell you that –

the other policeman seemed to feel it was something he should know. A couple of gin and tonics, perhaps. We finished the white wine. Trey and Ruth played badminton, not with a net or anything, just knocking about on the grass. There was a lot of laughter. It was a happy day.'

Just before six, the elder son Gordon, thirty, arrived with his wife Sally, twenty-five. They had driven through from Glasgow where he was a partner in a firm of investment analysts. An hour later the six of them set off in two cars for the birthday dinner.

'Gordon took Sally and Ruth and me. Trey went with his father. Yes, John had been drinking, and, yes, he drove back and, yes, he'd had more to drink at the meal. No, none of us argued with him about driving back. Whether they should or not, in the real world people do. Yes, quite a lot more at the meal. John has been driving since he was seventeen. He's never had an accident. Anyway, as I said, it was a happy day. Why spoil it?'

When they got back it was almost one in the morning, but they sat up, it seemed, for at least another hour. It was the birthday girl Ruth who gave up first, then the wife went to bed leaving her daughter-in-law with the father and his two sons.

'I was dozing when John came to bed. No, I couldn't tell you what time it was. I came to the surface – I was sleeping lightly, I suppose, until he came – and when he did, I settled into a deep sleep. It was after ten when I woke up. I didn't think anything of John not being there. Why should I? I went downstairs and Gordon and Sally had left a note and gone. Ruth was there, hurrying Alistair who was making a late breakfast. She was fretting about missing the plane.'

'But she didn't,' Meldrum said. He'd let her tell her story without interruption, that was usually the best way. Now she paused, looking at him as if seeing him for the first time.

'She asked if her father would be down soon. John was supposed to be taking them to the airport. Yes, we were puzzled. Of course we were. They hadn't seen him, but they weren't long up out of bed. Somehow or other we got it into

our heads that he must have breakfasted with Gordon and
Sally. He was always up early, you see.'

'Did you think he'd gone off with them?'

'No! Of course not. I mean why would he?'

'Did you check if his car was there?'

'Not then. Ruth was in such a state about catching the
plane and— We decided John had forgotten about the airport.
Forgotten that he was supposed to take them and gone for a
walk. Does that sound stupid?'

'No.'

'It sounds stupid to me.'

She waited, but he didn't comment on that. He could have
said, if people are asked to describe what they did, it often
sounds strange, hard to explain, I've learned to allow for that.
He could have told her it happens people take evasive action,
not wanting to hear the voice inside telling them how badly
something has gone wrong.

After a moment, she said, 'They were already late for the
plane. Ruth had a class to prepare for on the Monday morning.
Alistair was going back down to London with her.'

'He's in the army, isn't that right?'

'No,' she said, and went on without elaborating. 'I took
them myself. We were just in time – but they always want
you there ridiculously early, don't they? I came home, and
phoned Gordon. I got his answerphone and left a message.
And that was it, really.'

'What time would this be?'

'It was the afternoon. I seemed to spend it just wandering
about.'

'You were on your own?'

'Yes, I told you so.'

'What about her?' Henderson asked, nodding at the door.
'The woman who let us in.'

'Hilda? Mrs Martin. She comes through the week. If we have
people to dinner, yes. But not that weekend – I was quite alone.
Some of the time I sat in front of the television. After all the
excitement of the day before, it was so quiet it was unbearable.
I couldn't tell you what I watched. I only put it on because the
house was so quiet. I went out into the garden for a while.

And then to the beach – I walked for miles. Looking for John,
I suppose, though I didn't think of it like that. I remember
telling myself he would be there when I went home.'

'What time would it be when you did get back to the
house?'

'I can't tell you.' She was impatient. 'Does it matter?' As if it
was stupid of him to ask. 'When it got dark, I put the lights on.
I didn't feel like eating. And then the phone rang. It was Ruth
to say what a lovely birthday she'd had. Not long afterwards,
it rang again and it was Gordon. He was worried because I'd
sounded upset. He asked me what was wrong.'

'You hadn't told him?'

'I left a message asking him to phone. That was all. To phone
me as soon as he came in.'

'What was his reaction when you told him your husband
was missing?'

'He told me to get in touch with the police.'

'Yes,' Meldrum said. He gave himself a moment to watch
Henderson, notebook in his lap, driving the big scrawled letters
across the page. 'That was good advice.' What he meant was,
why hadn't she followed it?

'I kept listening, imagining I would hear John's steps coming
through the hall,' she said as if reading his mind.

'It was the next day, in fact, before you got in touch.'

'I didn't want to, you see. And when I did, I lost the hope
that at any moment he was going to walk in and everything
would be normal again. Calling the police made it real.'

A long time, all the same, to sit and wait. From whenever
she'd spoken to her elder son through the rest of the evening
and the night till morning came.

'What made you finally decide?' he asked, and felt at once
that was stupid; a question to which there could be no answer.
He imagined misery like water falling drop by drop into a jar.
The moment must come when the jar had to spill over.

'When my son called again,' she said without hesitation.
'Naturally he was worried about his father.'

The call she'd made to report her husband's disappearance
had been timed at ten minutes past eleven on the Monday
morning.

CHAPTER THREE

If men were supposed to marry women who resembled their mothers, Gordon Bellman had broken the rule. Sally Bellman was small, not more than a couple of inches over five feet, with a face that was conventionally pretty apart from the sharp length of the nose. She had blonde streaks through her light brown hair and breasts that seemed very large, perhaps because of her lack of height. To judge from the way he kept determinedly not looking at them, Henderson was impressed. Meldrum, on the other hand, remarked the length of her nose and reflected sourly that women with thin fair skin shouldn't chain-smoke if they wanted to stay unwrinkled. He had a good excuse for being irritated.

'He didn't have time to phone you. I mean, you'd have been on the road from Edinburgh by that time. When his office called, it was important,' she said, stubbing out her cigarette and shaking another from the packet.

'More important than whatever's happened to his father?' Meldrum asked, and ignored the side-glance from Henderson.

It wasn't a question in the little blue book of police etiquette, but instead of being offended she asked, 'Have you found out?' No, they hadn't, which gave her set and match, except that it wasn't a game she seemed to be playing. 'Gordon hadn't any choice. The client wouldn't let anyone else handle it.' And with a touch of the proud wife: 'He insisted it had to be Gordon. But Gordon says I can tell you whatever you want to know.'

The leather under Henderson's backside creaked a warning about etiquette as he shifted his weight uneasily in the chair.

'In your own words then,' Meldrum said. 'Can we try that? I'll ask if there's anything I'm not clear about.' And added with elaborate courtesy, 'We'll do our best not to take up too much of your time.'

'Oh, I don't mind,' she said. 'It's so funny, isn't it? Him going off like that.'

'Is that what your husband thinks? That his father's gone off somewhere?'

She stared at him. 'Of course he does.'

'Does he have a reason for thinking that?'

'What else could have happened?'

Well, it would be nice if he was found in a ditch shot through the head, Meldrum thought. It would give me a reason for being here. That would be like real police work. I don't know why the hell I'm here.

Instead of sharing that with her, he said, 'That's what we're hoping to find out. Can we start with the Saturday? You were the last to arrive, isn't that right?'

'It seems ages ago, and it's not a week yet. We were supposed to be earlier, but Gordon went into the office in the morning. Then it was a lovely afternoon, and he cut the grass and tidied up the flowerbeds. It was well after four by the time we left.'

'You must have made good time,' Henderson said, checking his notebook.

Meldrum remembered Mrs Bellman saying they'd arrived just before six.

'Gordon drives like a maniac.' She laughed. 'I shouldn't say that, should I? Not to you two.'

'We're not from traffic,' Henderson said.

'. . . Anyway.' She blew out her breath and studied him through the veil of smoke. 'We said, Happy birthday! and gave Ruth her present. Gordon had got her a beautiful bracelet. She'd a gold watch from her father and mother. I thought that was old-fashioned – but she seemed pleased enough with it. And Alistair – sorry, I suppose you don't really need to know about the presents, do you? Then we left for the restaurant. Gordon's father had booked us in for dinner at eight. He'd had to book it up months ahead. That's what he told us. Months ahead. The food was all right, I suppose. Gordon and him went on for long enough about how wonderful it was. Sorry – don't suppose the meal matters either.'

'How would you describe Mr Bellman's mood?'

'Very good. For him.'

'How did he seem to you at other times?'

'What do you mean?'

'You said, "For him" about the good mood he was in. That seemed to suggest he was normally – what? Quiet? Depressed?'

She hesitated. 'When he talked, he had a loud voice.'

When it seemed as if she'd decided that covered the matter, Meldrum tried again: 'Was he often depressed?'

'I didn't know him that well! I mean, we've only been two years married. And I didn't meet his father before that. There wasn't much time. We'd a whirlwind romance.' She smiled as if liking the sound of that, then went off again at a tangent. 'Anyway, how can you tell? Americans are different, aren't they?'

'Americans?'

'Gordon's father's American. Didn't you know that? I'd have thought you'd have known that. If you're trying to find him. It would be part of the description, wouldn't it? Not that it would be much help. I mean, he doesn't have what you'd call an accent. He's been over here for years and years, since he was a young man. Well, I mean that was their thirtieth wedding anniversary. As well as Ruth's twenty-first. Two or three days before, not Saturday. We sent them a card.' And with another change of direction, 'You could hear him all over the restaurant. I suppose that's American, isn't it? Or the other thing – more like the other thing.'

Patiently in pursuit of wheat among this flurry of chaff, Meldrum decided against asking about the 'other thing', whatever that was. 'Would you say he had a lot to drink?' he asked.

'Not more than Gordon. And a lot less than Trey.' She

laughed, 'Not that *he* showed much sign of it. I suppose they must get a lot of practice in the army. At drinking, I mean.'

'And when you got back to the house?'

'Oh, yes. They opened another bottle of wine. And the men had a whisky – more than one. And Ruth, more than one. I remember thinking it must run in the family. But, of course, it was her birthday. I warned Gordon we had to be away early in the morning and left the men to it.'

'How early would that be – when you left on the Sunday morning?'

'Before ten. And we didn't see Gordon's father. We took it for granted he'd still be in bed.'

'Did you? And yet Mrs Bellman described her husband as an early riser.'

'It had been a late night. We slipped downstairs, took some breakfast. There wasn't a sound in the house. Of course, we thought they were all still sleeping.'

'After a night like that. And with it being a Sunday morning. You said your husband stayed up after you'd gone to bed?'

'Yes. And he wasn't pleased at having to get up – he'd have been glad to snore on. But I wanted to visit my son Tony. I hadn't seen him for – too long.'

'Your son?'

'When I was seventeen. By my first marriage. A mistake.'

'So you were going to your ex-husband's . . . Where would that be?'

'I've no idea where – last I heard he was in London. Where we were going was a Home in Aberdeen. Capital H. Not that he recognises me. I go just so the staff will know somebody cares what they do to him. My son's brain-damaged.'

'I'm sorry,' Meldrum said, the automatic response, like answering a cue.

Shortly afterwards, they were on the doorstep, then out in the street, hunching against a thin drizzle.

'Slag,' Henderson said. 'Peddled her arse into a nice set-up.'

Meldrum could see you might describe it that way: the house wasn't as grand as the father's, but substantial, detached, in a street of the same; and Giffnock had a claim to being the best district in Glasgow. He was thinking, though, of Sally Bellman's handicapped son. If she'd had him when she was seventeen, the boy Tony must be eight by now. 'Because Ritchie was a musician,' she'd said, 'he beat Tony with his feet. He had to be careful of his hands.'

He opened the door and slid behind the wheel. Busy with his own thoughts as he drove, he was surprised when Henderson broke their silence. It was odd how quickly a new relationship established its customs.

'Lost? What gives you that idea?'

'Well, that was the turn back there,' Henderson said. 'Or is there another way on to the Edinburgh road? If we carry on like this, we'll finish up in the middle of Glasgow.'

'Last I heard,' Meldrum said, 'that's where Bellman's office is.'

CHAPTER FOUR

They could have had a walk in the park, Meldrum supposed, if they could have found a park, or done some window-shopping along Sauchiehall Street, or gone to the public library and read the magazines. On the other hand, he decided, if two detectives had to put in some waiting time, in the real world there was a dreary inevitability about them ending up in a pub. From Gordon Bellman's office, they'd found parking space at the top of Buchanan Street and, meandering down, past vast concrete building sites, down by the subway station with grass growing in the cracks of a flight of steps, an empty bottle of Buckfast rolling from a doorway, finished up in this cavern. An empty pub was the emptiest space on earth. In the shallows of a wet afternoon, swinging Glasgow had swung to a stop.

'Another one?' Henderson asked. Even his invitations came out dourly. He gave the impression of a man fighting a grudge match with life.

Coming out from the Gents, Meldrum had an angle along the bar that showed him Henderson knocking back what looked like a double whisky before he picked up the pints. He wondered if he'd been doing that every time.

If he had, he didn't show much sign of it as he settled himself down again and complained, 'Horse's piss.'

'It's all right.' Meldrum took a long swallow. In fact, it wasn't a bad pint. 'We'll make this the last,' he said.

'Case we miss him? Likely he won't be there.'

'We'll see.'

'He wasn't before. Waste of time.'

A secretary had told them Mr Bellman was seeing a client. No, not here in the office; if that's what they'd been told, someone had made a mistake. Mr Bellman had gone to visit the client, who lived in Kilsyth.

'We'll chance it. He should have been at his house when he said he would be. Not messing us around.'

'No,' Henderson said. 'I mean the whole thing. That's what's a waste of time. Some old cunt goes walkabout. Nobody says he's run off with the cash-box. He's only been gone for – what? – it's not a week yet. The whole thing's a load of shite. Maybe, way things are, you've to take it seriously. Not me. He'll be getting his hole somewhere.'

'Way things are,' Meldrum repeated, staring at him. 'What way would that be?'

Henderson didn't pause. Either when drink hit, it hit him hard, or this was something he badly wanted off his chest.

'Your coat's on a shoogley peg. We all know that, don't think we don't. I'm not saying we know why – not exactly. You were trying to get a guy out of jail – and then there was a cover-up. It was *politics*.' The word was spat out like a bite of rotten meat. It was the way most policemen felt. Theft, rape, murder, no problem; you joined up for that crap; it was how you were supposed to earn your corn. Politics was different. Politics was bad news. It was how he'd always felt himself, not that anyone cared. 'You should have been out the door – only you were being looked after. Way I heard it, three or four of the brass went to Baird himself and he told them, leave it. Chief Constable and *he*'d to toe the line – whoever was drawing the line. But they wanted rid of you. And they still do. You know that.'

But the thing was, he didn't. Or at least, if he did, it had been kept at the back of his mind, not something to be admitted. He felt the beating of his heart as if he was about to be attacked. Physical attack, violence he could have met with violence, would have been less traumatic. He'd been taken totally by surprise. For something to do, he picked up his glass and drank. Nothing of what he felt showed on his face, that was part of his profession. Ask him what he would do if he wasn't a policeman, he would have no idea of an answer. That's what he was. Not a do-gooder, a social worker, a campaigner. He'd cursed the day he finally knew Hugh Keaney must be innocent since it meant putting his life and career on the line to prove it. For him, there hadn't been any other choice. He'd been so grateful to be taken back into the fold a year ago, it hadn't been hard for him to find one reason or another to explain away how he'd been treated since.

'So they get you shovelling shite,' Henderson said, 'to sicken you off. But, oh no, not you. Chasing on – like we were after Jack the Ripper, eh? Big-time stuff. Like the stuff you used to do. Give us a break. From here on, you're going to get nothing but shite.'

That was one question answered, Meldrum thought. Henderson was ambitious.

'And you with me,' he said.

'You're in fucking Siberia. And now I'm there too.'

'Time we were on our way.' Meldrum emptied his glass.

Pick up your shovel, you bastard, he thought, and headed for the exit without looking back.

CHAPTER FIVE

Gordon Bellman was a long dry man. Almost as tall as Meldrum, with gold-rimmed glasses and thinning sandy hair, he gave an austere first impression. The wide, thin-lipped mouth didn't look as if it often relaxed into a smile. It was easy to imagine people turning to him for sound advice with a touch of caution about it. It wasn't difficult to believe clients would regard him as trustworthy. Taking all this in, on the other hand, it occurred to Meldrum that it was also true that people had a tendency to confuse the lack of a sense of humour with integrity. If there was prejudice in the thought, it came perhaps from the contrast between Bellman and his pint-sized wife with the large breasts, sharp nose, and cigarette curling smoke up from between her fingers. Meeting him, no one would imagine her; and most people, given a choice, might prefer to take advice about money from a man with no surprises tucked away in the background. Not that the clients would be likely to encounter Sally Bellman, and to be fair, a man's taste in wives might be felt to be his own business.

It was also possible that Meldrum's prejudice was due to nothing more complicated than being irritated by the receptionist.

'Mr Bellman?' She'd hesitated. 'You want to see him – Mr Bellman?'

Unless you've the Pope or President Clinton tucked out of sight back there, someone really interesting like that.

'Yes, thank you.'

'You had an appointment?'

'We covered that last time we were here.'

'He might not be back yet.'

The reception area wasn't large enough to overlook a returning partner.

'Why don't you check?' he'd suggested.

Instead of using the phone, she'd got up and disappeared through one of the doors at the back.

'Cunt's here,' Henderson had said, which Meldrum had worked out for himself – though, as the phone adverts allowed, it was nice to talk.

They'd waited almost twenty minutes before she came back. That made the question, was he reluctant to see them? Not that he gave any sign of it when they were shown in at last; apologising sufficiently if unsmilingly for failing to keep his appointment to meet them at home.

'Business worries?' That had brought the second frown. The first had been when he'd confirmed the reason his wife and he had left the parents' house early on the Sunday morning had been to visit her handicapped son. It was as if he resented having to admit the boy's existence.

'If someone disappears, money trouble is one of the things we have to think about. It's just routine.'

'My father didn't have any business worries.' He made it sound as if they'd been searching for pornographic magazines under a mattress.

'What line of business is your father in?'

'No line.'

'He's retired?'

Bellman straightened the papers laid in front of him on the desk, and spoke without looking up. 'Whatever's happened has nothing to do with money. I've no doubt about that. If you need it, I can give you a categorical assurance my father has no financial problems.'

'Do you handle his finances?'

'Why?'

'You were so sure.'

'I am sure.'

There didn't seem any immediate percentage in arguing

finance with a professional. Meldrum let the silence run, then changed tack to ground on which Bellman might be less assured.

'What about your father's private life?'

'Private life?' Bellman repeated, in the tone of sceptical distaste he'd used before.

'Private life,' Meldrum offered again. 'Can you think of anything there which might have a bearing on his disappearance?'

'Are you asking me if he had a mistress?'

Or a boyfriend, or a boy come to that. Or a mania for gambling. Or any of the other, countless strangenesses policemen got hardened to flushing out of these private lives.

'Did he, sir?'

'No. I find the idea offensive.'

'What made you think of the possibility, sir? I mean, it was you that mentioned it.'

'I'm not a fool.'

'What?'

'Don't treat me like a fool.'

'I didn't mean to,' Meldrum said, and added carefully, 'If I did anything to give you that impression, I apologise.'

'My father and mother are devoted to one another. Ask – there isn't anyone will tell you differently. And, in case you're wondering, yes, I am sure. Every bit as sure as before. More so, if I could be. No money worries, no secret love affairs.'

Meldrum nodded, agreeing, sympathising even. Lucky son.

'It's a puzzle, isn't it?' he said.

Bellman stared. 'What do you mean?'

'Your family gets together to celebrate your sister's twenty-first birthday. From all I hear, things went off well. A nice afternoon in the garden – that was before you got there, of course. The weather was fine – the family drank wine together – your brother and sister played badminton. "There was a lot of laughter" was how your mother described it. Then your wife and you arrived and you gave your sister her presents. Then off for a good dinner. Back to sit around the fire and chat. It sounds like a fine way to celebrate a birthday. I could imagine your father going to bed a happy man. He'd had a good day. But when your mother woke in the morning, he wasn't beside her. And when she went downstairs, no one had seen him. And no one's seen him since.' He paused until Bellman looked up, then shook his head slowly, a plain man puzzled. 'It's hard to make sense of, isn't it? What do you think's happened to him?'

'I've no idea,' Gordon Bellman said.

It was shaping up as a fast run home, until they hit a tailback just past the Livingstone turn-off. They dropped through the gears and at last came to a halt. Stalled traffic stretched ahead out of sight. Meldrum waited in the confident expectation of Henderson offering the first words he'd spoken since they left Glasgow by cursing the traffic, their luck, his life. Instead, he came out with, 'You didn't get much change out of him.'

But that's where he was wrong. Meldrum couldn't have explained why, but he wasn't in any real doubt about it. He'd like to tell that to Henderson, who didn't understand. Henderson, however, when he'd got no answer, had turned gloomily from the traffic ahead to the view of fields inching by as they went from this standstill to the next.

Listening to Gordon Bellman talk of his father, Meldrum had felt an alerting of attention like the stirring of hairs on the nape of his neck. Now he wanted to know why the father had disappeared. Now he wanted to find him. From now, unreasonably, he was sure whenever, wherever, that happened, it wouldn't be in a hideaway with a woman or a case of amnesia. 'You're a good thief taker.' That's what Billy Ord, now dead, had called him. If any of them, from Baird down, thought this was a nothing job, they'd made a mistake. You have the instinct, Ord had said. It was the joker in the pack.

CHAPTER SIX

There shouldn't have been occasion to do more with the Bellman disappearance, not hands on anyway. He'd talked to the wife, seen the son, got nowhere; circulated the description, put out some written enquiries. Time to stick a pending note on the file, and get on with the mayhem piled in a foot thickness of brown case folders at the right side of his desk.

But then the nudges had come: a question about how things were progressing, a memo that was about something else but somehow touched on Bellman in passing; and because this was coming from different people and all of it was casual, you couldn't challenge, What's going on? Yet when you thought about who these people were, the ranks they held, and exactly because there was more than one involved, suddenly you were sure that, if the pressure was there at all, it had to be initiated from a source somewhere near the top. The other possibility, it was all in his mind. As an alternative that had implications for his mental state he didn't like to examine.

Meldrum held the phone to his ear and listened to the call tone. It was the third time he'd tried, and he was about to give up when a voice said, 'Hello?' on a little gasp of breath as if she'd been hurrying. Just then the machine from hell started up, tearing out another wall as part of the reorganisation of space on the top floor. They called it improvement, needed no doubt since the headquarters building was all of fifteen years old. When he got a finger in his ear and could hear again, the voice was asking, 'Mummy? What is it?'

He waited in case she added to that, then checked, 'Miss Bellman?'

After a moment's hesitation, she admitted that's who she was.

'Detective Inspector James Meldrum.' And, giving her again a chance to respond, he let a tick of silence go by before continuing, 'I spoke to your mother on Wednesday.'

'Did you?'

'Yes. About your father's disappearance.' And he waited. 'Haven't you been in touch with her?'

'You're the policeman who came to see her. Of course I knew. It was just that she didn't tell me your name. Why are you phoning me?'

Because you're his daughter.

'We know you must be anxious about your father.'

'Have you found him?'

'No. We haven't found him.'

'Do you want me to come back?' And rushed on before he could answer, 'It's difficult, you see. I'm doing *A Midsummer Night's Dream*. Directing, producing, *and* in charge of the costuming too – the way things have turned out. I'm rehearsing the actors and it's a big cast – there are twenty-two of them. And we have competition – Rodney College is doing *West Side Story*, which is ridiculous, musicals are ridiculous, for amateurs, I mean, but that doesn't mean people aren't drawn to them, thinking they'll have a good night out and not knowing till they get there what a disaster it's going to be. Is that unfair? Anyway, it's true, I think, and so we have a fight on our hands just to get the audience to *be* there. Do you know what I'm trying to say? I expect I'm not putting it very well, but I do feel responsible . . . I really do.'

The floodgate had broken and he'd let the wave wash over him. When she'd stopped, he said, 'You're talking about putting on a play.' He didn't say it with any emphasis, just slowly and left it at that.

'. . . And exams,' she said. 'I have exams.'

'Your finals, would that be?' He knew about finals, having

a daughter who was in her junior honours year at Edinburgh University.

'No, second year.'

He glanced at his notes. Ruth Bellman was twenty-one. Maybe they started drama college later, he thought, and then wondered what difference it made, second year, last year, whatever year, didn't she care what had happened? As a father, he had a prejudice in the direction of daughters caring.

'Your father's been gone now for almost a fortnight,' he said.

'Tomorrow's Sunday.'

'A fortnight tomorrow.'

'It's just that, today being Saturday, you took me by surprise— But that's silly – it's obvious when you think about it— As if criminals would take the weekend off.'

The wrecking machine along the corridor had stopped. He took his finger out of his ear, and heard a tattoo of banging. He didn't feel talking to Ruth Bellman needed any assistance from hammers to give him a headache. Wondering what she looked like, he had an image of someone undersized, with big blue eyes, maybe blonde, scatty, that would be the word, nice old-fashioned word. Sure of being loved.

A daddy's girl.

'It would be easier to talk to you in person,' he said. 'When will you – have you plans to come home – to see your mother? We could talk then. Have you an idea when?'

'It would have to be after the play.'

'And the exams.'

'That's right. Three weeks, we'd be talking about three weeks.'

'Fine ... Would you mind going over it with me now? It was your birthday, isn't that right? And you travelled up to be with your parents. It was going to be a family party. Could you tell me about it?'

'Just ask me. Anything you need to know. I do want to help.' And when he didn't answer: 'Well, you know what happened. When Mummy got up on the Sunday morning, he wasn't there.'

'Could you start from when you got home on the Saturday? In your own words. What you remember.'

She made an odd little snuffling noise. He hoped she wasn't crying. On the phone there was no way of telling.

'It would be easier if you asked me questions.'

'I expect I'll have some. Start with when you got off the plane. What time would that be?'

'I can't remember. Not exactly.'

'According to your mother you got to the house just before lunch. Your brother—'

'That's right, he'd met me and brought me home. He could tell you about all that.' But before he could respond, she set off again and this time, in the same way as before, the floodgate opened. 'The sun shone for my birthday. Gordon and Sally gave me a gold bracelet. Trey – sorry, Alistair, that is. Daddy called him Trey when he was small – and it stuck! Everyone calls him that, not just family, at school and in the army, all his friends. Did anyone tell you that? Trey, Alistair, gave me a collected works of Shakespeare – published in 1779 – so lovely, I could have cried. And Mummy and Daddy gave me a watch. I had a wonderful day. We went to the Trow Inn for dinner – you have to book months ahead. Everybody was having a lovely time. Daddy stood up and made a funny little speech about me being twenty-one. When he finished, people at the other tables started clapping as well. It was a lovely speech. When we got home he opened another bottle of champagne. And then suddenly, my eyes wouldn't stay open. Not another minute. They laughed at me – being the one who gave up first and it being my birthday. I was fast asleep the minute my head went on to the pillow. Next thing I knew it was morning.' She stopped abruptly. He could hear the sigh of her breath.

'And your father was gone.'

'Yes.'

'But you didn't know that at first.'

'I thought he was sleeping.'

'But I'm told he was an early riser. Always the first one out of bed. You didn't think it strange that he wasn't there when you came down? What time was that, by the way?'

But, not to his surprise, she was vague about that, too. 'Gordon and Sally were already down — she'd got him out of bed first thing, I expect. They'd eaten breakfast and Gordon was hoping Mummy and Daddy would put in an appearance before they had to go. But Sally was fretting — you know about her little boy? So they went off. And I had something to eat. And then Trey came down. And not long after him, Mummy appeared, still in her dressing-gown, poor darling, and not more than half awake. Daddy had promised to take us to the airport. But Mummy said she would take us instead. By then, I was frantic about missing the plane.' He almost asked what made catching it so important but didn't, not wanting to hear again about the play she was helping put on; or her exams, come to that. 'And we were so late, they were calling our names, Alistair and mine, as we came into the airport. If you asked, I expect they'll remember us.'

'You must have been angry with your father.'

'. . . People were glaring at us going down the aisle to our seats. Because they'd been kept waiting,' she said. And then as if she'd just taken it in, 'Angry?'

'Annoyed. Your father had promised to take you to the airport. And then he wasn't there. He'd gone off by himself instead. Isn't that what you thought?'

'Mummy said he'd probably gone for a walk along the beach.'

'Did your father often go for walks on his own?'

'It was a nice morning.'

'Would you say he was absent-minded?'

'What?'

'About promises. Like saying he'd take you to the airport.'

'No. I mean, he'd do something if he said he would.'

It struck him that she was speaking about her father in the past tense.

'What do you think might have happened — about your father?'

'I've no idea.'

'Do you think he might have met with an accident?'

'I don't see how. Not on the beach — I mean, you wouldn't have an accident and not be found. Your people looked, didn't they?'

On the other hand, she was talking about a promise that had

been made in the past. And broken in the past. For whatever reason. So why not the past tense?

'Did he usually take you to the plane?' he asked.

'Usually.'

'Yes . . . See you off. Tell you to take care of yourself in London. That kind of stuff.'

'Oh, yes.'

The stuff fathers did. He imagined she might be smiling.

'And then that Sunday he wasn't there. You must have been surprised. You'd have thought he'd want to see you off. With it being your birthday. After all of you having such a nice time together.'

He listened to the phone echo silence for a while and then her voice came, smaller and sounding further away.

'I don't know what we were thinking about that morning either. Or at least, I do, of course, I do – my head was full of the plane and how late it was. And we should have been asking, Where's Daddy? What's happened to him? Searching or something. But that's talking now, clear enough now. The thing is, none of us, Mummy or Alistair or me, we couldn't imagine this. Not that anything could be really wrong.'

He'd explained that difference to young detectives often enough. You could get yourself into a muddle paying the wrong kind of close attention to what people said. Same thing with the decisions of any ordinary day, put them under the microscope of a police enquiry, and chances were for most of us some of the things we'd done or omitted to do wouldn't make a lot of sense. Nothing sinister about it, people didn't live their lives by strict reason. Or talk by a rule-book. Take past tenses, for example.

If they did, why would Ruth Bellman finish up talking about her play again? He couldn't work out quite how, something to do with anxiety, but she'd got there

'I haven't been finding it easy to sleep,' she said. 'It was light outside and I was sick of just lying in bed. Then I had this idea for the first scene. Not on stage at all, but have it happening among the audience. I saw it just the way it could be done, and I was so excited I sat right up in bed. And, you know, I might have dozed off – just for a second. So I could have been asleep and it could have been a dream, which when you think about it would be marvellously appropriate. The more I go over it, the more I feel it's right. Main problem will be persuading the actors, it's hard for them having to change at the very last minute. But I'm certain it would be worth it. That scene is *so* dramatic!'

CHAPTER SEVEN

Monday morning, Harriet was quiet at breakfast. She'd made a pot of coffee and toast, which she was eating dry. He wondered if she was dieting. If she asked, he'd tell her dieting wasn't something she had to do. If anything, for his taste, she could put on a few pounds and look just fine. Either way she would look good to him, but if that's what she wanted he wouldn't argue. An advantage of being older than her, he'd learned not to give advice too freely. That was one advantage, there must be others. Offhand, he couldn't think of any.

'I went to bed,' she said, 'and read till I fell asleep.'

'What were you reading?'

'Nothing. A detective story.'

'Any good?'

'Oh . . . They send me to sleep.'

'I'm sorry I was so late last night.'

'Unsocial hours. It's your job.'

She watched as he got one of the frying pans out of the low cupboard where they were kept. He put it on the ring and set it at high, then poured in some olive oil. From the fridge door, he took a couple of eggs and holding one in each hand cracked them on the rim of the pan. A sizzle as they hit the pan would have been nice, but because he'd been impatient and the oil was cold they spread and went white round the edge.

'You'll get fat,' she said, watching him.

'Are you dieting? You don't need to diet. You look great just as you are.'

He cut more bread and listened to the silence.

By the time he had everything on the plate, she was getting ready to go.

'You do look good, you know,' he told her. 'There's something about women power-dressing. Very sexy.'

'Power-dressing,' she mocked him. 'Haven't you heard, we don't do that any more?'

'Creatures of fashion.'

'We've decided to go for the substance instead of the shadow. This,' she patted shoulder and hip, 'is what we call neat and tidy. Oh, feminine, too.'

'Sexy.'

'I'm in court today,' and she bent and kissed him.

'Love you,' he said.

'Are you going to see Carole?' It was casual; she was already on her way to the door.

'Why?'

'Didn't you see my note? She phoned in the afternoon. I left a note for you before I went to bed.' He shook his head. 'So you could give her a call, if it wasn't too late when you got in.'

'Did she say what she wanted?'

'She made it sound as if it was important.'

'If I can find a minute, I'll phone her.'

'Hmm.'

They looked at one another, and then she turned and went into the hall. He picked up a piece of bread and pushed it into the yolk of one of the eggs. Chewing on it, he listened to the outer door close. *Important*. As soon as he heard the word, he knew what it would be. His ex-wife had got in touch to tell him she was going to get married again. She would want to tell him herself, not have him hear from someone else. He wondered if Betty knew; then thought that was silly. Betty and her mother couldn't be closer. Of course she would know. When he thought about it, even to him it should have been obvious this development was on the cards. And who the lucky man had to be. An educational adviser, he'd come into

the school where Carole was the head teacher. 'My friend,'
she called him. My friend said this, my friend was telling
me that. My more than friend. He tried to think when he'd
last seen Carole. Not for months. That was natural, bound
to happen, since Harriet and he had started living together.
During their separation and even after the divorce, he would
visit Carole often, just to sit and talk. They were divorced,
but friends still.

The truth was, even now he felt more comfortable with his
ex-wife than anyone else on earth. They'd been married a
long time. None of which made it any of his business if
she had decided to remarry. None of which made it anything
but stupid to feel as if his heart had been squeezed. Civilised
people, he and Harriet would probably get an invitation to
the wedding.

Nice to be civilised.

Given the pressure of work, the gap he claimed to have found
in the afternoon was more invented than real. All the same,
over Henderson's objections, he decided they would use it to
look up the Bellmans' family lawyer.

'After all,' he explained as they drove along Queen Street,
'he got in touch with us.' A quick side-glance gave him
the satisfaction of Henderson struggling with his curi-
osity. He'd learned that for the sergeant silence was a pre-
ferred retreat, occasionally a weapon. Mostly, his objections
took the form of what the army would have called dumb
insolence.

'Why did he do that?'

'Checking if we'd got any word on Bellman.'

'. . . We haven't. So what's there to see him about?'

Meldrum took a left, then right. By the numbers, the lawyer
should be somewhere in the middle of this block. He pulled
in and parked on a double yellow line. He was a couple of
steps ahead as he went along checking until he found the name
plate. Going up the stone steps from the street, he deliberately
left the question unanswered. All Henderson had to do was
listen: let him work it out.

He'd expected someone elderly, a touch of white hair, but

when they were shown in, the man getting up from behind the desk looked not much more than thirty. Despite the tan and the rugby player's shoulders, he looked soft round the middle like a man whose good lunches weren't getting burned off any more.

'I'm sorry my father is unavailable,' he said. 'I'm Robin Parker. I'll be glad to help in any way I can.'

When he smiled, his cheeks creased into two little pouches like a squirrel getting ready to store its nuts for the winter. With the news there was no progress on the disappearance, they went away again.

'It's very upsetting,' he said. 'Of course, I don't know him as well as my father does.'

'Your father has had him as a client for a long time?'

'Oh, yes. From about the late Sixties, I think. I can remember meeting him when I was just a child. He and my father had got to be friendly. They played golf together occasionally – that kind of thing.'

'Were you surprised when you heard that he'd disappeared?'

'Surprised?'

'Sometimes in cases like this, people will say to us, I wasn't surprised. If they knew the person had been under stress. In business, say.'

'Oh, John Bellman isn't in any kind of business. He never has been.'

That was an item of information Gordon Bellman hadn't volunteered to spell out about his father.

'You're saying he's always had money, sir?'

'Oh, yes. Rather a lot of it. And well invested.'

'So you were surprised when you heard he'd disappeared.'

'Absolutely! I mean, he hasn't any troubles in that direction.'

'So we've been given to understand.'

'I can confirm it.'

'And, according to his family, he had no difficulties in his private life. As far as anyone in the family knows.'

'Difficulties? He wasn't the type for difficulties. If you mean what I take it you mean?'

'Sometimes in a case like this the man will have met a woman.

He can't tell his family, but feels he can't live without her. One morning he wakes up, the pressure seems too much and he walks away.'

Parker waved a plump hand in front of his chest. 'No, I don't think so. From all I've heard, he was devoted to his wife. A love match, my father called it. I gather both sets of parents were against it. The General came round after they'd married – or even before, to be honest I can't remember what I was told. But Mr Bellman's father never did reconcile himself. And again I couldn't give you chapter and verse on this, but I'm almost sure he was rich – the father, that is. Anyway, he disowned him.'

On the periphery of his vision, Meldrum had picked up Henderson's attentive body language as the talk turned to money. At a conference once he'd heard CC Baird describe the belief that money was at the root of most behaviour as one held in common by hard-headed policemen and old-fashioned communists. Meldrum's colleagues had laughed heartily, not least the ones he suspected would need to have it explained to them later. Amazing how much better a joke sounded when it came from a Chief Constable.

Henderson leaned forward. 'I thought you said Bellman didn't need to work because he had money of his own?'

'The money was his wife's. It's quite a story.' Parker looked as if he would enjoy telling it, then had an attack of discretion. 'Mr Bellman didn't get a penny from his father – or cent, I suppose it should be.'

Cent?

'Mr Bellman is American,' Meldrum remembered.

'Originally, yes.'

'But doesn't have an accent. According to the descriptions we've been given.'

'Does it matter?'

'If the man we're looking for has an American accent, yes, it would help to know that.'

'He doesn't have an accent,' Parker said, confirming what they'd been told by the elder son's wife, Sally Bellman. He sounded relieved like a man who'd solved a needless unpleasantness. 'He's been in this country so long, you see.'

As well as the daughter's twenty-first birthday, it had also been the Bellmans' thirtieth wedding anniversary. Bellman was sixty-one now. That made him thirty-one when he got married; his wife ten years younger.

As if reading his thoughts, Parker said, 'Some people never lose their accent. You know, they come back from America after fifty years and sound as if they've never been away from Morningside. I'd an aunt like that. But with others, they pick it up – wherever they're living, they just pick it up. Bellman was like that. I read somewhere it has to do with having a good ear, being musical, you know. And I dare say with his father being so opposed to the marriage – perhaps he just wanted to leave the past behind?' And added, 'It was quite bitter, I believe. Apparently, the father was an orthodox Jew and was furious at his son for marrying out of the faith.'

It seemed Parker felt he could allow himself to offer so much as a titbit, a sop perhaps for having resisted the story-telling impulse.

Five hours later, it was finally time to go home. He had a choice of homes. Being lucky that way, he would find one if he went straight ahead or turned right. Go straight ahead and he would be on his way to the house in Blackford. Go right, he'd be with Harriet in five minutes; in her flat, which was home now, truly home. But then finding first gear as a traffic light changed from red to green, he found himself turning left and wondered what the hell he was doing until he realised he'd decided to go and see Carole, who had something important to tell him. After all, there hadn't been time to phone her all day.

She had part of the ground floor in a detached stone house in Sciennes. As he waited for her to answer his ring, his attention was caught by the little window at the side, which in the old days must have lit a pantry. The top sash had slid down leaving a gap of three or four inches. As a result, he greeted her opening the door with, 'You still haven't had that window fixed, have you?'

Being Carole, she took this in her stride. Laughing, she said, 'It's nice to see you, too.' And looking over her shoulder as she led him into the living-room, said with sudden pleasure, 'It really is.'

While, being him, he kept on grumbling as he followed her, 'You're on the ground floor. You should have all the windows secured.'

'It's too small for anyone to get in.'

'Kids do most burglaries now. And the younger ones are the most destructive. It needs a bolt, something you can lock.'

'I'll get it fixed. Don't worry. Do you want a coffee?'

'That would be good. It's been a long day.'

'Weren't they always?' she said, and went into the kitchen before he could find an answer.

Taking the chair by the hearth, he thought of how often as a visitor he'd sat here with her on either side of a blazing fire. In Blackford, in the house they'd shared for so many years, after the separation he'd got into the habit of sticking on one bar or two of an old electric fire he'd recovered out of the garage. How much agonising there had been before he would agree they should put in an offer for that house! Betty was old enough so that Carole was back teaching, but what if she got pregnant again? Then he made detective sergeant and they'd decided to risk it. For whatever reason, Carole hadn't ever got pregnant again; and next year Betty would sit her final university exams.

Carole came back carrying two cups and settled down opposite him.

'Thanks for coming,' she said. 'It's been a long time.'

In Harriet's flat, where he lived now, there was what looked like a black iron stove which glowed cheerfully and created an illusion of leaping flames with a mirror and ribbons that blew in the draught from a fan. They didn't use it for warmth, though, since that came from the central heating.

'Harriet left me a note, but I didn't get in until late.'

'Hmm.'

He waited, then said, 'She'd the impression it was something important.'

She made the same little humming noise of agreement, but sat staring into the fire, seemingly not in any hurry to start. Tell me you're going to get married again.

'I was thinking about the house,' he said.

'What?' It was as if he had startled her out of her thoughts. 'What house?'

'Our house.' Let her smile and shake her head at him, that was the way he thought of it. Their house. 'That lawyer wasn't pleased with you.'

It was a jump back into the past, a connection almost at random, but before he could elaborate, Carole said, 'She thought I was a fool.'

Picking up on one another's thoughts; they'd been able to do that from the beginning, even before they had so much of a past to share; like mind-reading.

'She thought you were a traitor in the war of the sexes.'

But at that Carole frowned and said, 'I probably was.'

The lawyer had gained her reputation by making men pay for the harm they caused turning from the old to the new. Assets split. Houses sold up. A claim on pensions due in thirty years or so. For each of the scorned, whatever she could find: nannies, school fees, holiday trips: she summed into the account. But I'm the one who walked out, Carole had told her. Not because of another woman. There isn't one; hasn't ever been one. Because of the hours he works. Because of what he meets when he works, what he sees when he works, what he hears when he works. You'd be surprised how many police marriages break up. In their case, it had been she who was turning from the old life in search of a new.

'There isn't all that much left on the mortgage,' he said. 'We could sell . . . If you needed money for anything.'

'How long is it since you've seen Betty?' she asked.

Mind-reading didn't always work. His head had been full of, Tell me you're going to get married and get it over with.

It was stupid to be angry at her. Stupider to feel as if his heart was being squeezed.

'Not for a while. I phone her. Bother is, I always seem to pick a time when she's out, so I get Sandy instead. He's not a great conversationalist – not with me, anyway.'

His future son-in-law; just finishing at art college; who'd worn a ring through his nose until a policeman had torn it out during a political demonstration. He'd been one of the group that Betty shared a flat with; and now they lived together and claimed to be in love.

'He's a nice boy,' Carole said.

'Uh-huh.' His turn to fall back from words to sounds. In fact, pushed to it, he would have agreed ungrudgingly. He thought Sandy was a nice boy on his way to being a good man; and from what he'd seen of him a brave one. It wasn't hard to have a lot of time for Sandy Torrance.

'This isn't easy,' she said. 'I don't know how to tell you.'

'Just come out with it.' That was too loud. He lowered his voice. 'It's all right. I think I've already guessed.'

She stared at him in astonishment.

'That Betty's pregnant?' she said.

CHAPTER EIGHT

Driving out of Edinburgh again with Henderson, north this time, on the motorway that started on the other side of the Forth Bridge and headed for Inverness. Raining this time too, as it had been when they went down the coast to the Bellman house to start investigating his disappearance. Henderson wasn't grumbling about the weather, just staring out at the rain whipping across the flanks of the hills. For once, Meldrum was grateful for the silence.

He couldn't understand how it had escalated, calm one moment, a tempest of words the next, but then with his daughter he never had been prepared for the storms or able to work out where they'd blown up from. He'd postponed going to see her until he'd come to terms with the folly of her getting pregnant. It had all been quiet and sensible. Sandy sitting beside her on the couch, one arm protectively round her shoulders until she shrugged it away. Let him hold you, Meldrum had wanted to say. Protective is how he should feel; protective's all right. It wasn't what we'd planned, Sandy had said. And he'd thought, There's a surprise; and biting back the sarcasm caught his daughter's eye. At once, Betty had looked away, but that fraction of an instant was all it needed for him to know she saw what he was thinking and him to understand she appreciated every bit as much as he did the element of absurdity in Sandy's muttering. That had always been part of the bother between them, how alike they were.

'What?'

Henderson had said something and he'd missed it.

'I said, it doesn't stop, does it?'

'Sun was shining yesterday.'

'I'm not talking about the fucking rain,' Henderson said. 'This Bellman thing, it keeps trailing on.'

'He's still missing.'

'Come on! If we carried on like this about every cunt that went AWOL, we'd have no time to do anything else. Cunts go missing all the time.'

'No argument there.'

'I keep trying to work out why. And I've no idea. I don't like it when I can't sus what's going on.'

But when Meldrum didn't rise to that, he went back to staring out at the rain.

Hey! Meldrum thought, we've had a conversation, isn't that nice? And then, that it was just as well Betty hadn't been here, listening and ready to catch his eye.

They followed the sign off for Stirling, and from there relied on Henderson's map-reading. They ran through the little town, past the castle on its rock, an echo of Edinburgh. Those old kings knew where to set themselves up: a high rock and flat land around, see your enemies coming. Bannockburn was somewhere around here. This open plain of grass and trees looked worth fighting for; though back then it would probably have been marsh and bogland. After a while, they began to climb into the hills. Henderson bent to check the name of a church at the end of a village of a dozen or so houses. 'Take it slowly. There should be a turn-off on the left.'

But Meldrum had seen what he was sure must be the General's house. A mile away or maybe two, slightly above them, across fields of poor grass separated by stone dykes, a long low grey building set in front of a line of trees planted against the prevailing wind. With the rain like a curtain drawn back and forward, in the failing light under a grey sky, it struck him as a desolate place.

It was further away than it looked, and the road they found on the left, narrow enough to need passing places, looped around an endless series of invisible obstacles, dripping hedges brushing the car on either side. Meldrum had already done most of a day's work before they set out, and would be faced with driving back once they'd finished. However tired, he disliked being a passenger. The road swung back and forward like a hypnotist's watch. It was as if starting awake to come on gateposts set in a corner where two grey walls met. Turning the car in, he stretched his jaw in an involuntary yawn.

The door was opened by a stocky man with a stiff brush of iron-grey hair and a red-veined drinker's nose.

'The General expected you half an hour since,' he said.

The hall was small and gave on to a passage that ran ahead for about thirty feet and then turned left. As they followed along it, Meldrum had an impression of polished wood underfoot, walls papered in dark green, a few prints of horses and a group photograph of men in uniform on the steps of a large building. At the corner the passage widened, but there was no sign of a stair to give access to the upper floor.

The stocky man had paced ahead as if at the double march, and now was waiting, since they had refused to be hurried. When they'd caught up, he rapped on the door, opened it and gestured them inside.

'Policemen you've been waiting for, sir.' His tone did its best to conjure up stamping feet and a salute.

Oh, very bloody military, Meldrum thought, but had to stifle an impulse to put his shoulders back and look smart about it.

'Right you are, Robertson.'

There were two men standing in front of the fire. Tall, slim, upright, at first glance they might have been the same age. Ridiculous, of course. The younger of the two looked in his twenties, and he knew the other, the one who had spoken, was in his eighty-second year. Meldrum didn't just know his age; he knew his campaigns, his decorations, the date of his wife's death and his daughter's birth. He'd looked him up, when he'd been told to go and see Mrs Bellman's father, General Seton Gordon Gardiner.

'Inspector Meldrum, is it?'

Close up, the General's face was a net of fine wrinkles, but the blue of his eyes was a true unfaded colour still.

'Yes. And this is Mr Henderson.' Mister was label enough. He didn't feel inclined to offer any more ranks.

'I appreciate your coming. From Edinburgh, was it? Not the best of days for travelling.'

'You must be concerned about your son-in-law,' Meldrum said, his tone carefully neutral, thinking it would have been nice if he'd been given a choice about coming.

He glanced at the other man. Hands behind his back, gently rocking by the General's side, head bowed as if studying the pattern on the carpet. Which label should be hung on him? Adjutant? Aide-de-camp? Lover boy?

'My grandson,' the General said, 'staying with me for a bit.'

Meldrum wasn't normally stupid but, wits clogged with all the stuff about rank, he didn't make the obvious connection.

It was Henderson who filled the pause by asking, 'Would that be Mr Alistair Bellman, sir?'

The young man contented himself with nodding. Fleshy, rosy-cheeked, he had the look of someone who spent a lot of time in the open air, on a tennis court, on a horse, on a beach. Facially there wasn't much resemblance to his grandfather's great beak of a nose and high cheekbones; except that when he looked up, he stared at Meldrum out of the same vivid blue eyes.

'Any questions for him, ask them,' the General said. 'Isn't that what you came for?'

'We didn't know Mr Bellman was here,' Meldrum said.

The thin lips stretched. If it was a smile, there was no humour in it. 'Wouldn't have asked you otherwise.'

There wasn't any arguing with that. Different problem: Since Henderson and he hadn't known Bellman would be there, why had they come at all? Solution: because they'd been told to. Luckily, the question wasn't asked; unfortunately, the answer was too obvious. Power games. The General played power games, Meldrum recognised.

They were waved to a couch facing the fire, while the General and his grandson settled in two green leather armchairs set to either side of it. The couch turned out to be less comfortable than it looked. As unobtrusively as he could manage, Meldrum eased off what felt suspiciously like a spring gouging between his shoulderblades. To the slight stress of that position was added the dimness of the room, islanded by lights from standing lamps, and the brightness of the fire to which his gaze kept being drawn. During the next hour, he felt increasingly nostalgic for an interview room at headquarters.

On the other hand, there were no complaints about the way Alistair Bellman responded. He dealt with questions quickly, hardly taking time to think, but almost without exception managing to cover the ground at the first time of asking. It was an impressive performance. Military training. He's been debriefed before. Officer material. All of that, but allowing for it the main impression left on Meldrum was of natural intelligence. Bellman was a very bright man; which made it odder that in the course of every answer he would glance across at the General. It didn't seem to have anything to do with looking for instruction. That would have suggested some kind of preparation, which in turn, policemen having suspicious minds, might have raised the notion of a concocted story. But clearly Bellman's wits were too sharp to need help, and anyway there wasn't the slightest reason to suppose he wasn't telling the truth, straightforwardly too and admirably concisely. Maybe he just needed the old man's approval. A habit of deference? If so, it was a pity the General heard him out with no more change of expression than a saurian on a rock.

Towards the end, Meldrum asked, like an afterthought, 'One thing – have you been in touch with us at all?'

In full flow by this time, Bellman opened his mouth to answer, then paused and frowned. '. . . In touch?'

'Hmm. Wondering how the search was going. If there had been any developments?'

'I let people get on with their jobs. Put that down to the way I was trained.'

'I wish everybody would feel the same way. Well, you can imagine. People feel if they phone somehow they're doing something. Doesn't make a lot of sense, if you think about it. But people get upset. We're into the fourth week since the disappearance of your father.'

'If there was anything, I'd expect to hear.'

'And, of course, you'll be in touch with your mother. And your sister.'

'Yes.'

'When I spoke to your sister – that was over the phone – she was very helpful. Just as you've been. About the sequence of events over the weekend.'

'Yes,' he said again, and glanced at his watch.

'I asked her if she could let me have your phone number. But she didn't have it.'

'She'll have mislaid it. That would be like Ruth.'

'And she didn't have an address, or I could have had it looked up in the book. Your phone number, that is.'

'I'm staying with friends. I'll give you the details. In case you have to get in touch.'

'That would be helpful, thank you. When will you be going back to—'

'Within the week. A group of us are planning a trip.'

And then the General intervened before Meldrum could reply. 'To Nepal,' he said.

'Nepal,' Meldrum repeated.

Alistair Bellman smiled. 'As I said, we're just at the planning stage.'

'How long would you plan to be away?'

'Months. There'd be acclimatising. And training. We intend to do some serious climbing.'

'You'll be hoping your father is found before then.'

'In 1953, when Jack Kelly and I decided to take a crack at Everest, we had to go in illegally,' the General said. 'Rule then was, the Nepalese government kept you out unless you had Himalayan experience. But of course you couldn't get experience unless you went to the Himalayas.'

'Catch 22,' Bellman said. Like two different people, Meldrum thought. When he talks to me, he's brisk and formal. With his grandfather . . .

The General went on as if uninterrupted. 'They didn't want you there at all. But then we got a tip-off about a cache of food a previous expedition had left at Camp Two. That was enough for us. Five weeks' stiff training in New Zealand and then in we went. But when we got to where the cache was, food was gone. John Hunt's expedition had beaten us to it.'

'Great times!' the young man exclaimed. 'I'm terrifically looking forward to seeing it for myself.'

With his grandfather ... Like a bright schoolboy wanting approval. A pat on the head. No, that's what dogs got.

'Not much point going now,' the General said. 'Be surrounded by trippers. From what I hear, you can't see Base Camp One for the rubbish piled round it. I'd hate to see Everest like that. Spoil all the good memories.'

WITNESS

M e and the other boys called her Willful. And she called me Robba, when she was real small, I mean, too little to say Robertson. Robba. And to us, among ourselves, she got the name Willful. Not meaning anything by it. It was because she was called Willa, that was it, more than her being wild or anything like that. In a Scots regiment you know what it's like, guys from everywhere, Birmingham, Liverpool, Manchester, and none of us had ever heard that for a girl's name. Not even the guys from Scotland – we had some – not even them had come across a Willa. It's from Orkney, an Orkney name, that's where her mother was from, Orkney. Only the mother was dead, of course, died giving birth to her.

The General's been a widower now for more than fifty years.

This was just after the war. I'd been with the General, Major as he was then, in Africa, then afterwards in Italy, all the way— You wouldn't think it now, but I was a wild man when I was young. In and out of trouble, more in than out – I still have stomach trouble and it goes back to the glasshouse, getting all your grub on the one plate, stew and potatoes and custard in a oner, made me sick. For some reason, it sickened me. I'd come out of the glasshouse stone and a half lighter, swearing that was me finished. But it was the old story, sooner or later, a wrong word and I'd smash somebody's face in. Always fighting, I was done for. In the end, they got sick of me – I'd a lot of chances, I was a good soldier most of the time – but they were ready to kick me out.

God knows what would have happened to me then. Civvie nicks probably, downhill all the way, and end up one of those old blokes on a park bench – wrapped up like a fish supper in the *Daily Express* with four pairs of coats on top, eh? I think of that some nights I wake up in my warm bed listening to the wind howling outside.

But I was lucky. The war came along just in time. Lucky for me. Things was all right then, like I say I was a good soldier, I was always all right as long as I'd plenty to do. Bother for me was the slack times, army's full of slack times. I used to get bored easily. I got in trouble in transit camp – just before we were due to get shipped out. This bastard of an officer who'd be in charge of the court martial, he had it in for me – no way I wasn't for the high jump this time – war or no war. I'm an old man now, I can admit what I wouldn't have then, not ever, died first, I was frightened. I mean, I'd almost killed the guy. I was going down for a long time – and worse than anything they could do to me was how I felt about myself. I was trained to be a soldier, it was all I knew, the only thing I'd ever been any good at or had any reason to think well of myself about. And right when all that training was going to pay off, when it was for real, I'd be sitting safe somewhere in a prison cell while my mates were getting killed. I'm telling you no more than the God's simple truth, I think the shame of it would have finished me. And then that bastard of an officer got his back broken in a car crash. And Major Gardiner came into my cell one night. What he said'll go to the grave with me, don't ask. He took me apart, and when he put me together again I was a different man. And when the regiment sailed the next morning, I was on the boat. God knows how he managed it. This country's fighting for its life, he said.

Tell you the truth, we were fond of her. The child, little Willa, that's who we're talking about, isn't it? Right, then. Hard not to be, a motherless child. It was the General had her brought out, lots of men wouldn't have. How do I mean? Obvious, isn't it? Well, taking on the responsibility of a kid under your feet. And, don't forget, the mother had died having her. I can imagine some men might have blamed the kid. But not the General, no, that wasn't the General's nature. He did his duty by her. Fond of her? Well, he must have been, mustn't he? He wasn't a man who wore his heart on his sleeve.

She had a nanny, Scots girl, even if he'd have had a German, it wouldn't have been on, security and that. Unfortunately, the nanny, that first one that came out with the child, she got herself married. Same thing happened with the next one. Not surprising, young women surrounded by soldiers, and nice girls, not tarts. We didn't get to meet that many girls you'd want to marry. So from when Willa came out from England in '48, she'd just turned two, there was one nanny after another. The one who mattered in her life was her father.

And here, listen. About how he felt about her. I told you he wasn't the kind to make a show of himself. God, you've seen him. He is a great man, that's all there is to say. But, listen, there was one time . . . Don't misunderstand me . . . Maybe I did feel sometimes he was . . . I don't know how to put it. He wasn't ever unkind to her. Just set her standards and, well, maybe for a little child it wasn't always easy for her to know what it was about. Anyway, if I did think that he was hard on her, there was this afternoon, this particular afternoon, I can't remember how, I'd gone into the drawing-room thinking he wasn't there. And he was by the window, kind of behind the curtain, looking out.

And it was the children he was looking at – little Willa and one or two others. The soldiers had taught them to give the Nazi salute and shout *Heil Hitler!* at the Germans. Well, you can imagine, kids with adults, irritated the hell out of them. I can hear her yet. *Sieg heil!* When he heard me, he looked round and then he said, 'Get on with it, man!'

But I'd caught him smiling, just a little smile, and you know what I thought? I thought, He does love her.

Sieg heil! Sieg heil!

Little Willful.

BOOK TWO

Dead Man Laughing

CHAPTER NINE

Tore Braaten was tired of living at the Villa Borghese. For a month he'd been travelling. Ten days earlier he'd been in Vienna, a city he'd never seen before. He'd been impressed, the buildings, the crowded streets, the well-dressed women; if you had to kill time, that was a good city to do it in. From there, he'd followed the Italian's trail to the Slovak Republic. Bratislava had been less run down than he'd expected. The dust on the window ledge of his room had drifted from a building site opposite the hotel. If less nimbly than the Czechs, the Slovaks were breaking camp and moving towards the free market. Even so, anyone but a lunatic would cheerfully swap Bratislava to be in Paris. And yet forty-eight hours after moving in, he was tired of the Villa Borghese.

He dozed and wakened. He had his meals brought to his room. He lay on the bed and read *Hunger*. He didn't like Hamsun's politics, but it was in old age that his compatriot had been a Nazi. As a young man, he'd written like a dark angel about going hungry to be an artist. To hell with a good writer's politics. Anyway, it was the only book he had with him. He did press-ups, looked out of the window. Time passed slowly. He was waiting for the Italian's call.

It came late on the afternoon of the third day. Although he'd been waiting for it, the sudden ending of the silence set his heart pounding. He scrambled across the bed and snatched up the phone, said his name and waited. Nothing.

He said, 'I'm on my own.' And then after a moment of

listening to the silence, 'I don't play stupid games.' He put the phone back. It rang again at once, but after three rings, just as he was reaching, it stopped. Time started passing again, slowly at first, crawling like honey down the side of a jar, then slipping by so quickly an hour had gone. So what if the Italian didn't phone back? To hell with the bastard! Bravado, of course, since he knew perfectly well *so what*: so the trail cold again, so no reason why he should be lucky enough to pick it up a second time, so he might never learn the last pieces in the jigsaw. *So* fuck it. Bravado again. He lay getting steadily more depressed and more persuaded he'd made a big mistake in hanging up. Yet when the phone rang, again he let it go on for a time before picking it up.

The breathy voice of a fat man said, 'You should learn patience, my friend.' Locascio spoke in French, which irritated Braaten unreasonably since he knew the Italian spoke fluent Norwegian. He kept silent. The Italian said, 'Now who's playing stupid games?'

'I kept our appointment in Vienna. You were the one who didn't show up.'

'Can we make it French, please? We're in France not Norway. Let's aim at not making ourselves conspicuous.'

'Are you planning to put in an appearance this time?'

'That's better,' Locascio said. Braaten had asked the question in French. 'I'm sorry about Vienna. Something came up.'

'In the Slovak Republic.'

There was a silence, before Locascio said, 'How did you know?'

'Call it luck.' And leave it at that. It would be better if he could keep from Locascio the kinds of help he could call on.

'Holy Name of God's fucking Mother,' the Italian said. 'Did you follow me there?'

'I spent a few days in Bratislava.' He listened to the fat man wheezing.

There was the sound of Locascio sighing, then he said, 'Now I know what went wrong.'

'You were there to try to make a deal.'

'. . . I was there to meet some associates.'

'Ex-associates.'

'Things didn't work out the way I hoped. I don't deny that. Let me name a time this evening and a place. I'll be there. Trust me.'

'I don't have to trust you any more. I'm the only way out you've got left.'

'Not true. Put a guard outside, board up every window. There isn't a locked room in the world without a door marked exit. A little door in the corner, you have to bend to go through it.' He gave a chuckling laugh that trailed out in wheezing intakes of breath. 'I can always shoot myself.'

'You're not the type,' Tore Braaten said.

Later, waiting in the bar, he reflected that he, on the other hand, was: a man born to live with dark nights and short days, a man from the cold north. Not, of course, that it was the winter that got to you; you could survive the winter. In the bad times, it was the disappointments of spring delayed that did the damage.

At that point in his reflections, he decided he'd been shut up in one room too long. Nothing for it but to get another drink. Beer again. His third since he came into the bar. Thinking of this and that, deep thoughts like Norwegian winters having the advantage they made you too depressed to shoot yourself, he'd let the first two slip down absent-mindedly. He wasn't good at sipping beer, making it last. He glanced at his watch. Almost nine. Already Locascio was half an hour late.

The arrangements had been predictably paranoid. As instructed, he'd caught a taxi in the Place Lafayette and driven around; got out at the Pont de Sèvres and walked towards the Auteuil Viaduct; taken the Métro and got off in a district of ugly high-rises – the Parisian version of stack-a-pleb. He'd phoned the Italian at three numbers from different locations, every time being given a different number for the next call. The last one had taken him into a narrow back street where he'd walked past the bar, and then coming back had checked the length of the street again to make sure he'd got the instructions right. The mean frontage untypically gave no view of the interior. If this was a neighbourhood bar, it looked like a secret the neighbourhood wanted kept to itself. An uninviting place, he wondered how Locascio had found it.

During the forty minutes he'd been there, none of it had grown on him. Not the unwiped tables, the tin ashtrays overflowing, not the barman with the tubercular cough, not the tapes of Johnny Halliday clones, and especially not the clients. He didn't regard poverty as a moral offence; not every country could have North Sea oil and gas. Born before independence from Sweden, his father's parents had been poor, get-up-in-the-dark work-the-land poor. But the clientèle of the bar offered something else: lie-in-bed-and-stare-at-the-wall poor, on-a-hand-out poor, take-a-fix poor.

Spoiling-for-trouble poor; which, to be fair, rich or poor everywhere came with being young.

There were three of them drinking at the bar and when they started trouble with the man another two came over from a table to spectate. That made five, none of them by his calculation over seventeen yet. They came in different sizes but the sweat-shirts and loose-cut jackets made a uniform of sorts, like the prejudices he guessed at inside the shaven skulls. As a group they explained why a ghetto neighbourhood bar didn't have a black face in sight.

When he caught a trace of accent in the man's French, he tried automatically to place what might be his tongue of origin. Danish; no, German, more likely. From wherever, a foreigner, like himself. His first thought was, there but for the grace of God. Like a pack of dogs, the storm-troopers had picked on the stranger. No surprise in that, they'd been somebody's accident waiting to happen.

'I'm sorry,' the foreigner said again. 'That was clumsy of me.'

'Or maybe it was me. I could have bumped your elbow. Do you think that's what happened?'

It was what had happened.

Four of the group were thick-necked, meaty-arsed types. After the Napoleonic fashion, the smallest, the one who'd spoken, was obviously the leader. Perhaps because of the quality of his wit; more likely because he had the loosest grip on sanity. He was drinking Coke, something sweet to go with whatever he'd stuck into himself earlier. When he yawned, a cord of spittle lengthened between his lips.

It went on like that. The foreigner kept apologising. He pulled out a bundle of notes, laid it on the counter: Drink, for all of them, whatever they wanted. While the barman was putting bottles up, the Boy Napoleon made a show of counting the money, spreading it fan-shaped with one dirty finger, then poked the roll more or less in the direction of his side jacket pocket. A couple of notes missed and floated to the floor. Nobody tried to pick them up. None of the cash went to the bartender, which wasn't a surprise. They'd paid him nothing so far. The foreigner took his drink over to a table, carrying it with both hands, and sat with his head down.

Given the odds, that kind of reaction made a lot of sense, and if the performance was a touch degrading, put it down to the bad luck of being in the wrong place at the wrong time. That kind of bad moment could happen to anyone – except perhaps, Braaten's instinct suddenly told him, just perhaps not to this man. Stoop-shouldered, late twenties, maybe younger maybe older, in poor light it was hard to tell, leather jacket, good enough quality but seen a lot of wear, dark hair cut short at the sides. Nothing exceptional about him. A man who would pass in a crowd; and so well that Braaten couldn't decide whether the foreigner had already been here when he came in or arrived afterwards. Either way, without the altercation, he wouldn't have noticed him, and that was odd. On the alert waiting for the Italian to show, in a bar not more than half full, Tore Braaten would have bet his life against overlooking anybody. He didn't understand it, or come to that why the foreigner was still there, at the table by the wall, head bent, sipping at his drink. Already the five were grinning across at him, their venom held only in a fragile temporary check. It seemed to him that a man who'd been frightened like this one appeared to have been should take his chance to get out, go find somewhere else to drink or go home if his nerves were too badly shaken.

In his brief concentration on the stranger, he almost missed Giovanni Locascio's arrival; so much for being alert. One moment Locascio was just inside the entrance, the next he was by the table, nodding recognition; it was the first time they had met face to face. For a fat man, the Italian moved quickly.

'Same again for you?'

Braaten was about to refuse when he noticed that he'd emptied his glass, absent-minded again.

'I'm sorry to have kept you waiting,' Locascio said, pushing the fourth beer across, settling himself in the seat opposite, 'especially in such a shithole.'

He spoke without lowering his voice. His heavily accented French, as Braaten had learned over the phone, was clear and fluent.

And, obviously, idiomatic.

'A shithole for fascists,' Braaten said, no more quietly. 'You should feel at home.'

Putting it into words, the Frontist feel of the place, made him uneasy. Given the Italian's contacts, why shouldn't someone have put those thugs at the bar at Locascio's disposal? A glance showed them with their heads together, busy with their own concerns. The stranger, nowhere in sight, must have had a rush of common sense to the head and got out.

'It's good to meet at last.' Locascio padded a handkerchief into the palm of his hand and wiped his forehead. Sweat made dark patches under the arms of his white jacket. 'What's interesting you over there?'

'The Hitler Youth at the bar. I was wondering if they were why you chose this place.'

Locascio swivelled his massive head a fraction to get a view.

'Don't insult me,' he said.

Taken by surprise, Braaten laughed. It was a good-sounding laugh, a top of the hill on a fine day laugh, one from the chest that opened the lungs, the sort that did you good. A pure sound in an impure place.

The Italian blinked.

'I'm referring to their lack of class,' he said. 'Not their politics.'

'Not their politics,' Braaten repeated stonily, the impulse to laugh gone as quickly as it had come.

'I'm not a political man,' the Italian said, as if taking the moral high ground. 'I'm a businessman.'

'When I saw Kielland at the foot of the Hollmenkollen

Ski-Jump, he'd learned how dangerous doing business with you could be. He'd died quickly, but not easily.'

'Under the circumstances, you'll understand I don't care too much what Mr Kielland thought about anything. Not any more.'

'Luckily, he kept good records. That's how we learned he was Bellman's partner.'

'I don't know anyone called Bellman.'

'Then you won't know he's disappeared?'

He mopped sweat, the white slab of face expressionless. 'You have the advantage of me.'

'John Bellman. He disappeared weeks before Kielland was killed. And that gives us two choices. Either he's already dead. Or like you he's hiding from the Hunter, but went on the run early enough to have a chance. Was he that smart?'

'Smarter than Kielland wouldn't be hard.'

Braaten smiled. 'I was thinking of smarter than you.'

'You don't think I'm in shape for running?' Rolls of fat under his chin shook with his chuckling. None of the photographs Braaten had pored over had shown him like this. In the times they had spoken over the phone, he had never heard him laugh. Maybe Locascio had been irritated by him grinning – or just found his example contagious. A jolly fat man. Except that in the eyes where the twinkle should have been, two circles of darkness held steady like the muzzles of a shotgun.

'The kind of trouble you're in,' Braaten said, 'I'm listening to a dead man laughing.'

It seemed Little Napoleon also disapproved. To explain how much, he swung round, elbows resting on the bar. When it came to idiom, he had the native advantage. On the theme of 'fat fuck', he began to ring intricate changes.

'Let's get out of here,' Braaten said; but then wondered, as the Italian heaved obediently to his feet, whether after all this might be a set-up.

The odd thing was the silence as they walked out, not complete but almost, a hushing of noise, a diminishing as they passed each table, as if the patrons too were waiting to see what would happen next.

'I have a car,' Locascio said. 'Parked opposite the market. I thought it would be safer there.'

Their heels rang on the pavement as they walked. The lane was deserted, pools of shadow separating the pale lamps. Ahead were the lights of the main street, traffic and pedestrians like a mirage moving across the mouth of the alley. Glancing behind, he saw a figure step through the shadow between two cars to the pavement and turn in their direction. Unaware, Locascio was hurrying on. A second look back was in time to catch the figure held in a sudden shaft of light from the door of the bar as it opened.

There hadn't been any real doubt what Little Napoleon and his storm-troopers would do, Braaten realised. Even if they'd been closet pacifists, the expectations of their audience would have got them to their feet, there being no business like show business. Choreographed by Leni Reifenstahl, they came out in a wedge of unhurried menace. It was the yelp they gave, pack noise of hunters, that made him share their recognition of the man caught in the light. The foreigner with the German accent hadn't gone away after all.

Intent on what was happening, he felt rather than saw Locascio pad back to his side. The yelling must have turned him in his tracks. Glancing down, Braaten reacted instinctively at sight of a weapon. He chopped down hard, swinging across his body so the edge of his hand smashed the fat man's wrist outwards. Locascio grunted in pain and the gun clattered out into the middle of the road as if he had thrown it from him.

It was the same instinct that made Braaten then reach under his jacket for his own gun. All of it instinct, while his eyes were showing him what his brain disbelieved, the choreography of violence on the pavement outside the bar. Two of the youths were down, a third spun and fell. It was close fighting, some mixed style, karate-based, as taught to the elite of armies now, borrowing techniques to hurt from everywhere.

Locascio had him by the sleeve and was yelling, afterwards he couldn't have said what or in what language, Italian, French, Norwegian, belatedly to make him understand, *Do you want me to die?*

And maybe it wasn't words at all that made him understand.

The fourth one down was the little leader, not much more than a boy. Profiled against the light, his head went back too far for the neck not to be snapped. The foreigner was a trained killer.

And Braaten understood and began to move, herding the Italian who cried out as he ran without looking back, 'Shoot him! Shoot him!'

When they burst on to the main street, Locascio ploughed the crowded pavement like an ice-breaker. Braaten rode the other's wake in a spume of curses choked off at sight of the gun in his hand. No one tried to stop them. When the Italian got to the car, Braaten ran round to the passenger side. A red Subaru estate. Central locking. He pulled open the door and was inside as fast as Locascio. If the German was coming, he was masked amongst the crowd.

'Where is he?' Locascio screamed.

The car pulled away with a jerk that threw him round face front again.

'Look out!'

They'd swung across the road, oncoming traffic swerved past on either side.

'My wrist. You've broken my wrist.'

Locascio was driving with one hand. Braaten reached for the wheel. Locascio as if demented with the notion of being attacked jerked away from him. The wheel spun.

The world spun.

They mounted the opposite pavement. Smashed through a tumbling uproar of chairs, tables. A wall of light stood up in front of them. Was gone. Blackness.

He could only have been out for a moment. The seat beside him was empty. On either side were the ruins of a pavement café. The window was starred where something had hit it. Probably his head. A face looked at him, an old man bent forward to peer at him. An old man in a white apron. Holding a tray. The old man was inside the café and so was the bonnet of the car. What struck him as remarkable was that the old waiter should still have glasses on the tray he held out so steadily in front of him.

While he sat there, content for a moment to think about that, the door beside him was wrenched open. He was dragged out, slammed against the car, feet kicked apart, searched, handcuffed. Very fast, professional. Their 'fuck's, 'bastard's echoed to him from the far end of a tunnel. When he was turned, someone slapped his face. He tasted blood in his mouth. Blinked at the half-circle of uniformed men.

Fuck them too.

'I'm a policeman,' Tore Braaten said.

WITNESS

Said Tweed tae Till,
Whit gars ye rin sae still?
Said Till tae Tweed,
Though ye gang at speed
And I rin sae slaw,
Yet for ae man ye droun
I'll droun twa.

BOOK THREE

Looking for Bellman

CHAPTER TEN

'A sixty-one-year-old man hosts a family party to celebrate his daughter's twenty-first birthday – and as well it's near as dammit his own thirtieth wedding anniversary, just past at least. A pleasant afternoon, sitting in the garden, drinking wine, then off to a good restaurant for dinner. Come home, sit and chat, have a whisky or two. Off to bed. And in the morning, he's vanished.'

'That's it.'

'No mistress, no money worries. Or so you tell me.'

'So everybody tells me.'

'Teenagers disappear. For a variety of reasons. Mostly to do with their parents. Hearing the things I hear, it's occurred to me the human race would be less complicated if we could be born, say, age seventeen. And happier, really incomparably happier. Tough on mothers, you might say. Would have to be a different mechanism, of course there would. Something like budding, that might do it.'

'Budding,' Meldrum said. He rubbed his forehead and squinted down his nose to check the time. Unobtrusively. An advantage of wearing his watch on the inside of his wrist.

'Children are so vulnerable. Human beings are born too soon, you know that? Helpless and hairless neonates. So that we can get those big heads of ours out into the world without killing our mothers. Not like deer.'

'Deer.'

'Doe drops her little one and it's up and running. Keep up

with the herd or get picked off. So . . . Anyway . . . Point is, yes, point is. *Teenagers* run off. Peak there on the graph. And again among the thirty pluses, another peak. Been married young, have kids, it all gets to be too much. I'm talking disappearances, not just partner swapping. *That*'s getting to be the norm.'

'Sixty-one-year-olds?'

'Quite. You do get a thirty-year itch. And a forty-year one. Women walking out when the kids don't need them any more.'

'Mrs Bellman is a pretty formidable woman. Not that it's relevant,' Meldrum added. Since, after all, it was Bellman not his wife who had disappeared. Better than deer, though. At least, now they were working within the right species. Surely the FBI wouldn't have to put up with shit like this.

'That's how she struck you? But that's meeting her on her own. Minus, I mean, her husband.'

'He's disappeared.' Helpfully, Meldrum explained the obvious.

Knife pulled his glasses down his nose, gave him a shrewd look, then used his forefinger to shove them back up into place.

'You have to see a couple together to know what the dynamics are. Man can be a lion in the office and a mouse at home.'

'You think Bellman ran away because his wife was bullying him?'

'Hardly. Not having seen them together, any more than you have, I wouldn't be imprudent enough to claim anything of the kind. *But*,' he raised a hand against a purely notional interruption, 'it might be worth bearing in mind as something to test for when you talk to or about her, about them as a couple. It does happen. One pattern among many. I know, altogether too many for your taste at the moment. An embarrassment of patterns. The less information there is, the more patterns suggest themselves as possibilities. The more information starts to come in, the fewer patterns you can find will accommodate the facts. Like it or lump it, that's the way it is.'

The doctor's surname was Stanley, which explained why he was known to the detectives on the force as Knife. A reference also to his preference for the roundabout approach in discussion as against cutting to the heart of the matter. Henry Stanley was an apple-cheeked little man, not much over five feet, who dressed – suit, shirt, shoes – like a successful banker, but undercut the effect with a taste for ties loud enough to make a pimp worry about the decibel count. He was an academic; a psychologist who had turned to anthropology and then taken a sideways step into the sociology department of one of the city's newer universities. Eight years ago he had volunteered his services over a series of assaults on schoolgirls which had put the city into a turmoil of anger and apprehension. The profile he had done narrowed the search to one area of the city and was an uncanny fit to the attacker when he was caught; and though the catching when it came wasn't down to science or good policework but dumb luck more than anything, Stanley had got a measure of credibility and a lot of publicity. Since then the force had called on him a number of times. Even Meldrum, a sceptic in such matters, had once worked with him at the insistence of the late Chief Superintendent Billy Ord, a man with a shrewd instinct for throwing the press a diversionary bone when the jackals were yelping. That, however, had been somewhere in the lagging middle of a major murder enquiry – and by invitation.

This time he had phoned out of the blue to express an interest.

'As for facts,' Meldrum said, 'that's it. I'm surprised you heard of Bellman's disappearance at all.'

'It was in the papers.'

'Not for long. He wasn't any kind of public figure.'

Knife nodded a vague agreement. 'Caught my eye, you know. It's an area I've been giving a bit of thought to. Disappearances.'

That wasn't impossible; it was even plausible. Stanley must feel he'd been invited in often enough not to risk being rebuffed if he expressed an interest. All the same, asking around it didn't seem he had volunteered his help on a case before. Being first left Meldrum with the feeling, irrational or not, that someone up there was giving him another nudge on the Bellman case.

'The attitude of his children strikes me as worth a look,'

Knife said. 'The one you met at his grandfather's, Alistair, the younger son, the one who's in the army—'

'Was in the army,' Meldrum interrupted. 'I'm told he isn't any more.'

'And his grandfather's a general . . . Interesting,' Stanley said. 'Anyway, he's so concerned about his father he's planning an expedition to eat yak butter and climb mountains. The daughter Ruth is in London producing the Bard—'

'And sitting exams. To be fair.'

'Let's hope losing a parent doesn't upset her concentration. And the elder son, the accountant—'

'Financial adviser. Gordon.'

'Gets a call his father's gone, tells his mother to call the police – and doesn't check again until the following morning. Even for a cold fish that's taking things pretty calmly.'

'If the father's done it before,' Meldrum said, 'it's never been reported.'

'Made a habit of dropping out of sight. And coming home after a bit. That would account for the lack of, Oh, God, what's happened to Dad? and, Hold on, Mum, I'm coming to hold your hand. They'll be waiting for him to turn up again. But, then, if that was the case, why call in the police at all? If the wife never has on these previous occasions. Assuming, for the sake of argument, there have been previous occasions. So what made this time different?'

It was true the attitude of the daughter and sons had bothered him. Give Knife time and he tended to get there. 'Maybe his wife had warned him not to do it again. Maybe she's using us to find out who the other woman is.'

'Oh, yes,' Knife said appreciatively. 'I like that.'

A scorned woman using a police force as private detectives to hunt up evidence for the divorce. It was a nice idea. Too nice perhaps. The fact the Profiler liked it so much put Meldrum off. It was the kind of twist Knife might have come up with himself, which to a simple policeman suggested it was almost certainly over-ingenious. Meldrum, who had plenty of imagination and as much intuition as the next man, had found that on balance it paid to keep it simple.

'Except,' he said, 'my strong impression is that Mrs Bellman wouldn't be the type to make her troubles public.'

'For that type,' Knife said, 'murder might seem a better solution than divorce. Certainly, it did to respectable folk like Crippen and Ruxton. Granted, it seems absurd nowadays. I know,' the warning hand went up again, 'no body. No body, no murder. Come to that, as far as we know, no mistress either, eh? I wonder if that was the trouble. Daughter pretty?'

'Sorry?'

'Bellman's daughter.'

'No idea. I've only spoken to her over the phone. Why? Are you suggesting Bellman was having an affair with his daughter?'

'Why not?'

'No body.'

'No evidence, you mean. And, anyway, you don't like the idea?'

'It happens.'

'But?'

But not all the time, Meldrum thought. Not as something more likely than not. The world wasn't that sick, for Christ's sake!

'We're policemen,' he said. 'We keep it in mind.'

'Matter of fact,' Knife said cheerfully, 'what I was thinking was, the conjunction of his thirtieth wedding anniversary with sitting up drinking with two pretty young women – never mind that one of them was his daughter – is the older son's wife pretty? right – might just have made Bellman realise what he was missing. Got the hormones going. He goes upstairs but can't get to sleep. *I'm sixty-one – that's not old* – Time passes, hours maybe, the window gradually lightens. *That's not old – soon, though, I will be old, really old.* And he slips out from under the covers, creeps across to the bedroom door, careful as a cat burglar not to wake his wife. And disappears.'

'You're right about one thing,' Meldrum said. This time he glanced openly at his watch. Holiday feeling: in the morning, he had a plane to catch.

'What would that be?'

'Too many patterns. Too little information.'

'Truth is,' Knife said, 'families are like pots – you can't tell what's bubbling away until the lid comes off.'

CHAPTER ELEVEN

Going to the restaurant, the car had taken them past Buckingham Palace. The Berk had leaned over, peered out of the window and said, 'The Queen's not at home. The flag isn't flying.' The sun was shining, though, and the Guard was being changed. Small under the high railings, a line of people peered through at red uniforms wheeling about the courtyard. On the other side of the road, separated by heavy traffic from the spectacle, other spectators clustered behind police barriers. It didn't seem as if they could have much of a view, being a long way off and on a day when the flag wasn't flying.

Looking round the restaurant, Meldrum yawned, a furtive parting of the lips, a little sip of breath, and then was seized by the pleasure of letting go until he finished on the luxury of a sigh that stretched his jaws. Even the childhood ingrained notion of politeness that raised a hand to veil the second half of the phenomenon didn't deflect Harriet's frown.

'Early flight,' the Berk sympathised.

'Eight o'clock.' Up at half-six to get to the airport by half-seven. But the real damage had been done last night. Sitting till three in the morning in front of the television, half watching, jumping channels between old movies, wasn't something he normally did.

'It's a pity you couldn't have come down with Harriet yesterday.'

'Oh, yes,' Jenny said enthusiastically. On a brief acquaintance, she struck him as someone who went in for enthusiasm.

Jenny was Harriet's friend from student days. Even though she'd gone home to London on graduating they'd 'kept in touch'. You haven't seen her since university, why go all the way to London now? he'd asked, why not wait till they get married? Oh, but, Harriet said, we've always kept in touch. The Berk was the one who had just got engaged to Jenny, which was the occasion for the celebration; combined with a housewarming since they'd just moved into a new flat together. Three rooms, high ceilings, a kitchen with a pine table and a dishwasher that slid out on rails from a cupboard, the cloakroom in the hall with padding behind the door; he'd admired all of it and then joined a dozen others, twenty years younger, Harriet's age, glass in hand, to admire the view of the private gardens out of windows that went down to the parquet floor. It was a nice flat in a nice district. Getting a taxi to it from Heathrow had cost him £36. He'd assumed they'd be having lunch there, but instead taxis had been sent for and the company decanted to merriment and fluting cries.

The taxi had let them out beside a restaurant with a green painted front in a narrow Soho street crowded with traffic. There were too many to fit at one table, instead they had two big round tables for six set side by side. He'd ordered duck as a starter, so when the waiter brought a little plate with pâté and a patch of salad and a small fork to eat it with he was about to object until he noticed they'd put the same in front of everyone else: a taster on the house. The wine began to flow.

Before they took the duck away, he realised Harriet was getting drunk. She'd been drinking at the flat, even before he arrived, and presumably with the Berk and Jenny the night before. Blame the waiters who kept filling the glasses, blame her who kept emptying them. Half-way through the poached haddock, he realised she was getting very drunk. He knew the signs; when they met she'd had a problem. Then they'd fallen in love and she'd been all right. Love conquers all. Hell, it was a celebration; and if she was showing the effect most, none of them were sober. What was wrong with having a drink, they'd object if he tried to stop her. More wrong than any of them would want to hear. He pushed his chair back and stood up. 'A policeman's work is never done,' Harriet said, and someone laughed.

In the lavatory he splashed water up out of the basin and stared at himself in the mirror. He looked fine, like a man who'd just eaten an expensive lunch, no gloomier than usual. Under the mirror, there were piles of small fluffy hand-towels. He used three, dropping them in turn into the bin. In the hall, he didn't even hesitate as he passed the main dining-room. 'Goodbye, sir,' the man on the door said. The traffic in the street sounded louder, the brightness of the sun hurt. A breath of air, then he'd go back inside. It was luck, whether bad or good, a taxi edging its way along the narrow street just then. The driver caught his eye, and stopped at his nod. He got in and gave the address of the Hall of Residence.

A policeman's work was never done.

Blame Harriet. Blame the waiters. Blame himself for not being able to face going back.

'You know Yuri Geller?' the taxi driver asked, watching him in the mirror.

'Heard of him.'

'What do you make of him?'

'Never given it a thought.'

'Me, I always thought he was a con man. But I was listening to him being interviewed on the radio. And just at the end he says, If any of you at home have a watch that isn't working, pick it up, look at it, and say to it, Work! Well, it just so happened the girlfriend had a watch wasn't going. I got it out the drawer, and it started! Makes you think, doesn't it?'

'Maybe you gave it a shake.'

'No! It wasn't clockwork. Quartz watch, wasn't it?'

'Static electricity,' Meldrum said, hating himself for getting involved in this nonsense, 'from you when you picked it up.'

'*I* thought of that. Phoned the girlfriend. Here, I asked her, how long has that watch of yours not been working? Two years anyway, she said, since I came back from Canada.'

'It's a mystery,' Meldrum said, resisting the weak impulse to wonder aloud how many stopped watches might go if enough of them were picked up at any moment.

'More things in heaven and earth, eh? Mind you, he might still be a con man. What way is there of knowing? Listen to some people, they swear blind they can tell if somebody's lying. You know, body language? More to it than not looking you in the eye. Liars are the very ones who do look you in the eye, straight in the eye. I've talked to policemen who say *they* can always tell. Right, I tell them, right. And nobody ever gets out of jail on appeal, eh? You ever been to Frankfurt?'

'Sorry?'

'Only takes fifty-five minutes. Went with a friend to a second-hand car auction. Couldn't believe how quick it was.'

The Grace Pennington Hall presented a long front of yellow brick and ranks of windows that seemed too small for the scale of the building. He went up the flight of stone steps and through swing doors to find himself in a large uncarpeted hall with doors in front and to either side. There were pinboards with notices and an unmanned reception desk. Squinting across it to check what lay beyond the glass partition, he could make out a table to one side and a computer on a desk midway down a dim aisle between filing cabinets. What looked like a half-pint milk bottle, seemingly empty, was set on top of the last cabinet like a memorial to the presence of intelligent life. After a while, he noticed an electric bell on the counter and pushed, keeping his finger pressed down on it. Nothing seemed to happen. Maybe an alert buzzed behind the partition. Listening for it, he became conscious of the silence. The building might have been evacuated.

For want of anything better to do, telling himself he should give up, there wasn't any point in this, he walked from one side of the hall to the other. At each end, a glass door gave a view on to a long empty corridor of numbered doors. He crossed back again, and went into the first corridor, which wasn't any different from the second. There was the same grey carpet, worn thin so that he could feel the hardness of the concrete underneath. His head turned from side to side, looking at each door as he passed. Where the corridor ended, it met another at right angles. Same grey carpet, same dim ceiling lights behind wired glass covers. Behind him, a man's voice called, 'What are you doing, please?'

He'd come out from a door half-way back to the hall. As Meldrum walked towards him, he retreated inside his room, holding the door almost shut.

'Do you have business here?'

Young, thin, intent Indian face, glasses, wearing a jacket; must have been on his way out when he'd spotted a stranger lingering at the end of the corridor. Not to spook him into closing the door, Meldrum stopped four careful steps away.

'I'm looking for Ruth Bellman. Do you know her? She's doing drama and English.'

'Did you ask at the reception? All visitors should make themselves known. That is a rule.'

'Nobody there or I would have.'

'Nobody? Are you quite sure? That is very bad!' Something about Meldrum's quiet solidity must have had a reassuring effect, for he threw back the door, exclaiming indignantly, 'After what happened, it is criminal.'

Meldrum followed him back into the hall. The desk was still unmanned. 'Criminal!' the Indian said again. Then with a sudden change of mood he shrugged and smiled. 'But we can't waste our day on it, can we? I'll make a point of telling someone, when I come back. Did you say you were a friend of Miss Bellman?'

Meldrum shook his head.

'I thought you might be a personal friend.'

Did he imagine the faintest sly emphasis on the adjective?

'We've spoken on the phone.'

'She is expecting you?'

'I'm sure she'll want to talk to me.'

'This building is supposed to be secure. People who don't belong shouldn't be wandering about it.'

There was a temptation to avoid this irritation by showing his ID, but he could imagine the speculation that would cause. It was possible Ruth Bellman didn't want anyone here to know about her father's disappearance. Before he could make up his mind, however, the Indian gave the same shrug as before and said, '315.'

'315?'

'Miss Bellman's room. It's on the fourth floor, by the way, not the third. The lifts are round there to your left.'

'Thanks.'

He was turning away when the Indian said, 'You're not a rapist, are you? Of course not. Or a murderer? Nothing like that?' He seemed to put the questions seriously, but then gave his gleaming unexpected smile. 'When the sun shines outside, we shouldn't spend our time in here.'

No arguing with that. Meldrum got into the lift and watched as the red number reshaped itself from two to four. When the lift stopped, a long moment passed and it seemed the waiting could end with it going on up, or down again, or just as easily staying where it was for ever. Then the door opened and he stepped out into a corridor identical to the ones on the ground level, except that the floor had some kind of linoleum tiles instead of carpeting. Each door had a number but no name. The occupants would change, of course, at the end of academic years, maybe even terms, unless this was one of the places where they talked instead of semesters? Or perhaps it was for security. Maybe if they didn't put names on the doors, rapists wouldn't know whether they'd find a man or a woman inside.

It seemed probable 315 was identical to all the other rooms in the building. It had a narrow wardrobe just inside the door, a single bed hard against the wall, a desk with a shelf above it and a bend-over lamp. There was something wrong with the proportions, so that it felt too narrow, as if you could touch the walls on either side, like living in a corridor. There was a low padded chair with wooden arms, the kind you'd find beside the bed in a hotel, placed in front of the window. After opening the door to him, being told who he was, Ruth Bellman had gone to sit in it, turning it round so it faced into the room. His impression was she must have been looking out of the window when he knocked, though on a higher chair pulled out from under the desk all he could see as he faced her was a square of blue sky and one white cloud.

When he'd talked to her on the phone, for some reason,

maybe the unbroken excitement about putting on her play – what? something by Shakespeare? – he'd had a picture of her as small and blonde. The reality was quite different.

Barefoot, Ruth Bellman, he judged, would be not much under six feet if she straightened up; in high heels she could be almost at his eye level. Like many tall women, though, it seemed she found her height an embarrassment, slouching her shoulders as she led him into the room. In the chair, she let herself slide down and sat with arms folded across her chest, a hand clutching each shoulder. As she glanced up at him, heavy brows drawn together in a frown, he could detect something of her mother and even of the old General her grandfather – dark hair, big features, not conventionally pretty or in fact good-looking at all. Yet, seeing her, Meldrum thought differently of their absurd conversation on the phone. That seemed now to uncover someone more volatile than the reality of her raw-boned presence might have revealed. In a moment of insight, he saw inside to a girl who was emotional, trusting, easily hurt.

And in the next moment warned himself against the dangers of imagination.

'I'm surprised they let you come up.' Light and quick, her voice was that of the girl on the phone, so that for an instant one image superimposed itself upon the other. Her frown darkened. 'Did they let you come up because you told them you were a policeman?'

'There wasn't anyone there to tell.'

'But that's awful! After what happened to Miss Roache!'

'Miss Roache?'

'She was – is – the Warden. Nobody knows if she'll be able to come back. She might not even want to. I mean, they hurt her badly.'

'She was attacked in the Residence?'

'In her office. Things get stolen from rooms, people just come in off the street and wander around. Our Students Rep Committee told them, this place isn't safe, somebody is going to get hurt. Actually, it was mostly Miss Roache we complained to. After the attack on her, we were promised things would be tightened up.'

'Your Committee should ask the local police to come in and advise you on security.'

'Police!' she said dismissively. 'Sorry.'

He remembered the deserted hall, empty corridors, the silence as if the building had been abandoned. On a weekend afternoon an eerie place to be sitting alone staring at clouds changing shape.

'Why have you come to see me?' she asked.

He waited to see if she would add to that. It was the obvious question. He wondered why she hadn't asked it at once.

'I'm afraid we haven't any news of your father.'

'You came all the way to London to tell me that?'

'No. I had other business, but since I was here . . . Interviews over the phone aren't – I thought it might help if I spoke to you in person.'

'Help me?'

'Well . . . To see if there was anything else you might remember about the weekend your father disappeared.'

'There isn't anything,' she said. 'Why ask me? Have you seen Alistair?'

'I did think about it. But we've had difficulties with the address he gave us.'

'Alistair moves around. He's been restless since he left the army. He stays with different friends – then moves on. I've no idea where he is just now.'

'You don't keep in touch?'

'He'll phone me out of the blue.'

'When he does, ask him to get in touch with me. Your brother isn't an easy man to make contact with.'

'You know he's going to Nepal?'

'I've heard,' he said drily.

'Anyway,' she repeated, 'there isn't anything else I can tell you about that weekend. I came up for my birthday. We had a nice time. When we got up in the morning, Daddy had gone. I can't tell you any more than that. It's all there is.'

She sounded sulky and impatient. Slumped down, frowning, incongruously she reminded him of his daughter Betty in the years after she had turned, overnight it seemed, from a child he simply loved to a young adult, complicated as a minefield.

At some point as he persisted, she challenged him, 'What do you want me to say? That my father was doing something wrong, and that's why he ran away?'

'Was he?'

'It is what you want me to say!'

'It's what I have to check. Was there another woman? Were there money troubles? A serious illness diagnosed? In cases like this, we look for a reason why a man might go off of his own volition. So far we haven't found one.'

'I'm glad.'

'It would be better,' Meldrum said, 'if he'd gone off of his own volition.'

'Instead of wandering about with amnesia, you mean. Like one of those old black and white films.'

He could think of worse possibilities. Letting his gaze fall, he saw a stripe of grey on the floor just within the shadow of the bed. When he looked up, Ruth Bellman was watching him.

'Have you talked to my mother?'

'I had to, of course.'

'What did you think of her?'

'I don't know what you mean.'

'Did you think she was beautiful?' When he hesitated, not knowing how to answer, she nodded, chewing on her lip as she thought. 'It isn't the right word, I know. But you'd say she was remarkable?'

Remarkable.

'I imagine people will notice her.'

The girl laughed. 'You're so careful. As if I might quote you in evidence. Are policemen always so careful?'

Another couple of inches back, he noticed, and the grey stroke on the carpet would have been hidden by the bed's shadow. He thought about how careful it paid a policeman to be.

'I'm not remarkable,' Ruth Bellman said. 'When I was little, Mummy's friends would say to her, the child takes after you. And I believed them ... Of course, when I got older I could see how ridiculous that was. One day I asked her, Why did you marry Daddy? Go out into the garden, she said, and pick a rose for me. It doesn't have to be the first one you see, but once you've picked you can't go back and look again, you have to take it. I was away for a long time and when I came back, it was with a windblown rose. You see, Mummy said, if you go along waiting and waiting, looking for perfection, you may find you haven't much of a choice.'

Like a puzzle that resolved itself when you changed the angle of the picture, the grey stripe emerged out of the shadows as a used condom. Pulled off and dropped over the side of the bed.

There was surprisingly little comment about his vanishing act when he caught up with the engagement party. Perhaps because, having gone to the wrong restaurant for dinner, he didn't catch up with them until the theatre where the show was about ready to start. Possibly because they were such self-absorbed little shits they hadn't noticed he was gone. Perhaps because they were delicate about it for Harriet's sake. Fortunately, she didn't seem much the worse for the wear. Either she'd got on to a plateau early, that sometimes happened, or his going off had shocked her into drinking less. She didn't seem shocked, though, or indignant, or curious about where he'd got to, but sleepy and mildly affectionate, leaning her head against his shoulder as the lights went down for the play. He opened his eyes in the morning to find her up on one elbow studying him. They made love, quietly for fear of being heard by their hosts, and afterwards she whispered, 'I'll come home with you.'

That afternoon, though, he flew into Edinburgh alone. After all, she'd arranged to have the Monday off, and there was no point in giving up the time she'd planned to have with her friends. Very sensible and it was he who had persuaded her; but it didn't stop him from feeling low and wishing he hadn't.

In the taxi, raising his voice he said to the driver, 'It was raining when we left London.'

The man grunted, 'Uh-huh.'

'Yesterday was good, though. Sun shining just like this.'

'Uh-huh.'

'Been like this all weekend, has it?'

'Uh-huh.'

They left the Maybury Roundabout behind. In the sunlight the bungalows lined up like brightly painted boxes on either side. The flat would be waiting, empty and silent; and hot since he'd shut all the windows before he left. Cars were streaming out of the car-park beside the Zoo. Deer would be dozing under trees in the paddocks on the hill; and small boys, having the advantage of freedom, would be matching the yellow stare of the lion on the Mappin Terrace, trying to hold their gaze steady until his eyes watered and he looked away.

'You can learn a lot listening to the cabbies in London,' he said maliciously to the back of the driver's head. 'Guy on the way to Heathrow was telling me he bought a flat in Docklands in '89. Still hasn't recovered its price, but according to him what he'd been getting in rent for it meant he could take a small loss.'

'They pay forty thousand quid for a licence,' the driver offered. 'Those cunts down there make a fortune.'

'Uh-huh,' Meldrum said.

He slept heavily and woke somewhere in the small hours out of a confused dream. He saw a blue sky and a white cloud through a window and on the cloud a reclining woman who held out a condom. Against the light, he could make out a dark spoonful of its freight of sperm wasted in the dumb dangling teat.

CHAPTER TWELVE

'For what it's worth,' Henderson said, laying the list of names on the desk.

Despite the disclaimer, Meldrum caught something in the tone of voice which made him glance up sharply. Nothing so positive as excitement, of course; and the expression was as dour as ever, but he was sure there had been something. He was getting to know his lugubrious sergeant.

'What is it?'

'You weren't in on Saturday.' He paused, and Meldrum felt it, the detective's twinge of irrational guilt about working anything less than all the hours God sends. 'With you being away, I took the time to go over the Bellman file again.'

'I'd've thought you – we'd enough on our plate.'

'Right,' Henderson admitted in the dry tone of a man agreeing to the obvious.

'Harry was sounding me out last week about pulling you over on to the Craigie thing. I told him it was all right by me.' He grinned, watching Henderson's mouth pull down appreciatively at the corners as his eyebrows rose. Craigie was the advocate who'd been found with his head battered in and a coded diary in his safe. The lawyer's homosexual appetite hadn't been a well-kept secret, and the general opinon was, break the code and they'd have some of the best-known names in the city as suspects. It was a case that could do an ambitious policeman a lot of good. 'So, anyway, you were looking at the file. And?'

'Eh.' Henderson took a moment to get his mind back on track. 'I decided to check the British Midland passenger lists. For last month, Saturday 14th. London to Edinburgh, flying out of Heathrow at 10.50. Once I'd seen it, I told them they'd better let me have a look at the ones for flights two hours either side of the 10.50.'

'Don't tell me,' Meldrum said. He looked down at the list, turned the pages, not bothering to read them. 'She wasn't on any of them?'

'If she was, she didn't call herself Ruth Bellman. Before you ask, I checked British Airways, just in case.'

'Shit!'

'I thought you'd be interested.'

'What made you think of it?'

'One of those things,' Henderson said honestly. 'The whole thing was such a dead end. I was just fiddling around. Never imagined she wouldn't be listed.'

'Stupid,' Meldrum said. 'To lie about something that can be checked.'

'Except that we almost didn't.' And added with the generosity of a man who'd got it right, 'Who'd have thought she'd have any reason for lying about when she got home?'

'Easiest way is to ask her.'

'Fly down?'

'Phone first. See if she can explain.'

'Not the same as getting the questions in face to face,' Henderson said. 'You can tell a lot by watching their eyes.'

Meldrum shook his head. Money was tight; corners were being cut; he didn't want to get into a hassle about expenses. 'Shit!' he said, repeating himself. 'I was in London at the weekend. I spoke to her.'

'On your own?'

Good question. On his own. On impulse.

'I was going to write it up.' Whether he'd intended to or not, now he would have to get it on the record. *Cover your back*: rule one in the unofficial handbook. 'I was hoping she'd know where the brother had got himself to. But she didn't.'

An hour later, half a dozen calls hadn't turned up Ruth

Bellman. She seemed for the moment to have disappeared as effectively as her brother.

'If she was lying,' Henderson pointed out, 'he must have been too. He says he went to the airport on the Saturday morning, met her off the plane and took her home to the parents' house. But we know he couldn't have. So where did he fetch her from?'

'If Alistair fetched her at all – from anywhere,' Meldrum said. 'He *claims* he did. Same story from the mother. So, if Ruth Bellman was lying, then her brother and mother were too.'

'What about the other brother Gordon and his wife?' But at once Henderson was annoyed with himself for asking. 'Stupid. Sorry. They didn't get to the house until about six o'clock. By the time they arrived, she was already there.'

'Sitting out in the garden with her parents and brother, having a drink and playing happy families. Unless, of course, they're all lying.'

Henderson pulled a face of dismay.

'Couldn't agree more,' Meldrum said. 'Keep it simple as long as we can. We don't know where the brother is, the sister won't answer the phone, let's go talk to the mother. You can watch her eyes.'

Only twenty miles down the coast; compared to the cost of a plane trip to London, what was twenty miles among friends? It amused him that Henderson didn't even suggest phoning to see if Mrs Bellman was at home. Maybe he, too, was restless, needed to get out of the city, have at least the illusion of doing something useful.

Thinking this, he caught Henderson in the passenger seat glancing across at the dials for the second time.

'Something wrong?'

'How do you mean?' Henderson asked.

'You used to be in Traffic, didn't you?'

'For a while. Why?'

'Wondering if you thought I was going too fast, if you wanted to get your wee notebook out.'

'Don't have one. When I made plainclothes, I got myself a big one.'

Taking the right fork at Jock's Lodge, he went up the hill still too fast, squeezing through the lights on amber and, turning left, had to dab the brake for a woman with a pram.

'One thing I remember,' Henderson said. 'Hit a five-year-old at thirty miles an hour, he's got a chance. Hit him at thirty-three, he's dead. You wouldn't believe three miles would make that much difference.'

Meldrum took his foot up. Bastard. Never had an accident, he could tell him; but, of course, not being an idiot, wouldn't.

'By the way, that business about Craigie. Harry came back to me, said it was okay, he didn't need you after all.'

'Interesting,' Henderson said, surprising him by being intrigued rather than disappointed. 'You think somebody warned him off?'

'. . . Thought occurred to me.'

'Looks, right enough, as though finding Bellman rates with somebody,' and, staring out of the side window, Henderson began to whistle tunelessly through his teeth.

They were leaving Musselburgh on the road south before he spoke again.

'Ever been in Australia?'

'Where?' Meldrum had been busy with his own thoughts.

'Australia. I lived six months in Cairns – that's up in Queensland. Got there in their winter and couldn't believe it. Left Edinburgh in the middle of June and it was cold and miserable – flew into Queensland on the best spring day you've seen in your whole life. And it was the same the next day and the one after that. Like that all the time. If it rained, it lashed down, mile a minute stuff till the earth steamed, then it was over. Palm trees everywhere. There was a mango tree in the neighbour's garden – dropped the fruit into ours. Blue sea, beaches – four miles wide of sand and nobody on it. I thought it was the nearest thing to paradise I was ever going to find. At the end of the first week, I decided – I'm going to stay here the rest of my life.'

Meldrum listened to this with astonishment, not at what was being said – as a detective he'd spent what felt like half his life in a car, travelling or on the watch, night and day, to the accompaniment of men talking, gossiping, telling stories, to while the hours away. Not what but

who astonished him: he'd got used to Henderson's habit of
silence.

'But then the hot weather came. Forty degrees and seventy-
five to eighty humidity. I hated it. Stuck it as long as I could,
then I came home.'

'When was this?'

'I'd my eighteenth birthday on the plane coming back to
Scotland.' He stared absently out of the window and started
into the thin whistling he did a lot of the time. Meldrum had
developed the theory he didn't even know he was doing it.
Luckily, tuneless whistling didn't bother him. It seemed a pity,
though, just to go back to non-communication.

'So what made you go out in the first place?' The whistling
went on. 'You have relatives there?'

'You saying about Traffic put it in my head,' Henderson said.
'Reminded me of the road trains. My father was taking me up
to see this mate of his, guy called Cookie, worked as a car
breaker on the tablelands above Cairns—' He paused, added
at last, 'After he ran away from my mother, my old man went
on his travels. Set off from Gorgie to see the world. Anyway,
the road goes straight up and we're chugging along. Not saying
anything, the old man wasn't much of a one for talking. He'd
told me I could do the driving. He was teaching me, and I was
concentrating just on keeping straight, you know the way you
do when you're learning. Where the road met the sky, the air
shook in the heat. And you'd come over that rise and there
would be another one ahead of you, same thing time after time.
But suddenly, right in front of us, coming towards the top of this
hill—there's a lorry right way up and another one underneath
it upside down, filling the whole road, shimmering in the
heat haze. Enormous and getting bigger all the time. I started
yelling, but the old man didn't say a word. At the last minute,
he grabbed the wheel and swerved us off on to the sand at the
side of the road – and this antartex pulling two trailers, this
fucking monster roared past blasting us with grit. When we
swung back up on to the road, the old man was laughing his
head off. Looking back in the mirror, I couldn't see anything
for the cloud of dust we'd kicked up. I forget to tell you about
those? he asked. That's what we call a road train. Fourteen

gears – so he told me – and they have to come down through
all of them or they'd strip the brakes. Takes them four miles
to stop. They could knock you out of the way no problem, got
this big bar across the front. Right enough, all the way up I'd
kept seeing these dead kangaroos and wallabies. If anything
gets in the way, they just go through it. My old man said, If
the driver had gone off the road, frightened he'd hit us, he'd
have turned the lot over in the sand. Could have been half
a million pounds worth of dead cattle you'd be getting sued
for. Christ! I said to him, you take over the driving! Not me,
he says, fuck, I've only got third party insurance.' Henderson
gave a bark of laughter, cut short at once. 'We met another
two coming down before we got to the top.'

Over the next dozen miles, Meldrum made a couple of
remarks, got the briefest of responses and gave up. Whatever
had started Henderson on his talking jag had run its course.
When they arrived at the Bellman house, it was in silence
as usual.

As they approached the front steps, a crunching of gravel
drew their attention to a stocky, red-faced man wheeling a
barrow piled with cut branches along the path in front of the
house.

'Fine day! If you're looking for Mrs Bellman, she's in the
garden round the back.'

'We'll try the front door first,' Meldrum said.

'Please yourselves.' Then as the two men went up the steps,
'Police, is it?'

Meldrum turned and looked down at him. 'What's your
name again?'

'Bobbie Selby. I do the garden.'

'I guessed that. You just started?'

'Me?' the gardener said scornfully. 'I used to work for the
Frasers, them that had the house before the Bellmans. Fine
people. He was a surgeon at the Edinburgh Royal – this is
twenty years since, you ken.'

'Selby?' Meldrum was puzzled not to recognise the name.
'Has anyone talked to you about Mr Bellman's disappearance?'

'I'm only in the two afternoons a week. And at the time
it happened I was off for about three weeks. I got food

poisoning at my second daughter's wedding in Selkirk. Man, but I was ill. Terrible, I wouldn't wish that on my worst enemy.'

Meldrum became conscious from the corner of his eye of being watched. Turning his head, he saw the sour face of the daily woman peering out between the curtains of the nearside bow window

'Tell you the truth,' Selby the gardener said, 'when I got back I wondered what all the fuss was about. I said to myself, he'll be away on one of those trips of his. Mr Bellman was forever going away some place or other.'

As he conveyed this information, the door was opened by the daily woman.

'I was telling these gentlemen,' Selby cried, 'that Mrs Bellman's fiddling about with the fruit trees on the back wall.'

The woman scowled, whether at Selby or at recognising the two policemen there was no way of telling. She took them into the hall and left them with the air of someone asked to launch a search when she was pretty certain the lady of the house wasn't at home. A charmer.

'What's her name again?'

It annoyed Meldrum having to ask; usually he could count on his memory.

'Martin,' Henderson said, without hesitation which didn't help matters. 'Her husband's a farmer. She drives in every morning for half-seven. Monday to Fridays – and weekends when needed.'

'Except the weekend that matters.' The weekend of the ill-fated birthday celebration, Mrs Martin had been recovering from a bout of flu. She hadn't come back to work till the middle of the following week, which hadn't mattered until Henderson raised the question mark over Ruth's plane flight. 'No witnesses to when the girl got home except the mother and brother.'

'And the father, of course,' Henderson said.

Meldrum grunted, not feeling that worth an answer; finding John Bellman being, after all, the point of the exercise.

Waiting, he was conscious, as he had been before, of how quiet it was. The mute grandfather clock, the dark length of sideboard, the highbacked chair set under the mirror,

foundered in stillness. 'It was a happy day. There was a
lot of laughter,' Mrs Bellman had said. He wondered what
the house must have been like when Ruth and her brothers
were young. Looking from the dim mirror to the painting
on the landing, not one risking of green in its canny brown
landscape, it wasn't easy to imagine the laughter of children
in this house.

'Mrs Bellman asks if you'd mind going outside.'

Without waiting for an answer, the woman left them to follow
her through the hall. At the end a morning-room gave access
through french windows on to a patio. As he stepped outside,
Meldrum paused, for a second feeling the familiar oddness of
knowing so exactly the layout of what was after all a stranger's
home. Facing him, a curve of broad steps went down to a lawn.
Out of sight round to the left, the gable of the house gave shelter
to a kitchen garden. Out of sight, too, beyond the vegetable
plots, there were fruit bushes, netted at this time of the year.
After the fashion of rooms being partitioned, the garden was
divided by enclosing hedges, some of which he could put a
name to: privet, hawthorn, escallonia – over so many years
some of his ex-wife Carole's interest in gardening had rubbed
off. Beyond that walk of trees, the property ended at a high
wall, and he remembered standing under it you would hear
the sea and the crying of gulls.

Going over a property this size was routine in a disappearance, in case there had been an accident. Checking for
a body.

By the boundary wall, Mrs Bellman in gloves and hat was
at work, pruning fruit trees espaliered against the grey stone.
She was on her knees, and when she turned to greet them
the skin of her neck seemed to him very smooth and brown
against the white of her dress. Looking up, with the back of
a hand she brushed up the wide brim to bring her face out of
shadow. The blue-grey of her eyes was clearer and even more
remarkable than he had remembered.

'I can't stand being indoors,' she said. 'If you've come
with news of John, I'd find it easier to be told it out
here.'

'We haven't found him,' Meldrum said. His abruptness came

from the realisation she was afraid they had come to tell her
he was dead.

She bent her head for a moment. With the secateurs, she
lopped a side branch from one of the apple trees spread
pinned upon the wall. He noticed the steadiness of her hand,
the neat firmness of the cut. She laid the branch aside and got
to her feet.

'In that case?' she wondered.

'We wanted to check a couple of things with you. About
the Saturday morning.'

'Saturday?' As if puzzled, she looked from one to the
other. 'It was Sunday – sometime during the night when
John disappeared.'

'If you wouldn't mind. Just to go over it again.'

'What do you want me to tell you? When we got up
on the Saturday, John and I had breakfast together. He
went for a walk – but I've been over all that. It wasn't
unusual. He often went for a walk in the morning – along
the beach was his favourite. It was quite a part of his
routine.' It was true she had been over it all before, and
more than once. The first time, Meldrum had gone on the
alert at her repeated assertion of how normal it was for
her husband to go off walking by himself. Did he say
where he'd gone? he'd asked. Did he seem upset when he
came back? Now, when she repeated things in that way,
he recognised it as no more than a trick of emphasis,
and wondered instead how he could have overlooked the
pleasure of listening to her. She must have been by her
accent to some public school, girls only at a guess, but
her voice was low not loud, a husky music with a saving
shading of Scots on the vowels. 'I worked in the garden for
a while – it was a lovely morning. Alistair arrived with Ruth
and then—'

'What time was that again? When they got here?'

'Almost twelve. John had been back for ages. He couldn't
have been away walking more than forty minutes, maybe an
hour, not more than an hour.'

'And Alistair said he'd been to the airport and met Ruth off
the plane?'

Instead of answering, she waved to where a bench was set in the shade thrown by a lilac tree. 'Let's sit down.'

She sat at one end of the bench, and Meldrum had no choice but to take the other. The privilege of rank, although, uncomfortably half turned on the bench, he would cheerfully have changed places with Henderson.

'Now,' she said quietly, 'what's all this about?'

'Passenger lists have been checked for all the flights that morning from London to Edinburgh. Your daughter wasn't on any of them.'

'That's not possible.'

'There isn't any doubt about it,' Henderson said.

She glanced up. As if she'd just bothered to notice he was here, Meldrum thought.

When she spoke, it was to Meldrum. 'More than one airline flies to Edinburgh from London. And don't they come from Gatwick as well as Heathrow?'

'Checked them all,' Henderson said.

She ignored him.

'It's possible,' she said after a moment's thought, 'that I misunderstood.'

'You mean your son didn't say he'd met her at the airport?' Meldrum asked, allowing himself the faintest trace of puzzlement.

'Of course he did. No, I mean I may have taken it for granted that she'd come from London. Perhaps she'd caught the plane in Manchester.'

From Henderson's frown, it was a possibility he hadn't checked. But then why should he have?

'Why would she do that?'

'She has friends there.'

He thought about asking their names; did she have an address for these friends? The routine questions. The ones that came next by the book. He remembered reading somewhere about a police department – in America, of course – that had used a computer to question suspects. Experts had sat in on dozens of interrogations, studied the pattern of question and answer, and come up with the software. A surprising number of the suspects had confessed.

But as for who these friends were, why bother? If the daughter herself told them she'd boarded at Manchester, time enough then to put it to the test.

He heard Henderson ask, 'Could you tell us the names of these friends?'

'Valerie Kerr and Michael something. Valerie and Ruth were at school together. When Valerie married, they went to live in Manchester. No idea where. You'd have to ask Ruth.'

'The difficulty from our point of view,' Meldrum said, 'is your daughter told us she came up from London on the 10.50 a.m. British Midland flight from Heathrow.'

'BD67,' Henderson said.

The memory man. This time she didn't even spare him a glance.

'The difficulty is, she was questioned more than once. Even when I spoke to her two days ago she told the same—'

'Two days ago?'

'I had to be in London. I took the opportunity of going to see Ruth.'

Frowning, she began, 'I don't see any—' Then with an impatient shake of the head stopped herself. Had she been going to say, I don't see any need? If so, she was too intelligent not to understand that now certainly they would need to talk to her daughter.

'Not a word from her about Manchester,' Meldrum said.

She didn't respond at once, looking down at her hands where they lay lightly clasped in her lap. The wide brim of the garden hat hid her eyes from him; but the hands betrayed no sign of tension.

Henderson started to say something, but went silent as Meldrum shook his head for him to be quiet.

At last she said, 'If she's wasted your time, she'll have to explain her reasons to you. But,' and she turned to look at him, 'I don't see what this has to do with finding my husband.'

'Probably nothing. But it's a discrepancy. We can't ignore it,' Meldrum said. He carefully didn't look the sergeant's way, having a feeling Henderson would think the choice of 'discrepancy' altogether too placatory.

'Discrepancy.' She gave the word an emphasis of fastidious distaste. 'Do you have any children?'

Taken by surprise, he hesitated as if wondering whether he should answer.

'A daughter.'

'You should understand then.'

Understand what? That girls were different? Not to be taken seriously? What did she mean? Natural liars? Crazed by menstruation?

'According to your son Alistair, he collected her from the airport,' Meldrum said. 'So we have him telling the same story.'

'Ask him then! Ask her, ask him! And then perhaps you can get back to doing your proper job.'

By proper job presumably she meant, Finding my husband. Rather than hunting for armed robbers, sorting out grievous assaults, trying to solve run-of-the-mill murders.

They were so intent upon one another that Henderson's question took him by surprise as much as her.

'What about those trips your husband used to go on?' the sergeant asked.

'What?'

'We've been told one reaction to the disappearance was to wonder what all the fuss was about. At first, I mean. Because, as somebody put it, At first I thought Mr Bellman was away on one of those trips of his.'

'Have you been talking to Mrs Martin?'

'I seem to remember it was in her statement,' Henderson said, his flat tone making no concession to her flare-up of irritation. 'I'd have to check the file again, of course, to be sure.'

Remembering they'd heard it from the gardener, Meldrum noted that, when put to it, Henderson could tell a very smooth lie. No reason why that should surprise him; but it did.

'I think you should check. I can't imagine what the woman can have been thinking of.'

Meldrum decided to pick up on it. 'Was your husband away from home regularly? You understand we have to go over everything, if we're to find him.'

She met this sceptically, but answered at last, 'My husband

likes to travel. I'm not so fond of it. He was often away –
but not, I think, as often as Mrs Martin must have given the
impression he was. No doubt, with John's disappearance she's
let her imagination run away with her.'

'I can see how that might happen,' Meldrum agreed. 'How
often would you say then?'

'I really couldn't put a figure on it. Occasionally. He'd go
on a fishing trip to Ireland. Or visit France, Italy perhaps. As
I say, he liked to travel.'

'And the United States, I suppose he might have gone
there.'

'Why?' The word a single chip of ice to match the cold blue
of her marksman's eye.

'With him being an American . . .'

'No.'

'. . . I thought he might have family there?'

'He came to Britain as a young man.'

That wasn't what I asked you. What would her response be
if he said that to her?

It was odd neither his wife nor children telling them Bellman
was American. It had been Sally Bellman, the elder son's wife
– and Parker, of course – who'd mentioned it. But then Parker,
the indiscreet family lawyer, had also talked of Bellman's
father being opposed to their marriage. Of Bellman losing his
American accent, he'd said, 'And I dare say with his father
being so bitterly opposed to the marriage – perhaps he just
wanted to leave the past behind?'

Maybe his family not mentioning it wasn't so odd, after
all.

Let it go.

'Did he have a friend he went on these trips with?' Henderson
filled the pause abruptly.

'No one in particular,' she said.

'Not even on the fishing trips?'

'I can't think of anyone. The boys used to go with him, but
that was when they were younger.'

When they were finished, she left them to walk up to the
house by themselves. Half-way, however, Meldrum asked
Henderson to wait for him. He threaded the path between

hedges, aiming for the place where she'd been pruning the apple tree. When he came out between the trees, he stopped in surprise not to see her and glanced one way and the other along the wall. He was so sure she'd have gone back to her task. Still sitting on the bench, she watched as he approached.

'There's one other thing I wanted to ask,' he said. 'I hope you won't think it's an impertinent question, but I expected to find your daughter in an apartment. Maybe a place shared with friends. I wondered why she wasn't.'

'You're right,' she said. 'That is impertinent.'

In her mouth, the word irritated him enormously; but then he'd been stupid enough to hand it to her.

'The Grace Pennington Hall doesn't seem to me a place anyone would choose to live if they could afford not to.'

'But she can't afford not to. She insisted on going to London. Her father wanted her nearer home. As a result, he put her on a tight allowance. She'd always been Daddy's girl, you see.' And added as he made some kind of thanks and was turning to go, 'Ruth is named after John's mother, did your detecting people detect that?'

Going back up to the house, he thought about Ruth Bellman's story of how her mother had asked her to pick a rose. *I was away for a long time and when I came back, it was with a windblown rose. You see, Mummy said, if you go along waiting and waiting, looking for perfection, you may find you haven't much of a choice.*

The strange thing was that with all the garden's rooms, he hadn't passed through one that had roses in it.

CHAPTER THIRTEEN

'I've tidied up the garden,' Meldrum told his ex-wife. They were sitting on either side of the fire in her living-room.

'That's nice,' Carole said.

'Difficulty is, I'm not sure which are the weeds.'

'You were always better at vegetables,' she said. 'Recognise a potato at ten feet.'

'I leave stuff I'm not sure about in case it's something you planted.'

When they separated, they hadn't divorced, hadn't got round to it for years in fact; and if that was in part because Carole was a Catholic, he had thought too it might have something to do with the fact they'd loved and been together a long time. Hadn't stopped her walking out, though. You're married to the job, she'd told him. You don't need me.

What did they say? More in sorrow than in anger. Something like that.

'You should come over some time and tell me which is which,' he suggested.

'I don't think so,' she said.

'Remember how the back green was when we moved in? Dandelions and half bricks – a cross between a field and a building site. You made a great job of it. That garden was—' He almost said it, a labour of love. 'You should have stayed there.'

'What's this about?' The question was sharp, angry almost. Drifting along from one thought to another, he was pulled up short. 'I just meant, I could have moved out. I would have, if you'd asked me.'

'I'm going to make a cup of tea.' She got up and went towards the kitchen. 'Want one?'

'Fine.'

He sat staring into the fireplace. Odd how you did that even if it was too warm for a fire. This late in the evening and the sun was still slanting in through the window. He was here because he'd come to see his daughter Betty – and her about-to-be husband, Sandy Torrance – on neutral territory. To be honest again, because Carole had phoned and said, They're visiting me tonight, be there. It was strange to think of Betty pregnant. She was beginning to show, a soft roundness in the belly. She and Sandy had looked very happy, holding hands, side by side on the couch.

'You'd never have found a place. That's why I decided I'd be the one to leave,' Carole said, coming back in, a cup in each hand. She passed one to him, and sat again in the chair opposite. 'I know you, you'd still be in digs somewhere. In a bedsit with a one-bar electric fire. Still talking about looking for a place of your own. Anyway, this suits me. It's near the school.'

'You work too hard.'

'You should see the other Heads. Some of them tell me they don't get home till eight at night.'

He thought of saying, They should join the police. Changed his mind, said instead, 'I made a hash of it.'

He didn't have to explain.

'For two people who love each other,' she said, 'you and Betty rub one another up the wrong way.'

'I try not to. She picks up on something I say – and that's it. Next minute she's marching out – trailing young Picasso behind her.'

'And, of course, nothing she says ever annoys you . . . She thinks you're disappointed in her.'

'I wanted her to have a degree. I wanted her to have a career.'

'She'll have them. Don't worry, she'll make you proud of her yet.'

'I am proud of her. Bloody fools!'

'Maybe I said so too. But what's the good of that? There'll be a baby, and we'll love it, you'll see.'

The sentimentality induced a flush of pure irritation that made him want to ask her if she'd influenced Betty into shunning contraceptives for some rhythm method nonsense. Unfair, of course, since Carole like most Catholics had never been other than practical about choosing the surest way to plan their family. If anything, he'd been the one keen on having more children.

'You still seeing Phil what's his name?' he asked.

'He's an Assistant Director now. Outside Edinburgh.'

'That's nice for him.'

Into the silence, she said, 'I like Sandy. He's an admirable young man.'

'Maybe your friend Phil can get him a job.'

'Hmm?' she wondered on a note of warning.

'Well, he's applied for Moray House to train as an art teacher, hasn't he? Now he's going to be a father. Instead of going off to tour Italy on that scholarship he won. I hope he doesn't live to resent it.'

'Not being a saint, I'm sure part of him resents it now.'

'Takes two to tango,' he said, leaping to Betty's defence. Seeing her smile at the inconsistency, he sighed, '*I* like Sandy.'

'Want another cup?'

'No. Get you one. You want one?'

He went into the kitchen and washed out what was left in her cup, put in milk and poured tea.

'Tea, coffee,' he said as he came back, 'I'm awash with the stuff. Catching up on the paperwork. Case conferences. Didn't get out of the building today. I hate that.' He settled down again, watching her sip from the cup. 'Baird called me in to see him this afternoon.'

'Oh, yes.'

'The Chief Constable.'

'I know who Baird is.'

'You might have forgotten.'

'I've heard you moaning about him often enough.'

Over the years. Not recently.

He grunted. 'He's not the worst.'

'High praise.'

'All right, he is.'

'The invisible man.' She smiled. It was Baird's style, or nature, same thing perhaps, to be remote. He worked through his ACCs and two or three favoured senior officers. Conversation with anyone else in the Headquarters building was a rare event, and almost invariably left an impression of discomfort on both sides. The inner circle who worked closely with him respected his intelligence, worried about the unpredictability of his temper and had fallen into the bad habit of finding it easier to avoid disagreeing with him. A management style which kept him from the realities of practice and opinion among his officers meant the occasional initiative came to grief, sometimes spectacularly. 'So people don't stand up to him. It doesn't make him a bad person.'

'He called me in this afternoon . . .' he said again.

Picking up on the repetition, she gave him a look of concern. 'Something's wrong?'

'Something. I'm just not sure how much.'

'What did he want to see you about?'

'Couple of months ago a man disappeared. Baird wanted to know how the investigation was going.'

'Who disappeared?'

'It wasn't anybody you'd have heard of.'

'Unless they're politicians or on the television, most of us don't hear about people. Doesn't mean they're not important – big businessmen or whatever.'

'He wasn't important.'

'All right, I give in,' Carole said. 'Why on earth would Baird care about someone who disappeared months ago – was it in the papers?'

'Not for long.'

'To get you into his office and ask about it. Baird of all people.'

'. . . I don't know why.' To suspect wasn't to know.

'He didn't give anything away? Without meaning to?' She grinned as he pulled a face. 'You'd get more out of him than he would out of you. People don't realise how you put things together. Anyway, you're cleverer than he is.'

'That's why he's the Chief Constable and I'm—'

'All the same!'

Serious again, he shook his head. 'No, he's a bright man. Whatever else you can say about him.'

And his own man. He'd never heard a whisper about Baird jumping to anybody's tune. An arsehole in many ways; but an arsehole of integrity. That added to the puzzle of the afternoon's interview.

Maybe it would help to talk it through, he told himself. Since Carole had a tidy mind, he should really begin from when he'd first gone to the Bellman house. That would be easiest, and it might bring out something he'd missed. After all, sometimes talking brought things into a new focus. Truth was, it was a relief to put the Bellman case right at the centre of his thoughts. Pretending it would go away wasn't going to work any more. Like sounds in a mist turned suddenly into footsteps, the uneasiness he'd been denying for weeks had surfaced.

When he'd finished, she asked, 'What does Harriet think?'

'I haven't told her about it.'

After a moment, she said quietly, 'You should sell the house.'

'Why?' he asked, irritable at her going off at a tangent.

'You don't use it. You're living with Harriet.'

'Half of it's yours.'

'Fine. We could use some of what we get for buying wedding presents.'

From there, they drifted back to the when and where and hows of a wedding; and the why of it took them to Betty's pregnancy, and whether she was looking after herself. All the time, during this diversion as he thought of it, he kept waiting for them getting back to Bellman's disappearance, but somehow they didn't. At last, he realised Carole had decided it wasn't going to happen. That was a pity since he'd wanted to tell her about the interview with the Chief Constable. It never did any harm to check with someone you trusted. After all, his impression of what had been going on that afternoon might be a little paranoid. That was possible.

'And that's it?' Baird had said.

'As far as we've got.'

'Not very far.' Everything was squared away on the tidy expanse of the Chief Constable's desk except his hands, dropped palms down at its edge, fingers of one drumming turn-about on the other. Behind the barrier of the desk, he sat very upright, eyes fixed on Meldrum as they had been throughout. Meldrum alternated between holding this gaze and, when that got to be too much of a strain (for both of them, he'd felt), watching instead the fingers beat out their silent measure. 'You contacted the daughter by phone, you say?'

'Just before I got word you wanted to see me, sir. I'd been trying to get her since we found her name wasn't on the passenger flight lists. She admitted right away that she'd lied about arriving by plane on the Saturday. According to her, she knows that was stupid, but she didn't want her mother to find out what she'd been up to. Her story now is, she came up on the Friday. By train – not by plane. To spend the night with her boyfriend who lives in Edinburgh. On the Saturday morning, the brother Alistair covered for her with her parents. Picked her up from the boyfriend's flat, took her home and pretended he'd fetched her from the airport.'

'Telling the truth?'

'I'll have to check, of course. The call was just before you sent for me and—' He broke off as Baird nodded impatiently. The Chief Constable wasn't a man who needed to be told anything twice. 'I don't see any reason why she should lie about it.'

As soon as the words left his mouth, he knew Baird would offer some dry remark about lies being exactly what she'd told before. Instead, the Chief Constable nodded. 'So what do you do next?'

'We're having trouble locating the brother, but I'd expect the boyfriend to confirm her story.'

'*Apart* from that.' Late, but fully dried, came the arrival of the disparaging comment. 'Whatever's happened to Bellman, it's unlikely his daughter had anything to do with it. Didn't we just agree on that?'

'Still has to be checked . . . sir.' Ask him the theory of it, and Meldrum believed without question in the need for authority and hierarchy. In practice, it was his weakness to have the spine straighten, the dour brows draw together. He had the beliefs of a courtier and the gut instincts of an anarchist.

'*After* the boyfriend confirms some squalid liaison – stupid girl should be charged with wasting police time – what about finding John Bellman? I take it you've more or less run out of ideas.'

'Thing is, sir, there's a routine in a disappearance.' In a routine disappearance, was what he meant, like this is a *routine* disappearance. 'If it's a child, we search and keep on looking. If it's an adult, in a lot of cases the best we can do is circulate a description.'

'Never mind a lot of cases, I'm talking about *this* case,' Baird said, his voice dangerously quiet.

'What we're talking about here is a sixty-one-year-old man, no hint of foul play, no money worries – at least none have turned up and they tend to pretty quickly after a disappearance – no family problems. Nothing to run *from* as far as we can tell, so that makes it likely he's running *to* – a woman most probably. And there's no law against that.'

'Have you had any hint there's a woman?'

'If he's got one, he's been good at keeping it quiet.'

Meldrum's attention was caught as Baird changed from left to right hand, drumming on the backs of his fingers, little movements so controlled they seemed no more than a rippling of the flesh. He glanced up to find the Chief Constable frowning at him.

'You think too much attention's been paid to finding him?' Baird asked.

Meldrum hadn't expected to be picked up so directly. 'I wouldn't say that for sure. I mean, it has to depend on why he disappeared. But, of course, we have to find him to know that.' Chicken and bloody egg, he thought, I'm raving. He took a breath. 'Given the circumstances of the case, you could say, we've put an unusual amount of effort in.'

'Effort?'

Always one hundred per cent. Sir.

'Man-hours,' Meldrum said. And thought, Because of pressure from somewhere near the top. As it might be from you, sir. Or why else am I in here? Now you're going to tell me to step up the search. More time, more effort, right? But why? He wondered, if he pushes it, will I have the guts to ask him what the hell's going on? And, being a sensible man with no taste for martyrdom, knew he'd be a fool if he did.

'I agree,' Baird said. 'We seem to have spent more time on this than can be justified. Leave the file open. Stop work on it.'

Only a long experience of the oddities of courtrooms and interview rooms kept Meldrum's jaw from dropping open.

'Stop? When?' The only visible sign of his surprise was the baldness of the question.

'Now.'

From the beginning almost till that moment, Meldrum would have been glad to be called off the search for Bellman. Somewhere over the weeks, though, that had begun to change. There was a cop instinct and now, at the instant of being told to give up, it went into overdrive.

'I have to check the girl's story.'

'What for? The Bellman affair's taken up enough of our time, you tell me. I accept that. So stop.'

'Her story can't be taken at face value. It has to be verified.'

'Even though you believe her.' Meldrum didn't answer. Of course, Baird had to know it couldn't be left at that. 'Get your sergeant to talk to her boyfriend. You get back to more important things.'

'There are other loose ends. A day, two days at most, would tidy them up.'

'What kind of loose ends?'

Meldrum thought, There should be follow-up interviews. After the daughter's change of story, I should talk again to her mother. That made sense.

Instead, he heard himself say, 'I want to speak to the father-in-law again. General Gardiner.'

At the mention of General Gardiner, Baird's left hand rose

and smoothed the hair at the side of his head. It took no more than that.

Meldrum would have been hard put to explain why he had said he wanted to talk again to the father not the daughter. Afterwards, though, trying to account for it, it seemed no more complicated than that, for whatever reason, Mrs Bellman's first name had come into his mind as he imagined talking to her again. Willa. Unusual name. Why and where from? Family name? Where did the General's family hail from? And, thinking of him, blunder out the old man's name? As simple as that?

Yet perhaps something had been bothering him that he hadn't yet put his finger on. Or could it have been cop instinct again? Flattering to think so. For though Baird had picked up the thread again quickly, the pause and that involuntary movement of his hand had been enough to set Meldrum wondering if the pressure to investigate John Bellman's death could have come from General Gardiner.

Responding as Baird talked on, he thought it obvious that the General, if only for his daughter's sake, would want Bellman found. But even if, a big if, the old man had enough influence to get an investigation started, why would the Chief Constable suddenly want to stop it?

That it could be at the request of the General himself surely made no sense?

What reason could General Gardiner have for wanting to give up on his son-in-law's disappearance?

CHAPTER FOURTEEN

'Me, her boyfriend?' Frank 'Gibbie' Gibson said, hand held
up comically to fend off the suggestion. 'I think *not.*'

With this, heavily muscled legs showing very white under
the brief dressing-gown, he beat a retreat, presumably into his
bedroom.

However comically, DS Henderson decided, he was entirely
serious. In any case, the comedy was a touch too camp for his
taste. Detecting a hint of vulnerability behind the brashness,
he wondered if Gibson might be homosexual. In his book,
when a young man with the right accent and job to match
was wary of the police he had something to hide. To be fair,
a lot of people with blameless lives got uneasy when faced
by a policeman. Grown men whose mothers had threatened
a visit to the police station as an aid to toilet training had a
tendency to guilty sweats. On the other hand, why be fair? He
was running through other possibilities: drug habit, taste for
the kinky stuff, faking expenses, when Gibson came back in
jeans and trainers, pulling on a jersey thick enough for night
fishing off Shetland.

'Do you mind if we go out for our chat, Sergeant? I'm
ravenous, thank God. First time in a week I feel as if I could
face breakfast. Been off work with a virus, and there's nothing
in the house.'

So much for guilty sweats. Gibson, however, still drawled
'sergeant' as 'sa'ant' in best officer style. Thinks I'm in the
bloody army, Henderson thought as they ran down the stairs

from the flat to the street. It added to his irritation that he'd let himself be carried along by the younger man's easy assumption going out would present no problem.

'We'll have to go somewhere quiet,' he said.

'I've got the very place.' Without warning, Gibson swerved out to cross the road. Henderson had to wait as a car passed. He caught up at the opposite pavement. 'It's a favourite. No pretensions. I have a weakness for a fried breakfast.' As they came out into the wide thoroughfare of Leith Walk, there was a sudden sense of sky and space. Gibson pointed to the other side of the road. 'There we are. Get ourselves into a corner and we can be as private as you like.'

The café was cleaner than it looked from outside, with wipe-clean wooden tables and a couple of good-looking casually dressed waitresses, one dark and Italian, the other with a strong Australian accent, who smiled at Gibson and asked, 'Where you been hiding?'

'I've been a sick Indian.'

'Too much partying. The usual?'

'Everything. Need to get my strength back. And make it a mug of coffee.'

'I'll have tea,' Henderson said.

'Cup or mug?'

'They make good tea,' Gibson said. 'And wonderful coffee.'

It was larger, too, than the skimped frontage suggested. They went through an arch into a long narrow room and, going through it, found another smaller space with half-a-dozen tables. It was unoccupied. Gibson led the way to the table by the window at the rear. The glass was grimy and there were bars on the outside, allowing an obscured view of a grassed back area.

'Nobody will bother us here,' Gibson said. 'You can write in your notebook, if you've brought one.'

And lick my pencil, will I? Henderson thought; but didn't answer, postponing talk till after the waitress served them. He felt a certain grim amusement as at once Gibson began to fill the silence with random conversation and kept it up until the Australian girl came with the tray.

'You should have some,' Gibson suggested, mouth full,

spraying a little food, the second forkful already on its way as he smiled at the waitress, who was lingering ready for a chat.

Henderson shook his head at the girl, who took the hint and bounced off. In fact, the food seemed well cooked, mushrooms and tomatoes, lean bacon, the yolks of the eggs high and unbroken. It was the smear of grease, though, spreading at the edge of the plate, that caught his eye. It was his misfortune to see the flaw in things and people.

A mouthful of tea cut the feeling of mild nausea. He asked, 'You weren't expecting Ruth Bellman that night?'

'No!'

'You hadn't made any arrangement to meet?'

'Last thing would have entered my head.'

'Why – I mean, why would it be so unlikely?'

'I didn't know her all that well. I'll be honest with you, I'd say I hardly knew her at all. She was just Trey's kid sister.'

'Trey?'

'That's what we called Alistair Bellman. Didn't you know that?'

Henderson's grunt was non-committal. He worked on the principle he was there to ask questions not answer them.

'So when was the last time you'd spoken to her?'

'That's the thing, the last time was the first time. Sorry, that not make any sense? I mean, I'd only met her once. She was with Trey – Alistair.'

'Where was that?'

'My flat. I'd written to say I'd like to see Trey, this was after I came to Edinburgh. I knew his people lived not so far away, so I thought, when he's up, come and see me for old times' sake. I'd always a half notion I wouldn't make my career in the army – that's where we met. He was the one with the military background – you know about his grandfather?'

'The General?'

'Trey thought he was God. Talked about him as a great man. Not when he was sober, understand, not the type to wear his heart on his sleeve. It all came out when he was drunk. About the General. And what a shit his father was. He really hated—

Ah . . . Sorry, and all that. Shouldn't have said that. Bad taste, eh? Under the circumstances.'

'Did he say why?'

'Lot of men don't get on with their fathers.'

'Hated, you said.'

'Come on, you can't hold me to that. When he was drunk. And not every time he was drunk. A few times, at a certain stage of getting particularly, horribly drunk. I doubt if he'd even remember in the morning.'

'You did,' Henderson said. 'He must have made quite an impression for you to remember in the morning.'

Gibson blinked, opened his mouth as if to say something and then changed his mind.

'Always got on well with Trey,' he said after a moment. 'I don't mean we were bosom buddies – but we had some times together. I'd already got out, six months maybe, got the job up here, when I heard Trey had handed back the Queen's shilling. That was a big surprise. Always thought old Trey might finish up a general himself. So, as I say, I wrote back to this chap who told me about it, and he passed the word on and Trey appears one fine day. Ring at the bell and there he is, plus sister. I thought she was his girlfriend, then he introduced her. My impression, she'd decided she was going to tag along, and he was stuck with her. At the time, that made me smile. He was such a cold-blooded bastard – never had any difficulty I'd ever seen telling a woman to fuck off. This was the middle of the afternoon and we wandered around the town – had dinner, went to a club – and she was there till the death, two in the morning, jumped into the car and off they went. And that was it. Going home to their parents, and then back to London, I suppose. Didn't see either of them again. Not at least until months later – that Friday night you're asking about.'

'Let me get this straight,' Henderson said. 'You hardly knew Ruth Bellman. You'd met her once. Spent a few hours in her company. That's what you're telling me? Were the two of you attracted to one another?'

'Physically?'

'Okay, physically.'

'Christ, no. She's almost my height. You know what she looks like—'

'I've never seen her.'

'She's *big*. Not my type. I wanted to catch up with Alistair. Find out why he'd packed in his commission. Put a few pints away. Far as I was concerned, her being there was a bloody nuisance. And, before you ask, I didn't see any sign of her being hot to trot either. Might have felt differently if she had. *Might have* – like I say, she wasn't my type.'

'And then months later she arrives at your flat.'

'Buzzer goes. I pick up the phone and this voice says, Hello, it's Ruth Bellman, can I come up?'

'No prior phone call, no letter, no arrangement in advance. And according to you she spent the night?'

'Half an hour after she rang the bell, we were in bed.'

Gibson wiped up with a wad of bread, pushed it into his mouth and grinned.

'Although she wasn't your type.'

'When it's offered, I don't refuse.'

'On a plate, you mean.'

He watched crumbs of egg on the man's tongue as he licked his lips.

'Exactly. Half-ten on a Friday night, you know? You're sitting thinking you can't be bothered going out, and you don't bloody well want to stay in. And then, on a plate like you say. Didn't even have to buy her a drink. Slept like a log. Woke up in the morning and she was on the other side of the room with the phone in her hand. Stark naked. I looked at her for a bit – she's one of those women looks good with her kit off. Better than you'd imagine seeing her dressed. Hey! I told her, that better be a local call. She looked over and said, I'm asking Alistair to come and fetch me. Christ, my heart turned over.'

'Why?'

'Didn't know how he'd react to having his sister mounted.'

'Sounds as if you were afraid of him.'

'You could say that.'

'Big fellow like you? I'd have thought you could take care of yourself.'

'Listen,' Gibson said. 'Let me tell you about Alistair. I'll give you an example. We were all drunk, if that's an excuse. I expect it has to be, don't you? Not in a court of law, but it won't come to that, will it? Not when— What you're after is more important than anything that happened that night, isn't that right?'

'What night?'

'This thing that happened when Alistair and I were in the army.'

'I'm listening.'

'I mean, I know what this is about. A man disappearing, that can be serious. I read the papers. It wouldn't make sense for you to get side-tracked. Different if – if the worst had happened that night I'm going to tell you about. Christ, of course I don't know! I've never wanted to know. It happened one night up north when we were coming back from an exercise. But it doesn't matter, does it? This is just to make you understand about Alistair. This is just between you and me, right?'

'Of course it is,' Henderson said. 'Don't worry about the notebook.'

CHAPTER FIFTEEN

As he drove, Meldrum thought about Ruth Bellman. He wished he was back in Edinburgh at that moment, interviewing the boyfriend Gibson himself. Better, though, to leave it to Henderson, and give at least the appearance of following the Chief Constable's instructions. To the letter, never mind the spirit. He glanced at the clock, not registering the hour, thinking about time. He had another day on the Bellman disappearance, not any more.

He had been so busy with his thoughts that he was startled to realise he was already among the first buildings of the little town. Five minutes more and he'd be at the harbour. Instead he turned left on to the road that ran alongside an open space of links and led to the houses by the shore. Suddenly he pulled into the side and sat staring blankly at the roof of the Bellmans' house where it had come into sight high above its nearest neighbours. He wound down the window, then after a pause turned off the engine. He smelled salt on the wind. Blowing from the Fife shore, it swept across the Forth knocking tops off grey sea waves as it came.

He couldn't go in and face Willa Bellman. What had he imagined he was going to ask her? To the best of her knowledge, Ruth had arrived at the house from the airport on the Saturday morning. That was it.

What more could she tell him?

And as for what might have become of John Bellman, God knows, he had nothing to tell her.

Twenty-four hours, and he was wasting them.

That was what made him decide to talk to the people at the Trow Inn again. Instead of just turning tail back to Edinburgh, it gave his journey some point. True, not much of a point. He'd listened once to the owner describe how the Bellman family had come that Saturday night for dinner. 'To celebrate their daughter's twenty-first birthday,' David Hamilton had explained. He and his friend Leo had taken over a tiny pub dying as the village round it died, and turned it over the intervening twenty years into one of the most fashionable restaurants in the country. 'Her father made the booking a year ago. It was the only way he could be sure of a reservation.' Hamilton could remember what he'd cooked that evening; he had an extraordinary memory for food. If menu details helped find missing persons, he'd have been invaluable.

The road wound in slack curves like a dropped rope. Intermittently, it began to rain in single drops that burst in long trails down the windscreen. Views of the sea came and went. With every mile, he was further from Edinburgh and home. He put on the radio and ran the gamut: fragments of music, voices talking about themselves, to themselves. It sounded like a lot of people alone in a small room with a jug of water and a plastic cup. There was one voice, deep and slow, that sounded as if it might care about what it was saying and he listened to it for a while before switching off. It was a pity he couldn't speak Swedish.

There was no car parking at the Inn. There had been one round the back in the days of the pub, but now visitors to the restaurant had to street park. Apparently, since there were only eight tables, this wasn't a problem. He went past, pulled up two wheels on the pavement in front of a cottage with its windows boarded up and walked back. He knocked on the closed door, then shaded his eyes and peered inside. They didn't do lunches, he remembered, only meals in the evening. Giving up, he made his way round the side.

When they started, Hamilton and Leo had lived in a room behind the bar. With time and prosperity, they'd extended living quarters, taking them out from the back to leave the inn frontage untouched and buying land for a garden that provided fresh vegetables for the kitchen.

Before he had a chance to knock at the house door, a voice hailed him from the garden. He went down to the end of the path. The neatly kept lawn ended level with the building. Beyond that, everything was practical: plots, raised beds, fruit bushes, nothing that couldn't be supped or chewed or stirred in. A tall thin man in a tartan shirt, with what looked like the trousers of a lounge suit tucked into socks above a pair of cracked brown shoes, was standing in the middle of a herb bed.

'Tarragon is so pushy,' he said. 'Look at it. Push, pushing its way across. Chervil's in the wrong place, of course.' He took off a pair of gold-rimmed spectacles and wiped raindrops from them on the sleeve of his shirt. 'It's a school playground. Sort out the bullies and give the quiet ones a word of encouragement. If you're looking for David, he's gone to Eyemouth.'

'Do you know when he'll be back?'

'Longer he stays aways the better.'

'You're not expecting him soon?'

'Five, Leo, were the last words he said to me, five, *at the earliest.* Long enough, let's hope, for him to get over his bad temper. We don't open till seven.'

He should have known. It was turning out to be that sort of day.

'Thanks anyway,' he said, starting to turn away.

'Can I ask what this is about?'

'Sorry.' Meldrum showed his identification. 'I spoke to Mr Hamilton some weeks ago. Tell him it's not important. I happened to be passing and there were a couple of details.'

'About John Bellman,' Leo said. 'I'd have thought you'd want to talk with me. He's been one of our regulars for fifteen years. On high days and holidays, that is. Family events like his daughter's twenty-first. And their wedding anniversary, of course. Wonderful food is just part of a restaurant like this. The rest is caring, really caring, about people.'

'Making them feel special,' Meldrum said, faintly satirical.

'Exactly!' cried Leo, but the enthusiasm's dying fall coincided with the briefest narrowing of the eyes, come and gone in

a moment, but enough to suggest there wasn't much they
missed. 'Married thirty years, did you know that? They've
been married thirty years.'

'The Bellmans,' Meldrum said, playing catch-up.

'And what age is their elder son? . . . Exactly!' he finished
without waiting for an answer, and on a different note, sly
this time.

Thirty 'exactly' fitted Gordon. Matching that to how long the
Bellmans had been married wasn't the kind of thing Meldrum
was predisposed to pick up on. Getting pregnant, though,
was one way for a determined girl to overcome parental
opposition.

Leo had crouched to complete the filling of a trug with leaves,
nipping them off the stems with swift deft movements.

'Lentil and sorrel soup tonight,' he said. 'A pan filled with
sorrel reduces to almost nothing. Like spinach, you know.
David and I disagree on what you can do with spinach. Such
a *dull* vegetable. What did David tell you?'

Getting used to his conversational style, Meldrum made the
connection: not spinach, Bellmans. 'He confirmed that they'd
been here that evening. Got here about eight, left just before
midnight.'

Leo patted the leaves down, and stood up, an arm hooked
through the handle of the trug. 'Nothing else?'

'A happy meal, the way he described it.' Meldrum smiled.
'He told me the menu.'

'*Crème Flamande. Pâtes Fraîches au Caviar. Suprême de
Pigeons aux Choux. Tarte aux Noix,*' Leo said automatically.

'Everyone in good spirits. No sign of the father being different
from normal. According to Mr Hamilton.'

'Well, yes and no. I was never in any doubt the father had
a streak of the bully in him. Under the charm, you know. I
have an instinct for that.'

At which, he gave a brief difficult smile, duly noted
by Meldrum, who had more immediate concerns than the
humiliations of Leo, past or present. 'Who was Bellman
bullying?'

'Oh, when it happened, it was always the younger boy.'

'Alistair?'

'From when he was quite a child.'

'Physically? When he was a child, I mean.'

'Never, not here! I've no idea what went on at home, of course. We never do about other people, do we? Know what goes on behind closed doors. But if there had been anything physical here, he wouldn't have crossed our door again. He'd have been told, No reservations, sorry. Believe me, it wouldn't be the first time we've done that until someone unsuitable got the idea.'

'So this bullying was just verbal.'

'*Just*. Sarcasm, constant criticism, that can destroy a person. It doesn't make a bit of difference if it's done smiling. Bellman has what used to be called a hearty laugh. The best way I can put it – he takes up a lot of space. I could imagine that bigness, that loudness, that sheer physical presence, *pressing down on* an eight-year-old boy. The first time they ate here as a family, I said to David, that boy – the younger of the two – is afraid of his father. He told me I was talking nonsense. I never felt things really improved, but he could never see it.'

'You're saying, you believe Alistair is still afraid of his father?'

'The child we've been hides inside all of us. Yes, inside still.'

'And something like this was going on the night of the daughter's twenty-first birthday meal?'

'Very much so.'

'What about?'

'I don't hear so much. I'm in the kitchen mostly. David is more out front.'

'According to him, it was a happy meal.'

'Oh, plenty of laughter. There always was. But the father had a glass of wine thrown over him.'

'*What?*'

'David came into the kitchen and told me. Bellman had been going on about his son giving up the army – and suddenly Alistair picked up his glass and *whoosh*!'

'Mr Hamilton didn't mention that,' Meldrum said grimly.

'Oh, David could never see it! I mean, I made an excuse to go out and circulate. And the father was mopping up. And already it was an accident. A joke. Just moments later, and it was all laughter again.'

'Throwing wine at him. Doesn't sound like Alistair was afraid of his father any more.'

'Inside, who can tell? But, of course, Alistair is a big strong fellow now. When I said things change over so many years, I didn't mean they improve. Unless you feel changing fear for hatred is some kind of improvement.'

Hate was a word people threw around carelessly: *he* hated *his partner, she* hated *her husband.*

'You mean that?' In Meldrum's experience, when you challenged them it was a word people often would swap for something more cautious like 'dislike'. 'You're saying Alistair *hated* his father?'

'Oh, murderously!' Leo said.

CHAPTER SIXTEEN

Meldrum hadn't wanted to go out at all that evening, which made what he learned about General Gardiner all the more fortuitous. In the first place, dinner at that kind of place wasn't his scene. In the second, Harriet had made the mistake of telling him John Brennan would be there. She'd been one of Brennan's conquests before they'd met, and apart from work Meldrum tried to avoid the advocate.

'Gilchrist, Gilchrist and Myers only got involved because John Brennan passed some of the search work on to us,' she said. 'Whatever you think of him – I think of him, he's still important to me professionally.'

'Not emotionally?'

'Don't be ridiculous,' she'd said.

It turned out at first to be worse than he'd feared. Harriet had misunderstood and they'd arrived at the restaurant near the Pleasance to find that no one else, except the millionaire industrialist, had brought a partner. As host, accompanied by his wife, the millionaire was throwing his thank-you dinner exclusively for the lawyers and fund managers who had just made him even richer. Ten at the table had been the plan, but that was all right, the waiter brought an extra chair for him; and their host was nice about it, which made Meldrum homicidal with chagrin.

It didn't help that the millionaire, though undersized, was so rich he could afford to be self-effacing. As a result, Brennan – with his shock of white hair and actor's voice, the most

successful advocate in the city – was left to dominate the
table after his usual fashion.

'And then a couple of nights later, I saw the Dimbleby
programme on Chris Patten twisting arms on Legco. He was
like a less crafty version of Larry Hands. Christ, I thought,
tough on the Hong Kong people they didn't have Larry Hands
as Governor – he'd have got a better deal out of Beijing.'

Everybody laughed.

Except Meldrum.

Brennan said to him, 'It was on TV, Jim. We were talking
about it just before you got here. A documentary about this
Australian Larry Hands plotting to get enough votes on the
council to stay mayor of a suburb of Sydney. Lovely stuff, if
you enjoy a good conspiracy.'

'If you enjoy politics,' Harriet said. She was amused.

'I don't watch television much,' Meldrum said, who had
good reason to be wary of politics and politicians.

'No, busy man like you,' Brennan said pleasantly. 'I can see
you wouldn't have the time.'

'I was watching Billy Connolly in Australia,' the millionaire's
wife said. 'Very funny; but his hands give him away. If you
look at how he uses his hands, you can see he's been a
working man.'

The previous week Harriet had come home from advising
clients during a meeting with a local authority's Education
Committee. During it, apparently one of the Assistant Directors
had remarked on how she never had time to read any more,
because of the increasing scope of her responsibilities. Later
the Director of Education had made a point of describing his
own voracious appetite for books, which he read in bed and
travelling – 'always have at least two books on the go, at least
two'. Harriet had said, 'The destructive thing was, it's true.
He's the kind of man who seems to have more hours in the
day than the rest of us. I hope the lady took the point. Everyone
else did.'

Meldrum hadn't needed to intercept a glance between
Brennan and Harriet to *take the point*. Not only did he
not watch much television, he didn't in all honesty read
much either. Whereas, no doubt about it, Brennan would

effortlessly do both – another one with more hours in his day than everybody else.

While he was thinking this, the florid man across the table had begun to talk about tax and offshore investors. 'It's not just the interest rates that draw money into this country. Tax arrangements matter. Give you an example. I advised a client in Singapore to buy into a scheme in London dockside. The development finished up with 47 per cent purchasers from UK and elsewhere in Europe and 53 per cent from Asia. My chap bought twelve flats at prices from £300,000 up. He rents them, and there's an arrangement about offsetting against mortgage and taking rents abroad. I tell you, he's well pleased.'

By a thought process which evaded Meldrum, this reminded the millionaire's wife, an apple-cheeked fifty-something twice the bulk of her husband, of a visit she'd paid to her old school in London. 'About nine hundred of us turned up for the seventy-fifth anniversary. It was strange meeting people I hadn't seen since I was a child, and remembering the things we'd got up to—'

'Fun and games,' the millionaire said.

'Silly!' and they twinkled at one another. 'All harmless, like trying to see how many of us could climb up into the old apple tree. The thing was – and some people had come especially from abroad for the occasion – the school now is almost entirely black. They were terribly kind to us, the pupils and the staff, so pleased that we'd all come. The pupils put on a show for us, and you could see how hard they'd worked. The first item was a piece of music played on an instrument like a set of hanging files. The second was a little play about racial prejudice, and then there was one about drugs. We sat there and none of it had anything to do with us.'

'Surely that's not the children's fault?' Harriet wondered.

If her strongly felt feminism or disdain for racism and bigotry was provoked, her response could be emphatic. All the same, Meldrum knew his stab of anxiety was unreasonable. She had spoken quietly, and she had only sipped at her glass of wine. At once, he was ashamed of his impulse to check how much she'd had to drink.

The millionaire's wife, however, had heard only the word

'children'. 'I found my old home and it was being used as a youth residence. A black man came to the door, and I couldn't make him understand I didn't want accommodation but that I'd lived there as a child and just wanted to look around. I peeped in and asked if the cellar was still there. "Oh, no one lives there now," he said. It was the coal cellar where as children my brothers and I had gone down after a flood. We'd waded round and got covered in floating coal dust. My mother was furious!'

Round the table people smiled and laughed. Harriet frowned, but before she could offer a response, John Brennan said. 'It's an interesting point that when we think of ethnic minorities we think of their alienation and stresses, and rightly so, but here is an example of it from the other side – people in search of their past who can find no point of contact with this utterly altered present.'

'That's a nice phrase,' one of the two younger men said with a seasoning of irony, just enough to preserve his self-respect without losing the brownie point.

'Altered, all right,' said Ernest Myers, senior partner in Harriet's firm, the Gilchrists who preceded him in its title being long since dead or recently bought out. 'Matter of taste whether it's for the better.'

'I went with a friend to see her old house,' the millionaire's wife said. 'And she couldn't find it, the house she'd been born in. We walked through streets with not a white face. We finished up surrounded by street stalls. Later on someone told us it was the biggest Asian open air market outside Calcutta.'

'I'll tell you what makes me angry,' the man on Meldrum's left said, 'when my son tells me this country's finished.'

They agreed it wasn't, and as they went the circuit of the recent General Election, integration with Europe, the problems of the royal family, Meldrum got to a state of mild boredom that let him relax and even begin to taste the food. The millionaire was telling how as a boy in the South of England he'd watched American Superfortresses – and later Super-superfortresses, 'they had a longer fuselage' – come up and circle and set off for Europe, 'thousands of them, they darkened the whole sky'. 'Our finest hour,' came the quote pat on its moment from

the man on the left. Meldrum tried to catch Harriet's eye,
and saw that she was nodding agreement. He wondered if he
should mention *Hogan's Heroes*, but decided by this time they
probably didn't care how much television he watched and was
only half listening as, under the tutelage of the millionaire's
nostalgia, the past began to be cited as proof that the country
had a future.

Like Gardiner.

The phrase startled him awake. He couldn't even be sure
who had spoken the words. Brennan? Certainly, it was Brennan
talking now. As he attended to the big actorish voice rolling on,
he tried at the same time to reconstruct what he'd been only
half hearing. '. . . the rest of them had an army out of control',
something about, at time of Harold Wilson's election victory
(and another part of his mind tried to place when that was –
the Sixties or Seventies?) '. . . or controlled by such men in a
coup', *something about the Secret Service bugging members of
the Government?* '. . . could do in a country', *something about
the far Right, among them David Stirling, the SAS founder,
getting into the notion of a military take over?* '. . . the model
awfulness of the South Americans,' Brennan was saying. 'You
know, those armies which fail against real enemies – but like
Hemingway's Italians are coldly efficient against the weak.'

'Gardiner?' Meldrum said. 'Would that be General Gardiner?'

CHAPTER SEVENTEEN

W akening next morning in the grey hours just after dawn, he slipped out of bed taking care not to waken Harriet. She needed her sleep. They'd got back late from the dinner and then quarrelled for a while. She'd begun by wondering what Brennan had been talking about to him, heads so close together, after the millionaire left. From that, she'd got somehow to, he was a clever man, why didn't he have more ambition, he should take further qualifications. And he'd been tired enough to make the mistake of telling her there was no point, he'd gone as far as he would be allowed to go. And she'd told him he was paranoid – everything was back to normal, no one held his efforts to get Hugh Keaney out of jail against him. For her the fight to prove Hugh Keaney innocent was something in the past, over and done with – while he knew it never would be. He had never told her how ruthless the authorities could be, or of the deal he'd made to survive. He had kept it from her, and from the start that had harmed something between them. He should have known secrets were a poison. Yet, even if he had, what choice would there have been? He'd kept her in ignorance for the best of reasons. To protect her.

It had been a long night.

Downstairs he made a coffee and sat barefooted at the kitchen table to put on paper what he had learned the night before.

General Seton Gordon Gardiner, born in Hampshire in 1915. One of five brothers to be commissioned into Highland Regiments. His career intersected with pre-war empire – he'd

fought on the North-Western Frontier; and after the war with
the end of empire – he'd been in Malaya and Aden. He had
served in the war in Korea; and, so the story went, had got
into trouble for rashly making no secret of his opinion of the
Gloucesters' performance in that conflict. This had reminded
some at the time of his attack on those who complained of
being distressed by the sacrifice to placate the French of a
fellow Highland Regiment by Churchill before Dunkirk. The
difficulty had been not his defence of Churchill, but that the
vigour of it had given unwelcome publicity to something which
the authorities wanted to hide. Apart from that he'd had an
exemplary war. In France with the British Expeditionary Force;
in North Africa under Montgomery at El Alamein in 1942. After
the desert campaign, he'd fought in Sicily and took part in the
Allied landings at Normandy. A man of great physical bravery,
wounded three times, with the MC and a variety of decorations
from foreign governments. He had been tipped to go to the very
top; but hadn't – perhaps because of lingering memories of the
occasions when he'd been too outspoken. That had been the
public picture. Sensing there was more, he'd kept pressing
Brennan. If the advocate had a weak spot, it was the pride
he took in his sources (businessmen, bureaucrats, bankers, top
politicians in all the parties) and the encyclopaedic quality of
his memory. After some perfunctory fencing, he had filled in
the real black marks on Gardiner's record.

Meldrum arrived at HQ later that morning ready to share
what he had learned. Henderson, however, had his own story
to tell of Alistair Bellman showing homicidal tendencies during
what his mate Gibson described as 'a yob hunt'.

'So what does that prove?' he asked when Henderson had
finished.

'Proves he's a nutter,' Henderson said.

Meldrum thought about it. 'And he doesn't like his father
much.'

He told the DS about Leo claiming Alistair had thrown a
glass of wine at his father in the Trow Inn during Ruth's
birthday dinner.

Henderson whistled. 'Why the hell didn't his partner—' he
snapped his fingers, 'the other poofter—'

'Hamilton,' Meldrum said, deciding the *poofter* bit was less out of homophobia than Henderson's irritation at falling down on the Mr Memory role.

The DS shot him an I-remember look. 'Hamilton. What was he playing at not telling us that?'

'Didn't think it was important, according to Leo.'

'He wants sorted out. Wasting police time,' Henderson grumbled.

'I suppose.'

'Anyway, we know now. Alistair is getting stick about packing in the army. He gets pissed off and chucks a glass of wine over his father. Next morning the father's disappeared.'

'So?'

'Know what his army chum Gibson said? He told me every time Alistair got drunk he'd go on about how he hated his father.'

'If we believe Leo, Alistair was afraid of his father as a kid, finished up hating him.'

'There you are then!'

'Where would that be? Not sure I'd rate Leo as a witness.'

They sat in silence, chewing it over.

At last Meldrum said, 'You want to spell it out for me?'

'Sometime during the night? That's the way I'm thinking. They get back from the restaurant. The mother goes to bed, fair enough, she's older. But then Ruth does as well – and it's supposed to be her party!'

'Maybe she'd had enough birthday fun for one night,' Meldrum suggested. He wanted to test how far Henderson would push his theory. There was an eagerness about the DS that was new. Maybe it was just the chance to think about the possibility, however remote, of their having fallen into a murder instead of a routine disappearance. For an ambitious man, that would be a break.

'Look at it this way,' Henderson said, leaning forward. 'That leaves Alistair and his father with the older brother and his wife. But we know that Gordon and Sally have to leave early in the morning to see her kid in Aberdeen. So it makes sense they'd want to get to bed as well.'

'According to Sally, she went to bed – but that left Gordon still there.'

Watching Henderson scowl and rasp the back of a fist over his chin, Meldrum thought, maybe he'll suggest both brothers did it.

But, sticking to his task, Henderson offered, 'Suppose Gordon wasn't that long behind her. Suppose he left Alistair and his father drinking together. Wine and whisky. That's a hell of a combination. Especially for two men who've been arguing the toss already, eh?'

'Come on.' Meldrum got up and with Henderson following made his way out of the office.

After they'd collected coffees, he picked a table by the wall and set his chair with its back to the room, even though the canteen was quiet this early in the morning. It was like putting up a Do Not Disturb sign. He took a mouthful of the pale liquid, which as usual didn't taste much of anything, and sighed.

'Where are we going with this?'

'He could have beaten his old man's head in,' Henderson said, looking more animated than Meldrum had seen him. He remembered Henderson's story of going out to Australia in search of his runaway father. Maybe more than ambition fired him up on his murder theory. That father of his had sounded like an evil bastard.

'Let's take this back to square one,' Meldrum said. 'Was there a quarrel? Maybe there wasn't. None of his family mentioned a quarrel in the restaurant. Okay, so Leo tells me about a drink being thrown. Thrown? We can't even be sure of that. Suppose the family and Hamilton, even people at the other tables, either don't remember at all or only remember something about a drink being spilled. Places where people eat, even the fancy ones, drinks get spilled all the time. And everybody in the family – Gordon, Sally, Ruth, Mrs Bellman, Alistair himself – tells the same story. Happy families. A good night out. No trouble. "Plenty of laughter," Mrs Bellman says.'

'Jury would love her,' Henderson reflected gloomily. 'Put the poofter up saying there was a stramash and her saying, no, there bloody well wasn't, except she wouldn't say "*bloody*", being a lady.' He gave the thumbs down. 'No contest.'

'God's sake, man, that's the least of your worries.'

'Eh? Oh, right. No weapon.'

'No body,' Meldrum said and began to laugh, sure suddenly Bellman was alive by a pool somewhere with the sun shining down on him and an eighteen-year-old with her top off stretched out beside him.

CHAPTER EIGHTEEN

It wasn't a fishing pool. An abruptness of depth, the way the water ran, the steepness of the banks and the clustering of trees, meant that this pool was neglected. It couldn't be waded, and it was hard to get at with a line. That could have been fixed, somehow, on a river where a beat cost a Kuwaiti's ransom, except that you couldn't drop a fly anywhere with a good hope of it being taken. For no obvious reason, it was a pool fish didn't like. Maybe it had to do with nothing more tangible than angles of the light slanting down at them.

On the east side, a young rowan had sprung up from earth churned by the capsizing of an alder in some winter storm. Stripped by the seasons, the dead tree hung by its exposed roots, trunk pressed against the earth, branches splaying down the bank to the river. Held like that for so long, there seemed no reason why it should ever move. Yet under and around it there was constant movement, of wood as it rotted, insects, time's siftings of earth by water. The last tether of root was loosening.

A man came through the trees stepping from shadow to shadow as if pursued by moonlight. Nothing broke or rustled under his feet. At the sound of a voice, he froze.

The voice was the smallest whisper, audible because it was only a few feet away.

'He's gone.'

Intent on silence, the listener took shallow breaths through his open mouth.

A second voice answered, 'The bugger's hereabouts. Hit him, mind, hit him!' Then louder, still not much above a whisper, but the effect shocking, like a shout wanting to be heard. '*Sneddon! I'm going to beat the shite out of you. Can you swim, ye bastard?*'

And in the same instant a white beam split the dark like a searchlight. Voice and torchglare set the quarry moving, but didn't stampede him as had been intended. The man kept his nerve, moving fast but still in silence. He was lucky, the torch swung first away from him. As the light came back, probing, swinging back a little, jumping forward, he was trapped behind a tree, a new growth that gave little shelter. Even in that extremity part of his mind recorded the strangeness that the leaves in front of him had been burned off, then as the light came in a swoop he fell to his knees.

The ground dropped from under him.

The dead tree took half the bank down with him in a landslide. Stones and wood clubbed him a blow in the middle of the back, on the side of the face, then another on the arm as he threw out a hand to clutch at the earth. Tumbling, he saw the moon above him, below him, above, below, until he smashed upon its reflection in an uproar of earth and water and was dragged under.

Afterwards in nightmares he remembered the silence. Blood sighed in his ears like the taking of soft breaths. Looking up from somewhere near the bottom of the pool, he reached up towards the light. He started up, felt himself held, kicked and seemed free, threshed and in his panic was caught fast. Something in him, courage, craft, cunning, refused to drown. He folded, pulling himself down the leg to where it was gripped. His groping hands found where the trunk divided. Surely his boot had forced itself through. Surely that was the trap. But when he tore at it, the rotten wood shredding off in lumps, still his foot wouldn't pull free. And then he felt it, the knot of chains he had kicked into, one tight loop of it twisted like a tourniquet across his boot by a stick caught behind the heel. It took both hands but he snapped the stick, and the chain turned, unloosing him.

When he surfaced and saw the thing he was holding, he

screamed. Even when they got him out, sprawled on the bank, still clutching it, his two rescuers had difficulty understanding what he yammered at them through a jaw broken in the fall. As they explained to the police later, however, it didn't matter since both of them recognised the white stick as a length of human bone in the moonlight.

CHAPTER NINETEEN

'Science,' the General said, hands clasped behind him, looking out of the window at the rain slanting across his lawns.

Tall, lean, upright. From the back, he could have been half a century younger. General Seton Gordon Gardiner. A man with a distinguished war record. A chestful of medals. Kind of man who should in retirement have been the Lord Lieutenant of the County and all the rest of the bullshit. But hadn't – any more than he'd made it to the General Staff or the Field Marshal's baton he'd been tipped for early in his career. 'What I'm telling you is on file, you can guess where,' John Brennan had said, 'classed top red, *need to know only* stuff.'

Meldrum, offered a view of the eighty-two-year-old back, studied it thoughtfully. A dark green shirt, open at the neck, suggested blood that ran warmer than the thin stuff of the very old. Certainly, there was a fire in the grate, but at its best it must have been a small fire, and the dour servant Robertson had smoored whatever it had of cheerfulness or warmth under the dark mantle of a half bucket of coal before taking Henderson with him from the room. Standing close to it, Meldrum was chilled. In winter, couched in its lair of dripping trees, the house must leach cold out of the air.

'No doubt about it, I'm sorry.'

The General turned, something very military in the movement, hands still behind him. 'But this body had been in the water for weeks? And it had been burned as well?'

'An attempt had been made to burn it before it went into the water.'

'And they could still identify it as my son-in-law? Dental records? And what was the other thing? Pattern of old bone breaks? Science,' he said again.

'We were lucky.' He hesitated on the word. Not lucky for the widow. Or the daughter and sons. 'Your son-in-law had very full medical records.'

'But why him? Why check his records? Was it because you were sure he was dead?'

Meldrum shook his head. 'I was pretty sure he wasn't.'

'Like me, you thought he'd gone off with some woman. That's the type he was.'

Meldrum contemplated telling him their investigation hadn't turned up even a hint of another woman in Bellman's life, but let it go. He suspected nothing would change the General's opinion of his son-in-law; that being the type the old man was. Instead, he explained, 'It was the local police who started it off. The inspector on the ground raised some questions as soon as he got to the scene. Almost any other place on that river – even ones an outsider would take to be deserted – have regular activity. It's a fishing river busy during the season. There would always be at least a chance of a body being found. Not in this pool, though. For some reason, it isn't fished, and that made it the ideal place to hide the body. But it's awkward to get at, not all that near the road. The inspector didn't think it was a place you'd land on just by accident. Looking for people with that kind of local knowledge, he decided among other things to check fishing rentals. John Bellman was in a consortium that had rented on that stretch for years. The inspector picked up on the name, checked missing persons, the address fitted. He got in touch and we took it from there.'

He wondered how Henderson was managing with Robertson. See what you can get out of him, he'd told the DS. The General hadn't demurred when Henderson followed his servant out of the room. He'd have seen it as junior ranks making themselves scarce. Assuming it registered at all. Living with hierarchy all your life as a soldier could blind you to things under your nose. In the same way, far from being surprised by their unannounced arrival he'd appeared to take it as no more than his due and was accepting all this fullness of explanation matter-of-factly, as if at a debriefing.

'How was he killed?'

Méldrum hesitated. 'The condition of the body caused problems. The skull was intact. The best estimate is stab wounds to the chest.'

'So it might not have been murder at all? I mean, if you can't be certain how he was – how he died.'

Partly burned. Weighted with chains. Thrown into a river. 'We're treating it as murder.'

The General thought about that, snuffled air down his nose, nodded a brisk acceptance.

'Yes. He left the house for a walk on the Sunday morning. That right?' He glanced sharply at Meldrum's lack of response. 'You think that's when it happened? Somewhere on the beach. Some quiet spot along that stretch of beach?'

'That's one possibility.'

'Poor devil must have been attacked by a madman.' And when Meldrum didn't answer: 'You have difficulty with that?'

'Mr Bellman *could* have encountered someone when he went walking that morning. But if that is what happened, your son-in-law was very unlucky. To meet someone carrying a knife and ready to use it – we'd have to assume without provocation. Somebody as mentally disturbed as that – it wouldn't be the first time, or if it was they'd go for the thrill again quickly. There's no record of another attack.'

Pacing forward, the General flapped a hand towards an armchair. But when his invitation was accepted, instead of himself taking the chair opposite he stepped into the place vacated before the dull fire.

'Anything else?' he wondered, gazing down from his considerable height on Meldrum.

'I can't see why a madman would drive sixty miles to hide the body. In fact, I can't see why he would try to hide it at all.'

'Doing things don't make sense, would have imagined that was the point of being a madman. No?'

'It's not so easy. There are patterns to these things.' Patterns, Meldrum thought. Knife Stanley would be proud of me.

'You're the expert,' the General said, in the tone of a man who'd used many in his time, not all of them up to task. 'Tell you what else occurs. Drugs. Goes on up and down the coast, smuggling, from what you read in the papers. Suppose he stumbled across something like that. Saw something he shouldn't have? How that strike you?'

Like something I read in Enid Blyton when I was a kid, Meldrum thought. And added at once in fairness, Not that smuggling doesn't happen.

But to judge by his frown, it was some hint of that first response the General caught. So much for the poker face of a professional detective.

'It's a possibility we'll certainly be taking a look at. Among others.'

'Care to tell me what they might be?'

'In a case like this,' Meldrum said, and spread his hands in the air – so many possibilities. 'When I was here before, your grandson was staying with you. Is he here now?' The connection was crude enough. Meldrum was happy to let it appear that way.

'No,' the General said, with no change of expression. At last, however, he took the armchair opposite, a kind of small victory perhaps. Straightbacked, he sat with forearms at rest on the arms of the chair. 'Why?'

'We're anxious to speak with him again. You remember when I was here he gave me a contact address? He isn't there, hasn't been for some time. The friends in the flat claim to have no idea where he's gone. He'd only been there about six months – "off and on", they said. More off than on was our impression.'

'These friends, are they the ones he's going to Nepal with?'

'So they told us.' What they'd actually said was, *Could turn up, ready for the off, day we're leaving. That's Trey for you.* 'He seems to move around a lot. Staying with one friend or another – mostly in London. As far as they know, he doesn't have a place of his own.'

'He's been restless since he left the army.'

'So restless he doesn't keep in touch when his father goes missing? If nothing else, for his mother's sake.'

'She'll have heard from him, no doubt.'

'Did she tell you that?' The General stared at him impassively. 'I ask, because when I spoke to her, she told me she hadn't.' After a moment, Meldrum went on, 'As soon as we established the identity of the body in the river, I went to see Mrs Bellman, of course.'

'This is hard on my daughter.'

Meldrum made a sympathetic face. 'I've also spoken to Gordon Bellman and to Ruth. She's flying up to be with her mother.' The General gave no sign to acknowledge he'd been told of his grand-daughter's homecoming plans. What kind of family was this? 'None of them knows where Alistair is, however.'

'Remember the boy doesn't know his father's dead. Probably imagines he's gone off with some woman. Just the way we did.'

'I've thought of that. I've arranged for appeals on television and radio. The papers in England are picking up on the story. If he doesn't see it, someone who knows him will. I'll be . . . surprised if I don't hear from him. Soon, I mean.'

'It will be a shock for the boy.'

For the first time, the timbre of the voice, which had impressed Meldrum, thinned fractionally. The firmness of the voice, the erect carriage, the undimmed potential ferocity of grey-blue eyes, had made for the illusion of age defied. Veins the colour of the chair's leather writhed on the backs of his hands. He had seemed indifferent to the death of his son-in-law. There had been no indication of worrying over his daughter's grief, or that of Gordon or Ruth for their father. This was his first sign of weakness.

'Poor Alistair,' the General said.

When they were shown out, Robertson stood on the steps and watched them into their car.

Going back down the drive, Henderson glanced up at the mirror, then asked, 'He still there?'

Meldrum, in the passenger seat, twisted round to check.

'Uh-huh.'

'Cunt's making sure we're off the premises.' The curse word, though a favourite with Henderson, wasn't much used by him.

For a detective, he wasn't all that foul-mouthed. It was possible, of course, being looked down on from a great height by a general wasn't something he relished. As if reading his mind, the sergeant added, 'That Robertson thinks the sun shines out of the old man's arse.'

'Any sign of Alistair?' Meldrum asked.

Henderson jerked a thumb back to where the house had dropped behind its cordon of birch and beech trees leaning into the prevailing wind. 'Big place like that. Fucking boring to stay indoors out of sight, but if he did he could hide all right.'

Meldrum nodded. Stay out of sight in his room, keep away from windows, no walks. And in the evening . . . Who else would be in the house then?

'What about servants? Any live in? Apart from Robertson.'

'There's a couple of women come in to clean up. Wife of the forester on the local estate and her daughter – I got that out of Robertson, like pulling teeth. Husband drops them in the morning, picks them up about now. If the General's hiding him, those two are our best bet.'

'Only bet by the sound of it. Not much of a staff for a place that size.'

'Robertson does the cooking. Does the General's washing, ironing. Lays out his clothes. Wipes his bum, I shouldn't be surprised.' He stopped the car between the gates. 'Head for the village?'

'Back to Edinburgh.'

Henderson didn't move. 'Somebody'll be able to tell us where the forester's house is. We could have a word with the wife and daughter.'

'No,' Meldrum said. 'I'll get someone to talk to the women.'

'I don't get it,' Henderson said. He kept the car out of gear but, perhaps by accident, pressed the accelerator. The engine note coarsened briefly to a roar before settling back.

Meldrum scowled. Anyway, he hated being a passenger, which was why up till now he'd done all the driving.

'Get on to Edinburgh,' he said. 'Or come out of there, and let me do it.'

Henderson slammed forward and swung out on to the road.

'Just as well nobody was coming,' Meldrum said.

They drove for a long time in silence. It was Meldrum's nature that, having got the irritation out of his system, it was over and done with at once. He began to go over what the General had said, searching for anything he could have missed that might be significant. They were on the outskirts of the city and he was busy with his own thoughts, when Henderson, eyes fixed ahead, said grimly, 'I still don't get it.'

'Sorry? Get what?'

'When we were that far, why not go and see them?'

'Who?'

'The women that come in to do for the General.'

'Because if we talk to them, chances are they'll clam up out of loyalty.'

'Frightened for their jobs more like.'

'Whatever. I'll get a woman to talk to them, pretend she's after something else altogether and hope they loosen up. We need evidence of Alistair being there, and even then getting a search warrant'll be tricky.'

'No problem if we wanted to go into a shithouse in the Pilton. Mob handed.'

'People of standing in the community,' Meldrum reminded him.

'Can sue the arse off you.' Another quote from the unofficial police manual. With that, Henderson lightened up. With a grin, he said, 'Little Willful.'

'Eh?'

'That's what Robertson says the soldiers called Mrs Bellman, when she was a kid in Germany.'

'Tell me about it.'

After he'd finished telling the story, Henderson wondered, 'Where do we go from here?'

Pondering children and Nazi salutes, Meldrum didn't have an answer.

Any more than he'd had when the General asked him the same question.

'Where do you go from here?'

BOOK FOUR

A Spreading Evil

CHAPTER TWENTY

Sitting in the departure lounge at Aberdeen airport, the easiest point of departure for Oslo, Meldrum passed the time when the flight was delayed by watching a quiz on television. Competitors had to select from a variety of choices shown on a screen which powers of the monarchy were real and which invented for the game's occasion. Bells rang when they got it right; a horn jeered for choices such as 'can vote in elections' or 'behead whoever she wants to'. What intrigued him was the list of correct choices. In theory at least, the Queen could: Appoint anyone a bishop; Disband the Church of England; Make anyone a peer; Give away territory; Disband the army; Veto an Act of Parliament; Declare a state of emergency; Dismiss the government; Close down the Civil Service.

Idly, he wondered which selection of those options the group round General Gardiner and his fellow-plotters might have dreamed of persuading the monarch to use. Back then in the Sixties, their aim had been not just to get rid of the Government, but to snatch power in a coup. By so doing, they would thwart the plans of Prime Minister Harold Wilson, and save the country for their version of democracy.

'In their demonology,' John Brennan had explained, 'little Wilson was a communist double agent. Nonsense, of course. His biggest secret was, off camera he smoked cigars instead of a pipe.'

'It's all crazy,' he had said.

'They weren't mad. Well, not all of them. But if you want to con yourself some easy money, tell a right-wing millionaire you can save him from the workers. Doesn't matter how shrewd he is in business, he'll reach for his wallet. The tougher they are, the stupider they'll be about it. Understand, that makes them more not less dangerous. Like the wounded tiger.'

'Giving a donation's one thing. Plotting's another.'

'You're such a copper, Jim. Revolutions aren't possible, not in this country, is your line. Most people here think so – it's a long time since the English have had one, the Scots love a lord, and the Irish don't count. But what your kind of policeman believes in his bones is that they're not just impossible – they're not even thinkable. Not true. Anything that can be thought, there'll be someone to think it.'

'Aye, and you're thinking of South America,' Meldrum had growled. Being lectured at offended him. 'Tinpot generals and crackpots wouldn't get far here.'

'As far as Mountbatten. They held talks with him. That's the big secret in General Gardiner's file. Stopped his career in its tracks.'

'You mean Earl Mountbatten?'

'An actual Earl! I can see you're impressed.' Brennan's grin showed a strand of meat caught between white teeth big enough for a horse. 'I told you Scotsmen love a lord.'

CHAPTER TWENTY-ONE

The woman in the fur coat wrinkled her nose and shifted to another seat in the Tegel departure lounge. The fat man she'd been sitting beside smelled rankly of sweat. It ran down his cheeks, and spread in dark circles under the arms of his shirt. Giovanni Locascio was afraid.

He had been chronically afraid for a long time; but for the last eleven days the condition had been acute. Perhaps somewhere inside and unadmitted he'd started to be afraid from the moment they'd decided to steal the Mountain's money. The difficulty was it had been made so easy for them. Without trying, he had come up with half a dozen ways to siphon it off: 'From the top, from the bottom, from the sides,' he'd joked to Kielland. That it was like that didn't surprise him, for it was his opinion that politics was only a road to power, and the purpose of power was to allow those who achieved it to open a Swiss bank account as soon as possible. People motivated by ideology without regard to money, it seemed to him, had to be fools. No surprise then that they should make it easy to steal from them. As a Sicilian, though, he should have remembered fascists were serious people. Some part of him had known it, never doubted it, which was why he'd been afraid from the start. Just a little afraid. At the start. Not enough to stop, when they made it so easy. Just enough to be careful. To keep the stealing within bounds. Not to steal too much. That had all changed when the accursed Bellman got greedier. From then on, he'd known in his heart it was only a matter of time. Yet he hadn't stopped. He hadn't stopped even though the fear had been with him all the time like a pain around his heart. It was his nature to steal, and they had made it too easy. He blamed them for that.

'I decided to pay at once for my carelessness.'

The voice from just behind him, at his ear it seemed, took Locascio by surprise. The speed with which he swung round, unexpected for someone so bulky, alarmed the man, who took a half step back, trying to protect the two glasses he held. As he did, Locascio recognised him as the blunderer who'd knocked his elbow at the bar.

'Please,' the man said, holding out one of the glasses.

'No need,' Locascio said.

'I wish you would,' the man said again. 'It would make me feel better.'

Locascio knew the type. He'd met them before, young men, very polite, very eager to please; as if someone had told them Germans had the reputation of being arrogant and they were trying to live it down. At a calculation, he wouldn't be much under six feet if he straightened up. A scholarly stoop – wasn't that what they used to call it? – and one caused, chances were, not by books or scholarship of any kind, but by bending over a computer screen working out endless figures. He had blue eyes, though, and a touch of blond about the temples: so that was all right, Locascio supposed sourly. He didn't much care for Germans at the best of times. After ten days hiding in a lousy hotel near the Alexanderplatz, all he wanted was to get out of Berlin as quickly as possible. Another day and he would have gone crazy. He took the glass.

The man gave a little satisfied nod, and was turning away, when Locascio said, 'Join me, why not?' As if they spoke themselves, the words were out of his mouth before he had time to think. He was sick from being alone. No question of it, one more day and he would have gone crazy.

The man smiled and took the seat the woman in the fur coat had vacated.

Locascio ran the drink round his tongue. 'This is better whisky than the one I bought.'

'Malt whisky is a drink for the connoisseur.' The man held

the glass up and sniffed. 'An expert is able to tell one from the other just by the nose. This is a whisky from the island of Islay. That is an island off the western coast of Scotland.'

No bore like a German bore had always been Locascio's opinion. This tight-arsed young-old man was shaping up to be a prize example of the species.

'I can see you're an expert.'

Impervious to irony, the man held up his free hand in modest disclaimer. 'No, not at all. Apart from anything else, I don't have the opportunity. The bar here is quite typical in the limited range it offers. I was lucky to get this. No, no, we don't get the chance to educate our palates. For that you need to compare the malts from the Highland and Lowland parts of Scotland and the islands especially.'

Locascio stared at his glass, thinking how much worse pedantry sounded in German. In Italian, a pedant wound himself round your brain in coils of soporific music. In German, he drilled into your skull like one of those serial killers in America. Without ceremony, he poured the whisky straight down his throat; 'so that it didn't touch the sides', as the peasants said. Hopefully, he looked to see if the man had taken the insult.

'Without water,' the idiot noted approvingly. 'After the Scotch fashion.'

'And you say you're not an expert!' Locascio allowed himself the indulgence of a false smile.

The man made the same little stop-it-please hand movement as before, drooping and shaking his head modest as a milkmaid. 'Helmut Meckel.'

'Emilio—' Locascio forgot the name on his passport. 'Solmi.' It had lasted only an instant, a nasty instant. 'Emilio Solmi.' Who forgot his own name? Even for an instant? Fortunately, the idiot, launched again on malt this and malt the other thing, was too self-absorbed an idiot to notice.

Actually, a fool of this stripe could be oddly relaxing. After so much silence, there was comfort in the sound of a human voice. You didn't have to respond or even listen, just nod now and again as if impressed. It left you to get on with your own thoughts.

Eleven days ago, he'd crossed the border from Poland. On the way, he'd changed cars in Poznan, then gone north before swinging west to cross the Oder. Even now, thinking back, he couldn't see how he'd been followed. Then, he would have staked his life he hadn't been. In a way, of course, that was exactly what he had done. And almost lost.

'You're feeling it hot?' the polite young man asked.

Nodding irritably, Locascio scrubbed a handkerchief back and forward across the sweat that had broken out on his forehead.

Only by chance, not by his own strength or cunning, that he survived to bet his life again. The Hunter had found him. Couldn't have been waiting for him, though it happened so quickly after his arrival it felt that way. He hadn't trusted anyone with his plans, there was no one he could trust. It wasn't a matter of having made a reservation in advance. Driving past, he'd seen the name, and a sudden craving for luxury American style caused him to brake and cut across, horns shrilling from the traffic behind. Yet when half an hour later, naked except for his underpants, he'd heard as he lay resting on the hotel bed three deferentially spaced taps on the corridor door, he'd been afraid to open in case the Hunter was waiting for him on the other side. He'd told himself it had to be a porter or maid and that he was a fool. But as he stood trembling, listening, there came a scratching sound as the lock was tested. Then he'd panicked; and that was the second time his life had been saved by chance. In Berlin that night, and once before in Paris with Braaten.

'You're going?' the young man asked, so surprised by the suddenness of it he almost, but not quite, managed a reproach.

'I have a phone call to make.'

But the moment he got through and heard the voice answer in Norwegian, Locascio came to his senses and hung up. The last thing he wanted was Braaten meeting him at the airport in Oslo with a posse of policemen. He clamped his briefcase under his arm and, busy with his calculations, waddled back to the same seat.

'There's something immoral about being tired in the afternoon,' the young man said, closing the guidebook he'd been reading. He yawned and looked at the empty glass in front of him. 'I was thinking of having another one, but they've called the flight for Oslo.'

CHAPTER TWENTY-TWO

For Meldrum, the photograph came as an unwelcome complication. It arrived with a set that showed the body: firstly, at the Holmenkollen Ski Lift where it had been found; later in the morgue, close-ups of the chest, and of the head showing the entry and exit paths of the death wound; and, among the last, one of the face tidied up and given the cosmetic treatment, the dead eyes open and glistening. All of them identified on the back with a note which named the victim as Gregers Kielland, who in life had looked like a contented fox, if the photograph that mattered was anything to go by. Sitting at a table in some restaurant, laden fork half-way to his mouth, he had his head to one side, directing a sly glance at his companion and half laughing as if coaxing him to share the joke. Neither Kielland nor John Bellman seemed aware they were being photographed.

The whole packet had been faxed to Edinburgh with the briefest of covering letters. When he phoned the contact number at police headquarters in Oslo and asked for the officer who had signed the letter, Meldrum hadn't been in the best of tempers. It was a relief to find this Tore Braaten spoke good English; but, dragging a red herring across the trail of a case more or less solved, he was still a damned nuisance. After the polite preliminaries, their conversation had been abrasive.

'Go out? Why should I go to Norway to talk to you?'

'If you've looked at the material, I should have thought that was obvious.'

'Not to me.'

'You've seen the photograph of them together?'

'So they knew one another.'

'And they were both murdered. You think that's a coincidence?'

'Your man was shot. Mine was stabbed. Yours was thrown off this ski jump and left in plain sight in a public place to be found. With mine there was an effort to conceal his identity – the corpse was partly burned. *And* to hide the body – it was weighted before it was thrown into the water. I don't see any connection.'

'They were partners.'

'In what? What kind of partners?'

'That's what I'll explain when you come out.'

'Why can't you tell me now?'

'That wouldn't be suitable.'

'All right. You're the one that wants to talk. You come here.'

There was a silence. 'I'm waiting for someone to contact me. It's important that I'm here when he does.'

And you think I'm sitting here on my arse with nothing to do, Meldrum had wanted to ask. Twiddling my fucking thumbs?

Instead, spelling it out, deliberately patient, he'd said, 'This thing of mine is a domestic. You know what I mean by that? We're fairly – we're sure Bellman was killed by one of his family.'

'I don't think so.'

'Why not?'

'I'll explain when you come here.'

'I won't be doing that. Not unless you can give me a reason.'

Silence again. Long enough this time for Meldrum to wonder if he'd hung up. Then Braaten had said, 'I don't think you're the kind of policeman who would want to have an innocent man charged with murder.'

As he stared down out of the plane window, Meldrum saw on an unbroken snowscape of cloud the image of John Bellman as he'd been caught in that moment sitting across the restaurant table from Gregers Kielland. In a murder case, no matter how endlessly you went over the facts or read witness statements until you were sick of them, trying to guess what the victim had been like as a person was never easy. In life, meet anybody for the first time face to face, however briefly, five minutes might be enough, half an hour would be plenty, and you'd have a feeling about them. An accent, a handshake, shape of the mouth, of the eyes, anything could do it, like a sniffing dog you'd be on your way to liking or not liking, trust or mistrust. Never mind you might have cause later to change your opinion. Only the dead couldn't ever stop being strangers.

During the search, there hadn't been any lack of photographs of Bellman to brood over: family snaps, portraits in evening dress at functions, a souvenir cut from the local newspaper where he'd stood centre-front in a group protesting a plan to site a fish-curing plant near the golf course. And none of them had told him anything of what he needed to learn about Bellman; no more than watching a performance made a theatre audience intimate with what the actor might be like offstage. But in the restaurant, and that was the difference, unaware of the surveillance he was under Bellman had given up something of himself to the hidden camera. The body settled into the chair like a side of beef, the heavy shoulders a little forward, one meaty hand clenched round a glass, the brows drawn, eyes looking down and to one side, ignoring Kielland's coaxing but aware of it, aware of it all right, the petulant down-turning of heavy lips gave that away. All of that together with something tentative in Kielland, a hint of risk-taking as if he was prodding a bear with a stick, and Meldrum understood something about Bellman as surely as if he'd encountered him in life. The man had been a bully.

At Fornebu airport, he followed the crowd straggling through to the lower level where international arrivals were checked through customs. If you could divide the world into travellers and non-travellers, Meldrum was in the second group as far as going abroad was concerned. While he was married, he'd left airplane bookings and hotels and city maps to Carole. In a world on the move, he was as comfortable in Edinburgh as a limpet on its native rock. Coming out into the concourse, it was a relief to see his name among the half-dozen cards being held up to indicate the passenger being met. Among the hire-car drivers, the man holding up the neatly lettered card with his name was young, smart and well shaven. Even in plainclothes, to Meldrum's eye he had policeman written all over him.

In the half-hour journey, Oslo impressed him as probably a nice place to live, which was just as well since the driver didn't open his mouth and he had nothing to do but appreciate the passing view. He liked the wide streets. He liked the handsome solidity of the buildings. He liked it that the crowds were well dressed. Above all, he liked the way they stepped out briskly like people with a purpose in life. If there were beggars, he didn't see any or miss them. When he asked what the building over there was, the taciturn driver said, 'The Palace,' and left it at that. Twisting to look back, it struck Meldrum there were no walls or railings round the building and people were walking on the grass. Nothing like Buckingham Palace, he thought; then realised he'd no idea if Norway had a king or a queen or still had a monarch at all. Ignorant bastard.

Just at the moment the police driver turned left, he was thinking about the time he'd gone by the gates of Balmoral Castle in a bus. Not long married, Carole and he had gone on some daft bus tour up north. The police car passed under an arch into a courtyard. 'Here we are, sir.' The Queen's holiday home, Balmoral, Carole read out of some guidebook, sat in the middle of 50,000 acres. He followed the driver across the cobbled yard and into the building. All he'd been able to see from that tour bus had been trees; and the wall, of course, no such thing as an estate without a wall; couldn't call that getting close to royalty, not real close. The driver led the way up a flight of stairs, then into a lift, and he watched the indicator numbers change until the doors *shushed* open and he reckoned they must have arrived at the top of the building.

In Tore Braaten's office, he could see he'd guessed right about the floor. Behind Braaten, through a window set at an angle on the combed wall he saw, level with this room, slanted windows set into the roof opposite. Plainly furnished with pine desk and chairs, the office was smaller than his own back in Edinburgh; the usual computer and a couple of filing cabinets just about filled it. Bright, all the same, up here under the roof; though the windows were due a wash.

The theory about getting a feeling about someone if you met them face to face wasn't working too well. He couldn't make up his mind about Braaten, perhaps because he was a foreigner. Age between thirty and forty, conservatively dressed, softly spoken – the first impression was of a quiet, almost diffident man. Bespectacled, with the air of an accountant. For that last observation chalk one up for Sherlock. Braaten had a qualification in accountancy.

'We operate in something of the same way as your Special Fraud Squad. Go into the streets out there and you'll smell money. In the last twenty years, we've had our share of scandals, but we're learning all the time. With wealth comes crime, that's human nature. Since we became independent, we've always been prosperous, but not like this – oil has made Norway a different country.' He smiled. 'That's not a problem you've had in Scotland.'

'No,' Meldrum said, irritable at having to admit the obvious. 'Are you telling me Bellman was involved with this man Kielland in some kind of fraud?'

'Can we start with Kielland? He's had a colourful history. Ten years ago he had to declare for bankruptcy. In his time he's been through a number of businesses. Just turned twenty, he took over the family building firm after his father's death. It was old-established, by his grandfather, in a small way but solid. It took him five years of good-time living to ruin it and leave some very unhappy creditors. Then he got involved with a servicing outfit for North Sea rigs – a partner was glad to buy him out of that. He cropped up next floating an idea for a hotel project in Lillehammer to be ready in time for the 1994 Winter Olympics. That's when my Department got seriously interested in him. Our government was spending 2 billion kroner on the town's sporting facilities. For us, that is a massive sum – and it wasn't being spent to help Mr Kielland make a killing.'

'His hotel deal was a scam?'

'Put it this way, when Kielland found we were taking an interest – and don't ask me how that happened, it's not something I'm proud of – he wound it up overnight and bought a ticket on a flight to New York. When I found out, I went to the airport to see him off. "Business or pleasure?" he repeated after me, when I asked. "Call it a working holiday." The bastard was laughing at me. Fourteen months later, back he came – and I knew, the very same day he stepped off the plane, I was informed he was back. This is a small country, and Mr Kielland and I had unfinished business.'

By this time, Meldrum had him pegged as a policeman who did his work from behind a desk. He wasn't stupid enough to think there was anything wrong with that. Big crime now was about the number jugglers, not robbing banks. Gut feeling, though, couldn't help it, was that a real policeman had to be able to find his way around on the street. At some time have experience of what Billy Ord used to call 'going hands on'. Detective Superintendent Billy Ord. Now dead.

'Unfinished business,' he repeated, being matter of fact not ironical.

Whatever else, though, Braaten wasn't stupid. He let the silence run, leaning back in his chair, holding Meldrum's gaze, rubbing a finger back and forward under his mouth.

At last, he said, 'Look at the time. You must be hungry.'

'I ate on the plane.'

'Well, I need to lunch. Have something with me.'

Meldrum assumed they were going to a canteen in the building for a quick snack. When they emerged into the courtyard again, he stopped abruptly.

'Yes?' Braaten looked round over his shoulder.

'Where are we going?'

'A nice place for lunch.'

'I don't have time for this.'

'We'll take a car.'

Braaten spoke with a smile, but in the car, moody and unsmiling, staring out of the side window at the passing crowds, he said, 'You are a difficult man to deal with.'

Meldrum didn't see any need to respond to that. He'd been told it before.

Braaten leaned forward and tapped the driver on the shoulder. The car stopped and they got out. Braaten leaned back in and said something. Meldrum heard the words, but made nothing of them since they were in Norwegian. *Pick us up at*, maybe, or *we'll walk back*: hard to tell how far, distances were different in a car. Hopefully: *Be back soon.* Like the song said.

'You're remembering I have a plane to catch?' he asked.

They began to walk, moving a little faster than most of the crowd drifting under the trees on the promenade.

'The University.'

Braaten nodded at the long frontage opposite. Now I'm getting the guided bloody tour, Meldrum thought. But even for him it was hard not to relax a little, moving through the dappled air under the trees. A handsome building with Greek columns, young people wandering up and down its steps, the University could have found a place in his own city.

'What street is this?' he started to ask.

Cutting across him, Braaten was saying, 'I hadn't forgotten about your plane. I thought you might give yourself more time.'

'I'm booked on a flight.'

'For Edinburgh?'

God knows when *that* one would be, Meldrum thought.

'London.'

'Is going there to do with Bellman?'

'His daughter lives there.'

'And the son. The younger son.'

'Right.'

'The one you're having difficulty finding.'

On impulse, Meldrum said, 'The one who killed his father.' Hesitated, then added, 'That seems the likeliest assumption. At the moment.' Which made it a bit better. Not enough. He felt a temptation to explain, Don't get me wrong – I'm not the kind of policeman who makes up his mind and gets the evidence to fit. Idiotic temptation. Never apologise, never explain: one of Billy Ord's rules. Maybe I do need to eat, he thought.

He hadn't expected waiters in bow-ties or cutlery that gleamed. He hadn't expected chandeliers. Braaten ordered something with fish as a starter for them both, and recommended the duck breast. That was more than a snack; that was a lot more than a snack. He didn't even want to think what it would add up to: he'd been warned the kroner went fast, as if a hole had been cut in your pocket. When a bottle of white wine arrived, he growled, 'You must have some budget for expenses.'

Braaten blinked mildly at him. 'Adequate, not wonderful. If you'd stayed the night, we'd have found you a hotel on Skippergata. Nice, but not too expensive. The rooms are rather small.'

Meldrum chewed on a mouthful of fish. 'So this is the bed and breakfast money.' He gestured at the expensive bustle around them.

'No. This is my treat. We can take our time and talk here just as well as in the office. You've come a long way, and I appreciate that. I'd like you to have a good impression of my town. Even if you can't stay long.'

Disconcerted, Meldrum grunted, chewed, stared at the table. Favours made him uncomfortable. He had a thought and a glance up confirmed it. Braaten had on what looked like an expensive suit. You wouldn't wear too many of them to work on a policeman's wage packet. Bet he'd money of his own. It wasn't a gracious thought, but having it made him feel better about the lunch.

'You were saying about Kielland.'

'So I was.' Braaten took a sip of wine the colour of harvested straw.

'Unfinished business.'

'If I'd put a map on the computer back there in the office with lines to mark routes from Sicily inward and outward to the Americas and the rest of Europe, what would you think it was about?'

'Drugs. Though looking at the streets out there, I don't imagine that's a problem you'll have.' Know much about first hand, he meant. Hands on.

Braaten smiled. 'Oh, we have our addicts. Plenty of them at the other end of the street. But that map's about money. Of course, it's about drugs too. Since the Seventies, the Sicilian mafia has concentrated on drugs. And the profits have got bigger every year. I could have put up other screens for you – stock-market prices in New York, London, Hong Kong, currency rates, oil movements, trade indices – all the stuff of modern gambling on the market. It's a long time since the Sicilians stuffed their money in mattresses. They've learned from the Americans – who were taught by Meyer Lansky and Murray Humphreys – that money is for buying things. Hotels, factories, banks if the price is right.'

'You're telling me Kielland was mixed up with the Mafia?'

Braaten see-sawed a hand, a non-committal gesture. 'When he came back with money, that thought occurred to me. As I told you, the moment he stepped off that plane I was monitoring him. And he knew I was, yet within days there it was in the business pages – he was publicising plans for a major marina development. I said to my people, this is a very reckless guy. I have to say, even then, it made me uncomfortable. It was too easy. You know, that what's-going-on instinct? I get a bad feeling when something's handed to me on a plate. Then I learned that Kielland had got himself a major investor. Anders Svensen was putting money in. So I had my con man and now I had the victim. Svensen, you should know, is serious money – shipping, oil exploration, insurance. My appointment took me in to meet a trio of his smooth top management in a boardroom at the top of Svensen House. And that's where it went wrong. Yes, Svensen was putting money up, but not a half or a quarter of what Kielland was putting in. Of course, I wondered how real the money was, but they showed me enough documentation to prove it was there all right. More importantly, they didn't want to know anything I could tell them. I was as welcome as a polar bear at a penguin's birthday party. Very polite, but all they wanted from me was to forget it. Shut my mouth and keep it shut. I was interfering with business.'

Taking the chance to think, Meldrum kept his own mouth shut while the waiters brought plates and side dishes. When they were finished, he said, 'I don't see where you're going with this. If I understand what you're saying, you suspect Kielland was being used by the Mafia as a conduit for laundering money. What you said earlier, cleaning dirty money by putting it into legitimate businesses. But if he was, you couldn't prove it, right? So maybe he was, and maybe he wasn't. Either way, I don't see where John Bellman comes in. He wasn't any kind of big businessman. He wasn't setting up marinas or anything else. I still don't see the connection. Apart from that holiday snap you've got of them together. Where was it taken?'

'You don't recognise it?'

And the moment he saw Braaten smile and look round, he understood. It had been in this restaurant. In fact, when he turned his head and saw the mirror, that column, the two men in the photograph could have been sitting at this table.

'Who took the picture? One of your men?'

Braaten nodded. 'As a waiter.'

Meldrum noted the bow-tie bringing them coffee.

'He still working here?'

Braaten laughed and shook his head. 'If I want your photograph, I'll ask you for it.'

'They were at this table?'

'One of these ones, I think so. Along this wall, anyway.'

'I thought Kielland must have been in Edinburgh for some reason. I assumed the photograph had been taken in Edinburgh, don't know why.'

'Because you're hoping all this is a mistake? Because if Bellman was the one who did the travelling, perhaps their meeting was more important in connection with him than you want to believe?'

'I don't think that follows.'

'Neither do I,' Braaten said. 'But the mind works in funny ways. No, I knew nothing about Bellman until the surveillance we were keeping on Kielland turned him up that night in the restaurant. We checked on him at once, of course – put a tail on him back to his hotel. But he flew out the next morning. We discovered he'd been in Oslo for a week, but what he did during that time—' Braaten shrugged.

'So how can you say they were partners?'

'I didn't take Bellman very seriously. There were other leads, they seemed more important at the time. I sent off a couple of enquiries, and when the information came back – just what you were saying earlier, lived in small town, didn't work, quiet life, all that stuff.' He paused as the waiter bent over them, coffee pot in hand. Meldrum refused; Braaten had his cup filled. As he dribbled cream into it over the back of his spoon, he said, 'No one told me he was an American.' Before Meldrum could respond, ask why that should matter, if it did, he went on, 'You know what happens during an investigation, you have to prioritise. There aren't the resources to follow everything up. For all I knew at that point, Kielland and he were casual acquaintances. What we got of the conversation during their meal was mostly about rivers and lakes, salmon here, Scotland, all over the place – they were both crazy about fishing. Anyway, I left it at that. I made a mistake.'

'You find out different after Kielland was killed?'

Braaten blinked, as if the question was smarter than he'd expected. Nodded. 'We found papers in his safe. Correspondence. There wasn't any doubt. They were partners. But when I enquired about Bellman, he'd disappeared weeks earlier. I couldn't be sure there was a connection – maybe he'd gone off with some woman. I kept a watching brief. But then when his body was found, for me that had to be more than a coincidence.'

They sat weighing one another up. Meldrum broke the silence. 'This business you say they were in together. I have a feeling you're not going to tell much about it.'

'We're at a delicate stage. You understand how these things are.'

'That's the stage things are at in my investigation, too. You're a policeman, you understand.'

Braaten sighed. 'You don't make it easy for me.' He stared into his cup, swirled the coffee gently, took a sip. 'I'm trying to help us both.'

'You haven't given me anything that would affect what I do when I go back.'

'I've given you some indications.'

'Indications . . . Well, okay, let me think about those. Kielland might have been laundering money for the Mafia. Sorry, you've seen papers in his safe after he was killed. So Kielland *was* laundering money for the Mafia, isn't that right?'

Measuring his words, Braaten said, 'He was laundering money.'

On occasion his ex-wife Carole used to tell Meldrum she

wondered if people realised how quick on the uptake he
could be. In the early days, and even later – like the time
Billy Ord made Inspector – she'd get irritated and tell him,
you've got to let them see how good you are. Letting people
underestimate you isn't a bad move for a detective, he told
her. No, she'd said, but it's a rotten way to get a promotion.

It worked sometimes, though. Like now, when he'd picked up
on that careful choice of words. Kielland had been laundering
money, fine. But not necessarily, it seemed, for the Mafia.

Out in the open again, it was a fine day. The sun was shining
and the air felt fresh as though it had been hung out on the line
and cleaned in a breeze off the sea. They were walking along,
both thinking things out, but Braaten liked to talk while he
was thinking. Already he'd explained the geography. They
were walking from the National Theatre at Stortingsgate back
up Karl Johansgate in the direction of Slottsparken and the
Palace.

'Anders Svensen was going to be the key,' Braaten said
suddenly. 'When I heard his name, I thought I was going to
nail Kielland.'

Nail, Meldrum thought. The word sounded slightly odd, out
of fashion, to him. He wondered if Braaten polished up his
English on old black and white gangster movies on television.
On the other hand, for somebody who could only speak English
– couldn't even speak Gaelic (far less speak Lowland Scots, like
most of the other Lowland Scots cheated out of a good language
by history, snobbery and well-meaning schoolteachers) – for
somebody like that it didn't make a whole lot of sense to get
smart about somebody like Mr Braaten.

Who was saying: 'If this was May, Mr Meldrum, if this was
Constitution Day, this street would be full of children walking
to the palace to greet the king. Thousands of children. All
carrying our flag.'

'Like America on the Fourth of July. Minus the king, of
course.'

'You're making fun of me. That's all right. I understand that
in England you do pageantry better than anywhere else in the
world.'

'In London,' Meldrum said. 'You're thinking of in London.'

'Everybody sweeps and washes. Houses, streets, everything. Everywhere. The whole country. Washed ... And clean ... Can you imagine your own country clean even for one day, Mr Meldrum?'

'People carrying flags make me nervous,' Meldrum said, which wasn't particularly true but was the best he could come up with, under the aforesaid circumstances of history, as an expression of patriotism.

His eye was caught by a girl ahead of them. Blonde hair, straight-cut, worn long, swinging below her shoulders. Long brown legs, endless legs. Very short shorts. Hips twitching one way and the other as she walked. He wondered what her face would be like. Glancing at Braaten, he saw him as well watching that double handful of globes bunch and relax under tight white cotton.

'So what do you want me to do?'

'I don't understand,' Braaten said.

'In our business, you give something, you expect something back. In my experience.'

'I thought you were complaining I hadn't given you enough?'

'That's true. Still, you've given me some information.' Neither of them was watching the girl any longer. 'And your time.' In fact, now he looked he saw she'd disappeared. Maybe they'd passed her. 'And lunch.'

Braaten laughed, sounding more exasperated than amused. 'Don't worry about the lunch. I'll put it on expenses, if that makes you feel better.'

'You're the accountant,' Meldrum said. He'd been trying to make a joke, and now he was offended. 'Do what you like. Put it on your tax form.'

They walked on busy with their own thoughts. At the corner, there was a tap on a horn, and the police car eased to a stop beside them. Braaten climbed in without a word and Meldrum followed.

They were climbing the stairs back to his office when Braaten broke the silence. 'I've told the driver half an hour. That'll get you to Fornebu in good time.'

In the office, Meldrum took the same seat facing the desk, was offered coffee and refused. Time enough on the plane.

He stared out of the window; Braaten prowled about the room before finally settling down. Behind him, the sunlight was already leaving the roof opposite.

Braaten sighed. Meldrum looked at him and made a face. This was stupid, he meant; and my fault as much as yours.

After a moment, Braaten said, 'I'd've come to Scotland, but I really am waiting for someone to get in touch. A man who acted as a contact for Kielland. The first clue to him came from the papers in Kielland's safe. Some of the money that was put into the Svensen project – certainly, some of it – maybe most of it – we think was channelled through him . . . We had his name. Nationality – he's Italian. We started looking for him. And he found out – almost at once. I hated the idea there was someone I couldn't trust among my own people.'

Braaten fell silent. Tapping a finger against his lips as he stared down at the desk, he might have been running a list of names through his head.

Meldrum said, 'Italian. *Are* we talking about Mafia money? *Is* that what we're talking about?'

Again he had a sense of Braaten picking his words carefully. 'The money came from Italy. Some of it. And some of it came from Germany, and from Spain, some from France, some from Eastern Europe.'

'You learned all that from what you found in Kielland's safe?'

Braaten shook his head. 'His records didn't make things as easy as that. In fact, they didn't make things easy at all. They were designed not to make sense to outsiders. We cracked some of it, but it wasn't easy.'

'But you know where the money came from.'

'The Italian told us.' He gave a thin smile. 'He named the countries. That's all. What I want from him is the source in each of those countries. That's the big prize. You can understand why I don't want to miss him.'

'How did you find him?'

'He found us. Or at least I got a phone call. He offered the countries the money had come from as a token of good faith.'

'Why would he do that? Why should he help you?'

'Fear of death. After Kielland, he knew he would be next. He's being hunted. The Hunter – that's how he referred to the man who'd been sent to kill him – has come close twice. Once in Paris. Actually, that time I was an eye-witness. I'd arranged to meet the Italian in a bar. The Hunter almost got him, and in the confusion the Italian ran for it.'

'Let me guess,' Meldrum said, 'some of this money he was laundering stuck to his fingers. So whoever he was laundering the money for sent the Hunter to square accounts.'

'A *lot* of money stuck to his fingers. I think an astonishing amount. The difficulty is, Svensen won't co-operate, which means there's some guesswork involved. But money was siphoned off all right, by the Italian and Kielland. And Bellman, of course.'

'You're guessing about Bellman.'

'Fact: Kielland and Bellman are dead.'

Meldrum checked his watch again. 'We've been through that.'

'After Paris, the Italian disappeared. I'd lost him, and since then I've been waiting to see if he'd make contact again. I was beginning to worry that he'd been killed like Mr Bellman, but five days ago my phone rang. Believe me, I was talking to a frightened man. The Hunter had found him again, and he couldn't imagine how he'd done it. It wasn't possible, he said. Kept talking about how he'd covered his tracks. Over and over, he said that he'd chosen the hotel at random – how could anyone have known where he'd be? I could smell his sweat down the phone. He talked as though he was being hunted by the devil.'

'All the same,' Meldrum said, 'your hunter can't be that good, or the Italian wouldn't have got away twice.'

'Japanese tourists,' Braaten said, and gave a little snort that might have become laughter and then got choked off abruptly. 'They say it's better to be lucky than smart – a bunch of punks spoiled things for the Hunter in Paris. At the second attempt, in Berlin, apparently it was Japanese tourists. Both times, no one could have predicted it. The Italian has been outrageously lucky. Nobody can be that lucky for long, and he knows it. That's why he's running scared.'

Meldrum looked at his watch. The car to take him to the airport was almost due. Among all the other things chasing through his mind, a part of it had registered *running scared*: those old black and white gangster movies again.

'Don't worry, we'll make sure you catch your plane,' Braaten was saying. 'I'd be grateful – all I'm asking – is that you keep me informed about any developments in the Bellman case.'

'I give you my word,' Meldrum said, 'if we make an arrest I'll let you know.'

For what that was worth. It was his impression Braaten would anyway be told quickly. He had sources. It occurred to Meldrum that, despite what he'd said, perhaps the pressure at the beginning of the case to find Bellman might have come from the Norwegian. For an instant, he was tempted to ask him.

'Thank you,' Braaten said, but not as if he meant it much. He leaned back again, doing the finger rubbing under his mouth bit. 'When I speak of developments, I'm thinking particularly if it looks as if your investigation might be going to take you to America.'

'Why should it?'

Why the hell should it?

'I was thinking about Bellman being an American. I take it he has family out there? Isn't it possible the son Alistair might go out there if he wanted to hide?'

'Anything's possible,' Meldrum said, 'but if he's killed his father running off to that side of the family doesn't seem to me the obvious thing to do. I mean, why would he?'

Do you know something I don't?

There was a knock at the door, followed at once by its opening. At sight of the driver, Meldrum got to his feet ready to go.

'Give us a minute,' Braaten said, coming round the desk.

The man stepped outside and closed the door again.

As Braaten came forward, Meldrum assuming they were going to shake hands held his out. The movement seemed to take the Norwegian by surprise. As they shook, he said, 'Anders Svensen's father was a close ally of Vidkun Quisling. He helped bankroll National Unification, Quisling's fascist party. He became very influential when the Germans forced

Quisling on the country as Minister President in 1942. He should have been shot with Quisling at the end of the war, but that's not the way—'

The soft rapidity of his tone, quite different from anything before, with its odd impression of intimacy had a disorienting effect on Meldrum. Now as the ringing of the phone on the desk interrupted the flow of words, he disengaged his hand. Braaten loosened his grip slowly, looking down as if he'd forgotten they were shaking hands.

'Svensen worshipped his father,' he said.

Not much later, sitting in the car on the way to the airport, it occurred to Meldrum he might have told Braaten about Bellman's father-in-law General Gardiner. It was that word 'worship' – who'd said Alistair Bellman had hero-worshipped his grandfather? Didn't matter. What mattered was John Brennan telling the story of General Gardiner and his fellow-plotters in the Sixties. 'They were aiming at a coup to snatch power. Thwart the commie plans of Prime Minister Wilson, and save the country for their version of democracy.'

Maybe he should have told Braaten about that, but they'd got on to the topic too late, and he had a plane to catch. Anyway, there had been the phone call which interrupted them.

Braaten had gone over to the desk ready to pick up the phone. Reaching for it, he'd said, 'I hope you'll keep in touch.'

Meldrum took that as a dismissal. At the door, however, a thought made him turn for a last word. The avid look on Braaten's face, however, changed his mind.

Nodding as he listened, it was clear that this caller was one for whom the Norwegian had been waiting.

CHAPTER TWENTY-THREE

There had been a time when Giovanni Locascio prided himself on his nerve. As a boy, he had lived among men whose domestic anger was sudden and often violent. The second youngest of his uncles in particular was feared and admired because there was no restraint on his anger. Once roused, it was like a beast that could only be appeased by blood and broken bones. It was only later that he had understood that the old man in the big house outside the village who spoke softly and showed no emotion was the one to fear. The unmasked anger of his uncle and the others was for foot soldiers. As a child, he had felt the weight of his uncle's hand, and the weight of the hand of the old man. His uncle's fist had marked his flesh for a week, and led to a bitter quarrel among the family. Don Francesco's had been laid on his head like a blessing, and had sent him on the road he'd travelled; every turn and twist, it seemed now, taking him straight to this cursed day.

He put the phone back on its rest. He stared at the wall in front of him, and read and re-read the instructions without taking in a word of Norwegian or French or German. He'd heard of nervous breakdowns where that happened: you lost all your languages except the first one, your baby language. He counted to ten: *ein zwei drei vier funf sechs seiben siete ocho* – wait! – *trois quatre cinq six sept oito nove* – wrong! *eight nine* – *uno due tre quattro cinque sei otto nove dieci undici dodici tredici quattordici quindici* – heard as a child – *sedici*

diciassette diciotto – he could go on for ever – *diciannove* –
like this for ever – *venti venti venti*. Behind him, like a threat
he felt the open space of the arrivals hall. If he turned his head,
he would see the floor crowded with passengers, among them
the stragglers from his flight from Berlin. He held his hand
in the air by the phone and saw how it trembled. He hadn't
been so reduced as this in Slovakia, or even in Paris. He'd
always had good luck. It seemed to him he'd been tested for
too long, all the way back to when Kielland, or when Bellman,
no, earlier, earlier, all his life he'd been tested against the best.
He'd always been lucky. In Berlin, he'd been so lucky. It had
taken time to sink in how lucky he'd been. It seemed your
nerve was like the watch on your wrist. When you lost it, it
didn't go a piece at a time. You lost it all at once. It was a
possession you'd had, and now it was gone.

When the hand touched him on the shoulder, he couldn't
get up the courage to turn round.

'Are you all right?' He'd heard the voice before but couldn't
place it. 'Are you all right, Signor Solmi?'

It was the idiot from Tegel. The malt whisky idiot from
Tegel. The act of identifying him worked like the breaking
of a spell. With a little gasp of breath, he turned round.
Swing your shoulders, round you went. Nothing to it. The
tall stooped young German bent towards him, concern in his
smile. Blue eyes, the hair shot through with grey but blond at
the temples. Blue eyes, blond hair. What was his name? Not that
it mattered. If your memory started to let you down, though,
that was dangerous. What the hell was the idiot's name?

'Helmut Meckel.'

Of course it was.

'I was phoning a friend.' Locascio was surprised to hear his
own words; it wasn't his way to explain himself to idiots. 'I
was arranging to meet a friend.'

As he spoke, his eyes flickered past Meckel to assess the
figures moving behind him, then to seek for people standing
still, anyone looking this way; lastly, most importantly, for
single figures. A man on his own.

A man on his own looking for a man on his own.

On impulse, he asked, 'Are you being met?'

The young German smiled and nodded. But said, 'Although it's beginning to seem as if something has gone wrong. That's why I'm still here. The company I'm doing business with was sending someone to meet me. But he wasn't at the gate. I've tried the information point. I was going to phone them, when I saw you. And thought perhaps you were unwell – I'm sorry for the intrusion.'

'We could share a car in,' Locascio said gripping him by the upper arm, urging him to get moving. 'You could phone them from your hotel. Where are you booked?'

'The Rica Victoria.'

'There you are. So am I. Why should you wait here, eh? Tell them it's not good enough, keeping you waiting.'

He resisted a diffident tug as the other tried to disengage his arm, as if somehow he could pull it free without Locascio noticing. Looking around vaguely, Meckel expressed polite anxiety, 'But if he comes, and I've gone?'

Tough! Let the cunt rot!

'He'll have learned a lesson on the importance of punctuality,' Locascio said, letting go of Meckel's arm to lay finger to lip with a smile. Humorous, that's what he was being. But not too much of a smile, just a little smile, really no more than a twitch, quite small enough to give a hint of grimness. Humorous, but earnest. Morally serious. Punctuality is not mocked.

Punctuality. The magic German word.

Meckel's glance managed to respond at every level, grim certainly, but not lacking a certain playfulness. The Italian was reminded of those Disney elephants dancing ballet in pink tutus.

'As a professional man it does me harm, if I'm treated disrespectfully,' the German said. Without further coaxing, he started to move, falling into step as he went. 'I think you're right, he's due a lesson.'

'Maybe his car's broken down,' Locascio said, absent-mindedly magnanimous because he'd got his way and, without appearing to, was busy scrutinising everyone within a dozen yards of the nearest exit.

'No excuse. I'm not a believer in bad luck. Cars can be serviced. For a professional, luck shouldn't come into it.'

As he stepped out under the awning, Locascio felt a sting of fresh wind on his cheek. He took what felt like the first full breath he'd drawn in days. He glanced at his watch. Braaten was waiting for him to call back. No way, he'd told the Norwegian, no way would he go to police headquarters. Not until they'd talked and cut the kind of deal he deserved for the information he could give.

In the taxi riding into the city, Meckel said, 'After all, maybe I'll leave phoning till the morning. I've never been in Oslo before. What would you recommend?'

He held up the book in his lap. Locascio glanced at the cover, and recognised it as one from a popular series of guidebooks. He remembered the German had been reading it in the airport in Berlin. Still trying to decide where he could arrange to meet Braaten, he said more or less the first thing that came into his head. 'Try the Munch Museum.'

'A museum doesn't sound very amusing. What kind of museum?'

'It's a place tourists go. Particularly tourists from your country. Munch did some of his finest work in Berlin.' The German looked back at him blankly. 'Edvard Munch? The painter?'

Meckel began to leaf through his book. When he'd found what he was looking for, he read for a few moments then looked up frowning. 'I don't think so,' he said. 'Listen to this. This is your painter describing one of his paintings.' He folded back the book, and measured off the lines with a forefinger as he read. '*I was walking along a road with two friends. The sun set. I felt a tinge of melancholy. Suddenly the sky became blood-red. I stopped and leaned against a railing feeling exhausted, and I looked at the flaming clouds that hung like blood and a sword over the blue-black fjord and the city. My friends walked on. I stood there trembling with fright. And I felt a loud unending scream piercing nature.*'

'I've seen that painting,' Locascio said. 'Stand in front of it for long enough, and you can hear the scream.'

The German grinned like a good sport waiting for the punch-line. When it didn't come, he let the smile go and suggested, 'You are meaning this as a metaphor?'

'Hear it over the chatter of the tourists,' Locascio said.

'It's such a beautiful day, the sun's shining,' Meckel said briskly. 'It's not a day for museums.' He laughed. 'Let's leave nature screaming till later. Isn't there somewhere in the open air to pass an hour or two?'

What he needed, Locascio decided, was some place where he could watch for Braaten and be sure he was arriving alone. Some kind of open space. A sudden inspiration made him smile. He'd thought of the ideal place for a meeting.

The German smiled back at him.

'I can see you have,' he said. 'Perhaps you could join me? Business can wait till the morning, eh?'

Locascio grunted. He would phone from the hotel while this idiot was booking in, and afterwards take him along. Chase him off, before Braaten arrived. It did no harm to have some camouflage. Anyway, it was true, the sun was shining. It was going to be a good day. It was as if a burden had dropped from his shoulders. Everything was going to work out; he was going to make it.

'What kind of business are you in?' he asked.

'The disposal business,' Meckel said. 'I arrange for the disposal of waste products.'

CHAPTER TWENTY-FOUR

There had been a heavy spell of rain lasting for about twenty minutes. The guidebook had been lying open and the rain had soaked the right-hand page. The left-hand page was dry, which made it easy to read.

... is Karl Johans gate. At its western end is the Royal Palace, where visitors can see the changing of the guard daily when the king is in residence. Nearby the nineteenth-century buildings of the University impress with their classical columns and imperial pediments ... And so on, and so on. At the bottom of the page, his eye was caught by a name. *Ranged behind Oslo are a number of hills covered with forests of spruce. One of these is Holmenkollen, on which stands a ski museum and the ski jump which was used for the 1952 Winter—* The rest of the sentence was lost to the blurring of rain on the next page. Even the most exhaustive guide couldn't be blamed for not getting everything in. You couldn't, for example, expect an account of how Gregers Kielland had looked spread out at the foot of the ski jump under a grey sky with his eyes open and lips drawn back blue against white teeth. It was only when he was rolled over you saw the ruin the bullet had made of the back of his head, not that the look on his face had ever much resembled a smile. A scream maybe. Like a guy in the cartoons falling arms out with a balloon saying *Aargh!* coming out of the black circle of his mouth.

In the middle of the dry page: *Among the city's attractions are the outdoor exhibit in Frogner Park by the sculptor Adolf*

Gustave Vigeland and the Edvard Munch Museum. In their
very different ways, both will repay a visit.

'Why there?' he'd asked the Italian.

'Why not?' Locascio had asked, and put the phone down.

Unlike Paris, there wasn't any question this time of not
going. Both of them knew, the stakes had got higher since
then. He'd thought hard about putting half a dozen men into
the Park, but decided against it. Though Locascio had set up
the meeting, he'd still be as skittish as a spooked horse. No
sense in frightening him off. He even hesitated about taking
his gun. It seemed that straightforward to him. He would offer
Locascio protection and a new identity. Time enough later to
worry about where. For the moment, he would tell him the
Spanish – or the English? – the Americans? – he'd tell him
the Americans had agreed to take him. Agreed in principle,
that sounded more convincing. If he co-operated fully, that
kind of thing. Out of options and with nowhere else to go,
Locascio would agree to come back with him.

Despite the sunshine, it had been cold in the park. The short
summer season was nearly at an end. He'd crossed the bridge
not giving the bronze figures a glance, but at the end aware
as usual, in some echo of childhood, of the dragon coiled
and eyeing him in readiness as he passed. They'd arranged
to meet at the monolith, but on the way he made a circuit of
the fountain as a precaution. No Locascio. Instead, checking
out the muscles on the six giants that held up the great bowl,
people wandering like himself through the pattern of tiles set
in the form of a maze around the base, their tourist chattering
rising against the fountain's white noise of overflowing.

'Is this the only fountain in the park?'

He'd turned at the touch on his arm. The question had been
asked by a tall man with dark glasses and close-cropped brown
hair shot through with grey, an overcoat slung over his arm.

Braaten, who'd done his share of talking to American
companies over the last few years, recognised the type. He'd
be on first-name terms within five minutes, make you feel as
if you were friends within ten; and a year later, you'd realise
that was as close as you were going to get. Oh, yes, and in the
first half-hour, if he ran true to form, he'd refer to something

he'd picked up during his time in 'the military': skill or insight rather than a dose of the clap.

'Can you imagine another one like this?'

The joke was a mistake, for as he moved off the American laughing fell into step.

'I know absolutely what you mean. Let me say I've done my share of travelling, and I've seen nothing like this any place else in the world. But – I'll be honest with you on this – I hadn't ever heard of Vigeland. It's just dumb luck I'm seeing this. What's that? Is that the monolith? That's the monolith, isn't it?'

Braaten grunted. That's what it was, all right, but again there was no sign of the unmistakable bulk of Locascio.

'Fifty-five feet high and made of granite. So the book here tells me,' he waved it in the direction of the monolith, 'but *you*'ll know that.'

'Not to the foot,' Braaten said.

Though as they came into its shadow, if he couldn't recall how many figures there were – 100? 120? – in the writhing clamber that reached from bottom to top of the pillar, he did remember the name of the schoolmaster who had gathered a class under it and told them that for Vigeland each and every one of those men, women and children had been 'climbing towards the light'.

'I guess he thought your country needed a larger population,' the American said, tipping back his head, 'and so he decided to supply her with one all by himself.'

But Braaten, overtaken suddenly by a superstitious certainty that the Italian was watching him from somewhere below, had started back down the path to a point where he could check the crowd around the fountain.

He might have taken half a dozen steps, when he heard the high breathy voice of a fat man cry in something like irritation, 'Herr Meckel?'

As he spun round, he'd seen Locascio with the American striding towards him.

Thinking about it now, at his desk, smoothing the page of the guidebook under his hand, it wasn't hard to see reasons for the way things went then, but those were exonerations others would offer. He was harder on himself.

The American didn't stop for more than a moment in front of Locascio. At something said perhaps, he gave a shrug and then had walked on with that raking stride which looks slow but covers ground deceptively fast. The Italian had been half turned away as if gazing after him. And he'd known something was wrong, but the surface of his mind was distracted, asking, *Herr? Why call an American*— And then Locascio was moving towards him, with one hand stuck inside his coat, like Napoleon, playing the Corsican not the Sicilian, in there at the top of his belly, and when it came out the blood followed it. Later the pathologist would say the blow must have lifted the fat man up on to his toes. 'A blow of tremendous force.' And when told how the American had stopped just for a moment, no more than paused, and then how he'd strolled on: 'to look so casual must have taken enormous strength'. Later a search of the park turned up nothing but the guidebook. At the time, it had seemed to him the first priority was saving Locascio, who died, however, without talking as the rain began.

It was getting late. In one of the windows on the roof opposite a light came on. Slates and stone, it wasn't much of a view, but he stood at parade rest, hands behind his back, watching without really seeing it for a while; until abruptly he turned and stared down at a photograph that lay beside the guidebook on his desk. He went to the door and put off the overhead light. At the desk, he switched on the lamp, bending it over to bear down on the photograph as he propped it upright against the out-tray. Like trying to catch an intruder unawares, from one angle then or another as he paced about the room, he'd lift his head or glance over a shoulder at the face in the picture, wanting to see it with fresh eyes.

It had never been any more than a long shot, even if one he hadn't been able to get out of his head since it occurred to him. The photograph he'd got sent from Edinburgh on a pretext had been meant to settle it one way or the other. What he hadn't allowed for was that the man in the bar in Paris and the American in the park wouldn't fuse into one image in his mind. More than that, though he was trained to see and remember, the image of each was already fading.

Nothing exceptional about either of them. Two men who were one man; a man who could pass in any crowd.

And so Tore Braaten, who would have bet his life on the accuracy of his memory, looked at the photograph and couldn't tell. And stubbornly kept on looking until exhaustion made him admit this third image alone could never be forced to tell whether or not the Hunter could possibly be Alistair Bellman.

BOOK FIVE

Fear of Falling

CHAPTER TWENTY-FIVE

Meldrum woke to the sound of a woman singing. Cautiously he edged one foot back and forward, which established he was lying in a narrow bed with his face to a wall. He opened one eye, the wall was painted green, and shut it again. The girl – something about the voice sounded young – had chosen a song he didn't know. This wasn't a hard thing to do. Apart, that is, from country and western, songs he liked for their lyrics about hard times and runaway women: poor white trash blues. Or runaway men, of course. After all, a whole bunch of country and western singers were women, bewailing men of the shiftless kind who stuck like glue, or the men who went to the pen, for murder or petty theft. Among them, the songs he liked tended to be sung by short busty feisty ladies, the traditional kind well able to belt it out Parton style. Hello, Dolly! clones, in fact, like that famous sheep from Roslin the scientists had got to go forth and multiply all on her own. Talking of which, his balls ached, and he doubted if he'd been kicked the night before.

Oh, God.

There was something about the green wall and the narrow bed that made him think of prostitution. When he'd joined the police, he'd gone with prostitutes for a time, an exact time he could measure. Before joining, he'd done an apprenticeship as a carpenter, and that had been a job he thought he'd follow for the rest of his life. He'd liked working with wood, but had come to dislike the repetitiveness of the tasks, a building site was an open air factory where a man who worked too fast found himself unpopular. When one of the building industry's periodic slumps came along, he was ready for a change and thought he'd give the army a try. Then he met a guy in a pub whom he'd worked beside on a couple of contracts. *The army? Fuck that for a bampot caper. I'm putting in for the police. Twenty years, you're on a pension. Wee job as a security man. Got a future, see what I mean, Jim? Fancy giving it a go? You and me, eh? Go together, right?* As it turned out, the bampot who spelled out these golden possibilities missed them, not being able to pass the written entry exam. Even when Meldrum put on the uniform, he'd felt it as a kind of charade, as though it should have gone to the guy who'd suggested the idea to him. I'll give it a buzz, he'd thought without much enthusiasm. His own feeling had been that he wouldn't last a year. In his bones, he'd been pretty sure that sooner rather than later he'd pack it in and go to be a soldier. His father had been a great man for patriotism, and head still full of stuff like that he'd fancied going off to defend Queen and country. By chance, though, there wasn't a war on offer. Apart from Northern Ireland, which didn't strike him as seeing the world. And so he'd stuck the job from month to month, and when he took off the police uniform it was to be a detective. Very fast, then, it had become the most important thing in his life. Half puzzled, half pleased, Carole had told him, You've found your vocation. Somewhere, though, in that earlier unsatisfied time, he'd taken some of the easy chances for sex that came a policeman's way. One chance, in particular; for about five months, he'd kept going back to one prostitute. A girl not yet twenty, she'd been like an addiction. Every time he'd say he wasn't going back; every time he went back. It was the best sex of his life and the worst guilt. Then one Sunday morning, lying in bed together side by side, Carole had told him she was pregnant. From then until they'd separated, years later, he'd never been unfaithful to her again, or even wanted to be. He'd talked to the girl, though, only once more, late at night in Rose Street where she'd called after him. *I've been missing you*, she said. At that he'd flown into a rage – suddenly terrified, for his marriage for his job, hard to tell which, both of them mixed up in his head together. Her crying so that her nose ran. Miss me? he'd sneered at himself afterwards, no bloody wonder; straight sex and no violence, no bloody wonder she missed me. A month short of a year later, a client killed her. It happened.

He'd never been entirely sober when he saw her, and afterwards he'd been racked with guilt.

'Are you awake?' He opened his eyes. 'If you are awake, I wish you'd stop just lying there. I mean, it would be nice if you said good morning.'

He recognised the voice, and knew where he was.

He was in the Grace Pennington Hall, a residence for students, some of them studying for a first degree, some of them doing postgraduate work, many of them foreign. He was on the fourth floor. He was in Room 315.

He was in Ruth Bellman's bed.

Not married any more, he didn't have to worry for his marriage.

The terror he felt was unmixed. A fear like falling he would lose the job that had become his vocation.

He rolled over. She was at the window, that seemed to be her favourite seat, sipping out of a mug she was holding with both hands.

'Good morning,' she said.

'Have I been here all night?'

'You don't remember? That's flattering.' She drank again, watching him over the rim of the mug. It was blue with white letters making a message he couldn't read. There was a chip out of the rim. 'Don't worry,' she said. 'You used a condom. Though you didn't want to. I had to help you on with it.'

'Was that out of the supply you keep?'

'Oh, it was a fresh one. I mean, not used or anything.' She slumped in the chair, head slightly bent, as if habit made her try to disguise her height even sitting. 'In Casanova's day, they used to use the same one over and over again. Silk or sheep's stomachs or whatever they were. Washed them and hung them up to dry. Must've looked funny on the washing line, between the ruffed shirt and the knee-breeches. Mind you, I don't know if Casanova himself used one. Doubt if he would. They don't

much, do they? Casanovas, I mean. What is it they say? Like
having a bath with their boots on.'

'Give it a rest.'

'You had a bath with your boots on.'

He kicked off the sheet and rolled up to sit on the edge
of the bed. It gave him some satisfaction to see how the
convulsion of movement made her jump. Some of her drink
spilled. He noticed the size of her hands, big knuckles, long
fingers wrapped tight round the mug.

'Where's my clothes?'

'On the chair.' It was pushed in under the desk at the head of
the bed. She pointed to it, and laughed. 'You folded everything
neatly as you took it off. Trousers, shirt, underpants – no, vest
first, underpants last. Very modest. I thought, he hasn't done
much of this.'

Unlike you, he might have said. Almost did. Didn't because
he'd been rude to her once, and didn't want to have anything
else he would be ashamed to remember.

As he started to dress with his back to her, he said, 'I
wish to God I'd caught the plane for Edinburgh at Heathrow
yesterday.'

'Better have a shower first,' she said. 'You smell of me.'

Out in the corridor, the building felt as unoccupied as the
first time he'd been in it. She'd said there were lavatories and
showers at either end, but he must have turned the wrong way
for the corridor seemed to go on for ever. Not a sound, blank
closed doors. The lavatory when he found it was before the
corner, still somewhere in the middle of the endless passage.
Pissing into the bowl, he stared at rings of black ball hairs curled
on the white porcelain shelf. Unwanted evidence. Some future
geneticist might be able to reconstruct an approximation to a
human being from them.

The next door in the corridor stood open on to a small shower
cubicle. He took off his shirt, trousers, vest and underpants,
laying them folded on the chair in front of the curtain. Neatly
folded. What was wrong with being tidy? Head bowed, he felt
the hot water beat down on the tight muscles at the base of
his neck.

When he'd got off the plane from Oslo, he'd been tired. Tired enough to be tempted to try for a seat on the Edinburgh shuttle and to hell with the plan. The plan on leaving Edinburgh had been a neat two-birds-with-one-stone trip: see the Norwegian and then spend a day in London checking one more time on Ruth and the friends of Alistair Bellman. In his wallet, he had the London hotel booking and the shuttle ticket back to Edinburgh for the day after tomorrow. They've been booked, they're on expenses, use them, he'd told himself. That the hotel was near the Grace Pennington Hall wasn't luck. It had been planned that way to save time. The bad luck was that after he'd eaten his tiredness went and he felt restless. He'd tried to phone Harriet to tell her how much he was looking forward to getting home, but got her voice going through the 'after the tone' routine, and when the tone came gabbled something or other, all the time expecting her to cut in. When he hung up, he couldn't remember what he'd said. Something bland. Not what he'd wanted to yell: *Where are you? Why aren't you there? It's late. Who are you with?*

He went out without a coat. It was a mild night. There was a park opposite the hotel, and he crossed over and walked along beside it. For some reason a double wire, for lights maybe though there were no bulbs, had been slung over the path between two trees. On the wires, a dozen, thirteen, seventeen swifts perched; he stood by the railings and counted them. Against the pale luminous sky, they were a tune waiting to be played. When he turned away, a bunch of people were crowding along the pavement in his direction, laughing, maybe at him, maybe not, no need to number them, enough that they were black and young and men, three counts against them. *What you see in there? Looking for a woman? What good that do you? No good, you can't get it up! Hey, you get it up?* And then they were past. They'd surrounded him and flowed on. Nobody had jostled him. There hadn't been any physical contact. Just voices and white teeth grinning. Yet the rage he felt was a battering rage, the homicidal kind. It lasted only a moment, but it shook him that he felt it at all. That stuff wasn't his style. Walking on, he'd told himself it was because he was tired. He was off his own patch and far from home. Maybe it was because they'd spoiled the moment

of magic, the birds against the sky. Those were the reasons he
came up with, and they satisfied him. Yet the truth was that, far
from being tired, the encounter tingled in his blood like pulses
of energy. The mild heavy air seemed to glow. He'd found a
pub and drunk whisky for a time. Later, he'd walked across
a darkened square and knew it for the hub around which the
great city spun like a wheel under the stars. Making his way
back, just where he'd expected to see the hotel he recognised
instead the long frontage of the Grace Pennington Hall. He
was far from home.

He turned and held his face up into the stream of hot water.
Last night he'd drunk a lot – had he? How much? He'd taken
a fair amount. But he hadn't been as drunk as he'd let himself
seem to be. Not just to the girl. Let him seem to himself. He
hadn't been drunk on whisky, but on his stupidity and the risk
of it and her surprise and that she didn't send him away. He'd
been drunk on her youth and an arm under the lamp as she sat
by the window and the sound of her voice. A cunning drunk,
he'd reminded himself if she was after information to tell her
nothing that mattered. He'd been drunk first that she should
be willing, then on her eagerness, at last on the whiteness of
her skin, the firmness of her flesh.

Walking back along the corridor, he had the same sense
of a profound and deserted stillness. When a door in the
corridor opened, his heart pounded like a burglar's. He had
dried himself carelessly in too much of a hurry, so that his
shirt stuck clammy against his sides.

When he went in, she was still sitting by the window.
Probably she hadn't stirred out of the chair since he left.

'I like the way you knocked before coming in,' she said.
'Nice old-fashioned manners. Kind of thing my mother would
appreciate.'

He picked up his jacket from where it was draped over the
back of the chair. All he wanted was to get out. Perversely
then he wondered if she'd gone to bed with him so that he'd
feel like that and not question her. He sat on the edge of the
bed with the jacket across his knee.

'How were Frank Gibson's manners?' he asked.

'Who?'

She stared at him, puzzled.

'He was in the army with your brother.'

'Oh, him. Only met him once, when Alistair and I were in Edinburgh for the day. I don't really know him. His manners? No idea, why should I?'

'He'd be disappointed to hear that.'

She frowned and then understood. 'Oh, I see. Because I fucked him. Well, I told you about that when you asked, didn't I? Yes, I came up to Edinburgh by train. No, *not* by plane on the Saturday morning. Yes, by train on the Friday night. It was stupid of me to lie about it. But I felt Mummy had quite enough on her plate without having to contend with my life.' Her mouth twisted. 'My sordid life.'

'Difficulty is,' Meldrum said, 'when you told me about it, you called him your boyfriend. That wasn't true.'

'Big deal.' She sounded like a sulky child.

'It might be. It makes sense coming up a day early so you could get a night in with the boyfriend. It doesn't when it's somebody you hardly know. Gibson says he was amazed when you turned up.'

'He got over it,' she said.

'He told my sergeant he doesn't refuse when he gets it handed to him on a plate.'

'I take it back about your manners.'

'If we could stick to the point,' Meldrum said. Dry and official, that was the trick. 'If you didn't come up on the Friday night because you wanted to be with Gibson, why did you come?'

Elbow on the arm of the chair, she laid her cheek against her fist. Her face tilted to the side like that, eyes cast down, the effect was childlike again. 'I kept putting off getting the plane ticket. All those cheap flights if you book ahead, you know?'

He waited, but she sat eyes down as if that was all the explanation he would need. It struck him something didn't fit between what she'd just said and her mother's happy families version of that visit.

'You didn't want to come up for your birthday?'

'I didn't say that!'

'But you kept putting off getting your ticket booked to come home.'

'I just kept forgetting. And then I'd spent the money I was going to use for the plane, so I came up by train instead. It was cheaper.'

'Forgetting your birthday?'

'I had the *Dream* to think about. I have a one-track mind, everybody says so. I get so involved.'

'Sorry? What dream?'

'Oh, for God's sake! *A Midsummer Night's Dream*. It's a play by Shakespeare. That's William Shakespeare.'

'I remember,' he said. 'You couldn't come home to be with your mother, and that was the reason you gave me.'

'And exams!'

'Exams.'

'It was a total fucking disaster, if you care,' she said. 'I had this wonderful opening, but they made a shambles of it. I had the idea too late, you see, so they didn't have time to rehearse it properly. My fault completely, so that's no surprise.'

She was self-pitying and self-absorbed. Just as she'd been that first time on the phone. Her father had disappeared off the face of the earth and she'd been absorbed by a bunch of amateurs putting on a Shakespeare play. That was William Shakespeare. She was a Martian he'd been to bed with, made love to, whatever. Fucked, she would have said. He shifted to ease an erection that he hadn't expected or wanted. The brainless thing had a mind of its own.

'Are you hungry?' she asked.

'What?'

'I wouldn't mind some breakfast.'

'You came up by train on the Friday night,' he said. 'Why didn't you go home?'

'Really!' She gestured impatience. 'I had the impression you were quick – not educated, but quick. I came up on the Friday so I could make it seem I'd come by plane on the Saturday.'

He didn't feel like pursuing whether that made sense or not. The point was whether it made sense to her, and how could you disprove that?

'But why Gibson?'

'I'd no money for an hotel,' she said. Ask a silly question. 'Look, I really am hungry.'

Why not? They couldn't throw you out of the force for having breakfast with somebody. They went down in the lift in silence. On the steps of the Hall, she took a deep breath and said, 'Another nice day.' It was hard to hear her over the noise of the traffic. Ten minutes' walk took them to a café with sandwiches made up to order and five kinds of coffee. No bacon and eggs. And they had to eat side by side on stools facing a wall.

'I could help you,' she said. 'Alistair's friends are more likely to be helpful if I'm there.'

'You know them?'

'Hmm.'

'I don't think so.'

'I do! I visited Toby's place when Alistair was staying with him.'

'I meant I couldn't take you with me.'

'Why not?'

'Come on!'

'It wouldn't be appropriate, you mean?' She took a big bite out of the middle of the baguette, chewed and said not too distinctly, 'Was last night appropriate?'

Meldrum had been told that Toby Sullivan, unlike Alistair and the other two who made up the projected trip to Nepal, had decided at an early stage in their training that he could envisage a better future at this late point in the century than being an officer in the British army. The fifteen floors of Spion House, a sleek pencil of concrete and glass set between larger neighbours, suggested he'd probably had the right idea.

Ruth's usefulness had been that she knew it was only one stop on the Tube, so there was no point in looking for a taxi.

Sullivan, according to the background memo, was on the editorial team of *Girl Talk*, the longest established of the Spion magazine titles; and the register in the lobby put that on the seventh floor. When they got out of the lift, Meldrum said, 'How am I supposed to explain you? He's going to think it's strange.'

'I'm one of the victims,' Ruth said.

The double glass door opened on to a reception area that smelled of new carpets. Pink and blue colour scheme and not one but two receptionists. Meldrum turned on his heel and went back into the vestibule. By the time Ruth, who'd gone in ahead of him, realised and came out again, he was by the lift pressing the button.

'What are you doing?'

He didn't answer. After a moment, the lift doors slid back.

'Either you get in or I do,' he said.

For a moment, he could see her think about refusing, then she stepped in.

'This is silly.'

'No, appropriate,' he said, but the doors were closing so perhaps she didn't hear him.

When he pushed through the doors again, both receptionists were looking his way expectantly. No doubt, hoping Ruth would reappear. A woman's magazine, gender conflict would be the butter on their bread. One was young and blonde, the other on the left dark-haired and middle-aged. It was nice to have a choice. He went for the soothing one. The dark hair framed a kindly face. When he asked for Mr Sullivan, she looked faintly let down. Perhaps she'd been hoping for an urgent request for the Agony Aunt.

She spoke on the phone, head cocked, eyes on him: 'Mr Sullivan asks what it's about, Mr Meldrum?'

'Not mister. Detective Inspector.'

She repeated the message, very professional, not a flicker of expression.

'Would you have a seat, please? Mr Sullivan will be with you in a moment.'

Putting in the time by avoiding furtive glances from the receptionists, he noticed that the panelling round the walls of the room was unbroken. Apart from the entry there wasn't another door. The mystery was solved when two of the panels folded back and Sullivan appeared. Five eight or nine, stockily built, bounced as he walked, cheeks that shone as if they'd been shaved and then polished. He was in denims, the shirt a shade pastel for an army type, but the grip was firm, too firm, one of those test of strength jobs, see whose eyes watered first.

'If you'd come through.' With a glance at the receptionists who had each found something important to do, too busy to be curious. Wary of him perhaps. Jekyll and Hyde type. Jokes in the bar and give the girlfriend a black eye. Or maybe not. Maybe just a stupid irritating bugger who shook hands too hard.

It was a surprise to find that the panels were held up on the other side by struts braced against the floor. There was just about space to walk between these and a series of cubicles partitioned in glass and roofless. Sullivan set a brisk pace, so that Meldrum had the odd impression of being rushed along the comb of a hive past the cells of the worker bees.

Just round the corner, Sullivan opened a door.

'We can talk in here.'

Meldrum expected to be gestured into Sullivan's office, and was taken aback to step into a broom cupboard. In fact, it was larger than that and instead of mops and buckets there was a table with a coffee urn, a cardboard box and an unplugged computer.

'Privacy's hard to come by in this place,' Sullivan said.

'Like the army, I expect.'

'Nothing like. I miss the army. But I'd no intention of being like some of those poor buggers you see bowler-hatted at forty. "Please, I've been an officer, I know how to organise." You know the kind of thing – creeping around somebody's arse for a job. "And what age are you? Forty, oh dear." And fuck off's the answer after that. Army's a mug's game, unless you've got the right contacts.'

'Like your friend Bellman.'

A slight hesitation before Sullivan answered. Maybe that's what the flow of words had been about, putting off having to answer questions about his friend Bellman.

'Oh, absolutely. Grandfather a general and all that. Trey would have been all right.'

'But he did the same as you. Packed it in. Why did he do that?'

'You'd have to ask him.'

'He never said why?' Hesitation again from Sullivan. 'After he came out, didn't the two of you share a flat?'

'For a bit. Trey moved around. Sometimes you'd have no idea

where he'd got himself to.' Sullivan laughed, stopped with a wry look. 'But you know that. I take it you still haven't— No. Obviously that's why you're talking to me again. As I said before, if he turns up I'll say you want him to get in contact.'

'You must have talked about leaving the army, plans for the future, that kind of stuff. It's what friends do, isn't it? I take it you were good friends.'

'The best.' And hurried on, 'I've had good times with old Trey. Drinking and women. Any sport you care to name. He's a hell of an athlete, Trey. A competitor, if you know what I mean. Hates to lose. Wonderful man to have on your side. I'd pick him to be on a mountain in a storm with, every time. But when I think of it— Since your people spoke to me last time, I have been thinking about it. Truth is, when I put my mind to it, struck me that with Trey the other chap was always the one did all the confiding. I don't mean he didn't talk. He did, talk the birds out of the trees if he was in the mood. It's just that at the end of all the talk you didn't know any more about him. Put it this way. What I came up with, Trey was a comrade more than he was a friend. If you've ever been in the army, you'll know what I mean.'

'When do you leave for Nepal?'

Sullivan blinked at the change of direction. 'Nepal?'

'You are still going?'

'Oh, yes. Absolutely. Just the three of us, though. Given up on Trey!'

'So when would that be?'

'We fly out week after next. Looking forward to it. Done all our shopping.' He laughed. 'Mickey got bolshie about paying five pounds a time for the rehydration sachets. Made up his own with salt and cremola foam.'

'What happens if Bellman turns up at the airport?' Meldrum asked unsmilingly.

'He isn't booked on the plane.'

'He could have made a booking for himself.'

'Why would he do that?' But Meldrum could see him thinking about it. 'I suppose it would be easy enough for your people to check if he has.'

'Give me the flight details and I'll see that's done.'

'Can I send them to you?'

'Soon as you can. I'll give you a fax number.'

Sullivan said, 'You're going at this pretty seriously, aren't you?'

'Seriously?'

'If he's told you all he knows, can't see the point myself. Shouldn't you be getting on with finding who killed his father, and leave Trey in peace to sort himself out?'

Meldrum studied him in silence. Sullivan tried a smile, then he rocked up on to his toes a couple of times, a boxer waiting for the bell.

'Seriously?' Meldrum said again as if there had been no interruption. 'I saw his father's body.'

At that, Sullivan's eyes fell and his tongue wiped quickly across his lips.

'I'm investigating a murder. And let me give you a piece of advice seriously. Don't let yourself get mixed up in it. If I was you, I'd put that comrades stuff right out of my head.'

He hadn't thought of Ruth waiting for him, but when the lift doors opened he knew at once he should have expected her to do that. They took the Tube to Oxford Street. She didn't ask him about Sullivan and, perhaps because of that, perhaps because tiredness had caught up with him, he let things drift. When she got hungry, they found a pub. Deciding what to have from the blackboard kept them occupied, and then they could busy themselves with eating and drinking; anyway it was too noisy and crowded for conversation to be easy. Afterwards they walked, weaving among the crowds. At one point, standing in front of a Selfridge's window, she said to him over the heads of two Japanese girls, 'Maybe it's because we're both tall. Tall people respond to one another. Maybe that's why we fucked.' That was possible, though it wasn't a reason that had occurred to him. Hearing it discussed in the middle of Regent Street, one Japanese girl looking at the other in a way that suggested her English was good, he decided it was time to call it a day. Yet he didn't walk away, but went together with her to the Tube, where he bought tickets for them both, she telling him for which station; and when they arrived, instead of leaving her

even then, he kept company with her to the Grace Pennington
Hall. And there, she said it was too early to go sit in her room
by herself, and she'd walk with him in the direction of his
hotel. When they came to the park, he kept glancing through
the railings until they came to the gate where he turned in
without a word. After a moment of surprise, she followed,
catching up at once he was pacing so slowly. They went along
in silence, until he stopped and tipped back his head. Looking
up, she saw they were under a double wire strung from one
tree to another across the path, for lights or something like
that. When she glanced back, he was watching her.

'Did your brother hate his father?' he asked.

'That's a terrible thing to say.'

'Is it true?'

'Who would tell you such a terrible thing?'

'I'm not saying it isn't terrible. But is it true?'

'Of course, it isn't true. Alistair loved Daddy.'

'They did quarrel at the Trow Inn on the Saturday evening.'

Her hair flew from side to side as she shook her head.
'No, no, no, no. It was my birthday dinner, and it was
perfect.'

'Your father didn't start getting on to him about leaving the
army?'

She walked away and then swung round. 'Was it that horrible
man in the kitchen? And we've gone there for years. I'll never,
never go back. I'll phone David Hamilton and say we'll never,
never go back. I'll tell him, you should never, never let that
slimy creature out of the kitchen. His hands on the food,
people will be afraid of catching AIDS. Nobody will come
any more. You'll have to close down. Food isn't that good
anyway. Pretentious *moi?* You know what I mean?'

A Martian.

It was easier thinking of her that way; rather than as a bright,
confused, not very happy girl, whose father was dead.

A girl he'd bedded.

Thinking all that, he'd walked on, and found that she stayed
by his side. He kept expecting her to leave, but she didn't. He
wanted her to leave, but couldn't find the right words. It was
a mess of his own making.

They got to his hotel. He stopped on the pavement outside the entrance, afraid that she wanted to go to bed again.

'What is it?'

'I'm sorry about what happened.'

'You know how to make a girl feel good,' she said, in an odd accent, as if it had started out as a joke, a cockney parody, and changed its mind. In her ordinary voice, she said, 'Don't worry about it. You're not a bad bloke.'

Over her shoulder, he saw Henderson come out of the hotel and stop at the sight of them just as she came up on tiptoes to kiss him on the mouth.

CHAPTER TWENTY-SIX

O n the plane back, Henderson was sulking.

'I'm not a kid,' he said when Meldrum used the word. His tone was dangerously quiet. It had been a stupid word to use. Hard-bitten policemen don't sulk.

A stupid word to use to a hard-bitten policeman who'd just seen his superior officer getting a kiss from the victim's daughter. Meldrum, however, had hived that off into a part of his brain where he wouldn't have to think about it. It wasn't in his nature to compromise when he felt he was right in an argument.

'So Alistair's a loner,' he said, putting down the shelf as the stewardess passed across the breakfast trays from the trolley. 'If being a loner makes you a hitman, the country'll need a hell of a lot more jails.'

He split the little roll with his thumbs and spread on butter. It was an argument they'd already been through, hence the sulks. One that had started the day before when Henderson arrived with the news from Oslo. Braaten had sent a fax for Meldrum to police headquarters in Edinburgh giving the bare fact of Locascio's killing, but adding, 'Co-operation now a matter of urgency.' Enthused, Henderson had booked himself on to the London shuttle and got on the phone to Oslo while he was waiting. From Meldrum's point of view, he had then swallowed everything he'd been told, hook, line and sinker. Braaten, it seemed, had found a fellow-spirit in the ambitious sergeant.

He watched Henderson chase yellow shreds of scrambled egg and pile them on a slice of potato, and regretted that they were on the side with just two seats instead of the three across the aisle. Fear of being overheard might have got Henderson off the subject. They could have talked of football. Or the weather. He wondered if Henderson was interested in football. He didn't follow it much himself.

'That Kerr was a right plankhead,' Henderson said, going off at a tangent.

Late yesterday afternoon, they'd interviewed the second member of the Nepal group. In the evening caught up with the third member, Kerr, at his home. Sullivan, Marks and Kerr, all interviewed; call it a passable day's work. Then back to the hotel for a drink. That's when they'd started arguing; and it was possible a little edge on both sides had come from that unmentioned kiss Ruth had given Meldrum, that witnessed kiss. To bed after midnight, plane to catch in the morning.

'Coffee, please,' Henderson said. When they'd both got their cups filled, he went on, 'All I'm saying is, we know he's a violent man. And, like Braaten says, his father was in with Locascio and Kielland in this scheme to launder money for the Mountain.'

To his listener's disgust, he did everything but smack his lips over the last words.

Last night, Meldrum had had it explained to him as Henderson had been given it by Braaten. The Mountain: a shadowy right-wing group, with different aims in different countries, but interconnected by constant travelling between the faction leaders, that mixture of idealists, psychopaths and opportunists, who all over Europe had taken encouragement from the unstoppable tide that had run from the pulling down of the Berlin Wall to the falling apart of the Soviet Union. Most of the surveillance agencies dismissed the Mountain itself as a kind of clearing-house for information, not much more than 'a neo-Nazi post box for fanatics'. Braaten disagreed. The leadership of the Mountain, the men behind the public demagogues, included survivors of the generation who'd been secretly funded by the CIA as tools in the crusade against communism. They'd always had their own agenda, always used the Agency as much or more than it used them, he'd told Henderson; and mentioned the Spear in Italy, without explanation though Henderson – and Meldrum – had never heard of it. Now, he'd said, they're off the leash.

And, not unreasonably, it irritated Meldrum that Braaten should have opened up more on the phone to Henderson than he had with him face to face. Like this parody of the great English breakfast, his trip to Oslo gave air travel a bad name.

'Braaten tell you about Svensen?' he asked.

'Who's he?'

'A Norwegian millionaire. Braaten thought Kielland was swindling him. Kielland had a dodgy past as a company con man. But when he tried to warn them, Svensen's people didn't want to know. And it seems real money was coming into the scheme to match Svensen's. Money that was being channelled in through Kielland.'

'What are Svensen's politics?' Henderson asked, surprising Meldrum again with his shrewdness. He had a tendency to expect a certain slowness from his colleagues.

'Right-wing. His father was a Nazi supporter during the war, and not very popular after it. Svensen, according to Braaten, hero-worshipped his father.'

'That would fit. The way Braaten described it, this wasn't the usual money laundering. You know, taking crooked money, hiding where it came from and turning it respectable. This laundering was so rich supporters could disguise their contributions to the Mountain. Because it was for the Far Right, they didn't want it traced back to them. Apart from anything else, some of it was being used to fund terrorism. So they funnel it through legitimate projects – goes through the books as profits . . . Would that work? I don't know about this stuff.'

Meldrum shrugged. 'Not my line.'

Henderson was enthusiastic. 'Or set it up as a way of seeming to make losses. Then the money gets siphoned off and can't be traced back. Would that work?'

'Sounds complicated.'

'That's where Locascio and Kielland came in. The fixers. Only difficulty, they decide to help themselves. The Mountain finds out, puts out a contract on them. And on John Bellman and then—'

'No,' Meldrum said, not for the first time. It was the point where they parted company. 'I don't see any connection. Gregers Kielland was shot. Bellman was stabbed and—'

'Locascio was stabbed.'

Meldrum took a deep breath. 'A domestic may not be as exciting,' *as good for your bloody career*, 'as Braaten's stuff, but I haven't any doubt Alistair Bellman was provoked, lost his temper and killed his father. The only question is, who else in the family knows? And did any of them help him get rid of the body? John Bellman wasn't any kind of hot shot money man. As far as I can see, he spent most of his time fishing. What he *was*, if we've got it right, was a bastard to his son.'

To his annoyance, Henderson wouldn't let it go. 'One other thing he was.'

'That'd be?'

'General Gardiner's son-in-law.'

'We went over this last night.'

Round in circles. It occurred to him to wonder whether Henderson would have been so persistent if he hadn't seen him with Ruth. The thought was unpleasant. Unfair too, for chances were that he would have sunk his teeth in and not let go anyway. For Henderson, apparently, all this Braaten stuff was a shot in the arm, he was thriving on it.

'But look,' he was saying now, on an uncharacteristic note of pleading reasonableness, 'why shouldn't Gardiner be a member of the Mountain? That lawyer friend of yours, Brennan, everything he told you – all that conspiracy stuff in the Sixties – wouldn't it be worth pushing him on it? Find out what else he knows?' And when Meldrum grunted non-committally, hurried on, 'Just suppose the General is in the Mountain, it's not impossible, is it? Then there's a real chance he might have got his son-in-law involved – because of Bellman's family. I mean, Bellman's father would be an amazing contact for what the Mountain's trying to do.'

That had angered Meldrum more than any of Braaten's other omissions. He could understand the Norwegian not going into so much detail with him as he had with Henderson about the Mountain, particularly perhaps given his own resistance to it having anything to do with Bellman's death. But background information on the victim's family was relevant to any investigation. He should have been told about the stuff Braaten had on Nathan Bellman.

'He might be an amazing contact, but can you imagine John Bellman phoning his father and saying, Sorry I haven't been in touch for thirty years, but I've a little proposition for you? I don't think so.'

'Maybe he had been in touch. We could check on that.'

Round in circles.

'Suppose Alistair's dead?' Meldrum wondered, taking a malicious pleasure in pulling the sergeant up short.

'What?'

'Keep it simple.' From his frown, Henderson might be getting tired of hearing that phrase. It was just possible he used it too much. 'Alistair gets into a drunken quarrel, kills his father. Hiding the body, going here and there, being with his grandfather – all of that keeps him going. But when he's on his own, he can't live with what he's done. Think about it.'

'So he kills himself?' Henderson made it sound absurd. 'Where's the body then?'

'I can think of one possibility,' Meldrum said. 'The rock pool where his father's body was hidden. It might be worth dragging that again.'

The good thing was Henderson didn't respond. The bad thing was he didn't turn to the weather or football. Instead, for the rest of the trip he stared out determinedly at the clouds, not sulking, of course.

Meldrum was left with the feeling his sergeant was disappointed in him.

CHAPTER TWENTY-SEVEN

'A brother?' Meldrum asked.

'Thomas Bellman,' Baird said, referring to the e-mail. 'Younger brother of the deceased. He asks for, and I quote, "a full account of the manner in which the investigation is being progressed, and what hope there is of an arrest. If any." The last two words are underlined. New York address – import export firm – Nathan Bellman, President.'

'That's the father.'

'You knew about him, but not that there was a brother?' The Chief Constable was in his usual mode of polite scepticism, reserving judgements he was never slow to pass.

'Braaten talked about the father, he didn't mention any brother. We'd no occasion to find out about Bellman's family. He hadn't been back to the United States in years. Our information was that his father disowned him when he got married.'

'Why was that?'

Meldrum cast around in his memory. 'According to the family lawyer, it was a Jewish family. The father was angry at him for marrying out of the faith.'

'Ah, very Old Testament,' the Chief Constable murmured. 'Just now, when you were telling me about the Oslo trip, you didn't mention the father, is that right? Or did I miss it?'

'Braaten didn't say anything to me about Nathan Bellman,' Meldrum said grimly. 'Or much about the Mountain, either. I got most of the background stuff about it from Sergeant

Henderson. Braaten told him on the phone when Henderson contacted him about the murder of the Italian.'

'Locascio, yes. Why should Braaten confide so much more to Henderson than he chose to share with you? I find that odd.'

'Shock?' Meldrum speculated, trying for as bland a note as he could manage. His temperament wasn't well suited to internal politics, but he hadn't lasted this long in the police without developing some survival strategies. 'Braaten saw Locascio being murdered. I imagine that might have unstitched him a bit.'

Baird nodded. 'That seems plausible.' Not necessarily true, but plausible. Something that might account for Detective Sergeant Henderson getting conspicuously more from a contact than his immediate superior had managed. Baird emitted, not approval, but a kind of chilly satisfaction at encountering some reasonably quick thinking. 'Tell me what your sergeant learned about this American father.'

'The FBI has been trying to prove Nathan Bellman is Mafia connected. They've been trying for a long time – about twenty years, according to Braaten. That doesn't mean he wasn't connected before – maybe for as many years again – just that he'd managed to avoid attention for all that time. He seems to be pretty good at that. He owns that New York company the son e-mailed from, and has shares in others. But the idea is he's richer than any of that accounts for – maybe a lot richer. The thing is, the FBI can't prove it – and the tax people can't dent him either. If he is what they say, he's something of a genius at moving money around.'

'I think they call that laundering, Jim.'

'I can see that, sir.' Not being a complete bloody fool. 'I've been going over it since Henderson told me. Kielland and Locascio are killed. And maybe that was because they were stealing money from a group of international right-wing conspirators calling themselves the Mountain. And maybe the man Braaten witnessed stabbing Locascio was also the man who shot Kielland. And, yes, it's true that Braaten has a photograph showing John Bellman with Kielland. I'm not ignoring all of that.'

'Sum it up like that and maybe you shouldn't ignore it.'

'All I'm saying is that we shouldn't jump to conclusions.'

Baird, however, pursued his own line of thought. 'And from what you told me the tie-up with Svensen happened only after Kielland had been to the United States, and happened almost at once after he came back. Any check on whether he met Nathan Bellman when he was there?'

'Not as far as I know,' Meldrum said. 'But I imagine Braaten will be enquiring about that — if he hasn't already.'

'You should ask him. Don't you think so?'

Meldrum nodded. 'I plan to do that.'

'After all, it was Braaten who wanted to co-operate. Co-operation is a two-way process . . . Although so far, when you think of it, he could argue he's given you a good deal more than you've been able to give him. Would that be fair?'

'I don't think so,' Meldrum said. 'In fact, I don't believe he's given me anything to help with the murder of John Bellman. I agree it's strange that Bellman knew Kielland, but John Bellman wasn't any kind of financial expert or businessman.'

'I can see your mind is made up,' Baird said.

As the Chief Constable studied him thoughtfully, allowing the silence to lengthen, Meldrum cursed himself. It was Baird's horrible gift to put everybody on to the wrong foot effortlessly. 'Of course, I'm looking to co-operate with Braaten. It's important in a murder case to keep an open mind. But it's also important to give evidence its proper weight. Otherwise you can find yourself all over the shop. For example, from all we've been told Bellman hadn't spoken to his father for thirty years. But, on the other hand, we've been told that he quarrelled with his son Alistair the evening of his disappearance. And we have a witness who'll swear Alistair hated his father. And we know they sat up drinking — and that they'd both been drinking heavily. Given those circumstances, to me it makes sense to go ahead with this as a domestic quarrel that ended in murder. At least until we have any real evidence to the contrary.'

'So what do you want to do?'

'I think we should go for maximum publicity now. Here and down south. Stir things up. Make it clear we think he's done it – off the record, of course. Somebody must know where Alistair Bellman is.'

'Do it,' Baird said. 'And deal with this Thomas Bellman. Write him "Enquiries are progressing" into the death of his brother. You know the form.'

CHAPTER TWENTY-EIGHT

Not much of an hotel. Tin ashtray on the bedside table, despite the fact he'd asked for a non-smoker's room. Thin stream of lukewarm water from the shower. Brown stain in the toilet bowl. Watery scrambled egg, cold toast and the only visible staff a man with greasy hair and fitful English. The good life on police expenses. Driving home from headquarters, it seemed to him twelve months instead of twelve hours since he'd clambered out of bed in the hotel in London. He'd started with a plane flight and finished with a hastily called press conference. It had been a long day.

Looking up from the street as he locked the car, he saw no light in the windows of the flat.

He let himself in the street door. It was the space of these New Town flats that he appreciated. This outer hall, for example, with its tiled floor and door in the corner for the ground-floor flat, was as big as the living-room of the house Carole and he had spent most of their marriage in. The other door led to the stairwell with its steps covered in blue carpeting and on the first landing a painting of a landscape hung on the wall. Some nights he ran up. This wasn't one of them. He climbed slowly, looking up at the painting, and stood for a while in front of it. Fields and trees and water. On trips to galleries and to previews by painter friends of hers, Harriet had taught him that landscape didn't have to be like this; that it could be pulled apart and reassembled into a pattern that had to do with memory and emotion. He had the image and

shut it out of a chair with his clothes neatly folded beside
a student's bed; thought about why the light wasn't on in
the window and wondered where Harriet might be, who she
might be with.

Memory and emotion reassembled and pulled apart their
time together.

All the doors in the hall of the flat were closed. He went
into the kitchen, hung his jacket on the back of a chair and put
on the kettle. For lunch he'd had a bacon roll in the canteen at
headquarters. That and the meal on the plane: two breakfasts.
What did they say? All-day breakfasts. He crouched in front of
the fridge and poked around inside. A quiche from Marks and
Spencer's. A pack of meat that he turned round to read the label.
Ostrich. Christ! A hunk of cheese. All-day breakfasts. He found
a heel of bread in the bin and cut three thick slices of cheese
on top, made himself a coffee and sat at the pine table. No
sooner sat down than he thought about the radio. He should
have put it on, but couldn't be bothered getting up again. He
bit off about a quarter of the bread and cheese, filled up his
mouth with it, added coffee and, forearms resting on the table,
staring ahead at nothing in particular, chewed stolidly until he
could get it down. When he'd finished eating, he made another
coffee and sat again. After a sip, he got up and went into the
bathroom. He pissed and then poured the rest of the coffee
into the bowl and flushed. He went back into the kitchen
and ran along the stations on the radio. He listened standing
to four bars of a pop song, a couple of minutes of talk about
a composer who'd told the drummer for some reason to play
with a cymbal attached to the drum the way they did in the
fairgrounds wherever and whenever, a man singing in German
and he listened through to the end of one song by him and the
introduction to the next and— Gave up and went along the
hall to the living-room where the television was.

He hadn't seen it from the street because it was only a lamp
set on a small fireside table a long way from the window; that
New Town spaciousness again. A glass lay under the pool of
light, a bottle of whisky stood on the edge of it. The glass was
empty. He went round the couch and touched the bottle; the
seal on it seemed to be unbroken.

'Oh, really!' Harriet said.

He sat on the chair opposite where she was on the couch. It put him quite far from her, maybe ten feet away. High ceiling, polished wooden floor, a dining-table and chairs at the window end. It was a big room.

'How long have you been sitting here?'

'I came home early,' she said.

'Have you eaten?'

'No.'

He knew he should get up and sit beside her. Instead, he sat staring at the fire, the illusion of flames. He was tired enough to want to lie back and close his eyes. Let everything go until tomorrow. On weekday mornings, they were both out of the house by half-eight. It would be tomorrow night before they could talk. Twenty-four hours was a long time. It was hard to think straight.

'Did something happen?'

'I wouldn't have drunk it.' With one finger she touched the side of the bottle. 'You don't have to worry. I was in court in the morning. A shoplifter stealing to feed a drug habit. A twenty-year-old who kicked a sixty-year-old half to death. Just the usual legal aid stuff. Office in the afternoon, came home. No, nothing happened.'

'So why the bottle?'

'I bought it on the way home.'

Which was where not why. They didn't keep drink in the flat. When Harriet had lived here on her own, sometimes, too often in the last months, she'd got drunk alone by herself at night. She'd worked in John Brennan's law firm, and they'd become lovers and then it had ended and he'd found her a job in another firm. He had a timorous, compliant wife who bored him, and so he had affairs and if they were with pretty, ambitious young lawyers he found them jobs after it was over. He was good that way. If you took it too seriously that was foolish, since you knew he was a Knight of St Columba and you saw the picture of him on the wall of his office smiling beside the Archbishop when he was awarded a Papal Knighthood as a recognition of his work for charity. Let other Catholics get divorced, that wasn't his way. If you got obsessed with him, if you thought your heart was broken, if you started to drink too much, it was no one's fault but your own; which meant not only that you were an easy lay but one whose fine brain, the mind in which you took so much pride, hadn't worked out what would have been obvious to any shopgirl with street smarts. Your first-class honours degree hadn't been enough to work out that John Brennan had everything he wanted just the way it was, respectability, a comfortable home, success, a plain little pig-tailed daughter he adored, a mistress when he felt the urge and another in waiting when the urge changed. His timorous wife had him bound with hoops of steel to the end of the chapter. He had a lot to lose, and there was something cold at the centre of him that made it unlikely he'd lose it for love, this traditional life, the nineteenth-century *père de famille* with his little milliner, the plump smiling bourgeois in Vienna whirling from embrace to embrace to the one-two-three of a waltz by Strauss. And if that life of the past made for more social stability, if now it meant Brennan's moon-faced daughter kept Mummy and Daddy to make Lawrence's rainbow arch of security over her, who could say it wasn't worth some heartbreak among the milliners? Two cheers for hypocrisy and Grandma's backstreet abortions. Night after night in front of a whisky bottle she'd sat working it all out with that fine brain of hers. And then Meldrum had come into her life.

She held out a hand. 'Come and give me a cuddle.' And when he was beside her, an arm around her shoulder, she put her head down with a sigh and told him, 'That pair in court this morning . . . The girl's mother was an addict. The father deserted them when she was eight. The mother's on the game, put on it by one of the string of partners she's had since the husband took off. Tracey isn't going to stop, shoplifting, drugs, any of it. And the awful thing is, if she has any dreams at all, they're about Mr Right coming along. And that isn't going to happen. And if it did she'd mess it up. So I got depressed. I'm so tired of it. And then I came home and you weren't here.'

'I couldn't get back any sooner.' How often had he said that in his life? And apologised for it. He was tired of having to apologise for it. 'I'm sorry.' He resented having to apologise for it. 'How was—'

But she'd started to speak at the same moment, 'How was—
Sorry! You first.'

'I was going to say, how was your other case? Sorry. Stupid
question.'

'A thug. Started drinking in the morning, met this sixty-year-
old, drank half the afternoon, got a carry-out and went back
to the man's flat. They quarrelled, of course. They fought, of
course. And, of course, his defence was, the old man made
indecent advances to him.'

'Did you get him off?'

'Of course not. Never mind. How was Oslo?'

'Didn't see much of it. Weather was good.'

'Then you went to London.' It wasn't a question, he'd told
her about the two cities plan before he left.

'Henderson came down. We got some witness statements.
Hotel we stayed in was a real dump.'

A bad conscience made him hope she wouldn't ask what
else he'd done in London. To distract her, he could tell about
the death of Locascio. But then she'd ask who the Italian was,
and he couldn't explain without using some of what Braaten
had told him. And then one question might set off another.
A habit of discretion stopped him. When she began to speak,
though, it was to hark back to her morning in court. She
sighed and said, 'The old man's head was swollen twice its
normal size when they found him, but our brain surgeons are
wonderful so this time it was only assault. Try again later.
Always tomorrow, eh?'

'One of those days,' he said, rubbing her shoulder.

'If it was about bad people, I could cope with that. Legal
aid's not about bad people. It's an endless procession of feckless
people, people without any luck. You know what they say, Born
to lose. You get afraid losing might be contagious.' She turned
and pulled his head down so she could kiss him. 'Take me to
bed. Please.'

As they went into the hall, he said, 'I've left the radio
on.'

It surprised him that it was still the same programme. The
man's voice singing in German, the sound of the piano, felt
like a long time ago.

'Never mind,' she said, twining her arms more tightly around him.

'I'll put it off.'

'Forget it.'

'Won't take a minute.'

'Christ!' she said, and he thought it was going to turn into a quarrel. But suddenly she said, 'Fuck it!' And then, 'Take me to your *lieder!*'

She was still giggling when they fell into bed.

When he woke in the night, it was abruptly with an urgent sense of something that had to be done. He got up and, not wanting to disturb Harriet, felt his way to the door, one hand stretched out ahead of him. Still half asleep, he was in the kitchen looking down at the mute radio before he remembered Harriet with her arms around him giggling at some joke of her own as they bumped and stumbled together into the kitchen to switch it off. Then they'd made love. Scratching the nape of his neck baboon fashion, he yawned luxuriously and decided life had its moments.

He was gripping the handle of the bedroom door ready to go back in, when he thought of the bottle lying on the table in the front room. The fire hadn't been put off, the table lamp was still on, end of day routines left undone, so after all there had been something to wake up for. He thought about emptying the whisky down the sink, but that offended him, less because it was wasteful than because it seemed melodramatic. Instead he put it in the side pocket of his coat to take away in the morning.

In the bedroom, he went through the same process of navigating the darkness from memory, one hand stretched out in front of him. When his knees bumped the bed, he found the edge of the sheet and slipped under it, edging cautiously across until he felt her warm against his back. Then, just before she spoke, some instinct told him she was lying awake.

'John Brennan's offered me a job,' she whispered as if afraid of being overheard.

He listened to her breathing. He knew it was important for him to make an immediate response. Even a clumsy word

now would be better than anything he might find to say in the
morning. It was possible that what he said now might decide
their future, whether they had a future. After a while her breaths
came more slowly, and it seemed likely she was asleep. He lay
thinking of what she might say to him tomorrow. If her work
had become unbearable to her, then going to Brennan would be
like a salvation. No more legal aid, being with the best defence
lawyer in Scotland meant getting involved in the high-profile
cases that were Brennan's speciality. Sneering at that would
be stupid: anybody who worked all the time with people at
the bottom of the heap could get worn down. Ask ministers,
social workers, teachers. Ask policemen. And those who did
get worn down came from the ranks of the ones who tried
too hard and cared too much. She might say to him she was
a good lawyer and wanted the chance to use her abilities to
the full. And that was a good reason, too. She would tell him
that her affair with Brennan was over, in the past, she would
never touch him again, the thought of it made her sick. If she
was being asked back, it was because she was a good lawyer,
a very good lawyer, one of the smartest that had ever worked
for him. Anyway, hadn't somebody once told him, years before
he'd met Harriet, Brennan's too smart ever to go back once he's
dumped them. And so there was no need to be jealous. But
the best argument was the glass and the whisky bottle. He
wouldn't let that happen to her again. Aloud he said, 'It's all
right. If that's what you want.'

When he woke in the morning, he was stretched at the very
edge of the bed as if he'd spent the night trying to get away
from her. Why couldn't she just tell me, he thought. All that
stuff about the shoplifting girl, what was all that about? And the
bottle of whisky. You opened it or you got up and walked away
from it. What was that about? No one sat in front of a bottle for
hours that way. Moral blackmail, that was what that was about.
It went round in his head until he grew ashamed of his anger
and turned to put his arm round her. She wasn't there.

Ten past nine. He'd slept in for the first time in years. He
went into the kitchen, had a look in the bathroom, looked in
the living-room and even checked the little study room beside
it. She'd gone to work. Maybe she'd thought he could take

a day off after being away. That would be why she hadn't wakened him.

He made a pot of tea and drank a couple of cups. He took his time getting shaved and dressed. When he was ready, he found he was hungry and went back and made tea with a bag in a cup and ate half a dozen crackers and cheese. If he was late, he was late. He even stood on the landing for a minute looking at the picture. Peaceful countryside: that's what he liked. Fields, trees, water. What was the point of hurrying?

He'd put the car in a slot reserved for Zone Five residents, who had a little card they paid for and stuck on the windshield to show they were entitled. Not being a Zone Five resident, he didn't have one, which didn't matter since he was away before half-eight every morning and arrived back after half-five.

He'd got a parking ticket.

Some days were like that.

CHAPTER TWENTY-NINE

'He's just off the phone,' Henderson said.
'From where?'
'At his office, I suppose. Or maybe at home. He didn't say.'
'Glasgow, either way. It'll take him an hour at least to get here.' Meldrum checked his watch. Half past ten. 'What did you tell him?'
'That you weren't available, but I'd pass the message on to you as soon as possible.'
'Better than saying I'd slept in, I suppose.'
'He wants to know what the hell is going on.'
'That's what he said?' Meldrum was surprised. No reason why an accountant shouldn't curse, but Gordon Bellman had struck him as the buttoned-up type.
'More or less. Anyway, it's what he meant.'
'You should have told him I'd phone him back.'
'I did. He wasn't interested. He's coming through, and you'd better be there or else. Didn't say that in so many words, but—'
'I know, it's what he meant.'
Henderson nodded.
'Sun's shining. Nice day for a run down the coast.' Meldrum put on the jacket he'd just taken off, slipping it from the back of his chair and shrugging into it. 'Get some sea air.' He sat down and reached for the phone, thought for a moment and dialled the number from memory.

It was the housekeeper who answered. He told her what he wanted and there was a pause until a different voice asked, 'Is that Inspector Meldrum?'

'Good morning, Mrs Bellman.'

'. . . Mrs Martin doesn't always get names right.'

'I wonder if it would be convenient for me to come and see you.'

'You want to come here?'

'Yes.' Where else?

'When would that be?'

'I'd leave right away. I don't know if you've seen this morning's papers.'

His press conference had been well covered.

'I've had reporters on the phone.'

'I'm sorry,' he said.

'Last night and already this morning.'

'I'm sorry,' he said again, and caught Henderson in a sardonic glance. Mrs Bellman had the voice and accent which took apology as its due. 'There isn't anything we can do about that.'

'And you want to come here now?'

'If that's convenient. I will have to talk to you, at some point.'

'Whenever you like then.'

'My sergeant and I should be there about half-eleven,' he said, but half-way through heard the click as the phone went down.

'Tell them where we're going, and let's get out of here.'

Downstairs, where he caught him up after seeing the co-ordinator, Henderson said, 'I just said where we were going. I didn't know what else to say. Do you want me to go back up and leave a message with him to give Bellman when he gets here?'

'Don't worry about it. When the shit hits the fan with Bellman, I'll explain that you misunderstood.' Meldrum smiled. 'I'll say you didn't tell me he was coming through. All right?'

'Bloody marvellous.'

It was a fine morning and, once they'd left the city traffic behind, they made good speed. On one turn of the road,

ahead of them the wind swayed yellow corn ready for the
harvester, on another it sowed white caps on the sea. As he
drove, Meldrum remembered the story Henderson had told of
going to Australia to look for his father. He glanced across at
the sergeant, who hadn't spoken a word since they set out,
and felt a twinge of conscience.

'I was kidding about telling Bellman you'd misunderstood
about him coming through,' he said.

Henderson shrugged. 'All one to me.'

'Aye, that'll be right.'

For a couple of miles, it looked as though Henderson was
going to leave it at that. But just as Meldrum was settling into
a responsive mood of black irritation, the sergeant gave a kind
of mixed sigh and chuckle. 'I doubt if Bellman would have
believed you,' he said. 'Do you think he'll be there when we
get back?'

'Up to him. But I wanted to see the mother first.'

'I'm looking forward to being there when you explain why
we didn't wait for him.'

'Time enough. I'll think of something.'

When they came into the little town, Meldrum glanced at
his watch. Twenty past eleven. Not bad. He liked to be
punctual.

As they turned into the Bellmans' drive, he suddenly asked,
'What's the name of that woman again? The housekeeper.'

'Martin.'

Of course. Jobbing gardener, Bobbie Selby; house phone
number, no problem. Just that bloody woman's name kept
escaping him. He had these odd blind spots, which, in
the way of everyone with a very good memory, were worried over, probed like a bad tooth, for evidence of dying
brain cells.

Sour-faced as ever, Mrs Martin opened the door. *Hilda*
Martin.

Cheered by this act of remembrance, he followed her briskly
into the drawing-room to find Gordon Bellman standing beside
his mother's chair.

'Inspector Meldrum.' Unsmiling, Mrs Bellman had the sleek
menace of a very handsome cat confronted by a very small

mouse. 'I think you know my son Gordon. He came through yesterday evening from Glasgow to be with me.'

Despite being taller than Gordon Bellman, Meldrum had the impression the man was gazing down on him. Going forward felt like walking up a slope.

Unwelcome surprises produce odd effects.

'Your mother didn't mention you were with her, Mr Bellman.'

'Why should she? I was on the point of leaving to come and see you, when you phoned. I told your sergeant I was coming.' He frowned at Henderson. 'I don't understand. Didn't you tell him?'

Before Henderson could respond, Meldrum said, 'I doubt you must have misunderstood, sir. Anyway, I've saved you the trip.'

Bellman stared and, unblinking, with crooked finger and thumb adjusted and readjusted the gold-rimmed glasses on his nose as if trying for a better view.

Before he could speak, his mother said, 'Sit down, Gordon. And you on the couch, Inspector. Sergeant,' and Henderson was waved to a chair at the side.

It was done very naturally and in a moment they were all seated, Mrs Bellman in her chair, her son and the two detectives arranged as audience before her. Yet that second or two before she spoke left Meldrum with the image to think about later of Bellman staring at him as he adjusted his glasses.

'My mother was pestered last night by calls from reporters. After I arrived here last night to protect her from that, my wife phoned to say two journalists from the *Herald* had actually been to our house. I think we're entitled to an explanation.'

What was it he'd sensed in that interval? That the tinder-dry length of the man might conflagrate, like a stick bursting into flames? At once, the moment past, the notion seemed ridiculous, looking at the man in front of him, so cautious, self-contained, restrained.

'We have no control over the press, you understand that. But I'm sorry your wife and your mother were upset.'

'My wife can take care of herself.' Was he aware of the twist to his lip as he said that? 'I mean, she doesn't feel these accusations you've made as keenly as my mother does. That's only natural.'

'If a reporter made any sort of accusation,' he looked at Mrs Bellman, 'I hope you got his name.'

'Are you talking about suing a paper? Losing some nobody his job? What do I care about that?' Meldrum felt the force of those extraordinary blue eyes. General Gardiner's eyes. And the eyes of Alistair Bellman. 'Do you deny that you have accused my son of murdering his father?'

'Of course I deny it. You've got the morning papers there. We've put out an appeal for your son to come forward and help us with our enquiries. That doesn't—'

'What else does it mean?' she asked.

'Only what it says. No more than that.'

'It reads like more, a good deal more.' Gordon Bellman gestured at the papers lying on the table beside his mother. By the size of the bundle, he'd gone out and bought a copy of all of them. 'The way they feature it so prominently. What they find to say about my brother. What business is it of theirs that he left the army? Lots of men do – there's nothing sinister in that. It's all hints and implications. Nothing to seize on, but the impression left with the reader is quite unfair.'

Meldrum was thinking about eyes. Gordon, the elder son, had brown eyes. Same colour as the father's according to the description they'd been given. He wondered what else the son might have in common with his father. A bully? That pert blonde wife of his hadn't the look of someone who'd let herself be bullied by her husband; more like vice versa maybe. Temper? There had been some talk of the father being quick to lose his temper. Not hard to believe the son had anger inside him. Harder to imagine him losing his temper. Maybe he would be afraid to. There were people like that, afraid of what would happen if they ever let themselves go.

'There was a reference to my father,' Mrs Bellman said. 'I hope *he* won't be pestered. That would be intolerable.'

'Can I ask which paper mentioned General Gardiner?'

'More than one,' Gordon said. 'In connection with Alistair having been in the army. I imagine all this stuff comes from you, isn't that right?'

'That's not how it works,' Meldrum said. 'Newspapers keep libraries of material on people. Your grandfather is – was – a public figure. Journalists are used to working quickly. It doesn't take them long to fill in background. And, of course, they have their own sources of information.'

'Background?' Mrs Bellman asked sharply. 'What exactly does that mean? Where does it stop?'

While Meldrum attempted something soothing, he was wondering how far in fact it would go. His old army buddies, falling short of the high standards set by the friends of Lord Lucan, might start spilling some of those stories about Alistair's streak of violence. If reporters went to the Trow Inn to ask about the birthday dinner, they'd be told about the quarrel between Alistair and his father. Indeed, unless he'd been warned off by his more prudent partner, chances were Leo might even get on to the topic of how exactly, in his opinion, the son had felt about his father. If Alistair didn't put in an appearance quickly, there was a real risk of too much leaking into the papers. This wasn't France, or even England. Scottish courts took a rigorous view of the kind of publicity that made for the prejudicing of a fair trial.

Apart from all that there was General Gardiner's history of Far Right conspiracy. And things could get even more complicated, if the *sieg heil!* skeletons weren't just in his cupboard, but out goose-stepping around again. That was what Braaten thought, apparently, and he'd turned Henderson into a believer.

'You're supposed to be looking for a murderer. That's your job. I can't see any sign that you're nearer to finding him. None of this,' she waved at the table with the newspapers, 'is going to help. How could it? Alistair knows nothing about my husband's death.'

Before Meldrum could answer, another voice asked, 'Don't you wonder what's happened to him?'

Mrs Bellman turned her head just fractionally to Henderson, as if reluctant to acknowledge his existence.

'My brother will be staying with friends,' Gordon Bellman said.

Meldrum shook his head. 'Not the ones he was going on holiday with, I'm afraid. They've no idea where he is.'

'Unless, of course, he's planning to turn up at the airport,' Henderson said. 'Bags packed for Nepal.'

'What would happen if he did?' Mrs Bellman asked. Now she was looking fully at Henderson. 'Would you arrest him?' Henderson hesitated, then shrugged. Dismissing him, she turned her attention to Meldrum. 'If you did, you'd find yourself talking to my lawyers.'

'Your son hasn't been in contact with you since your husband's body was found.' Meldrum made that a statement. After all, it was what he had been told. But as he looked from mother to son, he waited, letting the silence continue until it took on the merest shading of a question.

'He has not,' Gordon Bellman confirmed.

'You must worry about where he is.' Deliberately he repeated the substance of Henderson's question to the mother.

'I'd be ashamed not to have confidence in him,' she said.

'He'll be practising technique half-way up a mountain,' the brother said. 'In Argyll somewhere or on Skye.'

'If he did turn up at the airport, Mrs Bellman,' Meldrum said, 'I'd assume it was because he knew nothing of your husband's death. Once he was told, I'm sure he would be more than willing to help us.'

'Even if he didn't get on well with his father,' Henderson said.

'*What?*' She spat the word out.

To Meldrum's ear, though, she sounded less surprised by what Henderson had said than indignant at something equivalent to mutiny in the ranks.

Himself feeling slightly hustled by his sergeant, Meldrum said, 'We do have information that your husband and Alistair quarrelled during Ruth's birthday dinner at the Trow Inn. Quite violently, according to what we were told. Is that true?'

'That is most certainly not true,' Gordon Bellman began, and stopped as his mother waved him to silence.

As she leaned forward, Meldrum was fixed by that cold blue gaze. 'But that's what you asked Ruth!' Had Ruth phoned? What had she told her mother? Meldrum felt as if he'd been punched in the stomach. He sensed Henderson looking at him, and could only hope he'd given nothing away. 'She *told* you there was no quarrel. Then you asked her a disgraceful question, and she gave you the only possible answer. If you won't accept it from her, I hope you will take it from me. Whatever poisonous nonsense that creature at the Inn told you, my son did not hate his father.'

'Oh, hate's putting it strongly. I'm sure no one talked about hate,' Meldrum lied in a good cause. 'We were told that Alistair's decision to leave the army had upset his father.'

'My husband had never been in the army.'

That didn't quite add up to an answer. While Meldrum was thinking about it, Henderson said, 'Alistair must have been proud of General Gardiner. Was that why he wanted to be an officer? So he could follow in his grandfather's footsteps?'

'Everyone who knows him admires my father.'

'Thing is, if he admired his grandfather so much,' Henderson wondered, 'what made him give up his commission?'

Gordon Bellman said, '*I* admire my grandfather, but I would never have dreamed of joining the army. I didn't see it as having the kind of career prospects I wanted. Alistair came to the same conclusion.'

'He left the army to do something better . . .' Meldrum said.

'I've had enough of this.' She stood up abruptly. 'Do you think we're fools, that you can ask us these questions? That we don't know the way your minds plod along on the one track? You have an idea and you can't let it go, however absurd it is. I've told you John's murder has nothing to do with my son. I tell you again, Alistair knows nothing about his father's death. Find who killed my husband. And, for God's sake, until you do, if you ever do, leave us alone!'

She was at the door by then, ignoring Meldrum's, 'I apologise if I've upset you. We are trying.' Just as she opened it, he said, 'I wrote your husband's brother the same thing. That we were doing all we can.'

She stopped as if he had laid a hand on her shoulder. 'What brother?'

'Thomas . . . your husband's younger brother?'

'He's not in this country?'

'Oh, no. He sent a message from New York.'

'How could they have found out? Who would have told them?' She looked at her son, who frowned, pursing his lips as if to share her surprise. 'There's been no contact between that family and your father for thirty years.'

For as long as they'd been married, Meldrum thought. Silver for a twenty-fifth wedding anniversary. What for a thirtieth? Apart from a knife in the belly.

He said, 'However he got to know, Mr Thomas Bellman wrote to the Chief Constable asking to be informed about how the investigation was going.'

'What business is it of his?'

What was he supposed to say? Blood's thicker than water? 'He seemed to be very concerned.'

'Those people had no *concern* for my husband while he was alive. They belong to an unforgiving tribe.'

Gordon Bellman walked them to the door.

On the step, as if it were an afterthought, Meldrum asked, 'The night of the disappearance, when the two of you sat up with your father, which of you went to bed first – you or Alistair?'

'Alistair, but you know that. Just as I told you before. Nothing's changed,' he said.

On the road back, neither of them spoke for more than half the journey, each busy in his own way going over what had been said.

It was Henderson who spoke first. 'About going down there instead of waiting for him, you didn't dump it on me. I appreciate that.' He used the slightly grudging tone of a man who was determined to be fair.

'What did you make of him?'

'How do you mean?'

'I just remembered something his wife told us,' Meldrum said. ' "Gordon drives like a madman," she said.'

'Wouldn't think it to look at him.'

'No, you wouldn't.'

Henderson met that with a snort of laughter.

'Just remembered, when I was in Australia, this minister turned up at my dad's place. Pastoral visit, you know? Surprised me, I didn't think churchgoing was the old man's style. Maybe he'd gone once and they'd got his name on the books. And, of course, this minister had just got his call from the congregation. I doubt he'd do many more pastoral trips to see the old man. He was half cut when Reverend Thompson arrived and got worse the longer he stayed. Couldn't entirely blame him. This minister was the most sanctimonious, narrow bastard you'd meet in a month of Sundays. Told us at one point, his father and grandfather had both been ministers. No surprise there. Anyway, I wanted to go into town for the weekend. The old man had promised to take me, but he'd reneged. Wouldn't let me take the car and go myself, I was still new at the driving. Anyway, this minister offered me a lift. I was never so scared in my life. I tell you he drove like a bloody madman. He'd said he would take me back on Sunday after the service. I was so worried, I spent the weekend trying to cadge a lift instead of enjoying myself.'

'What happened?'

'Sunday morning we're all sitting in church. I'm praying I'll get home in one piece. Time passes and the congregation's getting restless. No sign of the minister. After a while, I mean really a long time, they gave up and started to drift outside. Me as well, wondering how the hell I was going to get back. And there he is, the old man, sitting in the pick-up across the street. Wouldn't go in because he was in his work gear. He leaned out of the window and yelled over, "The gendarmes have just gone to fetch the bastard." Turned out he'd been on a job that morning and he'd come across the minister's wife walking along at the side of the road in her nightdress. Black eye, split lip. The old man had brought her into town. "You won't be getting your lift," he told me. "If I was you, I'd get in." '

'There a moral to that?'

'Don't know about a moral,' Henderson said. 'Goes to show you never can tell about the quiet ones.'

CHAPTER THIRTY

The Atrium was a nice place to have lunch. Meldrum sat in the corner on his own and read the menu. Pigeon breast at £9.80: more than he'd usually pay at this time of day. There was a natural ceiling on the cost of a bacon roll. The restaurant was busy. Tables stood in the spaces that led out into the hall, and beyond that to the stairs down to the Traverse Theatre and the bar. At one of them, John Brennan sat with a group of two other men and a woman. As he came in, he'd made a point of squeezing past them. Taking his time, he'd done it the awkward way, looking and listening, scrupulously avoiding Brennan's eye. The men were in their fifties, tall and florid, one Scots, one English, standard Edinburgh top business issue; the woman was striking, about thirty, with hair a shade somewhere between red and gold. Now, carefully dissecting his pigeon – very tasty (and filling, very filling; be open-minded, be honest, nice change from a bacon roll) – he observed how half the men in the room followed her with their eyes as she headed for the door at the rear; and how the other half picked up on her as she returned. When she came back the men got up and they went out into the hall in a group.

Ten minutes later, he spotted Brennan, unmistakable above the crowd with his height and the mane of white hair, on the far side of the hall. And then he reappeared and crossed to Meldrum's table, pausing briefly on the way to speak to a waiter.

'Better than the police canteen,' he said, taking the seat on the opposite side of the table.

'You're a mind-reader.' As always, the actorly booming of the advocate's voice drove him to the opposite extreme, murmuring his words so softly it was as if everyone round about must be trying to eavesdrop.

'Sorry to keep you waiting. Terrible bore, I didn't expect the meal there to go trailing on. I couldn't get rid of them.'

'If you wanted a short meal, you shouldn't have invited the redhead. They were drooling over her.'

'In discreet Edinburgh style. Napkins over erections.' Brennan laughed. 'She's a bore as well. But looking like that, you forgive her, though it's a pity she feels she has to talk. I'd like to tell her, just be beautiful, like a painting in a gallery – a Raeburn doesn't have to speak.' He paused as the waiter poured coffee from the pot he'd brought him. 'So what's it about?'

Meldrum leaned forward and spoke quietly, an example he hoped the other man would follow. 'That time you invited us for dinner. Remember afterwards we talked about a certain person? Someone I'd come across in connection with an investigation.'

'General Gardiner.'

Meldrum grunted. He couldn't lower his voice much more or it would take a passing bat to catch it. 'Those involvements of his with politics, are they—'

Puzzled, he trailed off.

Brennan was laughing. 'I got that one wrong,' he said. 'I thought you'd got me here to talk about Harriet.'

'If she wants to change jobs, that's up to her.' He watched the end of his fork: some pigeon, bit of this, little bit of that, getting the mix just right took concentration. 'Nothing to do with me.'

'As long as there isn't any misunderstanding. I hate to see a good lawyer wasting her time, and Harriet could be one of the best. That's why I asked her to come back. The only reason. As far as I can see, you two are good for one another. No point in me regretting or apologising for what's over and done with. Draw a double line under the past. Do you feel the same?'

'If that's what she wants.'

Not much of a response to all that straight-from-the-heart malarkey, but it was the best he could do. As the Highlander said to the Duchess of Sutherland – We can forgive, but we don't ever forget. Although, since Brennan's affair with Harriet had been over before he even met her, what the hell did he have to forgive anyway?

'. . . Fine, then.' Brennan ended his thoughtful contemplation with a brisk nod. 'Turn her loose on something worthwhile, and we'll have her running rings round the Procurator.' He grinned. 'Theft, robbery, murder. Take your pick. You catch them, Jim, and we'll get them off.'

'Shouldn't that be, Prove them innocent?' Meldrum wondered. The touch of sourness coming as much as anything from the fact Brennan usually did.

'Speaking of which.' The lawyer looked at his watch. 'You want to tell me what this is about?'

'You have more sources than anyone else I know.'

'True.'

'Have you heard anything about General Gardiner being mixed up with the Far Right? Not years ago, I'm not talking about back in the Sixties. I mean now.'

Brennan leant an elbow on the table and covered his mouth with his hand. When he took it away, he said, 'You're full of surprises, Jim.'

'Does that mean yes?'

'It's news to me. You must be the one with the sources. But, put it with something else I was told, and maybe you could make it add up to four – or five, of course. Just maybe, mind you, don't ask me to make sense of it.' He shook his head. 'Cold War warrior in his eighties. Climbs back up on Rosinante and gallops off again after the other three Horsemen of the Apocalypse? Could be. What sense do any of those maniacs make?'

'Something else you were told, you said. Going to tell me what? I know you'll not tell me who.'

'No problem. Farquhar Wood.'

Secretary of State of Scotland until his party lost the last General Election. Now Sir Farquhar, having got the traditional bauble to console him and make it easier to pick up the odd directorship. During his ill-fated effort to prove convicted murderer Hugh Keaney innocent, Meldrum had gone to

Farquhar Wood looking for help and protection; and got neither. Hearing his name, he felt a superstitious sinking of the heart.

'Could you trust anything he said?'

'Farquhar has a lot going for him,' Brennan protested. 'He's intelligent and hard-working and well read. His heart's in the right place, and he really would like to do good in the world. He might even manage it, if it wasn't that he loves a lord and needs a spine transplant. Latter comes with the job. Former's so rare as to be almost a virtue in the Tory new model army of estate agents and wide boys.'

Fuck's sake! Meldrum thought.

Aloud he said, 'Have I got it the wrong way round? Are you going to tell me about *who* till the cows come home and never get round to *what*?'

'The what won't take long,' Brennan said. He sipped his coffee. 'You know if you're doing business with the Saudis you've to take your time, talk about the weather? A man who sold weapons to them told me that. Not a gun-runner, he worked for the MOD. Arabs think it's uncivilised to go at things bull at a gate – if I can exchange agricultural metaphors.'

'I was trying to help. You're the one said you didn't have much time.'

'I accept your apology.' And now, pushing the cup to one side, he did lean forward, resting chin on hands folded into a double fist. 'Your Chief Constable's younger brother is married to Farquhar's sister. Did you know that? There you are! – he is, though. That doesn't make them intimate friends, you understand. For Farquhar's taste, Baird's too upright downright – and I'd suspect Baird finds Farquhar a touch too ... supple for his. Chalk and cheese. But blood's thicker than water, they're fond of their siblings, and so they see more of one another than you'd expect. One Sunday after dinner, Farquhar told Baird that the son-in-law of a friend was missing, and asked if he could have it looked into.'

'Farquhar Wood's a friend of General Gardiner?'

Brennan pulled a face. 'I share your incredulity. I doubt it – more chalk and cheese than ever. No, I think it's been one of those lords that Farquhar sniffs after. Some old chum of

Gardiner's from Rhodesia First days, who's invited Farquhar
for a country house weekend and told him the sad tale. He'd
be off like a puppy dog with a ball in its mouth, eager to show
what he could do.'

'So that's why a routine disappearance got priority.'

'Baird passed the word down and you got the job. But then
later, come another Sunday, and Farquhar tells Baird he's not
happy about the Bellman thing. Forget I ever mentioned the
name, he says. Baird went for him – this is according to
Farquhar, you understand – asking what he thought he was
playing at. But all that Farquhar would say was that he thought
they should both distance themselves from it.'

'Baird did try to pull me off – which seemed fair enough
at the time.' For all anyone knew at that point, Bellman might
just have got tired of his life and taken off, found a woman
or whatever. A lot of man-hours had been clocked up with
nothing to show for them. 'But then, of course, the body
turned up.'

Brennan checked his watch again. 'I'll really have to get
going. Any of that stuff help?'

'I appreciate it. Just one other thing – did Wood tell
you what made him change his mind about the Bellman
disappearance?'

Brennan was on his feet. Meldrum got up and started to
walk with him

Brennan said, 'You'll get arrested if you don't pay your
bill.'

'Damn. Did he?'

'No, not really. He told me he'd had another approach on
the same matter. But this time from someone he wasn't at
all sure of. When that happened, typical Farquhar, he started
worrying about Baird as much as himself. He really isn't a
bad guy.'

'He didn't say who this second approach was from?'

'I've got to go.' Brennan started off, turned. 'I don't think
it matters who. He could understand a man worrying about
his son-in-law, and trying to pull strings to get some extra
attention. That's a politician's world. But then a third party
asks, and for him that's one too many. Somebody he said "who

was too insistent". Enough to set the alarm bells ringing. He wouldn't tell me any more. My impression was the whole thing had suddenly made him very nervous. Whatever else you say about him, Farquhar isn't stupid.'

CHAPTER THIRTY-ONE

He'd wakened in the morning with the idea fully formed. Just on the edge of parting with sleep, he'd been filled by a warmth and contentment he hadn't known for a long time, a sense that everything was going to be all right. The responsibility was his and he was going to solve their problems. That was what being a father meant. He had wakened smiling, and lain like that for a while, reluctant to open his eyes.

Sitting now in the Blue Blanket nursing a pint while waiting for Sandy Torrance to come, it didn't seem so simple.

To distract himself, he thought again about what Brennan had told him earlier over lunch, and Henderson's reaction to it.

'I wish I'd been there,' Henderson had said. 'I'd like to have asked him what he meant by Wood being nervous.'

'You wouldn't have wanted to be there.'

'I can tell a knife from a fork.'

'If I told you what it cost me, you wouldn't have wanted to be there.'

Henderson began to gather up the witness statements he'd been checking against one another and the computer record. 'Couldn't be "nervous" as in afraid somebody was going to get physical? Nice idea, eh? One of the heavy mob putting the frighteners on the little shit.'

'No, of course not. And there wouldn't have been any point in asking Brennan. I believe him when he said Wood wouldn't spell out what made him shy off.'

Henderson picked folders off the bundle he'd put on top

of a cabinet and opened a drawer. 'What makes a politician nervous?'

'A rent boy and a photographer?' Meldrum asked.

Not a great joke, but he didn't make many jokes. Amazing what a good lunch did for your sense of humour. Henderson didn't smile. He hadn't had a good lunch.

'I was thinking,' he said, 'of the wrong kind of politics. That makes a politician nervous. Getting the reputation of being too far left used to be bad news. But for Sir Fucker the danger might be of getting mixed up with the far right. That's not the way to get ahead in the born again nice guys Tory party. And if that's what he'd got a whiff of, see what I mean?'

This was a new side of Henderson, and one that made Meldrum uncomfortable. He wasn't a stupid man, but he didn't like politics or thinking about politics. He'd heard radicals – his daughter Betty among them – argue the police were instruments of oppression, tools of the capitalists. Listening to her one time, he'd looked at his hands. Spatulate thumbs, palms padded with calluses; a working man's hands. All right, all right, it was a long time since he'd worked on a building site. Yes, the hands were softer nowadays. A detective's hands, if you like. But there'd been a time in his life when he'd got up at six, walked down for a bus, grafted, picked up a pay packet for making things. He didn't think of what he did now in terms of anything as abstract and grand as society, how it was organised, who it profited. He saw it as catching villains, dealing with thugs. And as he experienced it on the street, the poor were the ones who most needed the police, their thin line of defence against violence and stupidity. And yes, maybe he'd been lucky. He'd never been asked to strike-break. And yes, he'd listened in the canteen in '84 to young coppers boasting of putting miners 'through the mincer'. But there were bastards in every job.

He lifted the pint. As the dark heaviness of the beer flooded his mouth, pub sounds swam up again around him. He wondered what Betty would say to his plan. He couldn't ever predict how she would react, though Carole claimed they were alike in so many ways. And how had he got from Farquhar Wood to strike-breaking and miners? By way of Betty, of course. In his head he'd been arguing with her without even realising what he was doing: there are bastards in every job, Betty. Give your politics a rest, Betty.

'No,' he'd told Henderson, 'I don't know what you mean,' though he had a fair idea, not being stupid. 'We're policemen. How do we know how a politician thinks?'

Henderson had put the last file away and shut the drawer, a little too firmly, not quite a slam.

'I know you fancy Alistair for his father's murder,' he'd said. 'I think he's in the frame as well. But this other stuff keeps on coming at us. Just suppose Bellman *was* mixed up with Kielland and the Italian to launder money for the Mountain. And then he disappears. The General does the old pals act and Baird puts us on to looking for Bellman. But while that's going on, the real heavy hitters behind the Mountain start getting worried. Why has this guy disappeared? Is something wrong? What about our money? There's another approach to Wood—'

Meldrum had made a gesture of impatience. 'Right. What do we *know* happened? Twice Wood gets asked to help chase on the police into investigating Bellman's disappearance. First time it happened, well, there's no mystery about a man wanting his son-in-law found – the General could be doing it just for his daughter's sake. Second time, it's all vague. Maybe another old pal of the General wasn't tactful and put Wood's back up. That's *all* we know. I wouldn't try to put more weight on that than it'll carry.'

'According to Brennan, Wood wasn't annoyed, he was nervous.'

'The Mountain gets worried about its money, so it sends for the police?' Meldrum had been dismissive. 'I don't see it.'

''Who's got a better chance than us of finding somebody?' Henderson had said stubbornly. 'And it wasn't all they were doing. Even if they weren't suspicious before, with Bellman gone it makes sense they'd check the books. And when they find out what's been going on, Kielland and Locascio are killed.'

'So it's nothing to do with us, right?'

'Eh?'

'Only murder matters to us is Bellman's. And you've just

proved he was murdered before the Mountain knew about their money getting stolen.'

It shouldn't have been like that. You were a team; you were professionals; you went over the evidence, weighed it up. Personal emotions shouldn't come into it, or scoring points, or getting tired and pissed off. Personalities shouldn't come into it. And pigs would fly. Personalities always came into it. All the same, it shouldn't have been like that. There had been an edge, too much of an edge, and it had come mostly from him, the gaffer, the man in charge who shouldn't let it be like that; and just when he'd thought the two of them were getting on better.

It was a relief to see Sandy Torrance standing by the door, his glance searching round through the smoke and movement. Going over and over the same ground did no good. He put up a hand and waved to catch Sandy's attention.

'Is that eighty shilling? You want the same again?'

'Sit down, Sandy. I'll get them. What do you want?'

'No, let me.'

And he was off. Half-way up out of his seat, Meldrum let himself drop back. He watched his prospective son-in-law work his magic at the bar. No matter how many people were lined up, Sandy seemed to get served quickly. Meldrum hadn't drunk with him often, but each time it was something he'd noticed. Watching now, he saw the same thing happen. He was tall, that helped. Thin, though, and not one to push himself forward. When Meldrum first met him, he'd had rings in his ears, and a dressing over the wound where the one through his nose had been torn out during a demonstration. Not that he was political, probably even less so than Meldrum himself. Wounded by Cupid, he'd been on the demo because it had been organised by Betty, who was, oh indeed she was, political. Rings gone, all tidied up to be a student teacher, he should have blended into the crowd but had still got his two beers in quick time. Maybe it was because he seemed more alive than other people. There was a kind of glow about him. And, decided Meldrum who liked him, he had a hell of a nice smile.

'Poor student like you. You should take a drink when it's

offered,' he remarked ungraciously as his pint was pushed across.

'I'm a *good* student,' Sandy said.

'You were a good art student,' Meldrum said.

'Water under the bridge.'

'Or you wouldn't have got that scholarship to Italy. You must think about what it would have been like.'

Sandy shook his head. 'No. That would be a waste of time.' The thing was he could say something like that without affectation or a trace of self-pity.

'It was a good plan. While you were away, Betty would have finished her honours year.'

'I'd have missed her,' Sandy said. He was frowning, but suddenly smiled. 'Now I don't have to.'

'Could you still go?'

'What?'

'Could you get the scholarship still?'

'What's the point of asking that?'

'Because I think you could be a bloody good painter. I don't like to see you throwing it away.'

'And I don't know why you're going on about it!' The frown back, the boy was staring at him half-way between amazement and anger.

So Meldrum told him what he was going on about and, over his protestations, insisted on driving him back to their flat so that he could tell Betty as well.

On the way, despite deciding he should keep off the subject till they got there, when he broke the silence he heard himself asking, 'What's it like?'

'The College?'

'Training to be a teacher.'

It was odd how if you were held up at the first red light, the rest caught you in turn. He put the car into gear as the lights changed, and headed along Melville Drive towards Marchmont.

'It's all right.'

Stubbornly offered, the stock phrase made unintended a kind of admission. Meldrum hearing it knew he had to bring this off or he was only torturing the boy with hope.

Sandy said, 'What about your day?' From a different kind of man that could have been aggressive: to hell with probing how I feel, let's talk about you. How was your day? But Sandy couldn't help a little snort of laughter as if at a joke, and one more on him than Meldrum. 'Sorry. I know you don't talk about your work.'

Had Betty told him that? It wasn't true, not entirely; there had been a time when he'd talked about it to Carole. 'This afternoon,' he said, 'I was in the middle of a discussion with my sergeant, a kind of argument, when a policewoman came into the office. I'd asked her to check on whether this witness we want to interview was being hidden by his grandfather. She'd questioned the servants – this is country mansion, not the Pilton, we're talking about – and they swore there was no one staying in the house but the old man. But, being a smart girl, she'd left a contact number, just in case. And she'd got lucky – a phone call claiming the guy we want to talk to is staying with the grandfather after all.' Right turn second past Tollcross; he ducked his head to check the numbers of the closes. Pulled in and stopped. 'We're going up tomorrow to find out.' He switched off the engine. 'See, who says I don't talk about my work?'

Going up the stairs, Sandy said, 'It sounds like an exciting day for you tomorrow. I'll look forward to hearing what happens.'

'Well, thing is,' Meldrum said reluctantly, 'it's kind of confidential.'

'Thought it might be,' Sandy said, laughing as he opened the door.

It started well enough. Betty was pleased to see him. Leaning over the swell of her belly to kiss her cheek, he felt a flood of protective affection for his strong-willed, argumentative daughter.

Half an hour later he was infuriated by her unreasonableness.

'Have you asked Mum about this?' Cheeks flushed, she stared across the table at him. The microwave gave its three-note warning and Sandy got up.

'I just got the idea this morning.'

Sandy put the dish in the middle of the table and lifted the lid off with a cloth. He passed a big spoon to Meldrum. 'Help yourself,' he said. 'It's pasta and tuna.'

'But your mother would agree with me,' Meldrum insisted. 'She's said before now, I should sell the house.'

'No, she hasn't,' Betty said. 'She's told me at least there she knows you're somewhere decent and comfortable.'

'I'd be better off in a flat. The garden's too much for me.'

'The garden looked fine the last time I saw it.'

'When was the last time you saw it?'

'Not that long ago . . . I just happened to be out that way.'

'When was that?'

'Does it matter? You wouldn't have been in. I know you're not staying there.'

Sandy said something then, and they ate and even talked for a bit about something else. It wasn't finished, though.

He took it again from a different angle. 'I mean we owe practically nothing on the house. Compared to when we bought— Prices are ridiculous. Don't worry, I could give you enough to see the pair of you through for a year or so – and I'd still have enough for a decent wee flat.'

'Half of it belongs to Mum.'

'Well, I'm talking about my half. Jesus Christ! Do you think I'd try and cheat your mother?'

And that was them off again.

Later, in the car outside Harriet's, engine and lights switched off, he couldn't muster the energy to open the door and get out. Watching the rain inch down the windscreen, taking the time to himself before he had to go upstairs, he sat going over it. The idea seemed so right to him that he still felt there must be some better way he could have found to put it. Better certainly than blundering into asking, 'You don't want to be a teacher, do you, Sandy?' Or: 'Maybe you don't want to remember, but I've heard you talking about how good a painter you were going to be.' Or: 'I know about teaching. It's not easy. It takes up your energy. For somebody like your mother, that was right. It was what she was born for. But don't tell me, you're going to come home after a day's teaching and paint.' Or, oh God!: 'I don't want you looking back and blaming the baby.' He had made a hash of it.

Didn't matter how well you had meant, what you were left with was the hash of it.

Only the thought that Harriet might be looking down into the street wondering what was keeping him, got him out of the car to cross the street and climb the stairs with weary legs.

CHAPTER THIRTY-TWO

'I'd lay you odds General Gardiner is in the Mountain. One of their old guard. You can't tell me it's impossible,' Henderson had insisted.

No, you couldn't say it was impossible. You could say it was irritating because it wasn't an impossible idea. You could say that not being an impossible idea meant all kinds of new things had to be considered; which wasn't irritating but, for some reason, had produced a flush of something close to pure rage.

'For fuck's sake,' he'd said, 'don't you ever give up?'

Fortunately, that was the moment at which Mary Preston had knocked on the office door. She'd been given the job, after the visit they'd paid to the General following the discovery of Bellman's body, of going back up and finding out from the forester's wife and her daughter whether the General had anyone staying with him. If she did it straightforwardly as a police enquiry about the grandson being there, Meldrum had told her, he was almost sure she would meet resistance, perhaps even be lied to out of a sense of loyalty to the General. The thing about the country was that too many jobs depended on too few big houses. People grew up with the habit of cautious deference. Her best plan would be to offer them some harmless cover that allowed her to ask questions, but didn't come too directly at what she really wanted. The trick would be to let them gossip, and hope for truth slipping out incidentally, so much as an afterthought or aside they might not even notice how much they had given away. All very well, in theory; but she'd got nowhere.

'But all the same,' she'd said, 'I had a feeling.'

She had used as her excuse for visiting them a survey into the need for signs to indicate a 30 mph limit at the approaches to the nearby village. It had worked like a charm. She'd got a cup of tea, and a history of accidents, the latest a coach hitting the gable end of the old school-house, all caused by vehicles going at speed through the village. At some point, the question of the availability of work locally, its scarcity especially for young people, had come up naturally. There had been some self-satisfaction and comfortable laughter at the discovery that the mother not only had a job but had found one also for the daughter. Smoothly enough, too, that had led to how much work must be involved for the pair of them in such a large house. That was the point at which things had gone wrong. Perhaps she'd gone about it clumsily, or perhaps trying to make sure just meant you couldn't avoid asking one question too many. She'd suddenly found the mother being very positive about the General living alone in the house. Just him – apart from Robertson, who looked after him. Isn't that right? she'd kept asking, and the girl kept agreeing. But when the mother's attention was off her, the daughter stole anxious glances at the policewoman. By that time, it seemed to Mary Preston that the original excuse for her visit had worn too thin to worry about. When she produced the contact number, 'in case there's anything you want to tell me', she gave them not any local number but police headquarters in Edinburgh, and that had been done deliberately to put on the pressure.

All the same, hunches weren't evidence, and that had been that until yesterday when the phone call came, a young girl's voice asking for Mary Preston.

Now as Meldrum drove north, he amused himself with the thought of how alike the two of them were, Henderson beside him and the policewoman in the back. Young and ambitious and smart. Other things being equal, they had the world at their feet. Must be a nice feeling.

'Pity we couldn't have got a search warrant.' Henderson broke his silence.

'Not without talking to the girl,' Meldrum said. 'And if she checks out, we won't waste time. We'll head straight for the house.'

'She will,' Mary Preston said. 'She didn't have to phone me, sir. I'm sure she's genuine.'

As she leaned forward, he caught the faintest trace of perfume. He wondered if Henderson had. A side glance showed him looking dour as ever, staring ahead preoccupied with whatever calculations he was making. Pity. A nice perfume, too; not sexy, more like clean, fresh and, oh, not too obtrusive: a smart girl. Henderson could do a lot worse.

Somehow he'd got the impression from her that the forester's house was actually in the village. Following her instructions, however, they went through the one-blink-and-you'd-miss-it place, two larger houses like paired bookends bracketing a dozen or so mean cottages. About quarter of a mile on, she directed him into a road that came at once to a building of dressed stone seemingly about one room square and too small to be inhabited till you noticed the curl of dark blue smoke out of the chimney. From there the road turned into an unpaved track that bounced the car on its suspension. They went by a paddock with a mare and two foals grazing and a notice on a post, DON'T FEED THE HORSES. He was going to ask how much further, but the track swung up to the left and they were into a wood. Rhododendron bushes, once tended now spreading wild, bulked dark on a bank. Undergrowth choked a path on the right between the trees. Light filtered down on the track ahead. It felt as if they could be a hundred miles from people, instead of ten minutes from container lorries thundering north. What happens, he wondered, if you meet a car coming the other way? Would there be room to pass?

The forester's house was an anti-climax. They came round a corner to be confronted by a grey-harled two-up two-down box that could have been transplanted, complete with satellite dish fixed on the front wall, from any city council housing scheme. There was a lawn at the side with washing poles and a dug patch for vegetables, but not a flower in sight. As they got out of the car, Meldrum got a glimpse of a face watching from a downstairs window before the curtain was tugged across. The rain had gone off, and drops of water could be heard dripping from branches in the stillness.

'Not very cheery,' Mary Preston said.

'Cheery?' Henderson measured the word and found it wanting. 'We're lucky there isn't a halfwit playing the banjo.'

'I saw that film,' she said.

Meldrum led the way across the wet grass to the front door.

As he approached it opened, and the girl looked past him to complain, 'I thought you'd come on your own.'

'Hello, Claire. This is Inspector Meldrum, I told you about him, he's my boss. Are you on your own?'

'Mum's away up to the General's. I pretended I was sick.'

Claire Macpherson turned and stepped before them across the narrow hall into a room overcrowded by a three-piece suite and an enormous television set.

'You didn't say to your mum then about phoning me?'

'No! You said nobody needed to know it was me told you!'

Meldrum judged her as about seventeen. Round face, big eyes and cheeks red with excitement, not a bad-looking lassie; and not stupid he realised and chided himself for being surprised.

'When you were here before,' she said a number of times. Determinedly she addressed herself to Mary Preston, acknowledging the others only when they asked a question, as if trying to keep the policewoman bound to the promise no one would need to know it was she who had informed them about the return of Alistair Bellman.

'He wasn't staying, when you were here before. So there wasn't any reason for Mum to tell you he'd been there and wasn't that long away.'

'Had you been told not to mention he was staying?'

'No, not then. But I just knew it was him you'd come about. And I thought she should have told you. And so when he came back, I didn't want Mum to get into trouble.'

'He's staying in the house now?' She nodded, looking at Mary Preston, not at Meldrum who'd asked the question. 'How long has he been there?'

'He was lying in his bed when I went in to dust round on the Monday morning. He got a right good laugh at me. You nearly jumped out of your skin, Claire, he said. He hasn't done anything wrong, has he?'

'We just need to talk to him,' Mary Preston said.

'He's always been nice to me. I know he's got a temper.'

'Does he lose his temper a lot?'

'I didn't say that!' She glanced indignantly at Henderson, then went back to speaking to the policewoman. 'Robertson — you know? The General's man? — he's a dirty old devil, always looking at me. I can sort him out, I'm not frightened of him. It just . . . sometimes it gets me down. I was making up one of the beds, and I got touched, I hadn't even heard him come into the room. So when I came out I must have been upset, and Mister Alistair was there and he gave me one look and then he went in and he gave the old swine hell. This was before, the time he was visiting before. I really like him. I don't think anybody could help liking him. I wouldn't have rung you, I feel really bad about it. It's just that I don't want Mum getting into trouble. And when the General said not to tell anybody, it didn't seem right.'

'The General said you weren't to tell anybody about Alistair staying with him?'

'He didn't say anything to me. But Mum warned me. Nobody was to know.' And went on in the same breath, 'Would you like a cup of tea? If Mum was here she'd be giving me a row for not offering you a cup of tea.'

She was so busy remembering her manners it took their general refusal to coax her back out of the kitchen. With the door open, Meldrum could see out of the kitchen window. There were two or three trees spaced across the open park of a field, and at its end a car following a lorry along a road and open country beyond that. The deep wood had been an illusion, thin as gauze.

The last thing she said was, 'You won't say it was me?'

In the car Henderson shook his head. 'That was some set. What would you think? Must have been thirty inches, easy?'

'I commented on it when I was here before. Her mother said, Our Tam likes his television.'

'Better than banjos,' Meldrum said.

CHAPTER THIRTY-THREE

T he seven days between the visit to the General's house and the morning of the phone call from Toby Sullivan were fractious. Meldrum had never worked with anyone who got under his skin as much as Henderson. The red-headed sergeant never actually came out and said that they shouldn't have let Alistair Bellman slip through their fingers, but the suggestion hung above his head like a blacked-out speech bubble.

In fact, having a search warrant would have made no difference. They were beaten before they left the forester's house, maybe even before they arrived at it. Beaten, as the General put it, by the country way of life.

'In the country,' he said, warming his narrow buttocks in front of the fire in the the big room where Meldrum had first encountered him, 'there's no such thing as being unobserved. Things don't work like that here. I imagine in the city you can drive around as long as you like, turn up at a man's door and still take him by surprise.'

Meldrum took time to work out the diplomatic answer to that, then as he opened his mouth heard Henderson say, 'Only in the good districts. In the slums they put watchers on the roofs of the high-rises. See a police car and they send a warning. Got mobile phones, everything they need. There's a big profit in drugs.'

Christ! Meldrum thought, and braced himself for the explosion.

The General leaned forward, a little inclination from the

waist, and made a sound it took a moment to recognise as laughter. With two fingers of his right hand, clasped like the beak of a bird of prey, he pecked the air at Henderson. 'Hold on to this chap,' he said to Meldrum. 'It's often the insubordinate ones who turn out for the best. Of course, they have to be broken first and put together again.' And returning a smile for Henderson's frown added, 'Though sometimes all it takes is kindness.'

'Your grandson was here?' Meldrum asked, looking for confirmation of what had been implied, not actually said.

'Packed his bags and left half an hour ago.'

'Do you know where he's going?'

'Doubt if you could catch him. He drives like the devil. Or is that stupid of me? You could send out a message. Get your people to look out for him. Tell me, I'm interested, would that be going too far? After all, you haven't accused him of anything, have you? Could you get them to stop him as if he was a criminal?'

'Maybe not this morning,' Meldrum said, 'but I could now.' To Henderson he said, 'Use the phone in the car. It would help if we knew what kind of car your grandson was driving, sir. And which direction he was headed.'

The General shook his head. 'I didn't wave him off. Not my style. You could ask Robertson, but you'd have to wait till he comes back.'

'Did he go with your grandson?' Meldrum asked sharply.

'Why on earth should he? No, he's off on an errand for me.'

'Young man on his own, travelling fast, probably too fast. Say we'll get a fuller description as quickly as we can. Assume he's heading south.' And added, as Henderson made for the door, 'Check with Preston if anyone's attempted to leave while she's been watching the house.'

As the door shut behind Henderson, the General demanded, 'Explain yourself.'

'Sorry?'

'Said you wouldn't have tried to stop Alistair this morning, but you could now. What does that mean?'

'According to what you tell us, the minute your grandson

hears we're in the district he runs away. That doesn't seem like the action of a man with nothing to hide.'

General Gardiner turned his back, stretching out his hands as if to gather the warmth of the flames. 'If he hadn't left today, it would have been on impulse tomorrow. He doesn't plan ahead. He has a restless spirit.'

'That's not quite how you described it earlier, sir. Country ways, didn't you call it? We were spotted, and because of that he left in a hurry.'

'Tell you what,' the General said briskly, 'why don't I show you around while we're waiting?'

He opened each door in the long passage that formed the spine of the downstairs area, stepping back, waving Meldrum a step or two inside and when he came out closing the door behind him. In spite of a satirical silence being maintained during all of this, Meldrum began to feel as he stepped into one musty tidiness after another, swept clean of any sign of occupation, as if he was being shown round a museum. Standing just inside the dining-room, he felt as if an ornamental rope should have been looped as a barrier between him and the oak table and the twelve high-backed chairs with their faded brocade. At the end of the corridor, where it widened and a curious half-turn revealed a stair, the General stopped abruptly. Instead of going up, he chopped the air in a gesture of annoyance or apology and led all the way back to the front door to inspect a small cloakroom – 'Everywhere, eh?' – then returned to the rear of the house, passing and repassing prints of horses and uniformed men, for a look into the kitchen and pantry.

Except that he hung the briefest of explanations on each area – 'Robertson's quarters,' 'My bedroom,' 'Old dressing-room' – upstairs was just the same, as if life had been tidied away into drawers and cupboards out of sight. If Robertson's sitting-room was more individual, with slippers in the hearth and a set of woodcarving tools on a side table, there was an odd resemblance between the uncluttered plainness of the bedrooms of master and man. The open book by the General's bed was one difference; the other, a faint smell of old age in Robertson's room.

'Another spare bedroom.'

The woman making the bed looked up with a smile. She was in her forties, with the same wide eyes and red cheeks as her daughter.

'You know who this is?'

'I haven't met the gentleman, sir.'

'Tell him who was sleeping here last night.'

Her smile faded into a look of uncertainty.

'Is that all right, sir?'

'There isn't any reason why you shouldn't.'

'Mr Alistair. That's the General's grandson.' She looked at the General as if for some indication what this was about, and getting none offered Meldrum with the faintest touch of defiance, 'He's a fine young man.'

'Your daughter's not with us today?'

The change of topic disconcerted her. 'She wasn't well this morning. I explained to Mr Robertson. He said he hoped she'd be back tomorrow, and I said I was certain sure she would be.'

'I'll tell you what,' the General said, 'leave up here just for the moment. I'm sure you could find something to do in the kitchen.'

'I did the kitchen first thing.'

'Even so.'

Flustered, she gave a final tug to straighten the bedspread and went out.

Going downstairs, the General remarked, 'Nothing in this life is ever certain.' Something appeared to have put him in a better humour. As they came into the passage, Robertson appeared from the direction of the front door.

'Sent Macpherson round the back, sir. He should be waiting in the kitchen.'

'He's got his wife for company,' the General said amiably, and smiled at Robertson's look of surprise. 'Must be wondering what on earth's going on. We'll give them a bit of time to worry about it. Set me up a whisky and a tray in the study. When you've done that, tell him he can take her home. Work out whatever's due, and he can collect it on Friday after you've been into the bank in Stirling. I don't want to see her face or the girl's near this house again. If he wants to know why, tell him to ask his daughter.'

'Biscuits or oatcakes, sir?'

'Oh, biscuits, I think. I'll show out the Inspector.'

In all the trekking back and forward, the door opposite the dining-room had been ignored by the General. Meldrum got his eyes fixed on the handle of that room, which approached as slowly, it seemed, as if he waded through water. He wasn't even thinking about it, not until he took it in his fist, concentrated instead on hiding his anger at the way the Macphersons had been treated.

'Everywhere, didn't you say?' He pushed the door open, stepped inside and pulled up short in astonishment.

Chaos. There were books open face down everywhere, on the long table at the side, on the desk which sat in the window, even pushed in on top of volumes on the shelves that rose ceiling high on either side. Papers as well, piles of paper, and pamphlets.

Behind him, Robertson said, 'Here! This's the General's study! Nobody's allowed in here!'

'Get out!' he heard the General's thin bark, but when he looked round the order was being given to Robertson, who had followed them in and was beating a hasty retreat.

'Nobody includes that fool.' The General pushed the door over, almost not quite shut. 'Now we talk about search warrants and illegal entry.'

'I misunderstood. I thought you indicated I should go in. Because you'd said everywhere, you see.'

'*Now* we talk about a letter to your superiors.' He swung the door wide. 'Time to go.'

Meldrum didn't move. As well be hung for a sheep as a lamb. He asked, 'Why did your grandson leave the army?'

'I told him, get out if you must.'

'So he left because you told him to.'

'No, he bloody well did not. He turned up to ask me if I'd mind if he resigned his commission. Do as you like, I told him. It's not my army any more. No wars to fight.'

'So if you didn't tell him to, why did your grandson leave the army?'

'To spite his father,' the General said. 'Same reason he did most things.'

Partly to fix it in his own mind, Meldrum had gone over it for the two of them on the way back to Edinburgh. When he'd finished, Henderson had said, 'Hates his father stuff again. Do you think he realised he was putting the boy in the shit?'

'Whatever he is, he's not stupid.' He'd thought of the explosion of books and papers in the room no one was allowed to enter. 'You should have seen that study of his. Unbelievable.'

'You didn't see what kinds of books they were, sir?' Mary Preston had asked from the backseat.

'I didn't exactly have the chance.'

'*Mein Kampf* and *The Protocols of Zion*, I expect,' Henderson had said.

Stopping any fugitive on the description of a young man driving too fast would have taken a lot of luck. Even with the addition of the car details obtained from Robertson, it was a long shot that hadn't come off. Alistair Bellman seemed to have mastered the trick of vanishing off the face of the earth.

It was a long week that came to an end with the phone call.

'I got a postcard,' Sullivan said. 'It doesn't say anything much. Just wishing us luck in Nepal and saying he's sorry he can't be there as well. Not signed – but I'd recognise old Trey's handwriting anywhere, seen it often enough. There isn't an address or anything. Thought, all the same, I should let you know. Views on the front, usual postcard idea. Funny thing is, I come from Lincolnshire.'

'He's in Lincolnshire?'

'Sorry, no. The card came from the other one, that's what I meant. Not the Lincolnshire one. The other Boston.'

BOOK SIX

The House in the Woods

CHAPTER THIRTY-FOUR

A fterwards for Meldrum it was voices in a wood.

'Mr Thomas Bellman is on vacation. It wouldn't be possible to see him.'

'I have no record of his vacation destination.'

'Mr Nathan Bellman? Have you an appointment? One moment, please.'

'Mr Bellman isn't free. What is the nature of your business with Mr Bellman?'

'His son's dead? Where? But Mr Bellman only has one son!'

For the first time the surface cracks. She comes back

'Mr Bellman can't imagine why you would bring him that information.' Surface fixed again, smooth-polished and hard as basalt.

'What's your room like? I've never been in a hotel room where you can touch all four walls at the same time.'

'The NYPD will listen, but they won't break down any doors to make him see us.'

A voice behind him asks: 'Do you have a dinner suit?'

'What the hell – Braaten? What are you doing here?'

'I was going to eat till I saw the menu. Couldn't you find anywhere better? And this must be Mr Henderson, isn't it? We spoke on the phone.' As they shake hands, Meldrum can see it's a meeting of minds.

'If Alistair Bellman isn't involved with the Mountain, why

else has he run here? And if he is, where else would you expect me to be?' Braaten says.

And again: 'We know Alistair went to Nathan Bellman's office. The name Bellman caused a stir. But our informant was relying on office gossip second-hand, she wasn't even sure who he saw or if he saw anybody. But we know that was the same day his Uncle Thomas suddenly decided to go on vacation.' Who does Braaten mean by 'we', Meldrum wonders.

'We don't need all this Mountain stuff to complicate things. We've got the paperwork to set up his extradition for murder.'

'He wouldn't come just because they were related. The family was split after his father's marriage. He has to have another reason.' That's Henderson, eager as the Norwegian to counter Meldrum's scepticism.

'First we have to find him. With his uncle, wherever he is. Or on his own. How are we going to do that?' And Meldrum gestured around, not at the shabby diner but at the unthinkable sprawl of a continent beyond.

'Why don't you ask his Grandfather Nathan?' asks Braaten.

'If you can get us in to see him, we will.'

'No, tonight, I mean. In about, oh, an hour and a half. That's where the dinner suit comes in.'

Voices.

CHAPTER THIRTY-FIVE

Since Braaten had borrowed it at short notice, depriving someone in the Embassy of the wine and nibbles, Meldrum could see it would be ungracious to complain that the dinner suit didn't fit. It was all right across the shoulders, but short in the sleeves.

The bald man with the purple bow-tie and the Australian accent was complaining about Hollywood. 'Those people aren't sincere. I was leaving the studio when this guy came out of the executive suite. "Don't tell me," he says and puts his arm round my shoulders. "I recognise this man! It's an honour," he says. "I admire your work enormously!" We're all human, I walk out my feet aren't touching the ground. Then my agent Tony, whom I've known since we were at school together, says, "I can't believe he did that. Before you arrived, I told him I was lunching with you. He asks me, Tell me what's he's done. So I go through your films – and he's going, no, don't know that one, no, don't know that one." Believe me, that's typical. The way someone will say, no, and without losing a beat say, yes, if someone more important round the table is positive. You ask them, Do you think that would be a good idea? Answer: Does a bear like honey? Eh? What the fuck does that mean? Is that something out of the Yiddisher joke book? It's a town that kills you with hope.'

As they moved away, Braaten said, 'If he's trying to raise money, he should have learned that joke book he's talking about is the one they use in this town.'

In the next room, the pictures were bigger, but as far as
Meldrum could see no one was paying them any attention
in here either. He twitched his shoulders irritably and asked,
'Couldn't you have found someone with longer arms?'

'Not anybody junior enough to be bullied into lending his
dinner suit.'

'Are you sure the old man's coming?'

'He's practically the guest of honour.'

Nathan Bellman was a major patron of European art. Norway
and Sweden were in Europe. QED. The exhibition sponsored
by the two governments had taken over the gallery.

By Meldrum's calculation, they'd been at the preview almost
an hour. One of the things about short sleeves, they made it
easy to check your watch. When he looked up, he didn't need
Braaten to tell him that Nathan Bellman had arrived. The
bustle of attentiveness just this side of sycophancy helped,
but mostly what did it was the heavy body, shoulders carried
a little forward so that he walked like a boxer. Apart from what
looked a foot less in height than John Bellman's six four, this
eighty-year-old was unmistakably the father of the man with
Gregers Kielland at the restaurant table in Oslo.

Quarter of an hour later when they attached themselves to
the entourage, courtesy of Braaten's nod to the Norwegian
third secretary, something had been said to the little man
that more than confirmed the resemblance. One meaty hand
clenched round a glass, the brows gathered, heavy lips drawn
down at the corners, he looked every bit as much of a bully
as his elder son. All this was targeted at the Australian film
director.

'You think there aren't any poor Jews? I started out working
in a tailor's shop – one of a chain of shops owned by a guy
when he came to this country slept under the counter for five
years. And the manager, this particular shop I worked in – he
was a Jew, a Jew who couldn't make or keep money. Know
what happened to him, what he did? He set the shop on fire!
Drunk and smoking on a Sunday morning. He was a salesman
though. Only offer them a choice of two suits he'd tell me. Just
two – pick one or the other. And I got pretty good at it. But I
tell you – you don't have to believe me – I didn't like making

some poor woman buy that way – I did it, but we sold on credit
– what those lousy suits cost them! But I was a good salesman.
Only thing, I couldn't tie a parcel. Brown paper and string. And
always I'd get it shapeless, a mess. Those poor people going
out with a suit that just about fitted – and a sleeve hanging
out of the parcel! And they'd say, Thank you! I swear, they'd
thank me. It doesn't do to think about how weak people are. I
love this country. Learned that from my father. I'd have been
an America Firster –' he poked the Australian in the chest –
'if they'd've let me join, that is.'

He had a voice like a buzzsaw, the kind of voice that would
have been hard to interrupt, not that anyone in the group
tagging along showed any inclination. 'Is that a photograph?
I was at Mapplethorpe's last exhibition in New York. At the
Whitney Gallery. *And* at the last birthday party he threw
for himself. Gregory Hines, Sigourney Weaver, Prince and
Princess Michael of Greece, Tom Armstrong, of course, and
Mary Boone and the Earl of Warwick. Everybody in town
was there, well, he'd photographed most of them – some
of them with a bullwhip stuck up their butt. I tell you I'm
doubtful about photography being real art.' Even while you
said to yourself, Who the fuck cares, Meldrum thought, you
couldn't help envying somebody who could talk on like that,
sure people would listen. Or maybe that was just the taciturn
Scot in him. 'Press the button enough times and there's a
chance you'll get lucky. The big photographers get a chance
to photograph big people – or they're crazy bastards who take
chances with SM or going off to the wars. For myself, I'd
as soon look at Mapplethorpe's arse as at one of Mr Patrick
Lichfield's duchesses. Just don't call it art.'

Under cover of the laughter at that, Braaten moved forward
and said something to Bellman. Bending down so that their
heads almost touched, he spoke too softly to be overheard.
There was no problem, though, in hearing the rasp of the
buzzsaw in response: 'Outside, you bastard!'

As they started to follow him, one of the officials caught
Braaten by the arm and spat out what by his expression was
the same description. It didn't sound any more complimentary
in Norwegian.

As they wound through the crush towards the exit, Meldrum asked, 'What the hell did you say?'

Braaten smiled. 'I asked him if he really didn't know his two sons were laundering money for the neo-Nazis. Or if the profit was so good, he didn't want to know?'

In the car, Meldrum sat watching the back of the chauffeur's neck and left the talking to Braaten. The buildings went by on either side; crowded pavements; a neighbourhood of small shops; trees like a park, two joggers wearing bandanas; neon signs again as if they were making some kind of circuit.

'No money would make me deal with an anti-semite. I hate those bastards.'

'There aren't any anti-semites in the Mafia?'

'I tell you I never heard of these people.'

'This is an operation Thomas ran, and you knew nothing about it. Is that what you want us to believe?'

The old man was silent. As he sighed, Meldrum caught from him a heavy sweetness of aftershave.

'You telling me Tommy and John been in touch all this time, all this time?'

And that was what hurt, it seemed.

'John did wrong in marrying outside his religion. Cutting him off, I did the right thing. But I was far worse hurt by what I did than he was. I told him I'd never speak to him again, I thought I was on my deathbed. I had TB. I got better, I felt my faith had pulled me through. Only time I ever heard from my son since, he sent me a card the day of my wedding. His mother had been dead five years – so my second wife was a gentile, who can tell how the heart moves in a man? I won't tell you what that card said, I'd be ashamed for him. The truth is, I always loved him more than he loved me.'

As a professional, Meldrum admired the way Braaten picked up on that. 'I'm sorry your son John is dead. But if you know where Tommy is, you have to help us to find him. These Jew-haters want to kill him too.'

It wasn't Braaten's fault that it went wrong.

Nathan Bellman leaned forward and tapped twice on the glass. The car pulled into the side. 'Get out.'

When they had, standing bewildered by the suddenness of it, they saw the glass of the window roll down.

'They kill him, they save me the trouble. After what he's done, he's not my son any more.'

The old man didn't raise his voice, but the darkness inside the car meant they couldn't see his face.

The car slid away, silent as a boat from a night pier.

Christ! Meldrum thought, looking around him.

'It was worth seeing him, don't you think?' Braaten said. 'Like a dinosaur. It was interesting.'

'Do you know where we are?' Getting to the point, keeping his voice calm out of self-respect. Where the *fuck* are we? We're in the dark. On foot in *New York*! In *dinner suits.*

'No idea.' Braaten looked around vaguely.

Skyscrapers leaning towards one another with clouds drifting across the narrow spaces between and papers blowing in drifts thirty floors above the street. Store-fronts and crowded pavements and advertising. A residential district of grey stone buildings six storeys high with awnings and doorkeepers. Not so classy brownstones with people sitting on the steps. None of Meldrum's earlier images of the city had been anything like this. Behind them there was a length of blank wall, across the street there was more of the same interrupted by a high chainlink fence. Warehouses. As they began to walk, ahead of them steam came up in curls from the street.

A taxi.

Like water in the desert, he wanted to see a taxi.

He took a deep breath. 'Interesting or not, it didn't get us any nearer finding Thomas.'

'Don't worry,' Braaten said. 'I should have told you. I have a contact.'

In this city people lived down where the trains were. Maybe if you let yourself look down into one of the gratings as you went by, you would see a white face grinning up from below.

'He knows where Thomas is?'

How calm he sounded, the way a Scottish policeman should

sound. He congratulated himself. You're a hell of a man, Meldrum.

'No,' Braaten said. 'But he knows a man who knows where he is.'

CHAPTER THIRTY-SIX

'Lot of things to see in Boston,' the black man said. 'Once this is over, you steal some days to yourself before you go home.'

'Ben's a booster,' the leathery man, who was driving, said sardonically.

The two had met them at Boston airport, where Meldrum had arrived with Henderson and Braaten. Irritated by the Norwegian's refusal to answer questions, Meldrum had left him to sit beside Henderson and taken the third ticket which put him across the aisle by the window. Planes like toys on the runways as they took off, the New York skyline on the left, boats heading for the docks, condominiums set in a line by the shore, over the sea, into the clouds. He'd passed the journey listening to a man in the seat behind trying to sell hydrographic equipment to a German. The man had a deep voice and said everything loudly and with emphasis. The German spoke very softly, too softly to hear, but then he was buying not selling.

'Back in the Eighties,' Ben said, twisting round so he could talk to the three of them, 'this place was about ready to collapse taking Massachusetts with it. Over there! See that NOW HIRING sign? Those signs are everywhere, and not just in the restaurants and department stores. Telecommunications, you name it, healthcare, biotechnology. This city is motoring again.'

'This city,' the leathery man said, 'has freeways designed by

Mr Salvador Dali. Look at what's going on here – lanes coming at you from the left, from the right. They come up from under you, they disappear again. If Paul Revere had used freeways to get out of Boston, we'd still be paying taxes to King George.'

His name was Ray Finewater.

'That an Indian name?' Henderson had asked as they were shaking hands at the airport.

'Sure. By way of a Polish *shtetl*.'

'His grandfather's father was Big Chief Fiddler on the Roof,' his partner had said.

Now Ben Miller was saying, 'You'd love Quincy Market.'

'Tell him you've got a castle in the middle of your town,' Finewater said.

'We've got a castle on a rock,' Meldrum said, laughing.

Henderson said, 'And a palace.'

'In Oslo,' Tore Braaten said joining in, 'we have a palace has somebody living in it.'

Now they were all laughing. God knows why, they'd just met. Maybe it was because the others felt the same tingle he did from an instinct telling him there was action ahead. Maybe it was because this Ben Miller and Ray Finewater were easy to get along with. Maybe it was because they gave an impression of competence, and the five of them he assumed were in the same profession.

'I take it,' he said, 'Tore's been liaising with your people.'

'Which people would that be?' Finewater asked.

Braaten gave a little cough. 'They're FBI,' he said.

'Working for Uncle Sugar,' Finewater said.

Miller twisted round again, showing a lot of very white teeth. 'Ray here is so old, he was working for John Edgar before I was born.'

'I met Mr Hoover,' Finewater said, emphasising the *mister*. 'And his good friend Mr Clyde Tolland.'

'Don't start,' Miller said, sounding as if he meant it.

'Bonnie and Clyde.'

'Mr Finewater,' emphasising the *mister*, 'is disillusioned. He doesn't give a fuck for anyone. I, on the other hand, have bigger ambitions than calculating my pension entitlements.'

'Invest your money right,' Finewater said, 'you don't need to worry about the size of your pension.'

Maybe the good nature had been just because they were moving, leaving the city behind, Meldrum thought. He made himself sit back and relax. For what it was worth, he trusted Braaten and hadn't any choice but to hope he was right in believing the two Americans could lead them to Thomas Bellman. If they couldn't, Henderson and he might as well give up on finding Alistair. If this didn't work, they'd save the taxpayers money and go home. In the meantime, it was out of his hands and that was oddly soothing.

He'd listen to Miller and Finewater and watch the country-side go by until they got to wherever they were going.

CHAPTER THIRTY-SEVEN

The three of them came out of the hotel, walked across the grass and round the long bar and restaurant extension on to the road. They turned left away from the road they'd come in by and found themselves walking up between large houses and a hill slope with a fence in front of it. Looking through the fence, Meldrum saw a bird sitting on a dead tree near the top of the slope. It was big and he was about to ask Ben Miller what it might be, when a car came racing up the road, forcing them into the side. There was no pavement, of course. Exercise in America was golf or jogging, you could get arrested for walking. Or was that only in California? What the hell was he doing in a country where he didn't even know the rules for going for a walk?

Ben Miller said, 'We should have gone up to the head of the lake with Tore and Ray. I don't think walking up this road's going to be much fun.'

Henderson stopped. 'Let's go back and try the other way.'

There was a man by a car in the driveway of the nearest house. He stood with one hand on the roof watching them. Without moving his gaze, he reached down with his other hand and took hold of the handle of the door. Then stood again, not getting in, just watching.

Meldrum saw that Miller had noticed the man. He said, 'You should go over and tell him you're the law.'

'If I put my foot on his property, he might just reach a gun out of the car and shoot my black ass off.'

Henderson was already making his way back down the hill.

Without looking round, he said, 'It's not your arse he can see.'

They started after him. Behind them, they heard the car door open and close.

'Nervous people.'

'Nervous country,' Miller said. 'He probably thought I was Louis Farrakhan.' He glanced across, and after a moment gave a low chuckling laugh. 'You don't have any idea what the hell I'm talking about, do you?'

When they came round the other side of the hotel and got a view the length of the lake, Meldrum broke stride just to look. Miles of still water, blue under the blue sky, the air warm today though the trees on the hills and their reflection along the fringes of the lake showed red, gold and yellow, the colours of the fall. From the plane as they came in, he'd seen a carpet rolled out towards Canada as if in the whole of New England there was nothing but trees. It was an extraordinary sight, coming from a country where forests had been in retreat since the time of the charcoal burners.

Miller chuckled at his sigh of pleasure. 'Not just nervous, goddamn beautiful too.'

'I wouldn't swap it for Loch Lomond,' Henderson said.

They began walking on the grass that ran along the edge of the water.

'I was just kidding about that guy back there shooting me,' Miller said. 'This isn't Alabama.'

'You come from Alabama?' Henderson asked.

'Hell, no! I'm from Boston.' The denial was forceful and automatic but, the words out, at once he directed a frown of suspicion at the red-headed sergeant.

'That's right. Biotechnology and all that stuff,' Henderson said innocently. 'I forgot.'

Needling wasn't something Meldrum did, and a remoteness he wasn't even conscious of had always stopped people from taking liberties with him. Giving or taking, he didn't see the point of the exercise. In particular, needling a stranger in a strange land didn't strike him as a good idea.

Before Miller could respond, he said, 'What about Ray? Is he from Boston too?'

'No! He's from Arizona. Not an Indian. He's a fucking cowboy.' He grinned, good humour restored. 'The meet was fixed for today. But when Ray double-checked, this is at the airport before you guys landed, the contact had made himself unavailable till tomorrow. So we had time on our hands. That's why I was suggesting you guys could fit in some sightseeing. You see how that burned Ray up?'

'Is the contact coming here?'

'Hell, no. This is Ray filling in the time somehow. You watch, tomorrow we ride all the way back. Be nice if you thought this was some high-power Bureau shit to avoid surveillance. Pity he didn't have time to fix it so we could change cars.' Miller chuckled. 'Old Ray certainly doesn't like admitting there's been a fuck-up.'

The path came to an abrupt stop at a high fence that ran from the lake up to the road. Another evidence walking wasn't to be encouraged. They stood for a while admiring the view. Ben Miller, doing the booster bit, talked about how people came from all over to see the trees, birch, maple, oak, white ash, pine, spruce, fir, change colour in the fall. Henderson said he knew that. Meldrum, who hadn't, said nothing. For him as an ex-carpenter hearing these names there came unbidden to memory sheens and grains and the variety of ways wood offered to resist the cut.

Back in his room, reflected light shimmered across the walls and ceiling. The hotel was a long one-storey structure that hugged the shoreline, making the illusion if he could lean out far enough he just might trail fingertips in the water. There was a tree like a willow outside and sitting by the window felt like sheltering under its branches. He watched the lake darken as the afternoon wore through and afterwards couldn't recall any one of the things he had thought about.

At dinner Braaten and Finewater talked about salmon and trout fishing. They'd found an interest in common, Meldrum thought, and then from something Braaten said he wondered if they might have known one another before.

Perhaps in some overhang from the mood of the time he'd

spent alone, in the bar afterwards Meldrum drank a little recklessly, which wasn't his way. They drank beer and worked their way patriotically in turn through the bar's offerings of Scotch and bourbon.

'How many guys do you think are in the IRA?' Miller asked. 'I read an article there's only about two hundred with guns. Just imagine if the English army could get those guys out in the open to fight them, eh? And the army could ask the navy and the airforce to pile in, right? I mean if they felt they needed a little help.'

'Since when did you get to be a big fan of the Irish?' Finewater asked. 'You never hear the Micks talking about who ruined Boston?'

'*They* ruined Boston,' Miller said amiably. 'Before that it was Cabots and Lowells. You ever been in Ireland, Jim?'

'Yes,' Meldrum said, 'just once.'

'Jim's like me,' Braaten said. 'Neither of us much likes being away from home. Even if home isn't perfect. A poor country can't get rich quick without some of the old values disappearing. Ask the Arabs. Hardy simple sons of the desert one minute, Cadillacs the next and the princes getting lorryloads of malt whisky delivered over the border. Those Bedouin tents got to be pretty comfortable. Same thing with our Vikings. There's some gold-plated longships floating around.'

'Like the one your Mr Svensen's aboard,' Finewater said.

But Braaten frowned and sheered off that. '*Hame drauchtit.* You know that expression?' He looked expectantly at Meldrum then Henderson. 'There's a Scots folk singer who is also a scholar in Old Norse. He taught me that Scots expression. Isn't it wonderful? Not just homesick, but pulled back. Maybe northerners love their home more than other people, eh? Who else would have them?'

'East west, hame's best,' Meldrum produced after a moment's thought. He wasn't a great one for poetry.

In the way of such things it was turning into a longer session than any of them had set out upon.

Towards the end, Miller was saying seriously, 'This guy told me when he was a little kid at school in Nigeria, the teacher told them Mungo Park discovered the Niger.'

'So he fucking did,' Henderson said.

'Think about it. Mungo Park discovered the Niger. David Livingstone discovered the Victoria Falls. I said to him, did the kids in your class accept that? We were children, he said. If the teachers told us, it was so. They were the teachers. And in the books, it was there.'

'In black and white,' Henderson said.

'Have I shit in your hat and pulled it over your ears? I don't think so.' While Henderson thought about that, he continued, 'It was only when we were older, he told me, it occurred to us. Hey, we said, *somebody* must have been here first.'

Some time after that, Henderson was explaining, 'Went across to the hotel for a drink on my own. My father was working on his car. Amazing stuff, you got these old cars, looked great, take them into the paint shop every so often, they don't rust there, that's the point. Like the roofs, big barn my father built to work in, and here he wouldn't have been allowed, it would've fallen down – but there he didn't have to build it for snow loading or to take slates, that's the point. Stubbies or tinnies – that's the choice. Beer in little bottles or tins. The bottles come in a plastic cooler. Lay your money on the counter – when you want another beer, take the bottle out of the cooler, barman comes over, gives you another and takes your money, puts the change back. Just places for drinking, women aren't welcome. I went over for a drink – did I say that? Locals at the bar, in shorts, bare feet, nobody wears shoes there much. It was my last day. And he wouldn't come for a drink, that was the point.'

'Who?' Miller asked. He was the only one by that time who was listening with any real attention.

'My father.' Henderson rubbed a hand over his mouth, and looked round. 'Jesus, I'm away to my bed.'

Miller, irritated by Finewater, wasn't long in following him. Finewater, drinking more and showing it less than any of them, had arrived at the opinionative stage.

'When I was in the San Diego office, I'd listen to the news. Local, then they'd cover the day in California. Then the guy would say, And now for the world news. In New York today . . .'

Braaten laughed and got to his feet, 'I've heard you tell that
one before.'

'Sweet dreams,' Finewater said. 'You ready for another
one?'

Meldrum sat on his own studying the ring left by a glass on
the coaster until Finewater came back with a drink for each
of them.

'You know those right-wing bastards set up an e-mail
hotline for any bitch wanted to claim Clinton had been
in her pants? Keep up with the Paula Joneses and they'd
pass it on where it would do most damage. What the hell is
happening to this country? You get the liberals talking about
the Defence State – saying Truman in 1950 took us down
the road to a one-party-with-two-names state. Eisenhower's
military industrial complex, right? But what can we do? We're
the dog soldiers. And when that conspiracy shit gets into the
heads of right-wing crazies it turns into something else. It
turns into talk of ZOG – the Zionist Organised Government
in Washington – and I know where those guys are coming
from, I know *exactly* where those guys are coming from. I
can hear the rattle of trains going across Arizona to the death
camps. Then the bastards blow up a federal building and kill
women and children. It's not hard to go after them.'

Meldrum sipped his whisky. With one finger he turned
the coaster round and back again. 'I went to bed with this
woman.'

'What?'

'She was only twenty-one. It was wrong.'

'Sounds good to me.'

'My wife always said if she ever found I'd been with
another woman it would kill something between us. Trust,
I suppose.'

'So don't tell her.'

Meldrum thought about that, puzzled. 'No, no. We're
divorced.'

'That works all right.'

'But I live with this other woman Harriet.'

Finewater gave a broad grin, counting the women on his
fingers – one, two, three.

'And it's the same thing. There has to be trust.'

'I haven't known you for long,' he said, serious now, 'but you're a good man. I can tell these things.'

Meldrum pushed vehemently at the air in denial. 'I'm not good, if this is goodness, what's inside everybody else?'

Their glasses were empty. It was time to sleep.

'You should stop beating up on yourself,' Finewater said. 'That's what life is, a grotesque business, doesn't mean we shouldn't try to be good, just that we should also expect something less than the best from ourselves and something like the worst from other people. Life's a comedy, my friend. Enjoy the joke while you can.'

CHAPTER THIRTY-EIGHT

Miller had got it right. In the morning they did drive back south all the way to the other side of Boston. None of them felt much like talking, and Meldrum sat watching the route signs go past. Interstate 93 south to Route 3 and to US 6 and along the length of Cape Cod to Provincetown at the tip of the scorpion's tail.

They walked up off the harbour on to the main street. It was very bright and clean and the air smelled of salt. Passing a side street, Meldrum glimpsed a tower high enough to suggest a spectacular view from the top out to sea across the dunes. He had a vague notion the Pilgrim Fathers had landed here or somewhere nearby. He wondered about asking Finewater, but they were on serious business and he didn't want to be laughed at for behaving like a tourist. I'll get a book when I go home, he thought, and read up about it. Meantime, I'll look round and try to remember. It was easy all the same with the shops and restaurants and pleasant bustle of the street to be touched by a holiday mood. Finewater cut suddenly across the traffic. Taken by surprise, the other four turned and followed him. Like a flight of geese, Meldrum thought, and smiled to himself. The FBI man walked into a lane between two shops, a little blunt space with a house-front set across it. When they made to go after him, Miller stopped them.

As they stood waiting, he felt a touch on his arm and turned to see Henderson grimacing at him. 'Bloody hell, eh?' the sergeant said.

What? He almost asked him what was wrong with him, almost told him Finewater had the right to talk to the contact on his own if he wanted to, almost said they could do nothing about it anyway – but saw Ben Miller was grinning at them. The sergeant nodded around at the street. And then he saw.

Saw the plump man with the coiffured white hair being led by two poodles on a lead. Saw two young men hand in hand. Saw two women hand in hand. Saw the older man with the younger man. Saw the same again. And again. Fuck! He'd been walking around with his eyes shut. For a policeman, he was slow on the uptake about that kind of thing.

'Hope you ladies aren't shocked,' Ben Miller said.

It crossed Meldrum's mind to tell him that Edinburgh had been briefly the AIDS capital of Europe. Sometimes, though, patriotic pride, however natural, had to restrain itself. Anyway, that had been due to shared needles rather than sodomy.

Finewater came down the steps of the house frowning.

'Don't ask!' he told Miller, and set off at an angle back across the street, moving with a long loping stride that looked leisurely but was hard to catch up on. He went into a shopping arcade and half-way down it, before they did. The shops looked like the usual kind of tourist bait you'd get in small seaside towns at home, maps in one window, confectionery in another, pottery in the next. The window of the small shop Finewater entered had whips and leather masks and books about domination. He was out almost at once.

'Where is he?' Miller demanded. 'Do you know where he is?'

'He left a message,' Finewater said grimly. 'Wasn't that obliging of him?'

He didn't say any more until they were out of town and back on the road.

'This isn't what I expected.' He spoke to Braaten, now in the front seat beside him, but loudly enough so the others could hear from the back. Remembering what Miller had said about Finewater's dislike of admitting fuck-ups, Meldrum thought this might be as close to an apology as they were ever likely to get. 'We've been watching the Bellmans father and son for a long time. Old Nathan was our main interest, of course.

But then about a year ago, there was a sudden connection between Thomas and the Reverend Doctor Esau Maclean. As a clergyman, you Scots guys might think he was a joke. The "Reverend" came from one of those Southern colleges where they teach you how to wear shoes and then do a Bible class. But the name caught our attention. Wouldn't you say?'

'You could put it like that,' Miller said. 'The name certainly caught our attention.'

'As one of our home-grown fanatics, he comes pretty near the top of the list. He's got connections to every militia outfit in the country. He was one of the delegates three years ago when our extreme right-wingers had a summit meeting with their European friends. And he was one of the group that did the getting-to-know-you trip round Germany in '96. And now we'd tied Thomas into him. Tell you, it came at us from left field. A New York Jewish businessman like Thomas Bellman with a Yale law degree. That isn't your obvious candidate to shoulder his squirrel gun and go hunting a recipe for a fertiliser bomb.'

'Money now, for a New York etc., that's different,' Miller said.

'We made Svensen pretty fast,' Finewater said as if there had been no interruption, 'and that took us to van Aken and the rest of that bunch. But we were slow to get on to the brother in Scotland. By the time we did, he was dead. With what you gave us, Tore, and what we knew ourselves, by then we had a pretty good idea what had been going on. Kielland was dead. Locascio was dead. One killer for the three of them, and we weren't in any doubt he was coming for Thomas.'

'And Alistair,' Henderson said. 'Alistair wouldn't be here with his uncle if he wasn't part of the money-laundering scam.'

Meldrum caught Finewater glancing at him in the rear mirror, but said nothing.

'Maybe,' Finewater said, 'but it's Thomas we want.'

'So why didn't you arrest him?' Meldrum asked.

'That isn't the plan. We're going to use him as an informant until we've enough to put the Reverend Doctor and his rats' nest behind bars.'

'What would the charges be?'

'Suppose we start with conspiracy against the government of these United States, and go on from there. And before you ask, we had already moved in on Tommy Bellman. I'd offered him protection against the Mountain's killer. He promised me he had documentary evidence – and tapes, he claimed he'd taped more than one conversation with Esau Maclean. It looked good. He knew he was on the death list, and there was nobody he could trust – except us. He wasn't in what you'd call a strong bargaining position.'

'So why isn't he tucked away somewhere instead of running about the country?'

'He kept dicking us around because of his father. Telling us we had to find some way of handling it so his old man wouldn't have to know what he was into. I'd had enough. It was shit-or-get-off-the-pot time, but then he disappears. Our theory is the nephew spooked him.'

As he finished speaking, Finewater began to brake. Going along, Meldrum had been conscious of the scatter of buildings on the near side and the dense mass of trees on the other. Now, looking past Braaten in the front seat, he saw flags and an hotel sign and then, as the car swung in between the gates, the long building set back behind a rise of cropped grass.

'This it?' Miller asked.

'He'd better be here,' Finewater said.

As they came into the lobby, the receptionist behind the desk looked at them and reached under the desk. Pressing a button for her boss, Meldrum decided. He thought it couldn't just be because they were five men, and wondered if it was the speed they were moving. Maybe she could smell they were the law. Maybe it was the look on Finewater's face.

He spoke to the man who'd appeared behind the desk, and then was off again. He led the way along the side of a dining-room, then they came out into an open space. There was a tree in it growing up almost to the glass roof. The middle of the atrium was taken up with a swimming-pool. Near it a couple on a white bench were sipping drinks. On this side as they made their way along beside the pool, what were presumably the guest bedrooms sat behind patios, each divided from its neighbour by partitions and just wide enough to take a little plastic table and two chairs. Finewater knocked at one of the bedroom doors, waited and got no answer. He turned and scanned the people in the pool. There were two children in the shallow end, and a man and woman swimming up and down together. The man's arms swung over in turn and when his head came up out of the water his hair stuck to his head so that his skull shone white under the dazzling light from the glass roof.

They followed Finewater to the area at the rear where the toilets were and a door marked GAMES ROOM.

When the five of them went in, they crowded the small space. Straight ahead, a line of lockers and male and female changing-rooms; to the right, an open arch with a sign for a sauna; and on the left an area with weights and exercise machines.

It was empty except for a man in a swimsuit riding one of the bikes. He had thick white legs and was driving the pedals round very fast.

He said, 'You're not supposed to come in here with your outdoor shoes on.'

'How would you like me to punch you off that and hang you by the balls on the weights machine, you fat fuck?' Finewater asked.

'That might be fun,' the man said.

Using his open hand, Finewater slapped him off the bike. As much as the force of the blow, it was the noise of it that shocked. The man sat on the floor with his legs sprawled apart staring up at them with wide eyes.

'You were supposed to meet me. Yesterday you were going to tell me where Bellman was. I hope for your sake you know where he is today.'

'He's at his house.'

'You think I don't have people watching his fucking house?'

'Not his house in New York!' The man bumped backwards, pulling himself with his hands scrabbling at the floor. 'Jesus, what's wrong with you? His house where the party was last night! It's only ten minutes from here!'

'Party?' Finewater asked. There was a world of menace in his disbelief.

'That's why I put you off yesterday. If you arrested Tommy, there wouldn't be any party. I told myself, what difference can a day make? Let him have his party, if it's to be his last. Tommy's always had to be discreet, because of his father. He can only be himself when he's with friends.'

Finewater glanced round in irritation as Henderson asked, 'Was his nephew with him?'

'Alistair, oh, yes. Such a good-looking boy.' He recovered a kind of forlorn jauntiness. 'Uncle and nephew. I was quite sceptical.'

'Who's in the house now?'

'I was about the last to leave. Some of us stayed over, but mostly everyone left after breakfast.'

'So Tommy and Alistair are there now?'

'Not Alistair maybe. He was getting on Tommy's nerves talking about going for a drive. After a party, Tommy just wants to sit around.'

Being naked except for the thong trunks didn't seem to bother him, as Finewater marched him back through the hotel. 'Tommy and I go back a long way,' he explained as they went. 'The first time he came to my apartment, I woke up in the middle of the night. I went for a leak and there he was in the john. I tell you, he jumped a foot in the air. Believe me, I never saw a person look so guilty. I told him, I'm not your mummy, sweetheart, you want to pee in the sink, pee in the sink. Later he said, That was such a moment of relief for me, I tell you it meant more than sex.'

At the desk, the receptionist gave Finewater a small single-sheet map from a pile on the desk.

'Cross the highway,' she said, going through her routine while her eyes darted from one face to the other. 'And turn left, then down this road to the sea and back along here. Look. I'll mark it for you.'

Finewater reached out and took the yellow highlighter away from her. He looked over the man's shoulder as he marked the route and put a cross where the house was. When he'd finished, Finewater took the map back from him. He looked at it and shook his head. 'All that stuff you gave me in New York about how much you loved Tommy, you stupid fuck.

So now he's on his own in a house in the middle of the woods.'

They came out through the hotel gates fast, squeezing between a car one way and a truck the other. As Finewater took the left off the highway into the woods, Meldrum was astonished to see on a little white building not much more than an overgrown hut a sign that said PSYCHIATRIC HELP. At full moon did the forest people slip out of the gloom under the trees for a consultation?

The road was narrow and Finewater was pushing hard. They passed two or three houses, New England style, one storey high, porches with pumpkins and a witch hanging from a rafter, wood the colour of licked salt, set into the trees as if just enough space had been cut out to fit them in.

'Here?' Finewater said.

'Should be,' Miller said, in the front seat again, with the map spread out.

Next moment they all saw it, a house like the ones they'd passed, just where the cross on the map said it should be.

Finewater hit the brake and they swung in and slammed to a stop. They sat looking at the house. Something Meldrum couldn't put his finger on wasn't right. 'No car,' Miller said. No car, too late, no need to hurry. Meldrum wasn't in any doubt they'd find the house empty. 'Shit,' Finewater said. 'Let's go see.' Just as he spoke, the door opened and a tall man stepped out and started down the steps. He wore a plaid shirt open at the neck and jeans and had a jacket slung over his arm.

'That Alistair?'

'No!' Meldrum said.

'It sure as fuck isn't Tommy.'

Meldrum looked at Braaten at his side, the only one of them who'd seen the Hunter.

'It could be. I don't know!'

As they piled out of the car, Miller and Finewater and Braaten had their guns out. They ran at the man, the two Americans yelling, 'Get down! On your knees! On your belly! Down, down, down!'

Even as the man threw his hands up, and folded down on his knees and then down on to his belly in the grass at the foot of the porch steps, Meldrum knew it was a mistake. It was the look on the man's face, a purity of shock and bewilderment. All of them must have caught it for though Miller went through the procedure, patting him down for weapons, the urgency mysteriously and at once had leaked out of the situation.

'He lifts his head,' Finewater told Miller, 'blow his brains out!'

The rest of them followed him into the house. Party time. Bottles on tables and on the floor, some of the glasses still half full, a dish of white powder, a couple of pipes. But no smell of tobacco, Meldrum noticed, nice that these people took care of their health. They scattered into the kitchen, the bedrooms, looked in cupboards, checked out the yard from the windows. As Meldrum went into the big bedroom at the back, Henderson said to him, 'Some cunt's been enjoying himself,' and he saw all the sheets were thrown off the bed on to the floor. The kitchen table was covered in used plates and bowls. A loaf sat on a board with the knife stuck into it half-way through cutting a slice. The wreck of the *Marie Celeste*. Everybody gone. Party over.

The man was still lying face down, with Miller at a cautious distance keeping the gun on him. At Finewater's command, he rolled on to his back.

'I don't have any money,' he said. 'But I live just ten minutes' walk from here. I'll give you whatever you want.'

Braaten said, 'Get him to stand up.'

The man rolled on to his side and then scrambled up, everything awkward as if fright meant he had to consider each movement before making it. Meldrum went through Braaten's description he'd memorised of the man in Vigeland Park who had killed Locascio. Nothing about it seemed to fit. The man in front of him had long yellow hair and round glasses: things easily changed, but they belonged with the long face and the light-timbred voice with its educated accent. He seemed all of a piece.

Braaten said, 'The height, that could be ... My man in Oslo was taller, maybe taller.' He bit his lip. 'I couldn't be sure.'

'Is this a case of mistaken identity?' the man said. 'If it is,

I can prove who I am. My name is Bob Rankin. I work in insurance in Hartford. Can I put my hands down?'

'Nobody asked you to put them up,' Miller said with a grin.

Rankin reached into a back pocket, then into the other one. 'I don't have my wallet. God, I'm a fool. What would I need my wallet for? I mean, all I did was walk up to a friend's house.'

'Where is Tommy?' Finewater asked.

The man looked at him then at the rest of them. 'What do you want him for?' He seemed to have got some of his courage back.

'FBI,' Finewater said.

Bending forward at the waist, Rankin peered at the identification. Instead of reassuring him, it seemed to produce a fresh bout of panic. 'Am I under arrest?'

'What for?'

'I'm not really like this, I'm married. I don't take drugs. None of that stuff was anything to do with me. My employers—'

'Shut up! Listen to me. Listen! Where is Tommy?' Finewater asked the question slowly, spacing the words out.

'He and his nephew took the car. I don't know where they've gone. Tommy told me to shut the door behind me when I left.'

'You know Francis?' Finewater asked.

'Was he at the party last night? I got there late when things were getting to be quite . . . informal.'

'Francis says he was the last one to leave this morning. When he left, Tommy and his nephew were on their own.'

'Maybe that's what he thought. I was sleeping at the back. I must have been the last one to wake up. I'm not accustomed – I don't take drugs. When I went through, it was just Tommy and Alistair. They were arguing about going for a drive.'

'Where you say you were sleeping?' Miller asked.

'The big one in back. Why?'

'What did you do with the blankets?'

'Blankets?'

'Blankets, off the bed, what did you do with them?'

'Threw them on the floor. Is that what you mean?' His voice

went shrill with anger. 'Because I woke up and realised I was in his bed. Is that what you want to hear?'

Finewater studied him for a moment, then he put his gun away.

'Tell you what, Mr Rankin,' he said. 'Far as we're concerned, there isn't any need for your wife or employer to hear anything about this. If your identification checks out, we'll be happy to forget you were ever here.'

Since he'd walked up, Miller put him in the front seat of their car. Henderson volunteered to drive it, which let Miller keep an eye on him from the back seat.

'Find a place to park out of sight when you get back,' Finewater told Miller. 'Don't want Tommy frightened off.'

They watched the car back out and go in the direction of the sea, then went into the house to wait. It was almost two in the afternoon and simultaneously they discovered a ravenous hunger. While Finewater stayed to watch the road, Meldrum went into the kitchen with Tore Braaten and rummaged through the fridge for something to eat. They found a jar of pickles and settled for cold ham on slices of bread. Meldrum bit off a corner while Braaten made coffee. The bread was getting to be a little hard but was tasty enough.

'Geese,' Braaten said.

A skein of birds were flying over the trees at the back of the house.

'Do you know what Kierkegaard said about geese? He said defying public opinion was like being trampled by geese.'

When they went back through, it turned out that Finewater was familiar with the name. 'Ah, Mr Kierkegaard.' They'd pulled the couch over so they could sit low and see out without being seen. By the time he'd eaten his sandwiches, Meldrum was tired of Mr Kierkegaard. He edged off the couch and ducked away from the window. Coffee in hand, he wandered into the kitchen. No geese in sight. Rough grass ran out from the house to where the trees started. In contrast to his country of thinned woods and parks, they seemed to him very close and tight-packed. He thought of the houses they'd passed, shingles a strange grey-white as if the wood had leached salt out of the air. Fat orange pumpkins scattered across a front yard. A witch hung aslant on a porch. Hallowe'en country. But where were the children? No face at a window. Visitors not welcome. Little wooden houses shut in on three sides by forest.

He shook himself and was turning away when he heard it. A human voice in a single strange call. When he ran out of the kitchen, Finewater was coming down the hall. 'What was that?'

Braaten was crouched in the back bedroom. He looked over his shoulder at them. 'I think you should see this.'

As they came forward, they saw the pools of glistening blood.

'I'm so damn tidy,' Braaten said. 'I lifted the blankets to put them back on the bed.'

They found the body huddled close against the outside wall. Tommy Bellman had been tortured with the knife before it killed him. Forensics established that later. The Hunter had dropped him from the window when he heard the car, and thrown blankets over the blood on the floor. They worked that out later too, and the speed at which he must have moved and the great strength it had taken. Then he'd opened the door and, jacket over his arm, sauntered down the steps to meet them.

It didn't take them long to get there; he hadn't lied about the nearness of the house he'd been using. It stood at the edge of a steep drop where a broad wooden stair went down in two flights to the beach. He'd broken in through a porch at the rear and it looked as if he might have spent more than one night there. The grey shutters were up for the winter, and that made it hard to understand why Miller and Henderson hadn't seen at once that something was wrong. Their car was slewed across the drive, facing away from the ocean. However it had been done, he'd got Miller into the front hall and cut his throat.

It had been Meldrum himself who found his sergeant. He'd been crouched beside tyre marks in the soft earth inside the gate – wide tyres, a large car, must have had to swing off the path to pull round Miller's car – when the feeling came that he was being watched. Slowly he looked up. His heart bumped in his chest. Inside the car, on the driver's side, there was a white face, head oddly angled as if for a better view of him.

He could see that it was a dead man before he recognised it as Henderson, and he had to come up close to the glass before he saw that the strange tilt of the head was because the neck had been broken.

For all the searching that came afterwards, the Hunter left no trail by which they could follow him. Perhaps he was back in Germany again, gone to ground among the people he had served. Perhaps he was elsewhere in Europe, west or east. The only certain thing was that he had escaped into the woods and from there to the vast anonymity that lay beyond.

CHAPTER THIRTY-NINE

V oices.

Miller: I got sand in my shoes as a kid going down the beach to look over at the Kennedy place. Across the water the compound looks no bigger than a row of toy bricks. And there's Bush's house at Kennebunkport. He isn't there much, but that's the house he nominated to be guarded. You can see the Secret Service cars sitting all the time just inside the gate. And you pass on the road, watch what you say. They have an overhead satellite it'll pick up a whisper. Before you go home, I'll show you the sights.

Finewater: You're like me. Had a bellyful. Put me out to grass, Mr Hoover. Please. Any time you're ready. I don't make any secret of feeling that way. But the FBI is too smart to believe what you just up and tell it. Bureau has to find out for itself – and I can't get the bastards to bug me.

Braaten: Two men met on the coach to Copenhagen. One asked the other what line of business he was in. Oh, the man said, I deal in tea – I buy chests of it for ten kroner and sell them for nine kroner. Hold it! the listener said, ten for nine? that doesn't make any kind of sense to me. Ah, the man said, but you have to realise *I buy in bulk.* Kierkegaard could tell a good joke.

And Henderson: My father wouldn't come over for a drink, that was the point.

*   *   *

What point? Too late to ask. For Henderson, as things had turned out, there wasn't going to be an afterwards.

WITNESS

W e know the name he used when he first came to Germany (Finewater wrote in his covering note), and maybe – if we can trust the comrades – we have his Russian name, the one on his birth certificate; but for sure we don't know what he's calling himself today, or what he called himself yesterday or who he'll be the day after tomorrow.

We're told he was born in 1961. It may have been somewhere in the Stavropol region; but again that's if we can believe the information we were given. If it's true, it makes a neat fit for Yuri Andropov came from the village of Nagutskaya in that same region, and our man, the Hunter as Braaten calls him, was very much one of the new breed of smart young guys recruited from university when Andropov headed up the KGB. If his birth year is right, he might have been recruited in about '82, when Andropov left the KGB to follow Brezhnev as Soviet leader.

He must have thought that his future from there was straightforward. He belonged to an elite group. No more of that old KGB image as badly dressed brutes in the shadows. Andropov's boys were drawn from the high-flyers, the top graduates with at least one language, and offered not just the large apartments, the foreign travel, the high pay, but a vision of service. They were the last ones in their generation to believe in the Soviet ideal – but then they could afford to. He seems to have been posted to the First Chief Directorate in the new building that had just gone up on the outskirts of Moscow. From there, we can't be sure of the dates. He did

well, and then not so well apparently. It's possible he made
some enemies or one powerful enemy along the way. He was
a fierce believer in country and Party; and there's a hint that
he uncovered some kind of corruption by a superior. Could
be, who knows? But information from the source we're getting
this from never comes without some disinformation mixed in
– even if just for old times' sake.

Bearing that in mind, seems he went undercover for the KGB
in East Germany. This would be maybe late in the Eighties.
He was tasked to penetrate the right-wing groups that were
starting to network even then and build momentum. He got a
new identity – he wasn't a Russian any more, he was German.
Step by step he got himself close to one of the old SS men in
West Germany and then to the top men among the neo-Nazis
in the East. He won their trust by killing to order for them. My
guess is he liked killing; we know he was good at it. So there
he is in deep cover and year by year, then month by month
and at last almost day by day he watches like everybody else
while the process Gorbachev started destroys the world he
believed in. It's from that period we have a copy of part of a
letter he wrote to some girl back home. We've no idea who she
was, there's no record of him ever having married, childhood
sweetheart I'd guess.

The page is torn –

had skiing accident and the hospital believed me. Over
five months, they operated three times. After the last one,
they told me it was no good. They were going to have to take
the arm off. Just before the fourth operation, the surgeon (a
fat Saxon) touched me on the edge of my shoulder and
said, From here, it has to be. But when I woke up, I was
greeted by this smiling Vietnamese I'd never seen before,
who says, You'll be pleased to see you haven't lost your
arm. I was saved because he'd been trained in the Third
World and so massive infection wasn't unknown to him.
He knew what to do.

The letter seems not to have been sent – maybe he wrote it
knowing he couldn't ever send it; wrote it for himself because

he needed to – but since it came to us from a longtime asset in East Germany I'm inclined to believe it's genuine. What had happened to him? It's a guess – but I have reasons for it – that he'd been tortured. Maybe he'd botched a job. Maybe he'd made another of those enemies – he seems to be good at doing that. Or just maybe the neo-Nazis had got tipped off by the KGB he was one of theirs. If that was what happened, he's still alive because the neo-Nazi torturers converted him. Pain can convert a man. On the other hand, he'd lived inside that German fanatic's skin for a long time. If the KGB did betray him, maybe it was because they decided he'd gone native and they'd let his new masters take care of him. The world he came from was gone. What was he going to do in the new Russia? Work as a hitman for some Mafia scum in Moscow? Maybe he'd been converted for a long time and managed to persuade those Nazis it was genuine. Or maybe he fooled them. Information. Disinformation. How could they trust what came out of Russia? There might not have been any hard proof for them that he was KGB. His file in Moscow could have been pulled and destroyed during the period of chaos – say round the time of the assault on the White House.

If he fooled them, he's working for them because there isn't anything he'd rather do more. It lets him kill. One clue, I'm told he despises drink. Figures, it's the curse of Russia. But on occasion (after a kill?) he'll lock himself in a safe house and get drunk for a week.

I don't know how much this will help. But it's just for your eyes; try not to show it around. Remember – before Reagan, after Reagan, makes no difference – nobody is ever supposed to get told anything. Whole world's sick on secrets.

Anyway, my guess is the Hunter's on your side of the Atlantic by now. Looking for Tommy Bellman's nephew.

over from your Papa's old house. I stood on the hill above the village to take a photograph. Sunshine and corn stooks like yellow huts set down on a yellow sheet of stubble. I wanted something to take with me into the new life I had been ordered to take up. But then I thought, if the photograph fell into the wrong hands would it give me away? Would an expert looking at the houses, at the trees, the river, be able to tell not just that it was in Russia but the very place? I thought of those accursed spies in the sky and how every inch of the land of the world could be examined, and I left Russia with nothing that would betray me.

And that's it. If there's any more of the letter we don't have it. Maybe he told her he loved her. For what that would be worth.

BOOK SEVEN

Target

CHAPTER FORTY

'This fellow I was apprenticed to used to do all the farms up at the back of the village – until Sir David took them back. Sir David owned all the land round about where we lived. He was a mean bugger, though. Like I say, I was just an apprentice, and we were on a job at the big house. We had these floorboards up, so I got a saw and cut up the ones we'd lifted. Old boards that were done, no use to anybody. My mother had a coal fire then and so had her neighbour. I had all this wood cut up in bags. Right, I thought, I'll get that in the van in the morning. But next day, there's not a sniff of them. Here, I said, what happened to those bags? Oh, the gaffer says, Sir David's housekeeper had them taken away – they'll go on his fires. Would you credit it? And him a millionaire. And the son's worse from what I hear. What would you make of them?'

Meldrum made of it that Sir David probably enjoyed warming his arse at that fire all the more for knowing he'd had the logs sawed for nothing.

His new sergeant Bobbie Shields was about his own age, which in itself made a contrast to Henderson who'd been thirty at the most. He wasn't ambitious, another contrast; a bulky, pie-and-chips kind of guy who played the accordion in a band and knew how to keep his head down and his nose clean. Meldrum had seen him around off and on for years. Never had enough to do with him to like or dislike him. Unlike Henderson, it seemed he didn't have much taste for silence. Since the beginning of the trip through to Glasgow, he'd kept up a stream of chat; getting on at last to the old standby of how close he was to retirement.

Making it to the pension: another difference from Henderson, it struck Meldrum, and then wanting to get that train of thought out of his head he asked, 'Security guard job, maybe?'

The question was ironical. He'd listened to a lot of this retirement shit in his time.

'Fuck, no,' Shields said. 'Do more work with the band, take the wife holidays.'

'Flute band, is it?'

'Not at all!' he said brusquely. 'For functions! I miss half the engagements because of this job. I tell you, if it wasn't that the son-in-law can stand in for me, I couldn't do it. He's a good musician, mind, or it wouldn't be on. Five in the band, all first-class musicians. Once I'm retired, I can see us spreading our wings. Get a few engagements down south – or abroad even. Wives could come with us.'

The word was everybody liked Bobbie Shields. He was in the masons, which did no harm. Despite the difference in rank, he'd been one of the late Chief Superintendent Billy Ord's court of drinking pals. He was a man with a surprisingly wide range of contacts, and a fund of good stories.

As for example: 'I'm friendly with this guy works in the VD clinic. A doctor, you understand, soul of discretion. But one of the nurses in the clinic has a pal works for one of these fashionable doctors. No National Health, all private. So guess who was in with a dose of crabs? John Brennan!' And getting no response, 'Brennan the lawyer. There's only one John Brennan.'

'Brennan the lawyer,' Meldrum said.

'Body Lice Brennan. Unbelievable, a smart man like that. Probably claimed he got it off a toilet seat. Guess the shape of the seat!' He shaped a backside in the air with his hands.

And at that Meldrum started laughing. He knew he was going on too long, but he couldn't stop.

Sounding like a man wondering if he was being laughed at not with, 'Not that funny,' Shields said.

'Sorry,' Meldrum said. 'I was remembering something a guy

called Finewater told me. Life's a comedy, he said, might as
well enjoy the joke.'

'Finewater?' Shields tested the name. 'He a jewboy? Sounds
like a four by two.'

'No,' Meldrum said. 'He was a Red Indian.'

That proved to be a conversation stopper, for a while at least.
Maybe it confirmed suspicion about being laughed at; maybe it
turned Shields's mind to America and what had happened to
Henderson. If so, he might have been sobered by the idea of
filling a dead man's shoes; or just touching wood and offering
himself the old comfort of lightning not striking twice in the
same place. When he did start talking again, it was about the
Bellmans, and in particular Gordon and his wife Sally, which
was fair enough since he'd hardly had time to read the files. It's
what they should have been talking about all the way, Meldrum
thought, and blamed himself for how indifferent he was to his
new sergeant.

'Nice houses,' Shields said grudgingly. As an East Coaster,
he liked to think of Glasgow as a desert of high-rises.

Penrith Avenue, Meldrum was checking the street names
as they went.

'Giffnock,' he said. 'Businessmen, doctors, lawyers.'

'What does Bellman do again?'

Meldrum glanced at him. He'd already been told.

'He's a financial consultant.'

'What's that mean exactly?'

'A lot,' Meldrum said. 'I'm beginning to think for us it could
mean a lot.'

He waited for Shields to ask why, but the sergeant contented
himself with a grunt. From Meldrum's point of view the reason
for him not being asked didn't matter. Maybe already the man
was wary of him. Maybe he'd always been wary of him.
Meldrum knew his own reputation as a difficult customer. 'You
don't have many friends in this place,' Billy Ord had told him
once. None of that mattered. Not asking was unprofessional.
As far as Meldrum was concerned, if you didn't ask, you didn't
get told. If it was a test, Shields had failed it.

He checked the street signs again, turned right, then left.

The house was, as Shields had put it, nice. A substantial

house, detached, grey stone, plenty of chimneys, capped no
doubt for central heating, trees at the end of the lawn for privacy.
He remembered it from his first visit. What he'd forgotten was
how small Sally Bellman was. When she opened the door, she
struck him as being not so much as five feet tall. Maybe last
time she'd been in high heels. This time she was wearing
trainers and jeans and a sweat-shirt, and she'd been working
tidying out cupboards upstairs. 'Gordon says get Mrs White to
do it,' she said as they followed her through the hall, 'but I hate
sitting around.' Her boy's backside wiggled like a woman's, and
Meldrum watched it until he realised Shields was doing the
same. He remembered Henderson eyeing her breasts; and later
calling her a slag who'd caught a rich husband. It occurred to
him that there might be easier things to be than Sally Bellman
in a man's world.

'Gordon's in the garden,' she said. 'I'll tell him you're
here.'

She pulled open the patio door and went out through the
conservatory into the garden. He wondered if Gordon would
talk to them in this room. It was comfortable with chairs
and couch in green leather, and a painting of the Waverley
paddle-steamer set above the fireplace. For some reason, he
was reminded of the sitting-room in the General's house. A
bland public space. It even had a piano set in the corner;
though, to be fair, that wouldn't be a standard fixture in this
kind of room in the way it would have been fifty years ago.
Perhaps it was there to be played. For sure, not by Sally. Why
so sure? She wasn't the type. Was there a piano-playing type?
Sure, then, because this was unmistakably Gordon's house,
his room; and so, if there was a piano, his piano. Hard, all the
same, to picture him relaxing at the piano of an evening. But
didn't a gift for mathematics go with music? He'd read that
somewhere.

'Taking his time,' Shields grumbled.

No books or magazines lying around. The General's house
had been like that, too. A tidy house that gave nothing away.
It had been half luck, half smeddum, Scots chutzpah, that had
let him force his way into the room no one was allowed to
enter. The General's study. By whatever name he called it, the

grandson would presumably have one of those, some room where he could work when he was at home. Interesting if it, too, was a guarded place. Do not enter. And if you could?

The vivid chaos of the General's study. Had that shown what the real man was?

Through the glass of the patio door and the conservatory, he saw Sally Bellman walking with her head down, coming back on her own.

'Could you talk to him outside?'

Single-file they followed her out and round the house to the side lawn. As if he hadn't noticed their arrival, Gordon went on reaching out in a half circle to draw the leaves rustling and clicking to his feet, the wide springy tines of the rake clawing at the grass. The wet grass. Dry-shod on the path, Meldrum waited, watching him. When he'd finished, no doubt he'd explain raking leaves was a job you couldn't leave half done in case a wind got up; that would more or less do as a kind of apology. Accept it from the bastard and get on with what mattered.

Without looking up, Gordon said, 'If this is about my father being involved in sharp practice with money, I've been all through it and I won't listen to it again.'

'All through it? Not with me.'

'Of course, not with you. These people had some kind of claim to expertise.'

Special Branch. Involved through Braaten? Those bastards, those bastards, he hadn't been told. Those bastards tramping across a murder investigation, arming Bellman against anything he might say to him. Or Serious Fraud. Particularly high and mighty bastards, and, going by their failure rate, incompetent ones as well.

'It must have come as a shock.' The rake stopped. 'I remember you telling me when your father disappeared that he had no money secrets. Not from you, at least. I had the impression you handled his financial affairs.'

'I've been through that. I won't go through it again.'

'Let me make something clear,' Meldrum said. Gordon straightened to listen, looked at him for the first time. 'In my book, money is less important than murder. I don't care who else you've spoken to. I ask a question, I expect you to answer it.'

Beside him, he sensed Shields stiffening at his tone.

Sally said, 'It was really his mother's money Gordon took care of. His father didn't have money of his own.'

Gordon walked away. Meldrum was about to go after him, when he began, dragging the rake, to pull leaves back towards the pile he'd made. Maybe, Meldrum thought, he's done that to calm himself. He remembered his earlier impression of a man determined not to unleash his temper.

Gordon said, 'I've heard it all from your colleagues. They went through everything about the Mountain and their hired killer. If you've come like them to ask why my father got mixed up with Kielland, I tell you what I told them. I can't explain it. I can tell you he had no need to do it for money. My father's financial affairs were uncomplicated.'

'As far as you knew.'

'Ignore my wife. My parents as a couple had a very sizable income. My mother's family were Glasgow shipowners in the days when that meant something.'

'So you see,' Sally said, 'Gordon's father made a good marriage. Your grandfather did too. Old General Gardiner was the one who married into the shipbuilding fortune. For all the way he despises people, he did it as well – he married for money.'

'My wife takes an interest in these things,' Gordon said. His tone was cold not angry. Holding people in contempt seemed to be another family tradition. 'As for my father and mother, his money, her money, neither of them thought like that. They were a devoted couple.'

'The money wasn't tied up in any way? You know, in trusts or whatever.'

'It was held in the Campbell Trust, yes. But my parents lived within their income, comfortably within it. There was no problem with money before my father's death, and there is none now for my mother.' Without a pause, he went on, 'I don't want my mother troubled with any of this. Leave her alone.'

'She struck me as a very strong person.'

'I tell you she's had enough. She may not show it, but she is deeply upset. And now my grandfather is ill.'

'The General? I didn't know.'

With an impatient jerk of the head, Gordon dismissed that. 'The point is, she's not at home. There's no use you looking for her there. She's gone to look after him.'

'I can't promise I won't have to see her again.'

'Why would you have to? They told me you know who killed my father. The same man who killed the others. The man in America who killed my uncle.'

'Not just your uncle.'

'What? Oh, some policemen as well.'

'Two policemen,' Meldrum said. 'But I was thinking of Kielland and Locascio. And if your brother had been there with your uncle, he'd have killed him as well.'

'Why, for God's sake?'

'His job is to kill everyone who was involved in stealing money from the Mountain.'

Whatever Gordon might have responded was lost in a sudden clamour from his wife. 'Alistair probably started it – got his father into it. He's a madman, he'd do anything. He has a terrible temper, a wicked temper. I thought he was going to hit your father – I thought if he starts he won't know how to stop. And he could have got you into trouble. Into danger. You could have been in America.'

'Be quiet. You're embarrassing.'

'You could have been. You've been there often before.'

'Go inside,' Gordon said. 'If you get yourself so excited, you won't be able to make the trip on Sunday. Your unfortunate son will have to do without you.'

She stared at him, then turned and headed back towards the house.

'You went to the United States?'

'On business. I handle investment for American clients.'

'So on these trips,' Meldrum asked, 'you wouldn't have any reason to meet with Nathan or Thomas Bellman?'

'Absolutely not. When my father married, his family cut off all contact with him.'

'But Alistair went to see Thomas in New York. Then they went off together.'

'It was news to me. Don't ask me to explain what my

brother gets up to. But that family are strangers to me. Less than strangers, they didn't treat my father well.'

'You've been lucky then.'

'What do you mean by that?'

'Look at it from the Hunter's point of view. According to the FBI, your Uncle Thomas was certainly taking part in helping to launder the Mountain's money. But they're not at all convinced that he was involved in stealing it. In their opinion, he was too shrewd to risk that. He'd have been satisfied with a fat cut for his services. The investigation in Norway seems to suggest that Kielland and Locascio and your father were the ones creaming money off for their own pockets. But there's also a strong suggestion – this came from Locascio when he was dealing with the Norwegian police – that the "other man", your father, stole most of the money. According to him, he and Kielland panicked – they didn't realise how much your father was stealing. That puzzles me.'

'Why?' A small wind, that came and fell away again, picked leaves off the top of the pile.

'Finding ways to steal money under their noses, that must have taken – what did you call it? – expertise. He wasn't a money expert. Neither was Alistair.'

'But I am. Are you accusing me?'

'I didn't say that.'

'If you did, I could promise you a good deal of trouble. Your colleagues went through the possibility with me. They were satisfied. Don't get into an area you don't understand. You're out of your depth.'

'I agree. I know my limitations. The difficulty is that the Hunter probably isn't any more of a financial expert than I am. He tortured Tommy Bellman before killing him. It's possible he liked doing that – but the other victims weren't tortured. I think he was looking for information.'

Wind through the branches tore off leaves and scattered them on the grass.

'What kind of information?'

'Maybe anything that would help him find your brother. Or just maybe he wasn't sure Alistair was the one he wanted.

Maybe he was trying to find who he should really be trying to kill next.'

Gordon stared at his hands clasped on top of the rake. Dry-voiced, showing no emotion, he said, 'If you do your job and catch him, it won't matter.'

'He isn't an easy man to catch.'

As they left, Gordon had gone back to raking, but the wind was getting stronger and the pile was blowing away from him.

CHAPTER FORTY-ONE

When they got to London, Meldrum's first aim was to see Ruth Bellman on his own.

'We don't want to spend a lot of time,' he told Shields. 'We'll split and get through things quicker. You cover these – I've made notes, given addresses at work and home. I've marked the ones who're supposed to be away on the climbing trip in Nepal. Worth checking they've actually gone.'

Shields propped the list against the teapot and studied it without any obvious enthusiasm, as he piled marmalade on to cold toast. 'What ones are you doing?'

'I'll go and see the sister. She's our best bet. I'm hoping Alistair will have been in touch with her.'

'Should we not both go and see her then?'

'Just do it.' Hearing himself snarl. Not far off losing it.

A great way to start the day.

Yesterday, before they'd left Edinburgh on the last shuttle, he had spoken briefly to Ruth. He'd offered to meet her at the College. She'd said she didn't want anyone there to know her private business. Reluctantly he'd agreed to go to the Grace Pennington Hall.

It didn't look any better on a sunny morning: a great slab of yellow brick studded with mean little windows. As the taxi moved off, he realised he hadn't got a receipt from the driver. Getting a receipt for the expenses claim was supposed to be second nature; but then it wasn't every day you went to

interview a woman you'd slept with. Fucked, as Miss Bellman
had so gracefully put it.

He went up the flight of stone steps and through the swing
doors. The hall's echoing space was empty. No one at the
reception desk. Little wonder they had trouble with theft and
even assaults. He headed straight for the lift and pressed the
button for the fourth floor.

When the lift doors opened she was standing there. Although
she saw him, she took a step forward, as if so primed to hurry
into the lift she couldn't stop herself. As he came out, she was
forced to step back.

'Going somewhere?'

She had on a black cloth coat, very long almost to her heels.
It made her look slimmer and even taller.

'I have to go out.'

'Why?'

She shook her head. He took her by the elbow and began to
walk her back along the corridor towards her room. It wasn't
what he'd intended. The plan had been to get her out into some
public space, a bar, a café, as quickly as possible. Talking to
her anywhere except in public hadn't been in the plan. He
stopped.

'What is it?' she asked.

'We can talk outside.'

She pulled her arm out of his grip. He caught up as she
opened the door of her room.

'I want to get this over as quickly as possible,' she said. 'I've
no time to waste.'

Reluctantly he followed her inside. She stood leaning with
her hands on the back of the chair by the window. She hadn't
put the electric light on and blocking the light where she stood
made the room dark. At his side, he was conscious of sheets
and pillow twisted in a single untidy bundle. A musty smell
of flesh and talcum powder rose from the unmade bed. What
would she say, he thought, if I told her she'd given me crabs?
Laugh probably. Go to bed with a promiscuous student not
over fond of washing, you get what you deserve. He'd had
an itch in his groin, and gone to a doctor. What would she
say, if he told her that the doctor grinning had gestured him

to the microscope and shown him obscenely armed shapes swimming opaque in light? Ask probably if the doctor had thought him a fool, at his age, with his job. Answer, yes. Shaved and daubed: *iron your underpants for a bit.* Behave like a fool, be punished as a fool. What would she say if he told her he thought it likely he'd passed her lice on to a woman called Harriet and, if he had, that she'd lain with an old lover? Shrug probably, and say so what. Herpes. Chancres. Tell him, shit happens. HIV. Think of HIV, fuck's sake. Tell him they'd all been lucky.

'What is it?' she said. 'I told you I can't help you.'

Christ, he hoped they'd all been lucky.

And not least her. Big awkward girl, blocking the light, whose mother had told her pick the rose before it withers. He'd been full of anger and the indignity of self-pity, and now he was only tired, tired to the bone.

Now he just wanted to get this over and get out as quickly as possible.

'You're sure you haven't heard from your brother?'

And she turned a little more from the light. 'I told you on the phone. Can we leave it at that?'

She was lying.

'It's important we find him. Important for his sake.'

'Why can't you leave him alone? He wouldn't do anything wrong. You don't know what a kind heart Trey has.'

He pushed aside the bundled-up sheets and sat on the edge of the bed.

'What are you doing?'

'This is going to take some time. You may as well have a seat too.'

'Please,' she said. 'I can't help you.'

Her voice was thin with anxiety. Simply keeping her here put her under pressure. Where had she been off to in such a hurry when he stopped her?

'You didn't know your brother had gone to America?'

'No, I told you.'

'The first you knew of it was when I told you last night?'

'I said so, didn't I?'

'He didn't tell you before he went?'

'Obviously not, or I'd have known. Christ!'

'So you didn't know he was there?' For an answer, he saw her hands fly up in protest at his stupidity then fall to grip fiercely at the chairback. 'It's just that sometimes a brother and sister are close.'

'We're close.'

'He's older than you.'

'Sometimes only by a year,' she said. 'The way our birthdays fall for three months every year he's a year older than me, then after his birthday he's two years older.'

Big brother, little sister. And Gordon seven years older than Alistair, nine years older than Ruth. Big gaps, when you're a child.

He said it again: 'So you didn't know Alistair was in America?'

'How *many* times? I'll tell you a hundred times. No, no I didn't, no.'

'Funny, with you being so close. Remember Toby Sullivan? Alistair sent him a postcard and he was just one of his friends.'

The postcard was lying at the back of her desk in plain sight. He'd seen it almost as soon as he came into the room. A picture of a white mountain set in a ring of autumn leaves. He was too quick for her, reaching out to slide it from under her snatching fingers. The leaves were named: quaking aspen, basswood, sugar maple, sumac. Fall foliage in the White Mountains of New Hampshire.

He turned the card over. The message on the back was unsigned.

Love you, it read. *Light a candle for me. Or was that a different dream*?

She started for the door. He stretched out his arm and it took no more than that to stop her, at once so that they did not touch.

'That is his writing?'

'You know it is.'

'Your family aren't Catholics?' She gazed at him blankly. 'Light a candle.'

'It was a dream he had. He did parachute training. After he

left Fort George. He told me he dreamed he was in the stick about to jump. And he was almost the last to go. He watched as his friends stepped out and fell. And when it was his turn the chute began to candle—'

'Candle?'

'It comes from a roman candle firework – the parachute half opens and the chute begins to spin – beautiful to watch – but the parachutist is dead. Down into the ground. Smash. And he told me, As I was about to hit the ground, someone was shaking me, Come on! Wake up! And I opened my eyes, and I was still in the plane and we were going to jump.'

He turned the postcard in his fingers.

'Was that why he left the army?'

'What?'

'Because he lost his nerve.'

'For a dream! He dreamed and then he jumped. Trey hasn't been afraid of anything in his life.'

'It must have been the other reason then. Maybe he didn't have a choice. If he hadn't been well connected, maybe he'd just have been booted out. Did the General pull strings? No scandal, no tabloid headlines, so long as he left quietly?'

She sat down, holding the collar of her coat together as if she was cold.

'You've no right,' she said.

But said it with so little conviction, he knew he was right.

'You knew he was homosexual?'

'My father had two diaries,' she said. 'One of them sat openly on his desk at home. When we were little we'd sneak a look inside. Fishing trips and salmon catches. Or a trip to London with a note of the hotel bill and what he had for dinner. Deadly dull. The other one wasn't. It was hidden on a top shelf behind a set of the collected works of Thomas Carlyle. I suppose he thought it was safe there. Certainly, it would have been from the boys. I was only twelve, and I took it to Trey because I needed somebody to help me make sense of it. You could read in the diary that lay on the desk – say, one of those London trips – and then look up the same date in this one. Only where the desk one gave you the price of dinner, this one gave the cost of women he'd bought and what he paid them to

do. Afterwards I blamed myself. When I found out about Trey.
I thought maybe that's what had made him that way.'

'Not a chance,' Meldrum said. 'Doesn't work like that.'

'I know that really. After that afternoon we never mentioned
it. Not until that morning he came to fetch me home for my
birthday party. I was twenty-one – maybe that's why I reminded
him. What diary? he asked me. He'd forgotten all about it. So
you're right, it hadn't upset him the least bit.'

'Did he talk to you about why he'd left the army?'

She nodded slowly. 'We talked about everything.'

Playing hide the sausage with the batman. Or Alistair,
officer-as-god, overawing eighteen-year-old recruits in flight
from small-town dole queues. Alistair and friends.

Toby Sullivan, the rising young publisher at Spion House,
who'd made so much of his smartness in getting out and into
business. Toby Sullivan, who hadn't been able to hide how
much he missed the army; how much he despised what he was
doing in civilian life. Toby Sullivan, who suddenly Meldrum
would have been prepared to bet had come out of the army
not just at the same time as Alistair but on the same deal.
No scandal for the General's grandson. Or his lover. He had
too much of a history with Alistair. No wonder Sullivan had
been panicked into betraying him.

'Damn!' he said. 'I know where he is.'

And by her face, he saw that she did too.

CHAPTER FORTY-TWO

'Used to be council. They were rubbished. Graffiti, broken lifts, vandals. This developer paid the council washers, a steal because they were in such a state. But he wasn't stupid. Did them up, didn't he? Put a wall round – you know, guarding your own territory? I've read up on it. It's human nature, isn't it? You look after your own space, look after what belongs to you, your family, your own kind. Keep the rest of the world where it belongs – outside. Entryphones, got a caretaker. Your friend did himself a favour.'

Alistair had got in touch with his sister the day before. He'd taken refuge in Toby Sullivan's flat, using the key he'd kept from the time they lived together. No one except her knew he was there, not even its owner busy getting acclimatised somewhere south of Everest. She'd gone there the previous night, and would have kept her promise to bring him food in the morning if she'd got up earlier and been out of the Grace Pennington before Meldrum arrived.

Ignoring the taxi driver's short history of reclaimed tower blocks, she said, 'He'll think I told you.'

'If he hasn't done anything wrong, he'll have nothing to worry about,' Meldrum said. Where had he heard that one before? 'What did you talk about last night?'

'Just silly things. Things that had happened when we were children. That's all he wanted to talk about. I don't care if you don't believe me.'

'It never occurred to you to ask where he'd been all these weeks? Or what he was hiding from?'

'Alistair would never have hurt Daddy,' she said.

'All round's come up, since I was young here,' the taxi driver said as he took the fare. 'And it's got further to go.'

The tower block was set back from the road behind a stretch of new-sown grass. A wall of orange brick about shoulder-high had been put up at the front, and there was a fresh-looking sign pointing to parking spaces round the back. That's the second time I forgot to get a taxi receipt, Meldrum thought, as they went into the entrance. The uneasy feeling that had come on him during the journey was growing stronger by the moment.

As Ruth pressed one of the entryphone buttons, Meldrum pushed the door open.

'That was quick,' she said. 'He must have been standing right beside the buzzer.'

'The lock's off. Was it like that last night?'

'No.' And sharply, 'What's wrong?'

'Nothing probably. People do it all the time.'

The tiled hall smelled of fresh paint. There was a corridor going to the left of the double lift, and on the right a flat entrance with a nameplate JOHNSON, and under it a neatly lettered card CARETAKER.

He pressed the buttons for both lifts and asked as they waited, 'Did you see anyone last night? Coming into the building? Or when you left?'

'Nobody,' she said.

Watching the floor indicator, they went up in silence.

As they got out on the fifth floor, she asked him, 'What are you thinking?' but he didn't answer.

The corridor went in a square round the lift shaft, and she turned the wrong way so that they came back almost to where they'd started before she found Sullivan's door. She rang the little bell set into the wood of the frame and then she knocked and knocked again only harder.

'He wouldn't go out,' she said. 'Is this what you were afraid of? Can you knock down the door? Or have you got keys?'

Forms to fill if he did either of those. The caretaker must hold a set of master keys. Form to fill in even if he did that. It was possible her brother was standing behind the door listening; with him gone, might appear. Brother and sister could flee down the stairs while he was coming back up in the lift. Different form for that, different number, different colour. Not a good form to have to fill in.

But not the worst.

'Stay here,' he told her. 'I'll get hold of the caretaker.'

Who might have been out, but wasn't. Who understood quickly, and made no difficulties. As quick as that, they were on their way back up. Brother and sister would have had to get their timing just right, if it had ever been possible for them to make their escape.

'Please hurry,' she said when she saw the caretaker key in hand.

Meldrum knew she shouldn't be the first one into the flat, but as he led the way he heard voices and made the mistake of choosing the only open door. Five heroes landed out of a cartoon sky on the screen facing him. It took only a moment to register the living-room empty. By then she'd found the body. As he came out into the hall, he heard her, not screaming but sucking air in great gasping breaths. He pulled the caretaker out of the way.

She was standing just a step or two inside the bedroom. He went further in, edging to the side until he could see Alistair's face. The pillow under it was red from the wound on his throat.

Like an accusation, Ruth said, 'He's killed himself.'

But it wasn't suicide. Later, a search found the murder weapon wasn't in the bed or near it or anywhere in the flat. Instinct might have told Meldrum that at once, since a knife was the Hunter's weapon of choice.

Anyway, what made the idea of suicide absurd was the way the body had been folded up so that its naked backside pointed at the door. It would have taken a miracle for a man to cut his throat in that position, or get into it after the cutting. It was natural in her grief for the sister not to understand that; or perhaps, in the decorum of her grief, not even to see the two concentric circles in red around the bull's eye of the arsehole.

They were so exact and neatly done that they could only have been drawn after Alistair Bellman was dead.

CHAPTER FORTY-THREE

'The boy who sold *The Big Issue* is dead.'

Habit was a funny thing. The manager of the local supermarket where he'd gone to get food hadn't seen him for months, not since he'd gone to live with Harriet. Yet, instead of asking where he'd been, he took Meldrum's reappearance as a matter of course and without preamble told him about the young vendor.

On his way from the airport, too, it had been habit that had brought him all the way into town and down past Charlotte Square. He'd been going along Queen Street before he realised he was almost at Harriet's, and changed direction to head out to Blackford.

He'd put on the central heating, but the house was cold having lain empty for so long. He put on all the bars of the electric fire and crouched close, so that his face roasted while the back of his neck chilled in a draught. Taking a chip, picking off pieces of fish with his fingers from the half-unwrapped bundle in his lap, he tried to work out why fish suppers nowadays were always a disappointment.

When he started out of sleep, the supper had slipped from his lap and chips were scattered in the hearth. He'd come up out of a dream where he was still married to Carole, and he'd come home late from a case and she was sleeping upstairs and soon he'd go up quietly, careful not to wake her or his daughter sleeping across the landing. As his breathing settled, on automatic pilot his brain started to go over what Ruth Bellman had finally told him.

She had come up from London on the Friday to surprise her parents by being home a day early for her birthday. She'd used her key and crept in, smiling, very pleased with herself, smothering a fit of the giggles. Behaving like a child again, she'd said; but that's what happens when you go home. Before she could call out, she'd heard voices raised in anger, and coming level with the sitting-room had seen her father punch her mother on the side of the head as she fell.

When Alistair collected Ruth the next morning, she told him what she'd seen. She was frightened by how angry he was. But, of course, she'd got out of the house quietly the night before. Neither of her parents knew she'd been there. So it was possible to go through the Saturday as if nothing had happened. For their mother's sake, that's what she persuaded Alistair to do. Drinks on the lawn and lots of laughter. The drinks maybe weren't a good idea. By the time they got to the restaurant at night, the charade was wearing thin.

Sometime after Ruth went to bed, she woke up. Her room was nearest the garage. From her window she saw one of the cars had been backed out and Alistair coming round from the boot and getting in. In the morning all the cars were back in the garage.

That, she'd sworn, was the true account of what had happened that weekend of her birthday. It didn't matter any more, she'd said. Not since her brother was dead.

He half lay in the chair thinking of what had been done to Alistair Bellman. He kept telling himself to get up and go to bed. There had been something else he'd been told that day. It was important. What was it? Then he remembered.

The boy who sold *The Big Issue* was dead.

BOOK EIGHT

The General's Study

CHAPTER FORTY-FOUR

Meldrum was going to the General's house not by right, as to so many before it, but unofficially with an invitation issued by bad luck and passion and simple evil. The case was over. Alistair Bellman had killed his father. Mark the file closed. It told nothing of the beliefs of those who called themselves the Mountain. He had this fantastic image of the General leading him into his study and out of all his books letting him understand why Henderson and so many others had to die.

All the great causes. Not a man given to such thoughts, Meldrum as he drove, with no books of philosophy or versions of history to mull over, could only call to mind fragments of his own experience. Carole had taken him to a meeting at her church once, where a mother of seven with a face the colour of a used dish-cloth had rehearsed a speech she was about to give to some women's conference in France on the right to life. She must have got some part of the argument wrong, for he had heard an odd hiss of breath and looked round to see the priest involved with the campaign gesturing at her, chopping his hand up and down. He'd never seen so much impatience and contempt on a man's face. And once, drinking late at night in Billy Ord's house, he'd heard Billy's pal, the politician from Ulster, explain how the Protestants there were not only in every way superior to the Catholics, but that they were even of a different race and had travelled north by different routes in the lost past. The politician was a businessman and a wealthy landowner, far better educated than Meldrum, who had never found the Mountains of Scythia on a map or read a book on prehistory or a page of archaeology. He knew it was shite, all the same.

And he thought of his daughter Betty, whom he loved and had never been able to talk to. He wished he could protect his grandchild waiting to be born from the badness of the world. He would tell the child, Grandpa doesn't know much, but bad people have been his trade. Tell the child, that the bad always betray, because they hate those who play follow my leader almost as much as they hate themselves. Left or right, black or white, Protestant or Catholic, Muslim or Christian, native or incomer, your country or your neighbour's, the last division and the first is between the good and the bad. If you're going to follow someone, he'd tell the child, bear that in mind. And even then, keep something back. Keep something back, in the centre of you, something they can't touch, the thing my father would have called conscience. Bet that sometimes the good won't let you down. Bet on that, not for any great cause, but just as a way of trying to live decently.

But don't bet too much.

About a mile from the General's house, he saw a man in a field standing head down as if studying the earth at his feet.

After he'd pulled up and reversed back to the farm gate, enough time had passed for the man to look up or move, and since he hadn't it seemed better somehow to walk up than call to him. He climbed over the gate and started up the slope. There was a track from the harvesting and he followed it through the stubble. He almost put his foot into a long drag by the track's edge, like a twist of blue-black tar, only a shape of ears suggesting the rabbit it had been. Nearby among the stubble lay a very clean handful of sheep's wool, teased out like spun sugar and glittering with drops of moisture. White here, black there, an accident of arrangement, without meaning. Except that as he came up to the man the dip of ground in front of them was filled with whiteness, like a drift of snow left from an early storm. Then he saw a pair of small curved bones, clean as if they'd been polished, a shape where the eye socket had been, a pink rag of ear; and so not snow but wool again, which after all made a sort of connection between creatures which had been alive and were dead.

'I don't usually feel the cold,' Robertson said, 'but it's turned bloody cold.'

The General's bodyservant was wearing a jersey, but he was jacketless and without a hat.

'Robertson, isn't it?'

'I know who you are. I mind you fine, tramping about the house.'

'That's where I'm going. I can give you a lift.'

'No.' He shook his head, and Meldrum caught the sweet whisky smell on his breath. 'I'm in no hurry to get back.'

'The General's ill, I hear. I'd've thought you'd want to be with him.'

'Would you?' The question grunted like a dismissal; but there was no force in the challenge. Hardly pausing, he went on, 'Do you know what he said to me? Right out of the blue, he said to me, I go to bed every night frightened in case I don't wake up. What kind of thing's that to say?'

'If you're sick enough, things look different.'

'No, no. This was *before* he fell ill. I was disappointed in him.'

'When did it happen?'

'His laddie Gordon was here. They were in the General's room together and I heard him give a shout. When I went in, he was lying on his back.'

The wind was beginning to pack the sky with cloud.

'I wouldn't stand about here,' Meldrum said.

'You're too young to remember the war. You get some cunts get to my age they want to talk about it all the time. I've never been like that.' Sitting round the table getting drunk in the hotel by the lake, Finewater telling them what some Italian writer said about war; two out of his five listeners dead the next day. What good did talking about anything do? Shit happened. 'Makes no kind of fucking sense, any of it.'

'The only thing worse than losing a war is winning it.'

Curzio Malaparte. Finewater's Italian writer who'd said that. His memory was still working.

'What?'

'Just something a guy told me.'

'Come again!'

'The only thing worse than losing a war is winning it. He read it in a book.'

'Cannae see how he makes that out,' Robertson said.

Meldrum thought of Dachau and the mean-spirited, moral dullard face of Hitler. It occurred to him that the red-headed Henderson must have resembled many of the men of the Highland Division who died in the deserts of North Africa.

'Aye,' he said. 'You could be right.'

The daily woman who opened the door to him looked flustered when he told her who he was. Taking advantage of her dithering, he followed her along the hall and when she indicated the sitting-room knocked himself and went in without waiting.

Willa Bellman was on a low chair beside her father holding a spoon to his lips. The General was propped up with pillows on what was probably his favourite chair, the green leather one nearest the fire. Her eyes widened with shock, but she returned the spoon to the tray with a steady hand.

'It's no use your wanting to speak with my father,' she said. 'He understands what is said, but he can't talk. And since the stroke has paralysed his right side, he can't write either. If he hadn't had help at once, he would be dead. So, you see, you could have saved your journey.'

Like a hidden room in a house, a cell grew and bled until in a moment everything ended in ruin.

'I came to say I was sorry about your son.' Standing awkwardly by the door. Moving forward to stand again. Not asked to sit. 'And sorry your daughter was there when I found him.'

One of the old man's eyes was blurred, as if a veil had been drawn over it. The other, blue and bright as ever, turned its predatory gaze towards the tray. His left hand came out and the index finger like a hooked beak tapped on the air. She took up the spoon, dipped it in the bowl and held it to his mouth. She fed him, tipping as the liquid ran off the spoon.

When it came too slowly for his liking, he sucked and lapped clumsily with his half-paralysed mouth.

'I've told her she was a fool. You took advantage of her distress.'

'Because she told the truth?'

'When they finally give us back your brother, I told her, we'll bury his body. But the body is the least of us. Honour, reputation, the memory we leave behind. When she spoke to you, she took all that mattered of my son and buried it in dirt.'

'He might be alive now,' Meldrum said, 'if she'd told the truth from the start.'

'Why do you have to go on with this? You know who killed my husband and my son,' she said, in words he recognised as Gordon's. 'The same man who killed the others. The man who killed John's brother.'

'The same man for your son and the others, yes,' he said. 'But not your husband. It was dark, but Ruth is sure it was Alistair she saw driving away the car the night his father disappeared. And Alistair as a boy had fished that beat where your husband's body was found.'

Before he could go on, she stood up, blocking her father from his view.

'I want you to leave.'

'And maybe if your husband hadn't disappeared none of the other killings would have happened,' Meldrum said. Stepping to the side, where he could see them both again. 'That's when the scheme to steal the Mountain's money unravelled. That disappearance got Kielland killed. And Locascio. People you don't even know. Tommy Bellman too. And Alistair, it got Alistair killed – so, I suppose, in a way he committed a kind of suicide after all.'

'No kind of suicide at all,' she said. 'Not a murderer. Not a suicide. I won't have you add one disgrace to another for my son. I killed my husband.'

'Because he beat you?' he said, dismissing the possibility.

'You know, not for anything so shabby,' she said. 'Because he boasted about the money he'd stolen. And, yes, he struck me. He damaged everything my father had worked for, and I killed him for that.'

'Look at your father then,' Meldrum said. 'Look at his face. Can't you see how angry he is at your stupidity?'

The General's voice gurgled in his throat.

'What is it, Daddy?' she said.

The General's left hand chopped up and down.

'Did you know it was your father who advised Alistair to go to America?' It was a guess, but the old man let his head fall back. The General couldn't speak, but he could shut Meldrum out. Wipe him away as if he didn't exist. The lid on the good eye came down, but on the other twitched and quivered to leave a milky sliver exposed. 'He was just a wild boy – I doubt he'd've thought of it on his own. But it took suspicion away from Gordon. And that's what it was all about – protecting Gordon. The clever grandson, who was doing such a good job for the Mountain.'

'You're lying,' she said, and looked to her father as if he would deny it.

There was the sound of the outer door being banged shut. As if it had been a signal, she ran her hands over her hair in a tidying movement. Then she sat down again on the low chair beside her father and picked up the spoon. As it rattled on the plate, he opened his eyes.

'Gordon was so smart,' Meldrum said, 'maybe he was the one stupid enough to work out how as well as laundering the money they could steal some for themselves. Was that what your father was told when he had his stroke? Did he discover he'd sacrificed Alistair to protect the greatest traitor of them all?'

The General's bright blue eye was intent upon the spoon. She held it just out of his reach, perhaps because she was lost in thought. His lips munched stretching to it.

'The pity is he can't tell you,' Meldrum said. 'You're going to have to work it out between you.'

And he left them like that.

Half-way along the corridor, Robertson with folded arms was swaying out and back from the wall. The smell of whisky was stronger from him than before. His eyes teared and snot was leaking from his nose.

Faithful to the end, the good soldier was standing guard outside the General's study.